Praise for *USA TODAY* bestselling author Delores Fossen

"Clear off space on your keeper shelf, Fossen has arrived."
—*New York Times* bestselling author Lori Wilde

"Delores Fossen takes you on a wild Texas ride with a hot cowboy."
—*New York Times* bestselling author B.J. Daniels

"In the first McCord Brothers contemporary, bestseller Fossen strikes a patriotic chord that makes this story stand out."
—*Publishers Weekly* on *Texas on My Mind*

"Fossen delivers an entertaining romance between two people with real-life issues."
—*RT Book Reviews* on *Texas on My Mind*

"This is a thrilling and twist-filled read that will keep you guessing till the end."
—*RT Book Reviews* on *Lone Wolf Lawman*

**Also available from Delores Fossen
and HQN Books**

A Wrangler's Creek Novel

Lone Star Cowboy (ebook novella)
Those Texas Nights
One Good Cowboy (ebook novella)
No GETTING OVER A COWBOY

The McCord Brothers

What Happens on the Ranch (ebook novella)
Texas on My Mind
Cowboy Trouble (ebook novella)
Lone Star Nights
Cowboy Underneath It All (ebook novella)
Blame It on the Cowboy

To see the complete list of titles available from
Delores Fossen, please visit www.deloresfossen.com.

DELORES FOSSEN

NO GETTING OVER A COWBOY

HQN™

HQN™

ISBN-13: 978-0-373-80189-3

Recycling programs
for this product may
not exist in your area.

No Getting Over a Cowboy

Copyright © 2017 by Delores Fossen

The publisher acknowledges the copyright holder
of the individual work as follows:

One Good Cowboy
Copyright © 2017 by Delores Fossen

CONTENTS

NO GETTING OVER A COWBOY

CHAPTER ONE

Panties in a Bunch 'Cause Your Car Won't Start? Use Camel-Tow!

That's what was printed on the magnetic sign on the door of the tow truck. Next to it was a picture of a woman in tight white pants sporting a camel toe, complete with arrows pointing to it as if making sure no one missed it.

No one could. Garrett Granger was certain of that.

Garrett tried to call his sister and mom to see if they knew what was going on. No answer from either of them, but he left messages for them to call him back. Then, he got off his horse and walked closer to get a better look at things and make sure he hadn't misread the sign on the flamingo-pink tow truck.

Nope, no misreading.

And his eyes hadn't deceived him about the other things he was seeing, either. The person who'd driven that truck to the Granger Ranch had apparently not only trespassed but had also broken into his great-grandfather's house.

Such that it was.

Garrett had always thought of the place as more of an ancestral eyesore than an actual house. But hell in a big-ass handbasket, it was *his* eyesore. Or rather his family's.

His great-grandfather, Z. T. Granger, had built the monstrosity nearly a hundred years ago and had chosen it as his final resting place. Z.T.'s grave was in the backyard. The old guy probably hadn't counted on the place becoming a mecca for squatters or whatever the heck this was.

It wasn't as if the eyesore had a welcoming appearance, either. It was painted a dull shade of purple, the color of an old bruise, and the shutters were urine yellow. To complete the god-awful curb appeal, there was a slime-green front door rimmed with milky red stained-glass panels.

The place didn't scream "Y'all, come on in now and make yourselves at home."

Garrett went even closer to see if he could spot a familiar face or anything that would help him make sense of his trespassing-squatter-mecca theory. There was a woman sweeping the porch, another raking the yard, and he could see yet a third woman in a window on the second floor. She had a feather duster and appeared to be clearing out cobwebs. A little girl was playing in the area by the open gate.

They weren't sneaking around, weren't trying to hide, so if these were indeed squatters or run-of-the-mill trespassers, they were either bold or stupid. Or maybe this was some kind of cleaning fetish cult.

Still, why had they driven here in a tow truck?

Garrett heard the galloping sound behind him, and he glanced over his shoulder to see his cousin Lawson. Lawson dismounted before his horse had even fully stopped, and he made a beeline toward Garrett.

Together, Lawson and he ran the Granger Ranch, another of Z.T.'s legacies, and now the two of them stood side by side studying the Gothic house and the people meandering around it.

"What the hell's going on?" Lawson asked. "And why is that kid poking at that cow shit with a stick?"

Garrett didn't have the answer to the first question, but as for the second, he knew from experience that kids poked at shit. Even kids who wore pink overalls and had their hair in pigtails.

"I just got here," Garrett explained. "I came out to look over things for the work crew, and I saw them. I have no idea who they are or why they're here."

"Maybe they're from the historical society?" Lawson added. "They could be sprucing up the place since it's obvious we suck at doing that."

It was a good guess, but Wrangler's Creek was a small town by anyone's standards, and Garrett knew every female for miles around. Every kid old enough to poke at a cow patty, too. He didn't recognize any of these folks. Plus, there wasn't a woman in the historical society under the age of seventy. These "visitors" were all much younger. And then there was the tow truck. No one in Wrangler's Creek, possibly the entire state of Texas, would drive a vehicle like that.

"Or they could be those ghost groupies," Lawson offered.

Another good guess. Since the house looked like something out of a bad horror movie and because there were rumors of Z.T.'s spirit haunting the place, it had indeed attracted ghost hunters over the years. But as far as Garrett knew, they'd never resorted to trespassing. Or cleaning.

"Looks like they got here using the old ranch trail." Lawson, again.

His cousin tipped his head to the tow truck and the SUV behind it, both of which were parked about ten yards from the house. Once there'd been an actual dirt and gravel road leading to the place, but the pasture had long claimed that. Now, the only way to get to it was on horseback, walking a half mile from the main house or by driving on the trail. The last time Garrett had checked it out, there'd been more potholes than trail surface, and there were bushes growing in spots. It wouldn't have been a smooth ride to get here.

"How many of them are there?" Lawson asked.

"Four."

But Garrett was being optimistic. That was only the number he could see. Since the old three-story house had over twenty-five rooms, it was possible that the entire population of a small country had taken up residence there.

On his land.

All right, it wasn't all *his* exactly, but Garrett had always thought of the ranch as his domain. His sister, Sophie, ran the family business, Granger Western. His brother, Roman, owned a rodeo promotion company, and Garrett ran the ranch. He made all the key decisions and knew everything that went on here.

Everything except for this.

"As soon as I spotted the *visitors*, I tried to get in touch with Sophie and my mom," Garrett went on as he walked closer to the house. "Maybe they'll call back soon."

Unfortunately, there were dead zones for cell service out here, but Garrett didn't intend to wait for any more info. He could find out what these women, and the child, wanted and then send them packing. He had a work crew arriving first thing in the morning to expand the nearby pond, and he didn't want any hitches with that. Having people parked in the very spot he intended to dig would definitely qualify as a hitch.

The women had obviously spotted Lawson and him because the two outside were now huddled together, talking and pointing at him. A third woman came out of the house and joined them. The only one who ventured to meet him was the little blond-haired girl.

She still had hold of the crap-coated stick, but she also caught his hand as if he were a long lost friend. "I Kay-wee."

Garrett had no idea how to respond to that. None. But he kept walking toward the house with the hope that she'd let go of him. He wanted to put a quick end to this, and it might somewhat diminish his air of authority if he was holding hands with a toddler.

Plus, there were the other feelings that came. They always did when he saw a baby or a young child. It'd been three years since he'd lost his own daughter. Three years, two months and six days. He could have provided the hours if someone had asked. And yes, he was still counting.

Always would.

Some aches just didn't go away no matter how much time had passed.

"Cows," Kay-wee pointed out as they got closer to the house. Or rather t-ows.

She used the stick to point and point and point. She could have pointed for a long time since there was a herd just on the other side of the picket fence that surrounded the house and grave.

The cows were forever breaking through that fence,

and that was probably why there'd been a patty so close to the porch for the girl to poke. They would continue to break through, too, and that's why these folks had to go. Once the work crew had expanded the pond, they could reinforce the fence so he could bring in the new shipment of cattle.

"I'm Garrett Granger," he said to the women.

They stayed huddled, their heads together like conjoined triplets, and they continued to whisper.

"Gare-if," the girl attempted. She finally tossed the stick.

"This is the Granger Ranch," he added to the women. "It's private property."

More huddling, more whispering. Since the only one talking to him was Kay-wee, he looked at her. "Why are you here?"

She let go of him to lift her hands and shrug. "Mommy," she said as if that explained everything. It didn't explain diddly squat. She took hold of him again and started leading him to the porch.

The huddling women scattered to the side of the house and from there they eyed him as if he were a rattler ready to strike. Funny, because most women in town gave him sad, puppy-dog looks. Once, though, he'd been considered the golden boy of Wrangler's Creek. These days, Garrett felt more like that discarded shit stick.

For just a second he got a flashback of why he now had that shit-stick label. It wasn't often a man got to see a video of his wife blowing some guy in the backseat of a VW, but Garrett could add that to his list of life experiences.

Another woman appeared in the doorway, glared

at him and then scampered off. Garrett thought about doing a smell check of his armpits. He'd been working with a new cutting horse all morning and was sweaty. That might explain the scurrying and rattler looks, but if he did stink, maybe that would just get the squatters moving faster.

He walked into the entry and looked around. Not that he could see much in his immediate line of sight. The house was a wooden ant farm with some rooms that had no purpose other than to lead to other rooms. It was a time capsule of sorts since it still had all of Z.T.'s furniture and stuff. Some things also left behind by his great-aunt, who'd lived here long before Garrett was born.

"I'm sorry, but you can't stay here," Garrett called out to anybody who might be in hearing range.

The little girl kept hold of his hand, and with Lawson right behind them, they began to make their way through the room maze. Someone had indeed cleaned the place and taken off the old sheets from the equally old furniture. Not a good sign. In his general experience, people who swept and dusted had plans to be around long enough to enjoy their cleaning efforts.

They went through the parlor, the place where Garrett had lost his virginity to one of the ranch hands' cousins who'd been visiting the summer he'd turned sixteen. That'd been eighteen years ago. Mercy, a lifetime. But still it was a sweet memory.

There was also a library that conjured up some deflowering memories. Seventeen years ago, he'd brought a cute flute-playing classmate out here. One thing had led to another, and even though he hadn't known it was going to happen beforehand, she'd lost her virginity to him. Things hadn't lasted between them, neither the sex nor the relationship. A month or so later, he'd broken up with her so he could date the woman he'd eventually marry.

Those were his only sexual experiences in the place, but he was betting Lawson and his brother, Roman, had committed some serious debauchery here.

Judging from the manly grunt Lawson made, Garrett was right about that.

"I'll try to find someone who knows what's going on," Lawson grumbled. "One who can speak in more than two syllables." And he headed back out the front.

Garrett wished him luck, and the little girl and he kept walking. They finally made their way to the kitchen where Garrett saw yet another woman, this one in the process of mopping the floor. She wasn't the little girl's mother, though, since this woman was easily in her seventies or even eighties. Sugar-white hair and skin as pale as paper, she didn't eye him the way the others out front had. In fact, she smiled. And she spoke. More than two syllables, too.

"You're one of Belle Granger's boys, aren't you?" the woman asked but didn't wait for him to answer. "Let me guess which one. Garrett or Roman? Hmm." Tapping her fingers on her chin, she looked him over from head to toe, but her gaze lingered in his crotch area. "I used to diaper both of you boys."

Garrett hoped like the devil that she didn't want to do a boxers check to see if she recognized his equipment. "Who are you?"

"Loretta Cunningham." She smiled again, the way one would for a social visit. Which this wasn't. Come to think of it, crazy people probably smiled that way, too.

Garrett made a mental note to call the county mental hospital to see if they'd had any escapees.

"Look, if you're one of those ghost hunters—" Garrett started. But he didn't get far with that comment because Loretta interrupted him.

"Lordy, no." She pressed her hand to her chest. "Those shows scare the livin' daylights out of me." She stopped, glanced around. "You don't think there are actual ghosts here, do you?"

"Yeah, I do," Garrett lied since it seemed like something to get her moving out of there.

But Loretta didn't budge, and she smiled again. "You're pulling my leg, aren't you, boy?" And she just kept on talking. "Your grandma and I went to school together back in the day, but I moved to Beaumont when you and your siblings were just little bitty things. You're Roman, aren't you? Even when you were her age—" she bobbed her head to the little girl "—you always looked ready to pick a fight. And from what I've heard, you've done your share of fighting."

"I'm Garrett," he corrected.

"Oh."

That one little word said it all. Loretta Cunningham knew about the divorce. But she probably knew a lot more than that. Maybe about the baby they'd lost. But more likely her suddenly red cheeks were because she'd heard about his ex-wife's blow job in the VW. Had perhaps even seen the video. Apparently, she'd also seen the fight-picking expression on his face and had mistaken it for Roman's.

The little girl let go of him again and took off running up the back stairs. Good. Because Garrett was about to get blunt with Loretta, and it was best if the little ears weren't around for that.

"Who owns the pink tow truck and the SUV?" Garrett asked.

Loretta gave him a "what tow truck and SUV?" look before she snapped her fingers. "Oh, those. It's Mrs. Marlow's SUV. Cancer," she added in a whisper. "And the pink truck belongs to Lady Romero. Drug overdose," she added in another whisper. "That's not Lady's real name, hair color or bosom, by the way, but I don't make judgments about such things."

She also didn't make sense. Why had she added cancer and drug overdose in there as if it were necessary to this very confusing conversation? Apparently, questions weren't getting what he needed from her ramblings so Garrett tried a different approach.

"I'm sorry, but you have to leave," Garrett came right out and told her. "This is pasture land, *Granger land*," he added, "and tomorrow there'll be a work crew all around this place. It won't be safe for you or the little girl."

Loretta made another "oh." Then, paused. "Didn't your mother tell you?"

That was not a good start to an explanation. *Any* explanation. His mother, Belle, had some good qualities, if he graded on a curve and added bonus points for her giving birth to him, but good communication wasn't one of Belle's better skills.

"Tell me what?" Garrett demanded.

"Oh, dear." Loretta did another hand press to her heart. "Your mother said we could stay here."

"It's not her place to do that." Actually, it wasn't Garrett's, either. Not legally anyway, since Roman owned the ranch. But since Roman had no interest in anything to do with this ranch or the family, he left decisions like that to Garrett. Besides, Roman had his own business to run.

Garrett took out his phone to try to call his mother again and then cursed when he saw he was in another of those dead zones. "How long did my mother say you could stay here?"

"I'm not sure," Loretta answered. "Maybe you can speak to Mrs. Marlow about that. She's the one who talked to your mother. She's upstairs."

Maybe she was the cobweb duster. One with perhaps cancer. And Garrett would deal with her soon enough, but he held out hope that Loretta could give him some real information just in case this Mrs. Marlow turned out to be a tight-lipped scurrier like the women outside.

Garrett went with his next questions. "Who are you people anyway? Why would my mother have said you could stay here? And why the heck would you want to be here of all places?"

Loretta's mouth moved, repeating those three questions, and she held up her fingers one by one as she went through them. "We're friends. Because Belle's doing us a favor. And because it was big enough for all of us."

Well, they were answers. Sort of. But not the answers he wanted.

"Are you sure you're not Roman?" Loretta continued. "Because you look like you're ready to pick a fight again."

"I am ready to do that," he snarled. Then, he huffed and silently cursed. Being a badass was his brother's specialty. He was actually a nice guy. Most days anyway, but this didn't feel like most days.

"Look, Loretta, there's been a misunderstanding," he said. "One that I'm certain we can all work out. But trust me when I say that you can't stay here. The work crew will have some big equipment, including a bulldozer. It's not safe," he repeated.

"You're sure?" Loretta called out to him as he started for the stairs.

"Positive," he assured her and kept on walking. Then, paused. "Is this Mrs. Marlow well enough to talk? I mean, she's not bedridden, is she?"

"Lordy, no. Why would she be bedridden?" Loretta patted her chest again. "You think she's sick?"

Yeah, he had thought that. After all, Loretta had mentioned cancer, but perhaps she'd been talking about Mrs. Marlow's astrological sign.

The second floor was right out of a class project for a horror movie. A long, dark hall with a creaky floor, complete with burned-out wall lights and old paintings that were tilted and bowed enough to send OCD folks into a panic attack. He followed the hall to the room where he'd seen the woman in the window earlier.

Not there.

"Mrs. Marlow?" he called out.

Nothing. Well, not a voice anyway, but his phone rang, and he saw his sister's name on the screen.

"Sorry, I was out riding, and I just now got your voice mail," Sophie said the moment Garrett answered. "Are there really squatters at Z.T.'s house?"

"I'm not sure who they are, but one of them said Mom gave her permission to be here. You know anything about that?"

"No. Why would she do that? And why would any-one want to stay at that place anyway?"

"I asked first. Where's Mom?"

"In the family room." It wasn't the best of connec-tions, and there was plenty of static on the line. "I'm pretty sure she's eating lunch and watching her soap."

Which meant she had turned off her phone or else had the TV volume cranked so high that she hadn't heard it ring. Of course, the third possibility was that she was avoiding him because she knew he'd be pissed about this.

"Can you go to her right now and ask her what the hell is going on?" He added some profanity to that.

"I will, but I'll leave out all the language that'll make her lecture you at her earliest convenience. Hold on. I'm heading to the family room now." At least he thought that's what Sophie had said through the static.

"Do you remember Mom ever mentioning a woman named Loretta Cunningham or a Mrs. Marlow?" Gar-rett asked, and he got moving, too, past the rows of bedrooms on each side of the hall.

"Not that I can recall. Wait… I do remember Mom mentioning a Loretta. She used to babysit us, I think."

And apparently diaper them.

"Well, she's here," Garrett added. "She's the one who claims Mom said she could stay."

"Maybe Mom meant they could stay for the day or something. You know, for, like, a picnic." More static, more noise, too, and he thought some of that noise was coming from a TV. Since the static was hurting his ears, Garrett put the call on speaker and kept search-ing for the elusive Mrs. Marlow.

"Garrett?" he finally heard his mother say. "You've

had three calls on your office phone. All from women. I don't think they're calling about business, either. Now that you're divorced, I think they want to get in your pants."

Garrett groaned. That was the last thing he wanted to talk to his mother about.

"It's not right," his mother went on. "Those women just want to use you."

Yes, and if his mind ever got back to a good place, he just might let those women get in his pants until he could work his way through a jumbo box of condoms.

"And speaking of the divorce, Meredith called, too, when she couldn't reach you on your cell phone," his mother continued before he could speak. "She said she needed to see you about something. Wouldn't say what exactly. Needless to say, I don't approve. I don't think it's right for your ex-wife to want to get into your pants."

He'd been wrong. *This* was the last thing he wanted to talk to his mother about.

Garrett finally managed to get a word in edgewise. "Mom, I'm calling about Loretta Cunningham. I'm out at Z.T.'s house now, and she's here."

"Loretta's there?" She sounded overjoyed about that. And static-y. Since the static was only getting worse, he stopped walking, hoping that would help with the signal. "She used to watch you kids for me when I needed a break. She's the one who gave me that home-made ointment that cleared up the rash on your tushy."

He would have groaned again if it'd do any good. "Please focus, Mom. Did you tell Loretta she could stay at Z.T.'s place?"

"No, of course not."

Instant relief. He could be the asshole after all and demand that the women leave. He could even pay them for the cleaning they'd done. Then, he could get that work crew in to deal with the pond and fence.

"Any idea why Loretta thought you'd told her she could stay here?" Garrett pressed.

But the line went dead. While it would have been nice to hear what his mother had to say about that, it wasn't necessary.

"Garrett Granger?" someone said. It was a woman, and she stepped out from the last bedroom at the end of the hall.

Because of the shot lights, Garrett couldn't see her that well, but she started walking toward him. "Yeah. And you are?"

"Nicky Marlow."

Ah, finally. "There's been a misunderstanding." *On your part*, Garrett wanted to add. "My mother didn't give Loretta permission to stay here."

"No," she calmly agreed, and she took something from the canvas bag she had in her hand. It was still hard to see, but it looked like some papers. "But she gave *me* permission. Actually, she gave me a one-year lease."

Shit. His stomach landed near his kneecaps. No. This couldn't be true.

She came closer, thrusting that paper at him. The lease, no doubt. The one that his mother better not have signed. Garrett snatched it from her and had a look for himself.

His stomach flopped down to the dusty floor. Because that was indeed a lease, indeed his mother's signature.

He looked up to tell the woman that one way or another, the lease had to be broken. But the argument died on his lips when he looked at her face. That's because this wasn't Mrs. Marlow. This was Nicky Henderson.

The cute blonde flute player Garrett had deflowered seventeen years ago. And then dumped.

Not exactly good memories.

Apparently not for her, either. Judging from the way Nicky's mouth tightened, this was one woman in Wrangler's Creek who had absolutely no desire to get in his pants.

CHAPTER TWO

IT WASN'T EASY for her to stare down the man with whom she'd made her awkward sexual debut, but Nicky managed it. It helped that Garrett wasn't exactly giving her the smoldering looks he had the night of said debut. In fact, once he got past the initial shock of seeing her, he started glaring.

All in all, he was a good glarer, too. Sharp, precise and with a smidge of *I'm in charge here so get lost.*

Nicky hadn't seen him in seventeen years, not since they'd graduated from high school, but he hadn't changed that much. By some measures anyway. He still had the thick dark brown hair that looked as if he'd just climbed out of bed after having sex. The same sizzling blue eyes that coordinated well with the smoldering looks. But there was something different about him, too. Something she knew a little too well.

Life had smacked Garrett Granger upside the head with a proverbial two-by-four. She recognized the world weariness, the impatience. The slight F-you attitude.

"My mother was wrong to give you that lease," he growled. Speaking had to be hard with his jaw muscles that tight.

"She signed it," Nicky pointed out, and she took the lease from him because he looked ready to vaporize it with his glare. She had other copies, but she didn't want to have to go back to San Antonio to get them. That would mean a forty-five-minute drive.

He cursed. Stopped. And Nicky thought maybe he'd remembered that he was the "nice" Granger brother, but she followed his gaze over her shoulder where she spotted her daughter, Kaylee, who was coming out of the bedroom that Nicky had just been cleaning.

"Gar-if," Kaylee greeted. She went to Garrett as if they were best buds and took his hand. "See my room."

"How do you know my daughter?" Nicky asked at the same moment, Garrett said, "This is your daughter?"

Nicky nodded. Garrett gave her another dose of stink eye that he thankfully didn't aim at Kaylee. Because if he had, Nicky would have let her own F-you attitude kick in, and she would have shown him the door. It didn't matter that he was a Granger because he wasn't her landlord. His mother, Belle, was.

"I *met* Kaylee outside earlier," Garrett snarled. "She was poking a stick in a cow pie."

Nicky groaned, immediately tugged Kaylee away from Garrett and checked her daughter's hands. There was no visible poop, but she'd need the hand sanitizer. She should buy stock in the company as often as she had to use it.

"I thought Mrs. Ellery and her sisters were watching her," Nicky explained.

Later, she would need to give Kaylee a lecture about cow pies and staying closer to her since the Ellery sisters apparently weren't the stellar babysitters they claimed to be. Ironic since they were named for various goddesses of protection: Aradia, Diana and Hera.

Kaylee led Garrett back to the room. "It's pink," her daughter declared.

It wasn't. Well, except for one dust-coated doll in a pink dress sitting on top of the chest of drawers. Everything else was gray, drab and probably festering with mold and things Nicky didn't want to identify. She'd need the full year of the lease just to get the place clean.

Garrett looked around, managed a semi nod and equally semi smile for Kaylee. "You can't stay here," he added to Nicky.

Nicky made a show of running her hand like a magician's assistant over the lease. "This says differently, and I should know because I drew up this lease myself. Since I'm a lawyer, I can promise you that it's all in order."

That seemed to distract him or something, and he gave her a funny look. "You're a lawyer? You said you were going to be a doctor."

Nicky gave him a funny look right back because she was surprised he had remembered that. "My plans changed. I learned the hard way that I tend to vomit at the sight of blood, guts and bones." Not a very professional reaction, and her instructors agreed. "I see you've become what you've always said you'd be—a rancher. But you're also a business owner. Granger Western."

Or Cowboy Mart as most folks called it since it sold Western supplies in bulk and at a discount.

Nicky guessed that the business was making the Granger clan even richer than they already were. Especially now that they'd worked through the kinks of a recent setback and investigation.

"My sister, Sophie, runs the business," he provided.

She listened for any hint of his disapproval about that. There wasn't any. Interesting because she'd read an article about a codicil to his father's will that had ousted Garrett and turned the reins of Granger Western over to Sophie. Things like that could tear a family apart, but it appeared there'd been no tearing involved in their case.

Apparently his idea of "small talk" was over because Garrett took the lease back from her and pointed to the bottom line. "My mother doesn't have permission to sign this. The ranch belongs to my brother."

"Roman." She nodded. "Yes, he owns the ranch, but he doesn't own this house. I researched it, and according to your great-grandfather's will, he left the house itself to his wife who then left it to your grandfather. He left it to your father, and since your father didn't stipulate in his will who was to inherit the house, ownership passed to your mother."

The look he gave her could have flash melted sand, and it had no sexual components to it whatsoever. Not that she'd expected anything sexual from Garrett. After all, he'd rid her of her virginity and promptly dumped her. Still, it was impossible for him to be completely nonsexual since he was still physically hot.

"I'll have my lawyers look into the will, too," Garrett added, "because I can't believe my father didn't spell that out."

Neither could she, especially since his father had apparently spelled out everything else. It was possible he'd simply not cared enough about the place to bother with it. In fact, judging from the state of disrepair, none of the current Grangers had cared much about it.

Unlike her.

Just like that, the bad stuff came. Memories that Nicky wished would die the death they deserved. But at the end of that memory tunnel was this place.

This house.

She'd escaped to this place too many times to count.

That was something the Grangers didn't know. But she'd used it to recoup and in some cases to heal, mentally and physically. No way, though, did she want to share all of that with Garrett. It was one of her many secrets, but if she was labeling them, that was secret number one.

Apparently, Garrett had no plans to share anything else with her, either. He took out his phone, no doubt to call his lawyers, but he mumbled something she didn't catch when he saw that he had no cell reception.

"Why would you care if we're here or not?" Nicky asked. "Other than the current dead bug population, the place has been empty for decades."

"I care because tomorrow there'll be workers here to expand the pond. I care because I plan to use every inch of this pasture for cattle. And I care because this is Granger land." He'd gotten a little louder with each word, and by the time he made it to the last one, he wasn't shouting exactly, but it was close.

"Well, I care, too," Nicky argued. "And our being here won't interfere with your workers or the pasture."

She hoped. Though the place would be a beehive of activity. Temporarily, since she didn't need any literal or metaphorical beehives in her life. Neither did the other women.

"Dolly-baby," Kaylee pointed out, leading him farther into the room. "And boogs."

She meant *bugs*. And, yes, there were some dead

ones on the floor. Yet something else that needed to be cleaned. Nicky had decided to start with the highest points in the room and work her way down.

"Aydee." That was Kaylee's attempt at *lady*, and she pointed to the painting over the bed. Nicky had no idea who the woman was, but she was coated with dust, too.

Garrett glanced at the other things Kaylee was showing him—the bed, the lamp, the cobweb Nicky had missed when she'd cleaned the window. Even the trunk of old clothes that Kaylee had discovered. Then he snapped back toward Nicky.

"Who are those women downstairs and in the yard, and why are you here?" he demanded.

"Widows. We're all widows."

His gaze drifted to Kaylee.

"Well, with the exception of her," Nicky clarified. "No child-bride arrangements in Texas. And you know Loretta Cunningham. She said she used to change your diaper."

His nostrils flared a bit, and they flared even more when she glanced at the front of his jeans. An unintentional glance, but Loretta wasn't the only woman in the house who'd seen that part of Garrett's anatomy.

"As I've already told you, the other women are the Ellery sisters," Nicky went on. "Drowning. All three husbands went when their fishing boat capsized." Mentioning the cause of the widowhood was something that she and the others had gotten accustomed to doing when they made introductions to new members in the support group. "Then, there's Mrs. Batson. Heart attack. But you might not have seen her. She'll probably be skittish around you."

A term that described every woman currently in the

house but Loretta and her. Perhaps because she and Loretta were the only ones who'd seen Garrett without his underpants.

"Lady Romero is taking a walk," she added. "But she'll be back soon to help clean. Ginger Carson, *respiratory failure*, is in town getting some supplies."

His jaw tightened even more. "Why? Are? You? All? Here?"

Apparently, he was getting impatient for more answers, but he probably wasn't going to like anything she had to say.

"Because we're all in a support group for widows and divorcées, and we thought it would be a good idea for us to have an actual retreat for those who need it."

Retreat was such a tidy little word, but Nicky thought Garrett might not like to hear that it could turn into a place where women could fall apart. Women like her. A place where no one would be around to see them if they went bat-shit crazy.

No one except for Garrett, that is.

"Widows?" he repeated. That seemed to be a prompt for her to provide more. More as in personal stuff, but Nicky had no intention of getting into that with him. Not in front of Kaylee. Maybe not ever.

"Most of us are young widows," Nicky emphasized. "With the exception of Loretta, we lost our spouses or significant others while in our twenties, thirties and forties. The women need this house," she added, hoping it would help. It obviously didn't. Since Kaylee was volleying glances between them and hanging on every word, Nicky tried to make those words sound as pleasant as possible. "Some have rented out or sold their homes to come here. They've quit their jobs. They've rearranged their whole lives so they could have this experience and take the time to heal."

Of course, not all would be able to come here and do that. Those widows with school-age children hadn't been able to take off that kind of time. Others simply hadn't been able to come because it would have meant a loss of income that they couldn't afford. Nicky had been able to help some with that by covering all the expenses of the house itself, but it still wasn't enough to allow some of the widows to be here.

"This isn't a healing place. It's a pasture on a working ranch." Garrett didn't follow suit in the pleasant department. "I'm sorry, but you can't stay." It sounded like some kind of monarch's decree, and he headed out of the room and into the hall. Since Kaylee followed him, so did Nicky. "My lawyers will be in touch with you about negating the lease."

Nicky caught up with Garrett and stepped in front of him. "You'd really throw out a group of widows and a three-year old? How will that make you look? It'll tarnish that 'good guy' image of yours."

She perhaps should have held off on mentioning the image thing. But then again, he probably wouldn't have been pleased with anything she told him right now. Like about the furniture that was being delivered any minute. And the movers she'd hired to put some of the existing furniture and knickknacks into storage rooms. Or the painters or repairmen.

Nicky definitely wouldn't mention the cocktail/ice breaker party she was throwing and that his mother would be attending.

"You'll never even notice we're out here," Nicky added.

"Trust me, I've already noticed. No way can you have people living here with all the work going on," he said. "And as for my image, it's already tarnished."

A polite woman would have pretended she didn't know what he was talking about. But she did know.

Man, did she.

And it was best not to mention the firsthand knowledge she had of that situation. That was her secret number two. Besides, she still had an argument to win with Garrett.

"Your work crew won't be coming into the actual yard," she went on. "So, there's really no problem—"

"They're tearing down the fence and replacing it with a new one. There won't be much of a yard left when they're finished. In fact, it'll be more like a barrier to keep the cattle from getting in and trampling Z.T.'s grave."

Since the grave was practically at the back porch steps, it was possible for the newly designed backyard to extend less than six feet from the house. That definitely wouldn't give them much outside space.

"What would it hurt to keep the yard area as is?" Nicky asked. "I mean, you're getting by with the pasture you have now—"

"I'm bringing in more cows, and I need every inch of this land. It's taken me months to work out the deals to get the land surrounding the ranch, and the expansion of the pond is the next step."

Clearly, she was getting nowhere. "I'll talk to your mother about this." She headed for the stairs so she could find a spot where she had phone reception. "I'm sure we can work out a solution."

Nicky wasn't sure of that at all, but Belle Granger had to be more reasonable than her son.

"Mrs. Marlow?" Loretta called out. "Uh, I think you should come down here."

"In a minute," Nicky answered. She finally got some reception bars about halfway down the stairs so she stopped to make the call. Kaylee, however, bolted down the stairs, heading in the direction of Loretta's voice.

"It doesn't matter what my mother says," Garrett went on. He huffed and took out his phone again, too. "I'll look for a place for all of you in town. There are several shops that have gone out of business, and you can maybe use one of those buildings."

She didn't want a shop in town. Nicky wanted the privacy and quiet that she thought she'd get at the Granger Ranch. She'd healed here before, and she could do it again.

"Mrs. Marlow?" Loretta, again. "You really, really, really need to get down here right now."

Nicky froze for a moment. One *really* would have alarmed her, but the trifecta of *reallys* meant something was wrong. Maybe it was nothing more than a spider or a repair that needed to be done.

Garrett stayed on the stairs to make his call, but Nicky didn't press in his mother's number. Instead, she hurried to the kitchen. She immediately got confirmation that this was more than a spider issue or a repair. Loretta was even paler than she usually was, something Nicky hadn't believed possible. Kaylee obviously hadn't thought this was anything worth waiting around for because she was already playing on the back porch.

"What's wrong?" Nicky asked the woman.

Loretta shook her head and pointed to one of the

rooms off the kitchen. Nicky hadn't been in this one yet, and the door was shut.

"It's in there," Loretta said.

So, maybe a critter sighting and nothing major after all. Well, unless the critter was a grizzly bear. Pushing that uneasy thought aside, Nicky threw open the door. It was a small butler's pantry with cabinets and countertops on both sides. Loretta's flashlight was on the floor, and it was still on, blaring light around the narrow space.

In the center of the cabinet rows was yet another door. That one was open. And Nicky picked up the flashlight so she could aim it at whatever had spooked Loretta.

"Holy shit!" flew out of her mouth before Nicky could stop it.

"What is it?" Garrett asked. Until he spoke, she hadn't even known that he'd walked up behind her, and Nicky nearly knocked him over when she ran back into the kitchen.

"There's a skeleton in the closet," she managed to say. "A real one," she had to add when Garrett stared at her.

Nicky felt her stomach lurch. That was the only warning she got before she puked on the freshly mopped kitchen floor.

CHAPTER THREE

GARRETT NOW KNEW there was something worse than having a body buried in the yard. It was having a second body in a closet. Unlike Z.T.'s, Garrett figured this one wasn't there by choice.

It was certainly something he hadn't planned on encountering when he'd started his day. Ditto for the widows and the toddler. Just one of those things would have been bad enough, but the shit storm had provided three all at once.

Along with some sobs, tears and a few *oh my Gods*.

Garrett had to admit that he'd contributed to the *oh my Gods*. And he'd had some serious unsettling moments. That unsettling had eased up just a little though when he realized the dead body wasn't exactly fresh. It was a skeleton, an old one from the looks of it, and he was wearing men's clothes. Specifically, boxers with hearts on them and a straw hat. At least this wasn't someone who'd died recently.

Garrett didn't know anything about this man, but the sick feeling continued to roll through him. Not enough to vomit as Nicky had done, but close. A guy was dead. And it didn't help that his last minutes on God's green earth had been in this house on Granger land.

"Everybody stay back," Chief Clay McKinnon called out.

The widows, minus Loretta and Nicky, were peering into the kitchen from the back door. Thankfully, Loretta had had the good sense to take Nicky and Kaylee upstairs so they wouldn't have to be near the corpse.

Garrett stayed back, too, in the dining room. Far enough away from the puke smell but still close enough if Clay needed anything from him. Not that he probably would. Clay was not only his soon-to-be brother-in-law, he was also an experienced cop and knew what he was doing.

"I'll get the medical examiner in here," Clay said. "Along with a photographer. Did anyone touch the body after it was discovered?" he added to Garrett.

"No, I'm pretty sure no one did."

Even though Garrett hadn't actually been side by side with Nicky when she'd seen the skeleton, he knew from her reaction that she'd gotten out of there as fast as she could. He would have the bruise to prove it, too, since her head had slammed into his shoulder. As the high school quarterback, he'd been hit by two-hundred-and-fifty-pound football players who hadn't rammed into him as hard as Nicky had. And as for Loretta, well, she definitely didn't look like the corpse-touching type.

"Any idea who the guy is?" Clay asked.

Garrett had to shake his head. "No one's lived here for nearly fifty years, since my great-aunt Matilda." He paused, frowned. "You think he's been dead for that long?"

Clay lifted his shoulder. "Hard to tell without some testing. The fabric on the boxers and hat are rotting, but they're still mainly intact. There don't appear to be any signs of trauma to the body. No bashed-in skull, broken neck or bones busted from bullet wounds. There's also no dried blood around him, but over the years the rats and insects could have eaten that."

That brought on some more *oh my Gods* from the widows.

Maybe this would get them all out of there. Fast. Garrett cursed himself. These women had already had their spouses die so this was probably hitting them harder than it was him. Still...they had to go.

He hated to think about something like that now, but having them there wouldn't make this easier. Plus, Clay wouldn't want them hanging around while he was conducting an investigation.

"This is a clusterfuck," Garrett heard Lawson say as he walked up behind him. "And it's about to get more clustered. Belle and Sophie are on their way. They'll be here any minute."

Garrett groaned because his mother didn't usually make situations better, but she might know something about this. It was more than a little unsettling to think that, but it was equally unsettling to realize that over the years he'd camped out in this house. Had brought two girls here. Hell, once Roman and he had had a party. All while there'd been a dead guy in a closet.

"Your great-aunt was married?" Clay asked Garrett.

"No. Not that I ever heard anyway. She didn't stay here long. According to what my mother told me, my great-aunt moved off after only being here a few months, and then she passed away in the seventies."

Clay lifted an eyebrow, and Garrett immediately figured out why. Maybe the reason Aunt Matilda had moved was because she'd killed a man and left the body behind. Hell. Not exactly a good thought to settle his stomach.

"I'll search local records and ask Belle about it," Clay went on, "but since I haven't lived around here that long, maybe you can help fill me in. Are there any longtime missing persons that the older townsfolk have mentioned?"

"No," Lawson and Garrett said in unison. "Anything like that would still be gossiped about," Garrett added. "Maybe the guy was a repairman or something. He could have slipped and fallen, and Matilda might never have even known."

Yeah, he was reaching, but he didn't want to consider the worst. That a man could have been murdered.

"Decomposing bodies stink," Clay said. "If she was here when he died, she would have definitely known."

Another round of *oh my Gods* from the widows.

Garrett heard the footsteps behind him, and for a split second, he thought his mom and Sophie had already arrived. But it was Kaylee making her way into the dining room.

"Mommy puked free times," she said, and as if it were the most natural thing in the world, she took hold of Garrett's hand.

He glanced around to see if Loretta or Nicky was with her, but the toddler was alone. "Where's your mom?" he asked.

"Puking," Kaylee quickly answered.

Well, Nicky had said something about having stomach issues when body parts and blood were involved so he guessed this wasn't a surprise. Still, he didn't want the little girl around all the talk of rats eating blood or rotting bodies. Heck, he didn't especially want to be around it, either.

Garrett led Kaylee to the foyer, intending to take her

back upstairs to leave her with Loretta, but he didn't even make it to the steps before his mother and sister came hurrying in. Both looked alarmed and were out of breath.

"I tried to keep Mom at home," Sophie said to him right off.

Garrett silently thanked her, knowing there was nothing she could have done if their mother was hell-bent on coming here. Which she clearly was.

"It's true?" his mother asked. "Did Matilda really murder someone and put the body in the kitchen closet?"

Maybe his mother hadn't noticed Kaylee, and Garrett put his hands over the child's ears for part of that, but Kaylee had no doubt heard things a three-year-old shouldn't have heard.

"Either hold your questions or speak in pig Latin," he told his mother.

His mother's gaze finally landed on the girl. Landed, too, on the way Kaylee had latched on to Garrett's hand. "Who is she?"

"Kay-wee," Kaylee answered.

Garrett provided his mother with more information. "She's with the widows. You know, the ones you gave a lease? A lease that can't happen because of the expansion I've got going on."

If his mother was bothered by anything he'd just said, she didn't show it. She stooped down, smiled at Kaylee. "Well, you sure are a pretty little thing." She gave Kaylee's pigtail a gentle tug. "And look how you're holding Garrett's hand. That's so sweet. She obviously likes you."

That was code for his mother letting him know that

she wanted a grandbaby. She already had one. Roman's son, Tate, but he was almost thirteen now so her mother was apparently getting grandbaby fever.

"No," Garrett said to his mother, and he figured she knew what that *no* meant. There'd be no kids in his future. Not after... Well, just not after. If he wanted his heart ripped out again, he'd do it himself.

His mother stood, meeting his gaze. "You didn't used to be so negative, Garrett. Honestly, I don't know what's gotten into you."

Really? He wasn't about to rehash the last three years and two months of his life. Not when there was something new that needed to be dealt with.

Garrett's phone rang, and he glanced down at the screen to see Roman's name. Since he had the lease-signing culprit in front of him, a conversation with his brother could wait. He pressed the button to send the call to voice mail.

"Matilda," Belle repeated before Garrett could say anything. "I should have known she could k-i-l-l someone."

That got his attention. And he was thankful his mother had spelled out the key word. "You really think she could have done this?"

"Absolutely. Agoraphobia, my f-a-n-n-y. That woman had secrets, I tell you, and I'm betting the d-e-a-d f-e-l-l-a was one of those." Belle leaned in to whisper the rest. "Matilda had h-o-t p-a-n-t-s."

Garrett hoped that was a fashion comment, but he doubted it was. "Did she have men visit her here?"

"Well, of course she did. That's what women with h-o-t p-a-n-t-s do. Now, mind you, I don't know the names of those men, but Loretta might remember one or two of them. She was still living in Wrangler's Creek when Matilda was here."

Then, Clay would need to talk to both Loretta and his mom. And speaking of Loretta, that was Garrett's cue to turn this conversation in a different direction. Yes, the body was top priority, but Garrett had a priority of his own.

"Why did you give these women a lease?" he asked Belle at the same moment his mother asked, "Are the widows upset because of the d-e-a-d b-o-d-y?"

He huffed. "Of course, they're upset," he verified. "*I'm* upset. And you're not getting out of explaining to me how you could sign a lease without talking it over with me first. These women can't be here."

His mother patted his arm in a "there, there" gesture. "It was the right thing to do. They needed a place to stay, and it'll be so nice to have someone living here again. The house needs that. It needs some cleaning and repairs, too," she added, glancing around. "That cleaning crew I hired should have been here by now."

It took Garrett a moment just to form words and rein in his temper. He loved his mother, most days anyway, but this was not one of those days. "You'll have to break the lease. I'll pay—"

But that was as far as he got because his mother's attention was no longer on him. Smiling, she moved away from him and walked to the stairs. Kaylee did, as well, and that's when Garrett saw Nicky making her way down the steps. Judging from the tight grip Nicky had on the railing, she still wasn't feeling too steady.

"There you are," his mother said, and the moment Nicky reached the bottom, Belle hugged her. "Nicky Henderson, you look beautiful as always."

It shouldn't have surprised Garrett that Belle felt as if she knew Nicky well enough to hug her. After all, they'd probably talked face-to-face to make arrangements for the lease. Later, Garrett was sure he'd hear all about how those arrangements had come to pass, but now that he had both of them together, he could get this sorted out.

"This has to be so upsetting," Belle said. She broke the hug but kept her hands on Nicky's shoulders. "I had no idea about the b-o-d-y being here." She shuddered. "But Clay will sort this all out. He's the police chief, and he's marrying Sophie, you know? You remember Garrett's sister, Sophie, right?"

"Yes." Nicky's voice sounded as unsteady as she looked. "Congratulations on your engagement."

Sophie scrounged up a smile, nodded, thanked her and then excused herself so she could make her way to the kitchen, no doubt to check on Clay. Garrett would have liked for her to stay as his ally, but he could remedy this on his own.

Kaylee finally let go of Garrett and hurried to her mother. Or rather to Belle. She caught Belle's hand.

"You and your daughter are both pretty as pictures." His mother glanced around. "Where's Loretta?"

"Upstairs, cleaning. She'll be down in a minute."

"Can't wait to see her. We've got so much catching up to do."

"Catching up will have to wait. Clay is bringing in a medical examiner," Garrett explained to Nicky and his mother. "All of us are going to have to clear out."

"Of course," Belle agreed.

Finally, they were getting somewhere. But it wasn't the direction Garrett needed them to go.

"Look at you," his mother added to Nicky. Heck, Belle was smiling again. Definitely not a good sign. She leaned in, put her mouth closer to Nicky's ear. "There's a bond between people who were as close as Garrett and you were. I can see the way you look at him."

Everything inside Garrett went still. He wasn't sure how his mother had known about Nicky and him, but obviously she did. Things suddenly got a whole lot clearer. This wasn't about providing a place for widows.

Belle was matchmaking.

And he was about to stop it.

"I'll call some of the hands to get out here and help move the women's things," Garrett offered. Actually, it was more than an offer. It was a demand. There weren't any hotels in Wrangler's Creek, but there were some on the interstate back toward San Antonio. They could make their way there.

"No need. I've already taken care of that," Belle assured him. "The men are on the way here now."

Garrett blew out a breath of relief. But the relief didn't last. Because he saw the look on his mother's face, and he just knew in his gut that she was about to contribute to the shit storm.

"What did you do?" Garrett came right out and asked.

His mother patted his arm again. "Nothing that any other kindhearted woman wouldn't have done. I called Roman and cleared it with him since the ranch house belongs to him and all."

And then Belle added something that put the icing on this shit storm.

"The widows and Kaylee will be staying with us."

CHAPTER FOUR

"HAVE YOU LOST your sonofabitching mind?" Garrett asked his brother the moment Roman answered the phone.

"Some would say that I never had a mind to lose, sonofabitching or otherwise," Roman calmly answered. "And now that we've gotten the profanity out of the way, I guess you're calling about the widows?"

"You bet your ass, I am." Garrett wasn't through with the profanity just yet, and he shut the door to his office just in case some of those widows were around to hear him chew out his brother. "What the hell were you thinking when you told Mom she could let those six women stay here?"

"I was thinking the same thing I'm thinking right now with you. What's the fastest way to get this person off the phone? Because I don't have time for this. I've got a business to run, and I'm stomping out fires left and right while raising a tweenager with a bad attitude."

That was the pot calling the kettle black. Roman had had a bad attitude since birth. According to their mother, when he'd come out breech, he'd immediately kicked the doctor in the balls.

Garrett wasn't completely immune to Roman's problems. Yes, his brother had them, but at the moment so did Garrett. "You need to call Mom back and tell her you made a mistake, that the women can't stay here."

"Now, you see, that would take time because Mom would plead her case for the women. I'd have to dig in my heels, and that would only make her plead more. That would then lead to multiple phone calls, and if she didn't get her way, she'd show up here. Like I said, I don't have time for that."

Garrett was glad he'd shut the door because he cursed some more, throwing in some really bad words and insults. He cursed again when he looked out the window and saw some of the women pulling into the driveway behind the house. They had already started to arrive. And the first person out of the SUV was Nicky, of course.

"If you don't rescind your offer, it'll result in multiple phone calls from *me*," Garrett threatened. "And at least one ass-kicking visit. I'm still your big brother."

He couldn't be sure, but he thought Roman chuckled. "Look, think of this as getting a lap dance. Just sit back, relax and enjoy it."

That was the worst advice in the history of bad advice. "I can't enjoy it. There'll be six women in the house and a toddler. I can't go to Z.T.'s place because it's a crime scene."

"Yeah, Sophie just called and told me all about that. Seems I can't get off the phone today with people in my gene pool."

"Well, you're staying on the phone with me until we get some things straight. Do you have any idea how crazy things are here right now?"

Roman huffed. "I have an inkling. Sorry about the crime scene, the widows, the toddler and the inconvenience this will cause you and those plans you have to extend the ranch. But I'm not rescinding the offer because (a) it won't be for very long, (b) Mom said some of the women don't have any other place to go and (c) you can move to the guesthouse if you want to get away from them."

"Sophie has her office in the guesthouse," Garrett quickly pointed out. As CEO of Granger Western, she had an office in Austin, a huge one, but since getting engaged to Clay, she spent far more time at the ranch than she did in the city.

"Sophie's not using the bedroom in the guesthouse since she's sleeping at Clay's. So, there's your solution. Sorry that I can't fix the delay on the ranch improvements, but it's my guess that Clay's not going to let you bring in digging equipment until he's processed the scene."

Roman was right about that. Nothing anyone could do about it. That still didn't soothe Garrett any. There were only a few things he could control in his life, and the ranch was one of them. At least he had been able to control it until today.

"My advice?" Roman went on. "Since Nicky's there, burn off some of your orneriness by having sex with her."

That brought on more cursing. "How'd you even know Nicky was here?"

"Mom and Sophie told me. Plus, I ran into Nicky a few months ago at a rodeo in San Antonio, and she asked about Z.T.'s place."

Garrett couldn't believe what he was hearing. "A few months ago? You've known about it all this time?"

"If you were an engine, I'd say you were about to

blow a gasket. No, I didn't know she wanted to lease the house, but she did ask about it. Apparently, she's always had a soft spot for the place."

Hell. He hoped that wasn't because she'd lost her virginity there. But what else could it be? He didn't like the answer that came to mind.

"Did you take Nicky to Z.T.'s?" Garrett asked, and even though he didn't add it, Roman knew what he was implying.

"No." Roman stretched that out a few syllables. "You have a dirty mind, you know that? I liked Nicky, and I always felt a little sorry for her."

"Because of what happened between me and her?" Garrett didn't let him answer. "I'm tired of explaining myself when it comes to that. I met Meredith and fell in love with her. What was I supposed to do—stay with Nicky just because we'd had sex?"

"Again, you're in dirty-mind territory. I didn't feel sorry for Nicky because of what happened with you two. It's because she always had this sad look in her eyes. Even before you, she had it. It reminded me of a wounded bird."

Garrett tried to think back to those days, and yes, Nicky hadn't always been the happiest of people. He always figured that was because she had seemed so anxious to get the heck out of town. His classmates had fallen into two categories—those who were planted in Wrangler's Creek and those who thought it was a smelly Texas armpit. Nicky had fallen into the latter category. At least he thought she had until today.

"By the way, Mom's matchmaking with Nicky and you," Roman went on. "If you want to ease your suffering and rile Mom at the same time, then just start seeing one of the women in town. Sophie said half the eligible women in Wrangler's Creek want to have sex with you. Half of the ineligible ones, too."

Good grief. His sister and Mom were regular chatterboxes today. "No, those women want marriage and commitment. You're the one they want to have sex with." Roman couldn't argue with that, and Garrett gave it one more try. "Will you call Mom?"

"I will if and when you break your sexual dry spell with Nicky." And with that, Roman hung up.

Garrett stood there, staring at the phone, and he considered all the bad things he would like to do to his brother. He didn't want any word of what Roman had said to sink in, but Roman was right about one thing. He was ornery and had been since this whole mess with Meredith. A shrink would probably tell him that he was depressed about failing.

The shrink would be right.

The shrink would probably also say that he was overcompensating for that failure by throwing his heart and soul into the ranch.

The shrink would be right about that, too.

At least there was no need for therapy now since he'd diagnosed his own problems. Too bad, though, that there wasn't an immediate fix for this shit storm.

Garrett shoved his phone back in his pocket and started gathering up his things from his desk to take to the guesthouse. There wasn't a box, but the trashcan was empty so he used that. He also grabbed his spare jeans and shirt from the closet, and he draped those over his arm. He kept a clean set there just in case someone dropped in for a meeting. Of course, he'd have to eventually go to his room and pack some toiletries and other clothes, but that could wait.

"I'm busy," he snarled when there was a knock at the door.

But it opened anyway, and Sophie came in. "Are you okay?" she asked.

"Why wouldn't I be?" He didn't bother hiding the sarcasm.

"Failed marriage. The six widows in the house. The dead body. You had to put your extension plans for the ranch on hold." By answering that seriously, Sophie was adding her own sarcasm. "You haven't had sex in months."

"I'm not talking sex with you. Just had a little chat with Roman about that very subject."

She flexed her eyebrows. "I would have thought you already knew about the birds and the bees."

He was so not in the mood for her attempts to cheer him up. Garrett intended to wallow in it while he came up with a fix for this. "Don't you have some other place to be right now?"

Sophie gave a smile that only a kid sister could have managed. "Nope."

"Well, I do. I'm moving to the guesthouse. That means you'll be inconvenienced until those women leave."

She shrugged, started to help him gather up his things. "FYI. Mom's trying to hook you up with Nicky."

Apparently everyone in the known universe was aware of that. Well, maybe everyone but Nicky. Maybe if he mentioned it to her, she'd go running. It was worth a try anyway.

"Mom thinks you and Nicky have this permanent

spiritual bond since the two of you had sex," Sophie continued. "I told her if that were true, then Roman would have spiritual bonds with half the county. She didn't like that."

"I'll bet. How the heck did she find out about Nicky and me anyway?"

"Gossip. She has selective acceptance when it comes to the things she hears, though. If it's about me having sex, then it's a vile rumor. If it's about you, then it's true. She believes you've had sex with the other half of the women in the county that Roman missed."

"Not even close," Garrett grumbled. He tossed his laptop charger and some files onto the stash, then added his laptop on top of the pile.

"It was pretty sucky, though, what you did to Nicky," Sophie added.

Garrett lifted his head, looked at her. Or rather glared at her. "How do you know what I did to Nicky?"

"Please. I've got ears, and I might be four years younger than you, but I still heard the gossip."

Yeah, and he was betting none of that gossip had painted him in a good light. Not that it should. But there were things about that whole encounter that the gossips hadn't known.

Well, one thing anyway.

But Garrett didn't intend to share that with Sophie.

Grabbing the filled trash can, Garrett headed out. Part of him felt like a riled kid who hadn't gotten his way and was now running away from home. But it was more than that. He wanted his privacy, didn't want to have to face anyone new who would give him "poor pitiful Garrett" looks.

Sophie picked up some of the books on his desk and

followed him out. Maybe to resume a chat he in no way wanted to resume. In fact, right now he needed to focus on work, and that meant contacting the work crew and rescheduling. Contacting Clay, as well, to find out if he had a timeline for this investigation. Also calling the cattle broker to postpone delivery of the Angus he'd bought.

He encountered no widows along the way, but as soon as Garrett made it to the backyard, he spotted Kaylee. Hard to miss her since she was right there just a few inches from the steps, and she was holding a cicada shell in her hand.

"Boog," she announced. Clearly, she wasn't a squeamish kid since the shells always looked a little creepy to Garrett. "Mama twit puking."

"That's good." He heard himself say the words, but it didn't actually register in his head. But what did register were some bad flashbacks. Bad because they were good. Memories of Meredith being pregnant. Of the ultrasound where he'd first seen his daughter.

Oh, man.

It felt like a punch to the gut, and Garrett had to get out of there. He needed to get behind a closed door so he could stuff all of these emotions back down. No way could he deal with this now. Maybe not ever.

He hurried past Kaylee only to encounter another obstacle. Nicky. She was lugging a suitcase that she'd apparently just taken from her SUV.

"Sorry if Kaylee was bothering you," Nicky said, and it seemed as if she was about to walk right past him. But then she stopped, maybe because he looked as unsteady as he suddenly felt. "Are you, uh, going to throw up or something?"

Hell. He must have looked really bad. So bad that Sophie took the trash can from him. "I'll put this stuff in the guesthouse," his sister offered. She headed that direction, glancing back as if waiting for him to follow. And he would have, but Nicky stepped in front of him.

"Are you sure you're okay?" Nicky pressed.

"Fine. I'm just busy. How about you? Kaylee said you quit puking."

She nodded, mumbled something under her breath that he didn't catch. What she didn't seem to realize was the effect her daughter was having on him. Thankfully, Kaylee hurried into the house, babbling something about showing off the boog. Too bad Nicky didn't go with her.

"Yes, the puking seems to have run its course," she explained. "I told you I didn't have the stomach for bones, blood and such. Not for puke itself, either, which was why it went on for a while." Nicky paused, took in a weary breath. "Look, I know we got off to a bad start, but I'm asking you not to fight the lease."

Even though it was hard to think, Garrett forced away the flashbacks. He managed it, sort of, and came up with one argument he hadn't given her yet.

"You really want to live in a house where someone died?" he asked.

Nicky shrugged. "Your great-grandfather died there. So did his wife." She looked reasonably strong about that until she shuddered. "But yes, this does creep me out. It's one thing to have your great-grandparents die there, but this guy might have been murdered. In boxers with hearts on them."

Yeah. That'd been disturbing to Garrett, too. "Underpants like that suggest a lover's tryst."

She made a sound of agreement. "Or maybe he had bad taste in boxers. Or he could have just run out of clean undies and those were his last option." She stopped. "But you're right. It feels tryst-y. Which, according to Loretta, points to your Aunt Matilda."

"Loretta told you about her?"

She nodded. "While I was puking. It's possible I missed a word or two of what she was saying, but I caught the gist. Your aunt had h-o-t p-a-n-t-s, and I don't think Loretta meant they were really short shorts."

"No," he had to agree. Even though Garrett had never met his great-aunt, it was unsettling to think she could have killed a man. That "unsettling" wasn't limited to just her though. "I'm holding out that the guy died of natural causes."

Nicky smiled. "And here I didn't think you were a rose-colored-glasses kind of guy."

Her smile quickly faded. Probably because she remembered there wasn't much to be happy about. But while it lasted, he got a glimpse of the cute flute player she'd once been. In those days, she'd been a looker. Still was. And Garrett hated to notice that the years had settled nicely on her.

It was definitely time for him to get the heck away from her.

He stepped around her to do just that, but Nicky blocked his path again. "Please don't fight the lease," she repeated. "I sold my house to pay for the rent and expenses on this place."

"You sold your house?" he questioned.

She nodded. "It really wasn't a home where I wanted to stay. I'd planned on selling it anyway, but I need to give this a try first. I made a promise to these women that they'd have a retreat here on the ranch. I just hadn't counted on the retreat coming with so many...obstacles."

She looked him straight in the eye when she spoke that last word. Yes, he was an obstacle to her, but he wasn't the only one.

"You should know that my mom is playing matchmaker," he informed her. "That's the real reason she agreed to lease the place to you."

Nicky didn't hesitate in nodding. "I know. That's also why she hired me to do some legal work for her."

Garrett frowned. Again, this was news to him. And confusing since they already had a family lawyer. "What kind of legal work?

"She's redoing her will. Not a standard will, either. It's complete with elaborate funeral details and her obituary. She says it'll take weeks, maybe even months to finalize."

Yeah, definitely matchmaking. He could add another chat with his mom to his to-do list. He had to nip this in the bud before it bit him in the ass. He didn't want his mother throwing him together with Nicky—and Kaylee.

Nicky lifted the suitcase onto the bottom step, and Garrett didn't miss the slight grunting sound she made. The grunt got louder when she hoisted it to the next step. With eight more steps to go, she was going to give herself a hernia before she made it to the back door.

Of course, he helped by carrying it up all the steps and onto the porch. Thankfully, the suitcase had wheels so she shouldn't have any trouble getting it inside. After that, though, she was on her own.

"You're leaving?" she asked, tipping her head at the clothes he had draped over his arm.

"Moving to the guesthouse. I figure the house will get pretty crowded what with Mom, our housekeeper, a toddler and six widows."

Nicky got a strange look. A cross between "deer in the headlights" and "oh, crap."

"About that..." she said.

But that was all she managed before he heard sounds he darn sure didn't want to hear. Car engines. And they were all converging on the house like some kind of funeral procession. Garrett watched as they drove in one by one, and they just seemed to keep on coming. Trucks, cars and SUVs. Someone even drove up on a motorcycle.

"About that," Nicky repeated. She opened the back door, pushed in her suitcase. "There are more than six of us." And she ducked inside.

For a few seconds Garrett was stunned into silence. "How many more?"

"Twelve. Maybe thirteen. Fourteen, tops." Nicky walked away, repeating the biggest lie of all. "You'll never even notice we're here."

CHAPTER FIVE

IT WAS LIKE a metaphorical intestinal disorder. The widows just kept coming.

When Nicky had first thought of this idea, she'd envisioned a *The World According to Garp* type of haven for women like her who needed mending. Peace, quiet, space. She had none of those things. And even in a house as big as the Grangers', it was hard to find a place where she could go and silently scream.

Like now, for instance.

"Two bathroom toilets are clogged," Loretta reported, reading from a list like the town crier. The woman had a canvas bag filled with heaven knew what looped over her wrist and a small box tucked beneath her arm. "And the Ellery sisters and Lizzie bought the wrong kind of groceries. Did you know they were all vegan when you sent them to the store?"

No idea, but Nicky did have an idea that someone, probably her, would be making another grocery run first thing in the morning. Not that she had time. Apparently, she had toilets to unclog, room assignments to finish not just for here but for the Widows' House once they had the all-clear to return. She also no doubt needed to smooth things over with the housekeeper, Alice, because someone had almost certainly managed to piss her off by now.

"Lizzie's little boy, Liam, was running through the house, playing ninja, and he broke some stuff," Loretta continued.

That didn't surprise Nicky. She'd only caught glimpses of the four-year-old, but Liam always seemed to be running. Lizzie needed to try to get him under control or there were going to be even more problems. "Keep a list of the broken items, and I'll replace them," Nicky said.

The only bright spot in this day was that Kaylee was napping and hadn't wandered off to pester Garrett. But even that silver lining was tarnished. Since it was 6:00 p.m., it was too late for a nap and too early for her normal bedtime, which meant she'd be up half the night. That meant no sleep for Nicky at a time when she desperately needed it.

No one would certainly accuse Nicky of wearing rose-colored glasses right now.

It didn't help that she was in Garrett's office. Even though he wasn't there, she was still surrounded by his things and could almost feel those things scowling at her. Kaylee hadn't seemed to mind, and that's why she'd fallen asleep on the small sofa beneath the window.

"Ruby Billings," Loretta went on. "Suicide," she added in a whisper to indicate that it was what had made Ruby a widow. "She's already complaining about her roommate."

Nicky checked her list. There were five available bedrooms and a family room with a pullout sofa, which meant people had to triple up in some cases. In Ruby's case, she was sharing with D. M. Arnison— surgical complications—who'd arrived on a Harley.

Nicky didn't know D.M. that well, but the woman did have Tourette's which caused her to let curse words fly without warning. That might offend some of the other widows, but someone had to room with her. And it wasn't as if the woman could help what came out of her mouth.

"Ruby wants you to check with Mrs. Granger to see if we can use her kids' rooms," Loretta added. "Since they're not using them and all."

Nicky was shaking her head before Loretta even finished. "No. We've disrupted the family enough, and those are their own personal spaces."

Something she didn't have at the moment, but she would hold her ground on this. They would make do with the six rooms they had. Even if they had to cram sixteen widows and two children into them.

Nicky checked her bed assignment list again and grabbed a pencil to make the changes. She'd given up using a pen because the change requests were coming in on an hourly basis.

"Put Ruby in with Lizzie and her son," Nicky instructed. "Ask D.M. if we can move a cot for her in the big bedroom with the Ellery sisters. The sisters have said they'll share the king-size bed that's in there. If that doesn't meet their approval, then I'll start calling hotels."

It was something Belle had insisted she not do, but Garrett's mom maybe hadn't realized the logistical and plumbing issues involved with having eighteen houseguests.

She gave Loretta the revised list, and Loretta handed Nicky the list of things yet to be done. Some needed help getting luggage upstairs, dinner had to be fixed, and there'd be cleaning up after that.

"You're not on the bedroom list," Loretta pointed out.

"Kaylee and I will sleep in here. Garrett moved his office to the guesthouse."

Loretta eyed the sofa, which was smaller than a twin bed, and there wasn't exactly a lot of floor space, either. It didn't matter. As exhausted as Nicky was, she could sleep on the desk. But exhaustion would have to wait.

"Oh, and this came for you," Loretta said just as she was about to leave. She took the box from beneath her arm and gave it to Nicky.

There was a white satin ribbon wrapped around it, making it look like some kind of gift. But Nicky instantly got a bad feeling about it. "I'll open it later," she told Loretta, mainly to get the woman moving.

Loretta did, but only after Nicky started mumbling to herself as she looked over the new to-do list. The moment Loretta was gone, however, Nicky slipped off the ribbon, lifted the lid a fraction and looked inside.

Oh, God.

Two yellow roses.

Her stomach went into a spin, and for a couple of seconds, it felt as if someone had sucked all the air from the planet. But the oxygen was there, and Nicky took several deep breaths, hoping they would steady her. That was asking a lot of mere air, but it helped some. It helped even more when she tossed the box in the trash bag that she'd been using as a garbage can.

The roses were nothing, she reminded herself. *Nothing.*

It took a couple more repeats of that mantra, more

deep breaths, too, but Nicky finally gathered some composure. She didn't have time for games like this.

She glanced at Kaylee to make sure she was still asleep and then went in search of a plunger. She only got a few steps before she saw a familiar face headed her way. Gina Simpson, *car accident*. But this was one additional widow Nicky actually wanted to see. Gina was not only Kaylee's nanny, but she was also Nicky's best friend.

"There's a really hot cowboy unclogging a toilet." Gina hitched her thumb in the direction of the other side of the house. "Never thought of that as hot, but he managed to make it look spellbinding. He's got an audience, too. I think a couple of the women are hoping for a butt-crack showing."

With that, Gina pulled Nicky into her arms for a too-hard hug. Gina was built like an Amazon warrior and sort of resembled one, too, with that untamed mop of brunette hair and six-foot body. The tattoos helped with that image. She had one on her arm, another on her ankle, and a gold nose ring that always seemed to catch the light just right.

"What's wrong?" Gina said after looking at Nicky's eyes.

Nicky dismissed her worry with a wave of her hand. "Just tired, that's all." And to get them on a different subject, she added, "Who's the toilet-cleaning cowboy?" Because she couldn't imagine Garrett volunteering for that. Of course, she couldn't see him refusing to do it, either. Beneath all that growl and hiss, she suspected he was a nice guy. He just hadn't been a nice guy with her.

"Lawson Granger," Gina provided. "A brother?"

"Cousin. Garrett's brother doesn't live here at the ranch." Actually, Lawson didn't, either. He had a place in town.

"I got your messages about the dead body and the change of location." Gina glanced into the office, smiled when she spotted Kaylee. "Thought you could use some help so I picked up fried chicken and pizza. It's on the counter in the kitchen. Oh, and I hauled my camper trailer here. Figured you could use the extra space. It only has one bed, but I can double up."

Nicky could have kissed her. And she did. She kissed Gina's cheek. "Sometimes, I think you have ESP."

"Oh, I do." She winked, but it wasn't exactly a joke.

Gina did have a knack for anticipating problems, which made her an excellent nanny. It also made her a little creepy sometimes, and it was impossible to keep a secret from her. Not from others, though, thank goodness. And Nicky had some she wanted to keep secret. A couple of them she was trying to forget, two that could further complicate what she was trying to do here in Wrangler's Creek.

And one that could destroy her.

Gina leaned in. "So, how's it going with the ex-lover boy? Is he helping the women get settled in?"

Nicky was thankful for the question. It got her mind off those secrets, even though the new topic wasn't an especially happy one. "No. He's probably staying as far away as possible." Nicky sighed. "I told him he wouldn't notice we were here, but he definitely noticed."

"Poor baby." There was plenty enough sarcasm in Gina's voice. "Serves him right after the way he treated you. A teenage girl's heart is a fragile thing, and breaking it requires some getting even."

Nicky sighed again, something she'd likely be doing a lot. In hindsight, it hadn't been a good idea to tell Gina about the deflowering/breakup incident with Garrett. But there'd been margaritas involved, and Nicky usually got blabbery after a couple of those. Of course, Gina had taken her side on this. That's what friends did, but now that Garrett and Gina would be in each other's company, Nicky hoped her friend didn't dig up those old bones with Garrett.

"I think I made a mistake, trying to put all of this together," Nicky confessed.

She'd wanted a place of respite for women who'd lost their partners. Women who were trying to piece their lives back together. Something Nicky had been trying to do since her husband had died almost eighteen months earlier. Of course, her piecing together wasn't solely from grief. She'd had plenty of other things to deal with because of Patrick. By giving back to the women, Nicky had hoped she would work things out for herself, too.

"The Widows' House looked good on paper, but maybe I need to throw in the towel."

Gina dismissed that with a *pshaw*. Whatever that meant. "You're just tired and maybe still a little queasy. Did you throw up when you saw the dead body?"

Nicky nodded. "Three times. But it's more than the dead body." Something she thought she'd never hear herself say. "It's, well, being here around Garrett. I didn't think it would bother me this much."

"Again, that's fatigue." Gina shrugged. "And maybe leftover lust," she added in a whisper. "If he looks anything like his cousin, then he's lust-worthy. But you also know lust leads to crushed hearts."

Yes, she did know that. But knowing it didn't make her feel any better. She needed to heal, and it was best not to get broken again while she was trying to do that.

Gina put her arm around her. "Tell you what. Let's wake up Kaylee, get some pizza in both of you and then Kaylee can sleep with me in the camper. That'll give you that itty bitty sofa all to yourself." She paused. "That is where you planned to sleep, right?"

"Yes." And that wasn't exactly ESP on Gina's part. Gina just knew her well enough to know that Nicky wouldn't take one of the beds. Not when she felt personally responsible for this situation.

"Let me get that doll baby." Gina hurried in to scoop up Kaylee. The little girl protested, whined, yawned and then smiled when she saw Gina. Lots of hugs ensued as if they hadn't seen each other for days instead of just hours.

Nicky followed Gina and Kaylee to the kitchen, but before she made it there, her phone dinged with a text message.

Call me soon, the text read, and it wasn't from just any ol' somebody.

It was from Meredith, Garrett's ex-wife.

Nicky frowned. Then frowned some more. Meredith could be another complication that she didn't need, but sooner or later she was going to have to call the woman back. And tell Garrett all about this.

After another frown and sigh, Nicky opted for later.

GARRETT HAD FIGURED since it was four in the morning that there'd be no one in the house up and about. He'd figured wrong.

Mrs. Batson, heart attack, was on the back porch steps, and she was smoking a cigarette. She quickly snuffed it out, and as she'd done at Z.T.'s place, she skittered back inside. Well, at least she hadn't gotten in his way.

Garrett slipped inside, glancing around the kitchen. No one. But there were some pizza boxes on the counter so he helped himself to a cold slice and a Coke before he went up the hall toward his office.

He passed the family room along the way and spotted two women on the sleeper sofa. Heaven knew how many of them were scattered throughout the house by now. Or how long they would be there. But in a couple of hours he could start bugging Clay about getting Z.T.'s place cleared so the women could return to it. It had only been a day since they'd discovered the body, but maybe Clay could work extra fast on this.

By the time Garrett got to his office, he'd nearly finished the pizza, but he clamped the remainder between his teeth so he'd have a free hand to grab some files from his desk drawer. He opened the door.

And froze.

There was enough moonlight coming through the window that he had no trouble seeing the woman lying on his desk. She was curled up in a fetal position and was using a book for a pillow.

What the hell?

It was Nicky.

She lifted her head. In the same motion, she gasped, grabbed a pen and jabbed it at him the way a person would wield a knife. She missed, but a strange garbled sound left her mouth. Maybe trying to choke back a scream.

"Garrett?" Nicky said on a rise of breath. "You scared the bejeebers out of me."

He didn't know what a bejeebers was, but she'd given him a scare of sorts, too, because he sure as hell hadn't expected anyone to be sleeping in his office, let alone on his desk.

"Sorry," she added. "I'm still on edge." No doubt because of the body that'd been found.

Groaning and wincing, Nicky climbed off the desk, got to her feet and turned on the reading light. Her gaze met his, and she looked at him funny. Only then did he remember he had what was left of a pizza slice sticking out of his mouth.

Garrett yanked away the pizza so he could talk. "Why are you on my desk?"

"Because the sofa was too small, and I kept falling off." She made it seem as if that answered his question. It didn't.

"There wasn't a bed?" he pressed.

She shook her head and pushed her hands through her hair to move it off her face. He'd seen her face before, of course. Had seen most of her entire body actually. But there was something, well, intimate about having a sleepy-eyed woman just a few inches away.

One who smelled like sex.

That was probably his imagination though.

"Why are you here?" she asked.

"I need some files." And he went to his desk drawer to get those. To do that, he had to walk right past her, and that's when he noticed what she was wearing. Pj's. Specifically, his pj's.

"Oh," Nicky said, following his gaze. "My luggage seems to have gotten lost in the shuffle. I didn't have any clean clothes, and your mom checked Sophie's room for some, but your sister's already moved her things to Clay's. She got these for me instead. She said you don't ever use them, that you usually sleep in your boxers."

Well, Nicky had gotten in his pants after all. Which was a stupid thought, of course. Something a teenage boy would think, but that seemed to be the way his mind was going right now. That meant it was time to get out of there.

Garrett finished off the last bite of pizza, grabbed the files and was ready to leave. But Nicky stopped him.

"Uh, can I ask you a question?" She didn't wait for him to agree, though. "Are you and your ex-wife on good terms these days?"

Garrett was certain he looked surprised. Because he was. "No. We're not on any kind of terms because I haven't spoken to her in months." And he'd like to keep it that way. "You know about the video that ended up all over the internet?"

Nicky nodded, glanced away. He'd been positive that she knew, and that was why her question was even more puzzling.

"Why would you want to know about my ex?" he asked.

She lifted her shoulder. "I was just wondering. I remember her from high school, of course. She moved to Wrangler's Creek our senior year."

This was still confusing. "But you weren't friends. Were you?" Because if they were, this was the first he was hearing about it. Then again, that not hearing about things was going around.

"No," she quickly agreed. "She knew about what had happened between us and didn't especially want me around. Over the years though, I've run into her from time to time, and she's been friendly enough."

Again, first time hearing this. Meredith had certainly never mentioned it.

"Anyway," Nicky went on, "no one around here has said anything about Meredith, and I didn't know if you'd been able to work past what'd happened or not."

He hadn't worked past it, but there was no way he'd tell Nicky that. He was about to press her again as to why she had a sudden interest in his ex, but maybe this was part of some kind of therapy. A shared experience sort of thing. Except there was really nothing to share. Meredith was alive, and Nicky's husband wasn't.

Her husband, Patrick.

Yeah, he'd looked it up on the internet. There hadn't been an obituary, but there'd been a mention of him on social media from someone he'd done business with. It was one of those requests for prayers and hugs.

According to what Garrett could glean from that, Patrick had been a lawyer at the same firm where Nicky worked. He'd died from cancer and been gone almost eighteen months now. Not an eternity, but maybe the pain wasn't still as fresh and raw for Nicky. Of course, the flipside to that was Kaylee had been so young that she wouldn't even remember her father. That had to be eating away at Nicky, too.

Garrett knew plenty about grief. It was a hungry bitch. And if he could figure out a way to beat it, he would have already done it.

"I'm sorry," Garrett said before he even knew he was going to say it.

She nodded but seemed ready to ask him to explain that. If she hadn't also looked like sex, he might have hung around and added more. He headed out, but he nearly smacked right into Loretta.

"Good morning, Garrett," she said. "It's so good to see you again."

Loretta didn't look anything like sex, but she did seem wide awake. Awake, smiling and also wearing his pj's.

"Loretta's luggage got misplaced, too," Nicky volunteered.

Well, at least he wouldn't encounter anyone else wearing his limited nightwear because he had only two sets of pajamas.

Garrett mumbled a "good morning" and hurried out. Staying longer and looking at Nicky would only cause this tug in his belly to tug even harder. He wasn't overly concerned about belly tugs per se, but if that tug lowered to that idiot part of him behind his zipper, he'd be in big trouble.

CHAPTER SIX

NICKY WAITED ON hold for Clay McKinnon while she watched out the window. Kaylee and Gina were in the backyard, playing fetch with a golden retriever, and Kaylee was having a blast. Nicky couldn't say the same for herself, though. That's because her daughter and Gina weren't the only ones in her line of sight.

So was Garrett.

He was in the barn about twenty yards away, and while he wasn't exactly nearby, Garrett had a way of grabbing her attention.

Damn him.

He was wearing those snug jeans again and looking very much like the hot cowboy he was. A cowboy in charge since he seemed to be doling out orders to several of the hands. Judging from their body language, they were listening but weren't liking what they were hearing.

Nicky had wanted these old feelings to be gone by now, but instead they'd morphed into adult feelings. Specifically, feelings where she had no trouble noticing how attractive he was.

Would she never learn?

Apparently not. Two heart stompings weren't enough to teach her a lesson, and she wasn't sure she could survive a third one.

"You still there, Mrs. Marlow?" Chief Clay McKinnon asked when he finally came on the line.

"Nicky," she automatically corrected. "I'm here. I hate to bother you because you must be busy, but I just wanted to know if there were any updates on the body?"

Just saying the word *body* tightened her stomach, and Nicky hoped she wouldn't feel the need to vomit again. While she was hoping, she added that maybe she could get those images out of her head. Every time she closed her eyes, she saw the skeleton. She hoped those images went away soon since she still had plans to live in that house for the next year.

"The remains have been moved to the county morgue," Clay explained, "and the CSIs will start going through the place this morning. I don't expect them to find much, not after all this time, but you never know."

Nicky glanced out the window again to check on Kaylee. She was no longer playing with the dog but rather was running toward Garrett. That nearly sent Nicky bolting after her because she didn't want Kaylee to bother Garrett, but Gina was on her heels.

"As for the identity of the John Doe," Clay went on, "he didn't have any ID on him, and there weren't any clothes in the immediate area that could have belonged to him. The CSIs will look upstairs, though. Did you happen to come across any men's clothes when you were cleaning?"

"There are some in a few of the dressers and trunks, but I doubt he undressed and put his things away."

"No. Unless he was staying there. That's possible, of course, but it's more likely that someone moved the clothes."

She was glad he didn't spell that out for her, but Nicky's mind began to race with some really bad ideas. Like maybe the clothes had been blood-soaked or had bullet holes in them.

"If there's no ID and you can't get his prints, how will you figure out who he is?" she asked.

"I might not. That's the way these things turn out sometimes. Of course, I'll keep looking through the missing person's database. The Ranger lab might be able to do facial reconstruction, too. Until then, I'll keep following what little evidence I have. The guy didn't have any unusual dental work, metal plates or prosthetics, but he was wearing a wedding band."

That got her attention. She certainly hadn't noticed a ring when she'd seen the body, but then she hadn't lingered around for a long look. "He was married," she mumbled.

"Sure looks that way. The band was yellow gold," Clay continued. "And it had the words *forever wrapped around you* engraved inside it."

Nicky felt her heart flutter. Not in a good way, either. Because those were lovers' words. Unless it referred literally to the ring, that is. But she doubted it. No, this was likely a declaration of love.

"He was *really* married," she repeated. Nicky hadn't meant for there to be that much emotion in her voice. Emotion that Clay must have noticed.

"Are you okay?" Clay asked.

She quickly tried to regain her composure. Also quickly tried to figure out how to get this conversation back on track. A track that didn't include transferring her own feelings onto this situation. "I'm fine.

I was thinking, though, that his being married could be a motive for murder, right?"

"Could be. Maybe a jealous wife. Maybe a lover who got fed up waiting for him to get a divorce. I'm interviewing some folks today who knew Matilda. That doesn't mean she had anything to do with this. Won't know that until the ME can come up with a time of death."

Yes, that would certainly help narrow down the list of people who might have had something to do with this. Unless the John Doe was just some trespasser. One who'd gone into the house, stripped off most his clothes and gone into a closet to die.

"By the way, I just told Garrett all of this," Clay added. "He's not giving you any updates?"

Nicky hesitated. "No."

Even though it was only a one-word response, the chief must have filled in the blanks. "He's still not too happy about you and the other widows being there."

Bingo. "There are a lot of us."

"Well, don't take it personally. Garrett just has a lot on his mind these days. Plus, he might be having flashbacks when he sees your daughter."

"Flashbacks?" she blurted out.

Silence. Followed by some mumbled profanity. "I've said too much. I'll call you if I get any other information on the case. Oh, and first chance you get, I need you to drop by my office and sign the report on the dead guy. Loretta's already come in, but I'll need you to, as well." And before Nicky could say anything else, Clay hung up.

She stared at the phone and glanced outside again. Gina was obviously trying to coax Kaylee away from

Garrett, but her daughter had something in her hand that she was showing him. Nicky saw it then. The look on his face, the need to detach from this situation. Did that have something to do with the flashbacks the chief had just mentioned? If Clay hadn't added her daughter to that slipped remark, Nicky might have thought this had something to do with Meredith's sex tape, but it had to be more than that.

Nicky scrolled through her recent calls and texts. Two missed calls and three unanswered texts from Meredith. Maybe it was time to quit skirting around the woman, especially since Meredith might know what was going on. Nicky didn't feel especially good about contacting the woman simply to pump her for information, but she wanted the big picture of what she was up against here. If her being here was causing Garrett real mental anguish, then she needed to find a way to get all the widows, herself included, out of there ASAP.

She made another check out the window first. Gina had Kaylee by the hand and was leading her back toward the house. Garrett was still there. Not alone, though. One of the women was talking to him.

Lady Romero, the *prescription drug overdose* widow, who owned a tow truck business. One that specialized in tacky slogans.

Lady was young, beautiful and, on the surface, didn't seem to be mourning as much as her fellow widows. In fact, at the moment she didn't seem to be mourning at all. She was smiling and touching the front of Garrett's shirt, and even though Nicky couldn't actually see the woman's face, she thought maybe some eyelash batting was going on.

Oh, well. Garrett was a big boy and could take care

of himself. He definitely didn't need her to come to the rescue.

Meredith answered on the first ring, and she obviously knew who was calling. "Nicky, thank God. I've been trying to reach you."

"Sorry, I've been really busy—"

"Yes, I heard about the dead man in Z.T.'s house," Meredith continued. Which was probably a good thing because that prevented Nicky from whining about everything that'd gone on. "You must have been terrified."

"More shocked than anything else—"

"I would have screamed my head off." Again, the interruption was good because Meredith didn't need to hear about her dignity-reducing stomach issues. "It's awful, just awful. Does this mean you won't be opening the Widows' House?"

"I'm still waiting to hear what the police chief has to say, but I think the widows and I will be able to move in soon. Why—?"

"Clay," Meredith said. "He's the police chief, and he's engaged to Sophie. You remember her, right? Yes, I'm sure you do even though she was four years younger than us. I always felt as if Sophie was more like a sister to me than a sister-in-law."

This time the interruption wasn't so welcome because Nicky had been about to ask her the critical question—what the heck was going on with Garrett?

But Meredith remedied that when she continued. "Have you talked to Garrett since you've been at the ranch?"

"A couple of times. Not for long, though. He was at the house when one of the widows found the body."

"Loretta," Meredith provided. "When you didn't answer my call or texts, I phoned one of the Ellery sisters, and she filled me in. Poor Loretta. Poor you! My God, your daughter didn't see that, did she?"

"No."

And this conversation was sounding a little too friendly for Nicky. Not that she minded friendliness, but it felt strange coming from Meredith. Over the past seventeen years, they'd seen each other three times. Once at a fund-raiser. Then a second time when Nicky had run into Meredith in a restaurant. That's why it'd surprised her when Meredith had shown up at the widow's support group.

It surprised Nicky even more, though, when she'd found out what Meredith had wanted.

The woman made a sound of relief over Kaylee not seeing the body, and this time it was Nicky who interrupted her. "Look, Meredith, I've considered what we talked about at the support group meeting, but I don't think it's a good idea for you to stay at the Widows' House."

Silence. For a long time. "I see." More silence. "I know I'm a divorcée and not a widow, but I can promise you I need the therapy and quiet time as much as the rest of you. I've been through a lot, Nicky."

She didn't doubt that, and Nicky wasn't immune to the emotion she heard in Meredith's voice. A nasty divorce was a nasty thing. But Nicky also knew Meredith had brought some of that nastiness on herself. Unless...

Nicky went back to what Clay had said about the flashbacks.

She hadn't exactly spent much time combing the internet for info about Garrett and Meredith. A friend had sent her the sex video, and Nicky had read some articles about the troubles with the Granger family business. Trouble that had now been resolved, apparently, but she'd purposely avoided anything personal. Maybe that had been a mistake.

"Do you think Garrett will have any trouble being around Kaylee?" Nicky came out and asked. It was an out-and-out fishing expedition, and she didn't expect much. She got plenty though.

"Maybe," Meredith said right off. But like before, she paused. "Garrett hasn't said anything about our daughter?"

Daughter? "Uh, no."

"Well, he probably won't. We lost her, you see. Stillborn. And Garrett was never the same after that. Neither was I," she admitted, and Nicky thought the woman might be crying or close to it. "Anyway, Kaylee and our little girl would have been about the same age."

Mercy. Yes, that definitely explained the flashback comment. "I'm so sorry," Nicky said.

"Now you know why I need to be at the Widows' House. I've always loved Z.T.'s old place. Always felt a peace and calm there, and I'm hoping it'll help. I need to heal. I need to get better."

Crud. How was she supposed to say no to that? And she was about to give in. Then, she remembered Garrett and knew this would be just another thorn in his side.

"I'll get back to you," she told Meredith, and Nicky ended the call before the woman could launch into another tear-filled argument. One that Meredith would almost certainly win this time.

Nicky groaned and put away her phone. Her quest for peace and healing was turning into a huge poop pile. And now she needed to sign that report for Clay. Which meant she'd have to read all about the dead man. Hopefully there wouldn't be any photos of the body to accompany the report.

She stood, checked on Garrett again. Frowned again. Lady had leaned in even closer. Garrett wasn't leaning, though. He glanced at the office window and met Nicky's gaze. He shot her a glare, and that was her cue to get out there and rescue him from Lady. And no, it didn't have anything to do with Nicky being jealous. She just wanted to minimize the crud that Garrett was having to face because they were all there.

Nicky grabbed her purse and was on the way out the door when she heard the footsteps, and she hoped this wasn't another widow in search of sanctuary. If so, she'd have to turn her away. She looked in the hall to do just that. But it wasn't a widow. Heck, it wasn't even a woman.

It was Roman.

He came toward her, several widows trailing behind him. Not showing him the way obviously. Because he knew the way in his own home. No, she recognized the signs. They were starstruck or rather Roman-struck as she used to call it. He definitely had that effect on most women. Not her, though. Nicky had never had a thing for bad boys, and Roman was very, very bad.

"Nicky," Roman greeted. As greetings went, it wasn't exactly warm and fuzzy. "I've come here to evict you."

CHAPTER SEVEN

NICKY DRAGGED IN a long breath, one that she was certain she would need for the argument she was about to have with Roman. Obviously, his brother had gotten to him and convinced Roman to oust them. For a moment Nicky considered letting him do just that with no argument whatsoever from her, but then she remembered there were actually women who needed the Widows' House.

Including her.

"Roman, please, don't kick us off the ranch." Nicky figured she was going to have to say a lot more than that to convince him.

He shrugged. "Okay."

Nicky took another long breath, but that's because she was confused. The confusion didn't clear up any when Roman took some keys from his pocket and dangled them in front of her.

"A friend lent me his RV." He took her hand, put the keys in her palm. "It sleeps six so that means you won't have to spend the night on Garrett's desk again. I've also told Mom to put someone in my old room. Sophie insists someone use hers, too. That'll mean fewer women will have to double and triple up. But the RV is for you. Consider that my version of an eviction."

She hadn't intended to kiss him but Nicky did. The

kiss was purely chaste and on his cheek, but one of the gawking widows sighed.

"Thank you," she whispered to him. "But how'd you know I'd slept on his desk?"

"I got it from the horse's mouth when he called me about some ranching business. At least he said it was ranching business, but really Garrett just wanted to vent."

Of course, he did. She would vent if everyone else weren't doing the same thing. In fact, this had turned into a vent-a-thon where all the complaints were becoming white noise.

"I swear, we'll clear out of here as soon as I can manage it," Nicky assured him.

He shrugged again in that lazy way that most mortal men couldn't have managed. "My brother's going through some stuff."

That was a nice way of saying Garrett's life had taken a nosedive. "I knew about some of it," she said. "But if I'd had the big picture, I would have just bitten the bullet and sent all the widows away."

"Big picture?" he repeated. "You mean his baby?"

She nodded. "I only just found out about it. He must think about her every time he looks at my little girl."

"He thinks about her even when your daughter's not here. Nothing you can do about that. Nothing any of us can do," he added in a mumble. Roman tipped his head to the purse she'd looped over her shoulder. "Going somewhere?"

"Clay's office to sign a report." She followed his gaze to the window where he'd spotted Garrett and Lady. "But I can stay if you want to catch up."

"No. I should see Garrett." He checked his watch.

"I'll wait, though, about twenty or thirty minutes. I enjoy seeing him sweat a little."

Nicky had another look at Garrett, too. "Maybe he's not sweating. He could be interested in her."

Roman responded with a sound that could have meant anything.

At that exact moment, Garrett shot her another glare, and he must have also spotted Roman because he said something to Lady and started for the house. That was Nicky's cue to leave. She said goodbye to Roman, goodbye, too, to the trail of widows gawking at him.

Nicky made a quick call to Gina to let her know that she'd be gone for a while, and she headed out the front door. Her SUV was actually parked in the back, but this way she could avoid Garrett. Thankfully, she avoided not only him but anyone else who might have stopped her along the way.

She got in her SUV, letting the quiet wash over her. Ironic that this was the most peace she'd found in the past twenty-four hours. Too bad it would have to end with that report.

The drive to town was a blast from the past. She'd done this trip many times, first on her bike and then in the run-down Toyota she'd managed to afford by working summers and weekends at the grocery store. There'd been no real reason for her to make the drive since the Granger Ranch wasn't on the way to anything. It was just something she'd done, all the while thinking about how it would feel to be normal like the Grangers.

She passed Clay's house and then Vita Banchini's, the oddball fortune-teller who sometimes put curses on people. Vita definitely fell outside the normal range.

And, of course, Nicky saw the old house where she'd been raised.

It didn't sit right on the road, but since there were no trees in front of it, it was impossible to miss. She slowed, not intending to stop but stopping anyway. Maybe this was a moth-to-a-flame kind of thing, but she also wondered if it was time to confront a demon or two.

The place was vacant and apparently had been for years. Her parents had once owned it and then lost it in foreclosure just a few weeks before her high school graduation. It hadn't exactly felt like much of a loss at the time.

Still didn't.

The Penningtons had bought the place from the bank after that and had used it as rental property. That probably hadn't been a successful venture because Wrangler's Creek didn't have a big renters' market, but she hadn't been around to know for sure. In fact, she'd spent the next seven years of her life working her way through college and trying to forget this place ever existed.

In hindsight, that need to forget had been the reason she'd avoided any and all updates on the town and especially the Grangers. After what'd happened with Garrett, the memories had rolled together into one giant, smothering ball of hurt and misery. But all of that had happened seventeen years ago. A lifetime. Maybe it was lifetime enough for this place to have lost its hold over her.

She parked next to the yard that was more weeds than grass. There were no signs of her mother's rose-bushes and flowerbeds, and Nicky wondered if the weeds had claimed them or if someone had taken mercy on them and replanted them at a more hospitable place. She hoped it was the latter.

Something good had to have come out of here.

The screen door on the front was hanging on one hinge, and the July breeze caught it, causing it to make a creaking sound as it swayed. Definitely not welcoming, but she just kept on walking up the steps. Nicky only made it to the second of five steps before she had to stop. She couldn't make her feet, or her mind, go any farther.

Even though she was still a good two yards away from the front door, she caught the scent of the place. She got an instant slam of dust, mustiness and other smells she didn't want to identify.

She'd thought there couldn't be a place grimier than Z.T.'s house, but Nicky had been wrong about that. From what she could see, there was plenty of dust here. Dead leaves and other debris, too. The paint on the walls was blistered and peeling. The wood floors, pocked with nicks and gouges. Nothing the way it had been when she'd lived here. She and her mother had at least kept the place clean.

But clean places sometimes held a dirty secret. This one certainly did.

The memories came. Not as some old, watery images that she couldn't blink away, either. No. She wasn't that lucky. These were crystal clear.

Memories of her father and his drunken rages.

Memories of him coming home from whatever job he hadn't been fired from yet. Staggering through the door, his body slumped because he was too drunk to stand upright. It always put a knot in her gut to know that he'd driven home that way from some bar.

Grow a pair, Nicky!

He'd yelled it at her so many times that it was like a tattoo inked on her brain. He'd told her that anytime he was disappointed in her. Anytime she'd cried. Anytime things hadn't gone his way.

Which was often.

She hadn't even known what it meant until she was eleven or so and then had gotten a backhand across the face when she had tried to explain in earnest that she would never grow a pair of testicles. After that he'd amended it.

Grow a pair, you dumb bitch!

There had been no lamps in the house because he'd managed to break every one of them. Most of their dishes were plastic. Because when he was in a drunken rage, he liked to smash things.

It didn't happen every night. In fact, sometimes he'd stay sober for months. Just long enough to lull her mother and her into thinking that the monster wouldn't come back. But it did.

It always came back.

There were times, like now, when Nicky could feel his hand slap her face. Times when she could hear the slurred words that had made her feel broken. So broken that she might never fit together again.

Stupid. Bitch. Ugly. Whore.

He'd had other words for her mother, but those were the ones he saved just for her. They echoed through her head now. Through the house, too, and Nicky could have sworn she smelled the cheap whiskey on his breath. The old sweat he hadn't bothered to wash off before he'd started his slide into the bottle.

His name had been Walt Levi Henderson. And he'd died of liver failure at the age of forty-three. But not before leaving his mark on her. Several of them in fact. Nicky had the scars he'd given her along with the one she'd given herself. The one when she'd used a razor to cut into her own breast.

Cutter was such an ugly word.

But it wasn't as ugly as the word she'd cut into her skin.

That was another of her secrets. And it was a secret she could hide beneath her clothes.

Grow a pair, you dumb bitch!

She thought of her big brother. Kyle. He was five years older than she was and had run away when Nicky had only been twelve. Or rather ridden away on a motorcycle he'd built from spare parts he'd found in the junkyard. Sometimes, she'd resented him for leaving, for not trying to save her. But he'd been just a kid, as well, and he certainly hadn't gotten out unscathed. No. Kyle had scars, too.

The tears came, and she cursed them. Damn him. Damn this. Obviously, she was nowhere close to chasing away the demons. In fact, it felt as if she'd just cut herself again. As if she'd ripped herself open to let those demons back inside her.

Grow a pair, you dumb bitch!

She whirled around, ready to bolt off the step, and landed right in Garrett's arms.

Nicky heard the strangled sound make its way through her throat. It wasn't a sound she wanted anyone to hear. Especially Garrett.

"You scared me," she managed to say.

Nicky didn't look at him. In fact, she looked everywhere else because she didn't want him to see what was in her eyes. Not just the tears. But the broken pain.

He opened his mouth, and she braced herself for him to say something like *I wasn't the one who scared you.* Or *what the hell is going on?*

But he didn't.

Garrett closed his mouth, and she could almost sense him debating how to handle this. Her elusive gaze probably wasn't fooling him, and he likely knew something was wrong. Hopefully, he also knew that saying anything about it would be opening a particularly nasty can of worms.

"I picked you up a couple of times here when we dated," he finally said.

So, no worm-can-opening today. Good. Because Nicky thought that maybe talking about it would be the same skin-cutting experience as being inside the place. It'd been a mistake to come here, and like the other times she'd felt this way, she wanted to run. Not to just any ordinary place but to Z.T.'s old house.

Fifteen minutes. That's all it would take her to run there if she cut through the old ranch trails and the pastures. Fifteen minutes before she could hide in a safe, quiet place with no drunk fathers calling her names.

Of course, she couldn't go there. Not only because of the investigation but also because Garrett likely wouldn't let her start running without expecting her to explain what the heck was going on.

"The dust got to me," she lied, wiping her eyes. Nicky stepped around him and went into the yard. It helped. She could catch her breath, could try to tamp down all these stupid emotions.

She could leave.

And that's what she started to do, but Garrett stepped in front of her, blocking her path. Judging from the look on his face, he was getting that opener ready for the worm can.

GARRETT WASN'T SURE that stopping Nicky was the smartest idea he'd ever had. It was obvious she didn't want to talk about what was going on in her head. But that stark look in her eyes tugged at him.

Because he was likely the reason for it.

Not just his attitude about the lease but also their past. He couldn't undo the past and couldn't pretend to be happy about the lease so Garrett just chose another topic. One that might get her mind on something else. In turn that something else might get that look off her face.

"Why are you here anyway?" he asked.

"I was on my way into town to sign a report for Clay, and I couldn't resist a trip down memory lane."

He glanced around the place. "Sometimes memory lane is best forgotten."

That got the reaction he wanted. She smiled. It didn't last and probably wasn't genuine, but he'd take it.

"Your folks moved right around the time you left to go to college," he commented. "Where are they now? And what about your brother? Where did he end up?"

She glanced away again, and he wanted to curse himself for the nerve that he'd obviously hit. "Kyle's in San Antonio. My mother moved to Virginia to be closer to her sister. And my dad passed away." She paused only the span of a breath. "What about you? Why are you here?"

"I'm on my way to sign a report, too. If I'd known you had to come in, I could have given you a ride." Man, she probably thought he had multiple personalities or something. One minute he was trying to give her the boot. The next, trying to give her a ride.

She shook her head. "I had some errands to do, too."

He got the feeling that was a lie, but he didn't call her on it. "How'd your visit with Roman go?"

"Great." No smile, but she seemed relieved with not only the topic but the result. "He's letting us stay in the house, and I'm sure you saw the RV he brought."

Garrett nodded. He saw it and approved. Well, as much as he could approve of any of this. It would get Nicky off his desk.

"Should I ask why Roman doesn't live at home?" she said.

"No." He paused, looked away. Since that was rude, he felt the need to explain a little. "He owns a rodeo business in San Antonio and has a house there. But he also owns the Granger Ranch."

"Yes. I heard your mom mention something about that last night. And she said your cousins still own all the land north of here and are trying to buy more. Pretty soon Wrangler's Creek isn't going to be big enough for the Grangers."

It already wasn't big enough. The only saving grace right now was that his cousins didn't have a working ranch on their land. They had a large spread just one county over. That was in part why Lawson worked for him in Wrangler's Creek. Also in part because there was some feuding going on between him and his brothers. A feud Garrett didn't want to know anything about.

"How was your visit with Lady?" she asked.

Well, it hadn't been great, as Nicky had no doubt witnessed from the window. "Lady doesn't seem to be grief stricken."

"How so?" But it was a question meant to poke fun at him. Because she knew that Lady had been all over him.

"As my mother would say, she wants to get in my pants. That won't happen. So, I told her I wasn't interested." Of course, he'd had to say variations of that *not interested* several times before the woman got the message.

The silence came, and it wasn't a good silence, either. It was the awkward kind so he stepped to the side in case she wanted to leave. She did. Nicky immediately headed for her SUV and got in. She couldn't leave, though, because Garrett was parked behind her so he went to his truck and drove away. But not before giving the old house one last look.

What the hell had gone on here?

Because he was no longer certain that he was the one responsible for those tears he'd seen in Nicky's eyes.

Garrett drove into town and parked in front of the Wrangler's Creek Police Station. Nicky didn't, though. She drove past him, no doubt to run those errands she'd mentioned. Probably to avoid him, as well. Since he'd been avoiding her, Garrett couldn't fault her for that.

He went inside and made a beeline for Clay's office at the back of the building. Not a long walk since, like everything else in the town of Wrangler's Creek, it wasn't that big. He found his soon-to-be brother-in-law seated at his desk.

"Anything new on the John Doe?" Garrett immediately asked him.

"Not really." Clay stood, poured Garrett and himself some coffee. "It might be a week before the CSIs can go through the whole place. Did you know there were secret rooms?"

"Yeah. There's one off the library. Another in the master bedroom." Garrett was about to take a sip of the coffee, but he got a bad feeling. "Please don't tell me you found another body."

"No, but it just means there are more places the CSIs will have to examine and maybe process."

"Process? You're not talking about collecting fingerprints, DNA and things like that?" Garrett's mind went straight to a bad place.

He'd obviously seen too many crime shows, and a little porn, because he thought of all the possible DNA in the place. His DNA and Nicky's. Of course, it wasn't as if everyone didn't already know that Nicky and he had been together like that. Still, he doubted she would want that old water, old bridge brought up again.

"They're looking for the John Doe's clothes and anything else that will help us identify him," Clay explained. He lifted his eyebrow as if he'd known what Garrett was thinking. "If he was murdered, the killer could have removed them. But if something else happened, the clothes might still be around."

"Right. Of course." And Garrett hated that he sounded relieved about it.

"They'll collect DNA from the body. From his boxers, hat and wedding ring, as well. And his clothes, if they're found. Here's the report," he added.

Clay slid it in front of Garrett, and Garrett sat down so he could look it over. Everything was there. Everything that they knew so far, that is.

"By the way, Nicky seemed upset when I mentioned the guy might be married," Clay told him. "I think all of this might be getting to her."

Clay seemed to be asking Garrett to check on her. Which he had when he'd seen her SUV parked at her old house. Judging from what he saw there, she might need to be checked on again. First though, he'd like to know what he was dealing with.

Garrett read through the report, signed it and passed it back to Clay. "You don't happen to have any old files on Nicky's folks, do you?"

Clay pulled back his shoulders. "Not that I know of. Why? You think they could be connected to our John Doe?"

"No. It's not that." But he couldn't say what it was exactly. "It's just I remember some rumors about her father getting drunk, maybe even arrested. And her brother, Kyle, ran off when he was just a teenager. I figure that couldn't be a sign of a happy household for him to have done that."

Clay stayed quiet a moment, but Garrett could almost hear the guy thinking. And he was thinking like a cop. "Are you looking for something to help you evict Nicky?"

"No." Garrett huffed. The truth wasn't going to make this sound any better, but he went with it anyway. "I just saw Nicky out at the old house her folks once owned, and it seemed as if she didn't have good memories of the place."

Nope, the truth didn't sound better, and that's probably why Clay gave him a cop's stare. One where he was no doubt trying to figure out what the hell was going on.

"She was crying," Garrett added.

That got rid of the cop stare and, cursing under his breath, Clay sank down into the chair behind his desk. "Am I going to need to be concerned that Nicky's come back to dole out some kind of payback to her parents?"

Garrett had to answer no for a third time. "Her father's dead, and her mother doesn't live here so no payback. Could you please just check and see if her dad, Walt Henderson, had a police record? Since the guy's dead, you wouldn't be violating his privacy."

Of course, Clay would probably be violating other things like rules about sharing official information with someone whose argument was that Walt's daughter had been crying. Still, Clay started typing on his computer keyboard.

"Not all the files have been digitized," Clay explained. "So, even if he had a record, it might not be…" He stopped, started reading something he'd pulled up on the screen. "It's here. Drunk and disorderly." He made some more key strokes. "DUI. Two of them," he added. "He also had his driver's license revoked."

This certainly wasn't painting a pretty picture, but Nicky hadn't mentioned anything to him about it. They'd only dated for a month, though, and while that had been enough time for sex, it apparently hadn't been enough for her to share with him the junk going on in her life.

"There's more," Clay continued a moment later. "He was brought in and questioned about a domestic violence situation after the cops were called to his house. That happened about seventeen years ago."

Even though Garrett had just taken a sip of hot coffee, he felt the chill go over him.

"Nothing came of it," Clay added, "because the person refused to file charges against him."

"Nicky's mother," Garrett mumbled.

"No." Clay looked up from the screen and met his gaze. "The person he assaulted was Nicky."

CHAPTER EIGHT

GARRETT READ THROUGH the monthly financial report
on the ranch that their bookkeeper had just emailed
him. It was important because he needed to know if
the changes he was making to the livestock inventory
were causing the ranch to grow or if he was sending
profits in the other direction. Normally, he scrutinized
each line of the report, made notes, calculated adjustments that needed to be made.

Not today, though.

He'd read the report twice now, and the info just
wasn't sticking in his head. That's because he had a
distraction.

Nicky.

Not only because he was thinking about her and what
he'd learned from Clay, but also because he could see
her. She was sitting outside the loaner RV, working on
her laptop while watching Kaylee play. It was something
he'd watched her do for the past two days. What he hadn't
done was talk to her. That was because he felt like a dick.

Hell, he *was* a dick.

Here, she'd almost certainly come home to deal with
a shitload of old baggage. Some newer baggage, too,
since her husband had died and left her a single parent. Dealing with all of that wasn't easy, and he'd made
it hard on her.

"Are you aware you're mumbling?" Lawson asked.

Garrett had known his cousin was there, of course, since he was using his laptop to read the same financial report that Garrett had been. It was something they did together every week, but Garrett figured he was usually more attentive and not prone to mumbling.

"You said *dick* and *hard*," Lawson went on. "Two words that usually work well together." He turned, peering out the window that was in Garrett's line of sight. "Especially when you've got a view like that. Nicky's a looker."

Yeah, she was, but in this case *hard* and *dick* weren't because that was his physical condition. It was because he owed her an apology. Or two. It turned his stomach to think that her father had assaulted her around the same time that Garrett and she had been dating. And he hadn't had a clue.

"Is Roman starting something up with Nicky?" Lawson asked.

And it caused Garrett's gaze to slash to him. "Why would you say that?"

Lawson shrugged, but there was nothing casual about it. His mouth was twitching a little. "Roman only comes to the ranch for emergencies or when Sophie or you browbeat him into coming. Yet, he showed up here a couple days ago with that RV without so much as a prompt. When Roman gives a woman that kind of attention, it's usually because he wants to fuck her."

Garrett had never objected to the F-word, but it suddenly seemed vulgar. And possibly true. Roman might be a single dad, but he was still a bad boy at heart, and that drew some women to him. Probably not Nicky, though.

Probably.

"I need to take care of something," Garrett grumbled. "Let me know if there are any questions about the financial report."

"Will do, and say hello to Nicky for me."

Garrett considered punching that twitchy little smile off his cousin's face. Strange, since violence wasn't usually his go-to reaction. But it riled him that Lawson or anybody else for that matter thought that Nicky was ready for the taking. Anyone's taking.

He made his way across the yard, but before he reached Kaylee and Nicky, one of the widows walked past him.

"Asshole," she snarled and went on her way, not even making eye contact with him. Apparently, the woman knew he'd been a jerk to Nicky.

Loretta came out of Gina's camper and made a beeline toward him. "Don't take anything she said personally. That's D.M., surgical complications. She has tourniquets and says things she doesn't mean."

"You mean Tourette's?"

"Yes, that's it. I'm always mixing up those words. Anyway, D.M. is really shy, but she talked to me about it, and she said sometimes she can't control what she says. But she admitted she has some go-to words that she often uses whenever certain things happen. Like she'll say A-hole when she's mad at somebody and BS when she thinks they're lying. For example, there was the time when Lady said she didn't notice that the janitor who cleans up the building for our support group was well hung, and D.M. said BS but she didn't just use the initials. She said the actual words."

Garrett always felt as if he were enduring some kind of karma punishment whenever he talked to Loretta.

"Sometimes D.M. says donkey wankers," Loretta went on. "Except she uses another word for wankers, and she told me she says that when she's surprised. So, if she ever walks past you and says donkey wankers and BS, that means she's surprised that you're not telling the truth."

Well, at least he'd only gotten the A-hole.

"I don't know what D.M. means when she says cocksucker," Loretta went on. And she was serious, too. Maybe because she genuinely didn't know what it meant. "But I'm not one to judge." She leaned in closer. "Is there any news on the dead man?" She whispered those last two words.

"Not yet. The CSIs are still going through the place, looking for the man's clothes."

"Oh, dear." She wasn't wringing her hands, but it was close, and she was biting on her bottom lip. "It's just all so unsettling, you know?"

Garrett nodded and, because he didn't know what else to do, he gave her arm a pat. "Clay will get to the bottom of this. Who knows, it might turn out that the guy was just some homeless person who went into the closet and died of natural causes in his sleep."

"Yes," she said and added another, "Oh, dear. But he'll still be dead, no matter how it happened."

He couldn't argue with that. Nor could he stay and chat. That was because Kaylee spotted him.

"Gare-if," she called out, running to him. Garrett excused himself from Loretta and went to the little girl. The moment she reached him, she took hold of his hand.

Like the other times she'd done that, the punch came. Not a good punch, either, but her smile sure helped. It was hard not to smile back at that little face.

"There's a party on my head," she proudly announced, and she bent down to show him.

"A part," Nicky corrected. She motioned toward the part in Kaylee's hair. It was crooked, but he was relieved that the little girl didn't have head lice or something.

"Parted," Kaylee tried again. "I show you," she added and went running into the RV.

"Thank you for not laughing at her," Nicky whispered to him. "She's a little behind in her language development, and it embarrasses her when people laugh."

Well, hell. Of course, it would. And Garrett suddenly wanted to punch anyone who'd ever laughed at the kid.

"I've had her tested," Nicky went on, "and she's working with a tutor in San Antonio so she can catch up before preschool."

This was yet something else on Nicky's plate, and he was about to try to clear his own plate of guilt, but Kaylee came back out of the RV, and she was carrying a comb.

"Like dis," she said, and she proceeded to show him how she parted and then combed her hair. She only made her hair messier, but Garrett gave her a nod of approval anyway.

"It looks beautiful," Nicky told her, and she scooped her up for a kiss. Kaylee giggled like a loon when Nicky added a raspberry-kiss to her neck.

"Again," Kaylee pleaded, and Nicky gave her two more.

"I love you more than…" Nicky told her.

"Choc-it," Kaylee finished. "I wuv you more than…"

"Popcorn," Nicky answered.

They went through two more rounds with food answers—peanut butter and pizza. Clearly, this was a game they liked to play because Kaylee giggled through it all, and Nicky smiled. Not an ordinary smile, either. This one could light up a total eclipse. Motherhood definitely suited her.

"You always wanted to be a mom?" he asked.

"Yes," she answered without hesitation. But then something went through her eyes. Something sad, and Garrett was sorry he'd brought it up. Maybe because his question reminded her that she hadn't planned on having to raise her daughter alone.

"Kaylee?" someone called out. It was one of the widows, Gina, who was standing at the back door of the house. "Come on in for your lunch."

"Lunch," Kaylee repeated, more or less getting it right, and she handed her mom the comb and took off toward Gina, leaving Nicky and Garrett alone.

Garrett didn't think that was an accident. Nope. Gina smiled that quivery smile that Lawson had just given him. A red flag to let Garrett know there was more matchmaking going on. Normally, that would have bothered him, but this gave him a chance to talk to Nicky.

"I've only got a minute," Garrett explained. "I need to send Roman a financial report." One that Roman would immediately delete, but he'd still send it.

He watched Nicky's face, looking for any sign that she wanted to discuss Roman. Any sign that she wanted to have sex with his brother, as well. Nothing.

"Okay," she finally said. She didn't motion for him to continue. Not physically anyway, but he could tell she was confused by this visit. Nicky continued to stare at him and then huffed. "Do you have any idea how many people are watching us right now?"

"Two," he quickly answered. "Lawson and Gina. Maybe Loretta, too."

"Seven," she corrected. "The Ellery sisters are in the second floor corner window, and your mother is hiding behind the curtain in her bedroom. And yes, Loretta is watching from the camper. Probably listening, as well."

Garrett glanced around and spotted all of them. Way easier than finding Waldo, too. Sheesh. Some people, including his mother, clearly had too much time on their hands.

"Why don't we step inside, and you can tell me why you really came to see me?" Nicky suggested. "The gawkers will assume we're going to kiss or something, but that's better than having them watching our every move."

He agreed, especially since he wasn't sure what he was going to say to Nicky. Or how she would react if he brought up anything unpleasant.

The RV was a lot bigger than it looked, and when he went inside, he stepped out of the doorway so he couldn't be seen. Nicky went into the kitchen, took two bottles of water from the fridge and came back toward him.

"So, you've spoken to Clay?" she asked.

His hand froze for a second when he was in mid-reach for the water bottle. Garrett nodded. "Day before yesterday when I went in to sign the report."

"But not today?" She didn't wait for him to confirm that. "I just got off the phone with him so he'll probably be calling you soon. Anyway, the CSIs have cleared the first floor of Z.T.'s house, and they're going to let the cleaning crew get in there tomorrow. Once that's done, the widows can move their things to the bottom floor and some can start staying there."

That was good news. There were only two bedrooms on the bottom floor, but it would get some of the women out of the house.

"What ever happened with your work crew?" she asked, gulping down some water.

"They're still on hold for now, but once we get the okay from Clay, they'll go in and expand the pond. Not to the width that I wanted it—I've made some adjustments. Not just with the pond and the pasture but with the size of the new herd I'll be bringing in." That had involved plenty of paperwork. Garrett tried not to look too sour about it.

She sipped more water, did more staring. "Why did you really come over here?" Nicky sounded like a lawyer. Or a cop. Maybe she was sensing his guilty conscience.

"I also wanted to apologize. I was too hard on you that first day at Z.T.'s house. In fact, I was a jerk."

She didn't confirm or deny that. "I accept your apology, but I'd like to know what brought it on. I hope it wasn't what I just told you about Kaylee."

"No." Garrett answered that really fast. Which meant he now needed to do a follow-up. Hell, he might as well just spill the beans. "I heard some things. About your father."

There wasn't a huge change in her expression. Not at first anyway. Then, he saw a glimmer of that look in her eyes. The very one that'd been there when he'd seen her at her parents' old house.

"How much did you hear?" she asked.

How much wasn't a good sign. It meant more had

happened than just what Clay had told him. "Your father was a drunk, and he hit you." That was a little easier to stomach than the word *assault*.

"I see," she said. She had some more water, repeated her comment, then nodded. "He did. My father was an alcoholic."

Alcoholic was a fairly sterile label, but he suspected that her situation had been anything but sterile. With all the times her father had been arrested, there'd probably been more assaults.

"Things got bad," Nicky added. "My brother and he clashed a lot, and that's why Kyle left. I didn't have the courage to do that, too."

"Because of your mother?" That was the first thing that'd popped into his head.

She nodded. "In part. But also because I didn't have any other place to go. No aunts, uncles or cousins, and Kyle rarely called. It took us years to reconnect, and that was only after I'd finally moved out and was in college."

"When we were dating, you could have told me what was going on at home," he assured her.

"No. I couldn't have." She huffed, pushed her hair from her face. "Heck, in those days, I couldn't admit it to myself. No way would I have said anything to you. You were the high school star, and you'd asked me out. I was the girl in the school band who was from the wrong side of the tracks."

He could have pointed out that they'd both lived on the same side of the tracks, but that would sound smart-ass-ish. Best not to let his ass do anything but listen right now.

"We were dirt poor," she continued. "And you're a

Granger. I didn't want to do or say anything to blow it with you. I especially didn't want you to know that my life wasn't perfect, the way I thought yours was."

"It wasn't perfect. My dad wasn't a drunk, but he was an asshole. He never hit me, though."

"Lucky you." She didn't sound begrudging about that. "When things would get bad, I'd sneak over to Z.T.'s house. It was my sanctuary, you see, a place where I'd go to get away from things. The library especially. So many books, and I could sit there and read for hours." She paused. "That probably doesn't make sense."

Yeah, it did, because he'd gotten away there plenty of times. Most recently after he'd seen Meredith's sex video.

"I sneaked into the place," Nicky added. "That means I trespassed. If I'd known there was a body in the kitchen closet, I might not have been so eager to run there." She added a brief smile to that, maybe because this conversation had gotten too serious.

Garrett, however, wasn't ready to go light just yet. "That's not why you had sex with me, was it?" He shook his head when he realized he hadn't clarified that enough. "Did you have sex with me so you wouldn't lose me?"

"No. That was a hormonal thing. I was about to turn eighteen and was still a virgin. Metaphorically, I was ready to be plucked." She dismissed it with the wave of her hand.

Garrett frowned again. He wasn't sure he liked her thinking of what they'd done as "plucking." "Are you sure? Because—"

He didn't get to finish. That's because Nicky huffed, came up on her tiptoes and silenced him.

By putting her mouth to his.

NICKY KNEW THIS was a mistake. No doubt about it. It was a huge one, too. But sometimes making a mistake was better than the emotional bloodletting that would happen if Garrett kept up with these questions.

Besides, it wasn't as if she was actually into the kiss or anything.

She remembered the feel of his mouth, of course. That was because Nicky had catalogued everything about Garrett. His taste, his scent, the way his hand felt on her skin. And she hadn't been able to uncatalogue all of that after he'd broken up with her. Now, it all came flooding back.

Apparently, Garrett didn't immediately get caught in that flood because he stiffened, and for a moment she thought he might pull away and ask her if she'd lost her mind. He could flat out reject her for a second time.

He didn't.

The stiffness only lasted a couple of seconds before a husky sound rumbled in his chest. Maybe a sound of approval because Garrett put his hand on her waist, eased her closer. So close that his body brushed against hers, and she got another memory of what it was like to have Garrett take her.

Heck, she was into the kiss.

That was a huge flapping red flag, plenty big enough to cause her to step back. No way should she be doing this.

"That was payback," she said when she found her breath.

It was a lie, but it seemed to be a believable one

because his eyes narrowed a bit. At least the kiss had served its purpose of getting him away from those questions she didn't want to answer.

Or not.

"You don't want to talk about your dad," Garrett threw out there. "I get that. But my apology for being a jerk stands. So does my second apology for complicating that kiss. If I hadn't put my hand on you just now, you probably would have kept it as a little payback peck."

Mercy. It was as if he could see right through her. And Nicky wanted no part of that.

They stood there, probably still too close to each other, but for Nicky to leave, she'd have to touch Garrett to get past him. That wouldn't be a good idea, either, and she'd used up her bad idea quota for the day.

"That night we were together at Z.T.'s house," he started. "I didn't know you were a virgin. If you'd told me, I would never have let things go as far as they did."

Well, that was a mouthful of a confession. One that stung more than she wanted to admit. "So, if I had been the sort to sleep around, you would have gone for it?"

"Probably," he readily admitted. "Because I would have assumed that sex wasn't a commitment for you." He looked her straight in the eyes. "I wasn't ready for a commitment."

Not to her anyway.

"You *committed* to Meredith just a few weeks later," she reminded him. "Love at first sight."

His mouth tightened. "Something like that. But the point is, I wouldn't have been with you like that if I'd known the big picture."

They were talking about her father now, about the physical abuse. He probably thought she'd been vulnerable and that he'd essentially taken advantage of her by taking her virginity. It probably hadn't helped his outlook when she'd confessed to him that she hadn't wanted to lose him.

Well, heck. Now, she was feeling sorry for *him*. She blamed the kiss, of course. It had put a hole in an emotional barrier that needed to stay intact.

"It's okay," she assured him. "There's no reason for you to apologize. That all happened a very long time ago, and I don't even think of it anymore. And I didn't come back to Wrangler's Creek to punish you or to try to rekindle things between us. I only want us both to go on with our happy, separate lives."

That little speech was a mixed bag of truth and lies, and Nicky wasn't sure exactly which was which. Man, when she'd decided to come to the ranch, she hadn't thought that Garrett was going to be this much of a problem.

He finally moved away from her, starting for the door, but his phone rang, the sound shooting through the RV. They were still close enough that she could see Clay's name on the screen.

"He's probably calling to give you the same update he gave me," Nicky volunteered.

Garrett stepped outside, clearing the path for her to get around him without touching, and Nicky decided to head to the house to check on Kaylee. But Garrett put the call on speaker, and when she heard Clay's voice, Nicky stopped cold.

"I'm at Z.T.'s house," Clay said. "We found something."

CHAPTER NINE

GARRETT LOOKED AT the items that were laid out on a table in the library. The items that the CSIs had obviously found. Nicky was as focused on the stuff as Garrett was. Probably a little alarmed, too.

One of these things was not like the others.

There was a man's plaid suit, shoes, socks. All of them were old and dusty like the rest of the house, and they seemed to be from a different era. The sixties or seventies was his guess. The other item on the table was a delicate silver necklace.

It wasn't like the other things simply because it was jewelry rather than an item of clothing. And seemed to belong to a woman. It was one of those necklaces where the silver spelled out a name.

And that name was *Nicky*.

"These were all beneath there," Clay explained, and he tipped his head to the burgundy velvet chaise.

Yep, the very one where Nicky and he had had sex.

Garrett hadn't remembered Nicky wearing a necklace like that, but after one glance at her face, he knew it was hers. In that glance he also understood that she'd probably left it there on the infamous night, and that in turn meant they were going to have to explain this to Clay.

"The necklace was only about an inch from the

upper right leg of the lounger or whatever the heck you call it," Clay went on. "The clothes were neatly folded and tucked beneath it." He shifted his gaze to Nicky. "Should I guess what went on here, or do you have an explanation?"

"It's my necklace," she said at the same time that Garrett said, "She didn't know the clothes were here."

Garrett glanced at her again to verify that was true. No, she hadn't known.

"I used to come here to read when I was a teenager," Nicky added. There was no hint in her voice that she'd come here to escape. "I guess the necklace fell off or something," she added.

Probably the "or something." The foreplay that night on the chaise had been frantic, fast and had involved groping. The clasp had probably come undone and caused it to fall to the floor.

Clay looked at both of them, and he didn't have to be a cop to fill in the blanks, especially because Garrett was certain that Nicky and he looked guilty.

"You believe these clothes belong to the John Doe?" Garrett asked in part because he truly wanted to know but also he wanted to stop the glances that Clay was volleying between them. Those glances were making Garrett feel even guiltier than he already did.

"It's possible. John Doe's hatband is identical to the plaid on the suit."

It was. Garrett could see that now. He doubted that was a coincidence unless that color plaid was a fashion statement during that time.

"This was next to the pile of clothes," Clay went on, and he picked up a small plastic evidence bag from the back of a chair. He dropped it on the table next to the other items, and Nicky and Garrett leaned in to take a closer look.

It was a faded receipt from the town's only gas station. And it was dated twenty-one years ago. So, the John Doe hadn't been from the sixties or seventies after all. That meant this murder, death or whatever the hell it was had happened in Garrett's lifetime. Not exactly a comforting thought.

"It wasn't a credit card purchase," Clay explained. "No way to trace it. I've already called Arlo out at the gas station and asked if he remembers a customer dressed like this. Arlo didn't remember if he'd put on underwear today so I struck out there."

That didn't surprise Garrett. Arlo wasn't a bright bulb, but even if he had been, it would have been a long shot for him to recall a customer from over two decades ago. Someone in town, though, might remember the plaid suit, and he was certain that Clay would ask around about that. Garrett would certainly ask his mother, but he suspected she would hear the gossip before he spoke with her. The CSIs probably wouldn't keep this close to the vest since getting the word out might help ID the guy.

"There could be prints on it," Clay added. "If so, then it might help us get an ID on the John Doe."

"And maybe it doesn't even belong to the dead guy," Garrett reminded him. "Someone else could have dropped it over the years."

Clay nodded, acknowledging that could be true. "But you can see now why I asked about what had gone on here. You're both thirty-four, and that would have meant this guy was here when you were thirteen or so. Any chance the necklace got lost around that time?"

"No," Nicky and he answered in unison. It was Nicky who continued. "I didn't start coming here to read until I was sixteen."

"And Nicky and I weren't here together until two years after that," Garrett added.

Clay nodded and seemed relieved about that. Hell, had he really thought the two of them had knocked off the John Doe?

"And the times you came here, you didn't see anyone else or notice any odd smells?" Clay pressed.

Nicky put her hand over her stomach. Oh, no. He hoped this didn't set off another puking spell.

She shook her head. "No one was here. Not that I knew of anyway. And it was hard to smell anything with all the mustiness and dust."

That was true, which reminded him of just how bad things must have been for her at home to consider this a refuge.

"How about the guy's wedding ring?" Garrett asked. "Anything on that?"

"Not yet," Clay answered, and when Nicky made a sound of agreement, Garrett and Clay looked at her.

"I did some internet searches," she admitted. "I checked for anyone who might have posted anything about a ring like that on social media. Nothing."

"I put out some feelers, too," Clay added. "There are no police reports that mention a ring fitting that description, and none of the jewelers in the area have any records of an engraving like that. I'll do a wider sweep, though, because a jeweler could end up being our best bet. Especially since there are no missing person's reports that match our John Doe."

Maybe that meant the guy was widowed and didn't

have any family. Garrett doubted it was a situation where he was on the run from the law because that didn't explain the folded clothes. If a guy was going to hide out, he probably would have stayed dressed. But why place them under the chaise?

"This house isn't exactly on the beaten path," Garrett went on. "Either he got here by way of the ranch trail or the pasture since there's not an actual road."

Clay nodded. "That's why I questioned your hands. Only one of them worked here during this time frame. Hester Walter. And he doesn't know about a man visiting the place. He did say, though, that kids were always sneaking into the house and that you would camp out here sometimes."

Nicky looked at him, no doubt questioning why he would do that when he had a nice big house less than a half mile away, but since she knew his mother, and his situation, she probably understood.

"I used to walk here from the house where I lived," Nicky volunteered. "Maybe he parked a car somewhere in town or in the woods and made his way here on foot."

That was a good possibility, and Clay must have thought so, too, because he made a comment about doing a search of the area.

"Yoo-hoo?" someone called out, and a couple of moments later, one of the widows came in. Not Lady, thank God. It was Gina.

Except Garrett took back his "thank God" when the woman shot him what had to be a glare. Since she was Nicky's friend, that likely meant she knew all about what had gone on between Nicky and him.

"Is Kaylee with you?" Nicky immediately asked Gina.

"No. She's with Loretta. Loretta wanted to come herself, or rather she wanted to find out why the chief called you up here, but she said she wasn't feeling up to being back in here just yet. Loretta's trying not to let on that this dead guy thing is getting to her, but she's muttering 'oh, dear' and 'oh, my' a lot."

Well, the woman had been the one to find the body. That was enough to shake anyone to the core.

"Loretta might be too spooked to move in now," Nicky commented.

"I think she'll be okay. We just need to keep her off kitchen duty. The sisters have volunteered for it anyway."

Gina went to the table, her gaze skirting over the evidence, and that gaze paused a bit when it landed on Nicky's necklace. She paused even more, though, when it landed on Nicky herself.

"Uh, how much longer do you think you'll be here?" Gina asked. "Because we need to go over the new bed assignments."

Nicky opened her mouth, and Garrett could have sworn she wanted to ask "what bed assignments?" because she certainly seemed surprised by that.

"You can go," Clay told Nicky. "But this will generate another report, and you'll have to come in and sign it. That means you'll have to explain in accurate detail how your necklace got here."

Great. *Accurate* was code for don't fudge the truth, which meant Nicky's de-virging would now be part of an official police report. Garrett hoped like hell that none of the deputies would see it because they'd blab. Of course, most people in the town probably already knew, but it was a different thing to have it all spelled out for them.

The moment Nicky moved to leave, Gina took hold of her arm and got her walking a lot faster than it seemed Nicky had planned. He didn't know why Gina was acting like that, but something else had likely gone wrong. Garrett hoped there wasn't another rash of clogged toilets.

"Are you okay?" Clay asked.

The question confused Garrett for a moment, and then he realized he was staring at Nicky as Gina led her away. "Fine." He scrubbed his hand over his face. "Just distracted," he settled for saying.

The corner of Clay's mouth twitched a little. "Your sister's been distracting me like that since the day I met her."

Garrett frowned. "This is different."

"Yeah. Of course, it is." And with that totally inaccurate, smart-ass comment, Clay smiled. "You're free to go, too. I'll call you when the new report is done."

Garrett nearly stayed back to tell Clay that there was nothing going on between Nicky and him. Nothing but some lingering lust anyway—Nicky was a still-grieving widow, and Garrett wasn't anywhere near ready to get into a relationship. Maybe if he repeated that to himself enough, it would sink in.

He worked his way to the front of the house and immediately spotted Gina and Nicky on the porch. They were having a whispered conversation, and whatever Nicky was hearing, it had caused her forehead to bunch up. Garrett decided to give them some privacy and go ahead to his horse, but Nicky moved away from Gina and hurried after him.

Apparently, Nicky had something to say to him, but instead she just stood there, glancing around as if trying to figure out how to tell him something bad.

"What happened?" he came out and asked. Because that wasn't a good-news kind of look in her eyes.

Nicky took a deep breath first. "It's Meredith." Another breath. "She's here."

NICKY STILL HAD some secrets, but at the rate things were going, Garrett would soon know every little thing she'd ever tried to hide.

Every big thing, too.

And Meredith definitely fell into the big category.

Garrett stood there, staring at Nicky. "Meredith's here?" He glanced around. "Define *here*."

Nicky didn't know exactly where the woman was, but it soon became very clear. That was because at that exact moment, Meredith came up the side porch. Obviously, she'd walked up from her car, which she had parked on the ranch trail. Meredith smiled, and it wasn't tentative, either, despite the unfriendly look on Garrett's face. Of course, that look wasn't solely for Meredith. He was aiming it at Nicky, as well.

"I'll be inside if you need me," Gina whispered to Nicky, and she went back in the house. She wouldn't go far, though. Gina would stay near the door in case she felt the need to run to Nicky's defense.

"Want to tell me what the heck is going on?" Garrett asked. Like the glare, that was meant for Nicky, too.

"Nicky was kind enough to let me come," Meredith volunteered before Nicky could speak. She walked toward them, still smiling.

Unlike the other times Nicky had recently seen the

woman, Meredith no longer looked to be in "down in the dumps" mode. She was wearing a perky yellow sundress that skimmed several inches above her knees, and she had her blond hair pulled back in a sleek ponytail.

A reminder to Nicky that her own ponytail needed an adjustment.

Everything about Meredith's outfit was coordinated and perfect. As cool as glass, which Nicky had always thought described the woman perfectly.

"Don't be mad at Nicky," Meredith went on. "I sort of pressured her into doing this for me."

There was no "sort of" to it. Meredith had pressured her, and while Nicky didn't consider herself a pushover, she hadn't exactly felt comfortable telling a grieving woman that she wasn't welcome. Still, Nicky hadn't expected Meredith to show up while Garrett was around. That'd been their deal, that Meredith would steer clear of her ex-husband. Maybe Meredith hadn't known that Garrett would be here. Still, she should have called first to make sure.

Garrett didn't even spare Meredith a glance. "Explain 'pressured her into doing this,'" he snarled to Nicky.

Meredith opened her mouth, no doubt to provide that answer, but Nicky held up her hand. She'd gotten herself into this mess, and she'd rather use her own words to get out of it. Or at least try to smooth things over.

"Meredith called me a while back about the support group," Nicky explained. "We do have some divorcées in there from time to time, and she wanted to join."

Garrett seemed to release the breath he'd been holding. "So, that's all there is to it. Meredith's part of your support group."

Not exactly. And here was the part that was going to be very hard for Garrett to hear. "Meredith wanted to come here to the Widows' House."

No held breath this time, and his gaze snapped to Meredith. "Here?" And he didn't just say it once, but three times. "Why the hell would you want to be on the ranch?"

"I don't want to be on the ranch." Meredith didn't seem at all taken aback by Garrett's obvious anger. "I want to be at this house so I can heal and recover. I've never gotten over our baby's death."

That was almost verbatim what Meredith had told Nicky, and while it'd made Nicky feel sorry for her, it obviously wasn't having the same effect on Garrett.

"You know about the baby," Garrett said, looking at Nicky. His mouth tightened. Heck, all of him went even tighter than he already was.

Nicky nodded, but didn't get a chance to say anything, including how sorry she was about that, because Meredith spoke first. "I need some time to heal and recover, Garrett. Losing our child isn't something I can just get over. As you well know."

Nicky saw the grief in his eyes. Felt it, too. Yes, Garrett did know the death of a child was something that would never be made right. But along with that grief was also the anger. Probably because he knew this wasn't only about healing for Meredith. It was because the woman wanted a reconciliation.

"You agreed to having Meredith stay here?" Garrett snapped. Again, he meant that question for Nicky.

"I did," Nicky had to admit. "But Meredith knows

it wouldn't be a good idea for her to be at the ranch house." Nicky shot a stern look at the woman to make sure she did indeed know that.

Meredith dismissed that with the wave of her perfectly manicured hand. "Of course, I won't stay there. I'll be staying with a friend in town until Z.T.'s place is ready. Any idea when that'll be?"

Meredith seemed to think this was a friendly conversation. It wasn't. "Soon," Nicky assured her.

"Good. Because I'm anxious to get started. When will the therapist be arriving?"

"Soon," Nicky repeated, but her attention was still on Garrett.

She wanted to say how sorry she was to have this dumped on him without warning, but an apology wasn't going to fix this. And that bothered her. Far more than she'd expected it to.

Well, heck.

All these feelings were because of that kiss. It had broken down barriers that she'd spent way too long putting up.

"I can see you're not happy about this," Meredith went on, talking to Garrett. "But I'm truly not here to make things worse for you. I'm here for me. I need a fresh start, and I think I can get it at this place."

Garrett didn't argue. In fact, he didn't say anything, including an order for Meredith to leave. Nicky felt like a hypocrite, but she was almost hoping he'd do that because having Meredith here was only going to make things harder.

He stood there, his gaze shifting from Meredith back to her, and then he did something that Nicky could have guessed he would never do. He hooked his arm around her, pulled her to him.

And he kissed Nicky.

Not a little bitty peck, either. This was a real kiss. Well, real in the sense of it being French and hot. It involved some body-to-body contact, too, since with all that hooking and maneuvering, she landed against his chest.

It fired up Nicky's body and brain so much that she had to fight through the heat to realize what was really going on. This was some kind of payback. Aimed at Meredith. He wasn't kissing her because of all this heat and old attraction.

"I'll see you later," Garrett said when he finally let go of her.

Meredith made a strangled sound of surprise. It was similar to the one Nicky made. "I had no idea you two were seeing each other," Meredith added.

"Things change. People move on," Garrett grumbled. He stared at Nicky as if challenging her to rat him out. She wouldn't. Mainly because she still hadn't caught her breath enough to grapple with human speech. She could only stand there and look mute and stupid.

"Yes, I can see that." Meredith moistened her lips, glanced around. "I'm just surprised, that's all. I mean, considering…everything that went on with her brother."

Since Garrett still had his hand on her waist, Nicky felt him stiffen. Nicky was doing her own stiffening, too. No. Not this. Not now. But Meredith apparently was in a 'fess up kind of mood.

Which meant another secret was about to bite the dust.

"Her brother?" Garrett challenged.

Meredith nodded. "Yes, Kyle." She paused. "He was the man with me in the backseat of that VW. Nicky had to jump through a lot of legal hoops to keep his name out of the press and off social media. Wish she'd been able to do the same for me." Another pause and she must have noticed his poleaxed expression. "Oh, God. You didn't know? I would have thought Nicky had told you."

"Nicky must have forgotten to mention that," Garrett said without taking his stare off Nicky. Except the stare was now one of his infamous glares.

Nicky wanted to say that she would have told him. Once she figured out a way to do it, that is. But they hadn't exactly had time for long, "heart pouring out" conversations.

"I'll see you later," Garrett repeated to Nicky. And this time, he said it through clenched teeth as he walked away.

CHAPTER TEN

GINA STOOD AT the window and watched the scene play out in the side yard. Lady was moving in on one of the ranch hands, Jake Walter, who was just on the other side of the fence that divided the house from the pasture. While Jake could probably take care of himself when it came to a sexually aggressive widow, Gina knew she had to intervene.

Because of what Jake was carrying.

That little white box tucked under his arm could be trouble.

People had often accused her of having ESP, but it was just a simple matter of watching and guessing what could go wrong. Being married to a private investigator for six years had helped hone those observations a little. If the box contained what she thought it did, then it fell into the "things that could go wrong" category.

Gina went downstairs, smiling at Nicky when she spotted her in the kitchen. If she kept a straight face, no one would question why she was going outside in the boiling heat. But thankfully Nicky was distracted by a game she was playing with Kaylee so Gina got out and made a beeline for the cowboy. Lady was already swooping in on him and looked ready to unzip him. The cowboy looked ready to run.

"Jake," Gina called out. "Thanks for coming over."

Lady frowned. Jake's forehead bunched up. That's because he didn't know Gina. He'd likely seen her around, but that was about it.

"He didn't say anything about coming here to see you," Lady snapped.

"Well, that's probably because you didn't let him get a word in edgewise." Gina went to him, touched his arm with her fingertips and rubbed softly. It was just as effective as a peeing dog marking his territory, and after Lady sputtered out a few more huffs, she headed back to the house. No doubt to find her next conquest.

"She owns that," Gina said, tipping her head to the tow truck. "Enough said. But if you truly do want some mindless sex with her, I'll smooth things over for you."

He smiled, slow and easy. A dimple flashed in his cheek. The smile of a man who didn't have to try too hard to charm panties off women. "No thanks. I've had my quota of mindless sex for the week. Maybe next week, though."

Yes, definitely a charmer. And much too young to already have that particular skill set. Gina estimated he was twenty-seven, give or take a year or two. She was thirty-four, a widow and therefore immune to such smiles. Besides, she was here to mourn her husband and take care of Kaylee and Nicky. Her panties would stay right where they were.

"I'm Gina Simpson, by the way." This time she skipped the arm rubbing and went for a handshake.

"Yeah, I know." He tipped his head to the work crew by the pond and then did another tip in the direction of the ranch. "The women of the Widows' House are the hot topic in town right now."

Probably because of Lady. Or maybe the eccentric sisters.

"Everyone knows all your names," he added. "I'm Jake Walter."

She nodded. "You cowboys are the hot topic in the Widows' House. Hey, we might be in mourning, but that doesn't stop us from looking. Of course, some do more than look." She said Lady's name, covering it with a cough.

He smiled again. "So, did you come out here to rescue me?"

No, but when she felt that little tug in her body, she considered saying yes and flirting with him. It'd been a while since she'd felt that, a nice reminder that her lady parts hadn't ended up in the grave after all. Still, tugging lady parts weren't enough to let this go any further than conversation.

A specific conversation, at that.

"Is that box for Nicky Marlow?" she asked.

He did a double take as if he'd forgotten it was there. Maybe his man parts were doing some tugging, too. Or maybe he'd fibbed about reaching his quota for mindless sex.

Jake nodded, handed it to her. "It came to the ranch house, and Miss Belle asked me to bring it out."

Gina lifted the lid, had a look. Two yellow roses, just as she'd suspected. No card, again as she'd expected. That didn't mean Nicky wouldn't know who they were from.

She would.

And so did Gina.

She took out the roses, glanced around and spotted the perfect place for them. A huge pile of cow shit. She tore up the flowers as best she could, dropped them into the poop, located a stick and swirled them around until they were no longer recognizable as flowers. To a passerby, it would look as if the cow just had a poor digestive system.

Now, this was when most people would have asked what the heck she was doing or maybe would have even tried to stop her. Not Jake, though. He just lifted his shoulder in a gesture that was as slow and easy as that smile.

"You want to go out with me Saturday night?" he said.

Now, this was when Gina would have normally had a snappy comeback, because she would have anticipated he was going to say that. But she'd missed the signs. Perhaps because the scent of the cow poop was a tad overpowering.

"I'm a widow," she reminded him, though she was certain he needed no such reminder. "My husband died just eleven months ago."

"Car accident," he provided. "The gossip consensus is you had a good marriage and that you're not here for mindless sex, a vacation or because you like to look at cowboys."

The first two were true. She was beginning to bend a little on the third. But not bend enough to go on a date.

"I'm not too young for you, you know," Jake added. She got another dimple flash. The man certainly knew how to use that facial indentation.

Jeez. Had she been drooling or something to make him see that she found him attractive? "I'm thirty-four."

"I'm twenty-eight. See? Not too young."

In her way of thinking he was, and as long as she kept that in mind, Gina had to decline. "I'm sorry but no."

"How about Sunday then?" Of course, he smiled.

Gina had to fight back her own smile. "No. Widow." She pointed to the wedding band that she still wore. "If you see me without this, then you can ask me out."

"Deal," he agreed as if she'd be doing that in the next hour or so. She wouldn't be. Sadly, she might be wearing that ring to her own grave.

"By the way, don't mention the flowers to anyone," Gina said.

"What flowers?" He winked at her. The man really had some weapons in his panty-removal arsenal.

"Also, please burn the box first chance you get," she added, and she started back for the house.

"Will do. Does any of this have something to do with Garrett's ex-wife?"

That stopped her, and Gina turned back around to face him. "Why would you ask that?"

He lifted his shoulder. "It's just I was going through Spring Hill a couple of days ago. That's a town not too far from here, and I saw his ex at the florist there. Thought it was strange since we have a florist here in Wrangler's Creek."

Strange, maybe. Though it could be just a coincidence, especially since Meredith shouldn't have an idea what the roses meant. Or who'd started sending them. Or why. Still, if Meredith had learned that, she could have sent the flowers as a way of messing with Nicky's head.

On the walk back to the house, Gina took out her phone to make some calls.

"WHO IS I?" Kaylee asked when she stepped into the office Nicky had set up at the Widows' House. She struck a pose, outstretching her hands.

"Who *am* I?" Nicky automatically corrected.

Obviously Kaylee had been playing in the old trunk of clothes that she'd found in her room because she was wearing a very baggy white dress that she'd tried to cinch with ribbon. She had puffed up her hair, too. Or rather put knots in it so that it frizzed around her face.

From the looks of it, Kaylee had used a marker to attempt a drawing on her neck and arm. Hopefully, it wasn't a permanent marker. And the finishing touch—she had a loop of what appeared to be aluminum foil hooked on her nose. If it hadn't been for the foil and the tattoos, Nicky wouldn't have known the answer.

Nicky pretended to give it some thought though. "You're Miss Gina."

Kaylee squealed and clapped as if it had been a huge accomplishment, and she ran to the window seat to pick up her coloring book that she'd left there earlier. Despite the insanity of her day, Nicky took the time to smile and tell Kaylee how pretty she looked.

But her daughter was the only thing pretty at the moment.

There was a chanting fortune-teller in the front yard. A bulldozer in the back. And Nicky was reasonably sure that the knocking sound she heard was Lady having afternoon sex against the wall with one of the repairmen.

She couldn't do anything about the bulldozer. It was there to stay until they expanded the pond. Which could take days. Nicky had struck out with the fortune-teller, too, because Vita Banchini had assured her that this was the only way to get rid of the spirit of the dead guy in the heart boxers. Nicky wasn't sure of that at all, wasn't even sure there was a spirit, but since it was rare to win an argument with Vita, Nicky had saved her breath.

However, she wouldn't do that for Lady.

Now that Kaylee was in the room, she didn't want her daughter learning at such a tender age about a horny woman who had a penchant for yelling "Camel-Tow" during her climax.

Nicky banged her hand on the wall her office shared with Lady's bedroom. The response was a faster rhythmic thumping, followed by some orgasmic moans. Nicky's response was more banging, and while she would have liked to believe that it'd worked on the second try, it was simply that Lady and her repairman lover had finished their little afternoon tryst.

"Camel-Tow!" Lady yelled.

Yep, they'd finished. Maybe it'd be another hour or two before Lady felt the need to have someone un-bunch her panties.

"Gare-if?" Kaylee asked, getting Nicky's complete attention.

Nicky hurried to the window seat where Kaylee was coloring and looked out. From the second floor, she had a good vantage point of the front and side yards. She saw two repairmen, Vita, Ruby, one of the sisters. But no Garrett.

"Gare-if," Kaylee proudly announced, and she showed Nicky the stick figure drawing she'd made in a bare spot on the coloring page.

It looked like him. Well, as much as a stick figure could look like a real person. Kaylee had given him the right color hair, eyes and cowboy hat, along with three arms and very large ears, but it was a good attempt.

"Very nice," Nicky told her.

And she hated that she felt so disappointed that Garrett himself hadn't been out there in the yard. Not that she could expect him to be. No. He wouldn't come near this place.

It'd been over two weeks since Meredith had spilled the Kyle secret, and despite Garrett's semi threat of "I'll see you later," he hadn't done that. He hadn't called or come by the Widows' House. In fact, the day Nicky and the widows had all finally moved in, Garrett had been away in east Texas on a cattle-buying trip.

Nicky had tried to call him, though, just an hour or so after he'd heard the Kyle bombshell, but the call had gone straight to voice mail. That said it all. Garrett was done with her.

Great.

The ache came, spreading through her chest, and suddenly she was seventeen again and feeling lower than hoof grit because he'd dumped her. Maybe one day she would learn to guard her heart better. Maybe one day there'd be a vaccine to cure her of Garrett-itis.

There was a knock at the door, but before Nicky could say come in, it opened. Not Meredith, thank goodness. It was Gina.

"Still moping?" Gina asked her right off.

Nicky tried to fix her expression so that it didn't confirm Gina's moping accusation. But Gina didn't notice the expression fix because her attention went to Kaylee.

"Who *am* I?" Kaylee asked her, doing her outstretched pose again.

The foil nose ring had fallen out and was on the floor now, but Gina still got it. "You're me." She clapped and squealed with Kaylee. "How am I ever going to tell us apart?"

Kaylee giggled and giggled some more while Gina spun her around. Thankfully, the noise they were making drowned out some of the kissing sounds that Lady and her beau were making as she said goodbye to him. Nicky got up and shut the door.

"Please tell me no one else wants to move rooms," she said to Gina when the giggling and spinning stopped. "Because I've already redone the room assignments three times."

"No room complaints. That's about all the good news I can give you, though. The washer overflowed, Loretta has a panic attack every time she sees the kitchen, and the guy who's supposed to be checking the plumbing checked Lady's plumbing instead. And someone from the historical society called to complain about Lady's truck. She objects to the camel toe picture."

"Yes, I heard. I'll talk to Loretta. Lady, too." But she wouldn't mention the picture complaints because Lady being Lady, she would likely change it to something much worse.

"Oh, and the sisters are complaining about Vita," Gina added. "They say she gives them the creeps and that she smells like old cheese."

Probably true. Vita's pockets could be filled with smelly cheese or some kind of homemade charm to ward off whatever she was trying to ward off. With Vita, you just didn't know.

"Anything new on the d-e-a-d g-u-y?" Gina asked.

Nicky shook her head. "Nothing from those posts I

put on social media. I was really hoping that someone would recognize the engraving in the ring."

"They still might. All it takes is the right person to see it and get in touch with you." Gina went to Kaylee, ruffled her hair and smiled at the picture. "Now, that's a hot cowboy."

Kaylee grinned. "Gare-if."

"It sure is. Seems to me that your mom should show this picture to Gare-if. Would you like that?"

Kaylee eagerly nodded, but Nicky gave her friend a blank stare.

Gina stared back. "Take it to Garrett while Kaylee and I have some playtime. Stay as long as you like. Overnight, even."

"Overnight?" Nicky practically howled. "Not a chance."

"Well, it should at least be on your radar. Look, everybody's noticing that you're moping. Why don't you just go to Garrett, have a good air clearing, maybe kiss him again, and all will be right with the world?"

If only it were that easy. Her world wasn't something to which she could apply a quick fix. But the idea of a kiss did sound like a compelling start to an argument.

"Plus, I think your visiting Garrett would get that sneaky smile off Meredith's face," Gina added. "She's the only one in the house who's not moping about this rift between Garrett and you. A rift that she caused with her blabbering. I hope you know that she wants her man back, and that this is step one toward accomplishing that."

"I suspected it." It felt a little like a sucker punch, though, to hear it voiced aloud. "But she's also grieving the loss of her child and marriage, and she might get some help here."

"You're too nice." Gina handed Nicky the stick-person picture. "I, on the other hand, have no such character flaw. If she tries to mess things up for you, then I'm putting butter and full fat milk in her oatmeal. A few extra pounds should put a dent in her oversize ego."

It probably wasn't a good idea not to scold Gina for a threat like that, but Nicky didn't.

"Have you gotten any roses that you didn't tell me about?" Gina asked.

That grabbed Nicky's attention, and she studied her friend's face to see what had prompted the question. "No, only the one since I've been here. Why?"

"Just making sure. Now scoot. You've got a cowboy to visit."

Nicky hesitated a moment to see if Gina was going to add anything else to that, but the only thing she added was a shooing motion with her hands. Nicky shrugged. Maybe this was just Gina's way of watching out for her and there was no ESP involved. Because Nicky certainly didn't want another reminder in the form of flowers.

With Kaylee's and Gina's full approval, Nicky took the drawing and headed out. The place certainly didn't have that air of serenity yet, but it was getting there. Soon, maybe in a week or two, this would be the haven that Nicky had envisioned.

She passed by the parlor that was already set up for the first group session that would take place tomorrow. Cassie McCord, a therapist from nearby Spring Hill would be leading the group, and Nicky couldn't wait to get started.

Vita was still in the yard, a cluster of feathers in one hand and some smoking weeds in the other. Like

Z.T.'s house, she looked like something from a different era in her ankle-length drab gray skirt and white embroidered blouse.

"Donkey dicks," D.M. mumbled when Nicky started to walk past her.

Nicky stopped. That's what the woman often said when she was surprised, and yes, Vita did fall into the surprising category. "She's harmless, really."

D.M. lifted an eyebrow. "She offered to *anoint* me with a potion to help with my Tourette's. Apparently, it cures acne, ingrown toenails and hemorrhoids, too—should I ever have a need for a cure for those problems. I told her I'd rather seek out my anointments from folks who've actually gone to medical school."

Nicky patted her arm. "Good for you." But she hated to tell D.M. that logic probably wouldn't stop Vita from trying to dole out her so-called treatments.

"The dead guy's spirit won't bother you after I finish this," Vita announced as Nicky went to her.

"He's not actually bothering us now." Nicky hoped that would get the woman to hurry up and leave so there'd be no more complaints about the smell.

Vita stopped her prancing, looked at Nicky. "Of course, he is. Women are complaining, and the mood around here is dark and gloomy."

Well, they were widows. All but Meredith anyway. So dark and gloomy came with the territory. As for the complaints, Nicky was learning that was the norm, too. The idea of a retreat was wonderful. In the idea stage. But logistics, overflowing washers and chanting fortune-tellers somewhat diminished that idea.

"Can't do anything though about the shit flowers," Vita went on.

Nicky doubted there were actual flowers by that name, and she waited for Vita to elaborate. "Shit might hide the scent, but it'll come back," Vita finally said.

All right. Since there probably wasn't anything else Nicky could say to Vita that would make this conversation any clearer, she just thanked the woman and went on her way. Her SUV was parked on the trail, which meant she had to walk close to the bulldozer and the work crew to get to it. It was loud and a couple of the men were gawking at something.

Lady.

She was now sunbathing in the backyard. Apparently, she was in search of her next orgasm and figured she'd showcase her assets to potential orgasm givers.

Nicky didn't want to take the time to walk the twenty minutes to get to the ranch house, so she got in her SUV. Plus, it was hot, and she didn't want to arrive all sweaty. Her confidence, however, wasn't nearly as high when she got there. That's because she saw several women on the front porch. Not any of the widows. These were women from town, all young, all attractive, and judging from the gossip she'd heard, they were all after Garrett. Maybe this was why he hadn't contacted her.

Sophie was with the women, and the moment she spotted Nicky she came down the porch steps and headed straight for her.

Nicky didn't get out of her SUV and kept the engine running. "I'm sorry if I interrupted a get-together—"

"You didn't. God, I could kiss you." Sophie glanced back over her shoulder at the women. "They just showed up, all looking for Garrett. They're worried about him." She put "worried" in air quotes. "*Worried* is code for they're looking for a permanent hookup."

Just as Nicky had suspected. "I can leave."

"Please don't. Just get out of your car and make sure you look sad, like you need to talk to a friend."

Nicky didn't even have to change her expression. She was sad, and a chat with a friend sounded like a good idea. The moment she stepped out, Sophie pulled her into a hug.

"You poor thing," Sophie said in a much louder voice. "Ladies, this might take a while. I'll see you on your next visit. Which hopefully won't be too soon," Sophie added to Nicky in a whisper.

With her arm still around Nicky's shoulder, Sophie led her into the side yard and then to the back porch. "Garrett's not here," Sophie went on. "But please tell me you came here to talk to him."

"I did. I want to apologize."

"That's going around. Meredith was here earlier to do that same thing."

Nicky hadn't meant to scowl, but she did, and Sophie must have noticed because she laughed. "My sentiments exactly." Sophie opened the back door and led her into the kitchen. Both Alice and Belle were there, and they were peering out one of the windows.

"Those women want to get in Garrett's pants," Belle said without greeting. "Is that why you're here?" she added to Nicky.

Nicky nearly choked on her own breath. Thankfully, Sophie answered for her.

"We just need some girl talk, that's all," Sophie explained, and she led her to a room that Nicky knew well. Garrett's office. "So, what the heck happened?"

Sophie asked the moment she shut the door. "It's all over town that Garrett kissed you on the porch at Z.T.'s house, and he did that right in front of Meredith."

Where to start? Nicky took a deep breath and decided to simplify this. "He kissed me because he was pissed off at Meredith for being at the Widows' House. A few moments later, Meredith told him that the man in the VW with her was my brother, Kyle."

Too bad those images of Meredith in the VW were branded in her head. Garrett's, too. Heck, it was likely branded in plenty of heads since the video had gotten a ton of hits on the internet before it'd finally been taken down. It'd been a miracle that Kyle's face hadn't been visible. That was because the photographer filmed him from the back. Hours later her brother had confessed to her that he was the costar in that particular show.

"There were some things a sister should never see," Nicky explained, "and one of those things is my brother getting a blow job from my ex-boyfriend's wife."

"Yeah, that would definitely be on my not-to-see list." Sophie took her own deep breath and sank down onto the edge of the desk. "That explains it. Garrett is moping again, and he's doing that because he feels as if you lied to him."

"In a way, I did. I didn't tell him or anyone else the truth. And Kyle didn't have to own up to it because there wasn't a clear image of him on the video."

"Hard to believe," Sophie mumbled. "You'd think if anyone's image would be unrecognizable, it would be Meredith's. I mean, since her mouth was occupied."

Both Sophie and Nicky made a face. It was definitely a yucky subject when family members and a male "member" were involved.

"Meredith also told Garrett that I'd worked to keep Kyle's name out of the press. I did," she admitted. "I called in plenty of favors when the gossip started that he was the one involved. But I did that because Kyle was married at the time, and I didn't want it getting back to his wife, Ivy." Nicky groaned. "I know, I know. It was wrong to keep something like that from her."

And it hadn't helped because Ivy had filed for a divorce just a few months later.

"You weren't wrong to do that," Sophie assured her. "You were trying to protect your brother. I would have done the same thing if I'd been in your place."

That was generous of Sophie. "I'm sure Garrett doesn't feel that way."

Sophie made a sound of agreement. "All the hurt from the past three years has gotten balled up together, and now you're a part of that ball."

Great. Another discussion about man parts. But Nicky knew what Sophie was saying was true. "Maybe I should just stay away from Garrett. Permanently."

"God, no. That's the last thing you should do. Since you've come here, I've started to see some signs of the old Garrett." Sophie lifted her shoulder. "Well, until two weeks ago anyway. But you can fix that."

Nicky wasn't so sure of that at all. "I'm not sure I'm the right person for Garrett. He hurt me back in high school, and whether or not it makes sense, that's part of that *ball*, too."

Sophie stared at her. "Do you want him?"

Nicky wished Sophie hadn't phrased it like that. It made Garrett sound like an ice cream cone or a hot stone massage. "I just want to feel something again. Something that isn't depression or sadness."

"Yes! Well, there you are. You know what you have to do then."

Uh, no she didn't have a clue. Nicky shook her head.

"You have to stop what's about to happen," Sophie provided. "Come on." She took Nicky by the arm again. "Those porch women should be gone by now so we can leave."

Nicky had to shake her head again. "Leave and do what?"

Sophie didn't stop, didn't slow down. "We have to stop Garrett from making a huge mistake."

THIS WAS A MISTAKE. Garrett was certain of it.

At least it was a mistake he was making while drinking a cold beer. And he was drinking that beer with Roman at the Longhorn Bar in town. All in all, if he was going to do something to screw himself over— or be screwed—then, this was the way to go about it.

"No strings there," Roman reminded him as he sipped his own beer. He tipped his head to the blond-haired woman in one of the booths. From their vantage point at the end of the bar, they could see pretty much everyone in the room. Everyone who came through the front door, too. "You could spend some time with her, and if you don't want any more *time*, then she'll be fine with it."

Garrett knew the no-stringer, of course. He knew everyone in town, and this was Tara Lynn Whitlow, a woman who made no apologies for enjoying her rather busy sex life. She hadn't been one of the women in the "trying to get in his pants" category because she'd probably seen more interesting pants around. Ones that didn't come with so much baggage.

Which got Garrett thinking.

"If we weren't Grangers, women might not be so interested in us," Garrett said.

"Speak for yourself," Roman grumbled.

Coming from any other man, that would have sounded cocky. It still sounded that way coming from Roman, but it was the truth. Roman still had that bad-boy edge that caused women to flock to him. Maybe some wanted to tame him, but Garrett suspected his brother just had pants that plenty of women wanted to remove.

"Well?" Roman prompted. "What about Tara Lynn? And FYI, if you dismiss her the way you have the other four women I've suggested, then I'll just keep suggesting. Because one way or another, you're getting laid."

Roman had already made that crystal clear.

"I'm sick and tired of seeing you so down," Roman added.

"Hell, I'm sick and tired of it, too. And if getting laid will help with that, then I'm all for it. Just not with Tara Lynn." Garrett paused. "Or those other four women." He paused again when Lady walked in, her hungry eyes already scoping out the place for her next conquest. "Not her, either."

Roman gave him a flat look. "Anybody else on your no-sex list?"

His brother had meant for that to be smart-ass, but Garrett answered it anyway. "Yeah. None of the women who keep coming to the house."

"You're significantly whittling down your prospects," Roman pointed out. "My advice—instead of whittling, be more, well, inclusive. It's sex, not a marriage proposal." He drank more of his beer. "Do you plan to tell me what's going on between Nicky and you?"

"Nothing's going on." It was an honest answer. Well, honest from one perspective anyway. There certainly wasn't any sex going on. Or kisses. "She didn't tell me it was her brother who had been with Meredith. I had to hear it from Meredith herself."

"Seems to me that's who you should have been hearing it from. If you wanted to hear it, that is. Kyle is Nicky's brother. Of course, she wasn't going to spread shit about him."

Garrett paused in midsip. "Did you know it was Kyle?"

"No. But it's not surprising. I know Kyle from the rodeo circuit. He used to ride broncos, and wedding rings and vows don't mean much to him. Obviously not to Meredith, either."

They did to Garrett. Roman, too. For all of his brother's sleeping around, he didn't keep company with married women.

"Besides," Roman went on, "you need to cut Nicky some slack. Shitty parents, shitty brother, shitty husband."

Garrett turned to him so fast that he would have sloshed his beer had the glass been full. "You knew her husband?"

"Knew of him. Let's just say that Nicky's brother didn't keep things as close to the vest as Nicky does. According to Kyle, the guy cheated on her."

Well, hell. That hit Garrett a lot harder than it probably would have if he hadn't known just how deep the cut felt from having a spouse step out on you. At least Nicky's hadn't been on YouTube, but that probably meant she hadn't been hurt. That also perhaps explained why there'd been no obituary online. Maybe she just hadn't felt the need to share the demise of a man who'd treated her like dirt.

"Please don't tell me the cheating happened when she was pregnant with Kaylee," Garrett said.

"Don't know the timing. Her brother quit riding for me about four years ago, before Kaylee was born."

That didn't mean the cheating hadn't continued. Damn. No wonder Nicky had needed a place to come and heal. She'd been dumped on by everyone in her life. Including him.

"Back to sex," Roman said a moment later. "I think you should have a go at the next woman who comes through that door. No wait, make it the second woman who walks in."

At that moment, the door opened, and Sophie walked in. Nicky was right behind her, making her woman number two.

Some men might have thought that was an eerie co-incidence or maybe even fate. Garrett knew the real reason, though. Roman had almost certainly seen their sister and Nicky through the window.

Sophie scanned the room, spotted them, and walked toward them. Nicky was right behind her, but she didn't have the same "woman on a mission" expression as Sophie.

"I knew I'd find you here," Sophie greeted, but her attention landed on Roman. "You're trying to set up Garrett with one of these barracudas."

"I am," Roman readily admitted. "And you're here, trying to set him up with Nicky."

Nicky looked stunned, as if Roman had just handed her a vibrating dildo. She probably would have slunk out of there if Sophie hadn't had a grip on her arm.

"I don't object to that, by the way," Roman went on, "but Nicky's got doubts about how all of this will play out."

Garrett had equal doubts. Especially because Nicky was the only person with more emotional baggage than him.

"It's okay," Garrett assured her. "Roman has no filter."

"You agreed to come here and get laid," Roman reminded him. It also proved that no-filter thing.

"And Nicky agreed to come here and stop it," Sophie explained.

"Well, not really—" That was all Nicky managed before his sister continued.

"Sex for the sake of sex isn't going to fix anything." Sophie stared at Garrett when she said that. "What you need is to have a good talk with Nicky."

"Talk instead of sex," Roman mumbled. "Yeah, that'll work. They've been dancing around this attraction since Nicky came back to Wrangler's Creek. They need to just take out their frustrations in bed."

Again, no filter, and this wasn't doing anything to ease those doubts Garrett had. But those doubts didn't extend to Lady. She finally set her sights on him and began to saunter his way. Since he wasn't in the mood for another flirting session where she kept bumping herself against his dick, Garrett finished off his beer, stood and took hold of Nicky's hand.

Her surprised expression went up a notch but then she saw Lady and must have realized why he was doing this. It made him a dick to use Nicky this way, but he really wasn't ready for another round with Lady. Or another round of Roman's suggestions. And besides, he was feeling sorry for Nicky.

"Leaving so soon, Garrett?" Lady asked, her bottom lip lowering to a mock pout.

"Yeah, Nicky and I have a date." There, he'd marked his territory. Sort of. It would get the likes of Lady off his back, maybe his mom, too, but he didn't want to put Nicky through another wringer.

Garrett tossed a twenty on the bar to pay for the beer and headed out with Nicky. "Sorry about that," he said as they made his way to his truck. "The date thing just popped out of my mouth. And I think both of us were ready to leave."

She didn't say a word. Nicky just stared at him while she put on her seat belt.

"We can drive around for a while, and then I can take you back to Z.T.'s house," he added. He hoped that would cause her to look relieved.

It didn't.

She kept staring at him. "What did Roman tell you about me?"

Man, he had to be wearing his emotions on his sleeve. Or maybe she just knew Roman and his penchant for not holding anything back. However, Garrett intended to do some holding back.

"Roman knows your brother," he settled for saying. There, he'd just put the ball in her court. If Nicky wanted to add more about Kyle, she could.

"I see." That's all she said for several snail-crawling moments. "And the reason you said we had a date was to get Lady off your back?"

He nodded, started driving. "I can tell her the truth if you want."

"No." She didn't hesitate that time. "This way, Meredith will hear and will maybe quit smiling."

"She's smiling?" Garrett wasn't. He was frowning.

"Gina seems to think so. I believe Meredith told you about Kyle to make sure there was a wedge between us."

Shit. If so, it'd worked. For two weeks anyway. Garrett wished people would start wearing signs to show their real intentions. Except he didn't want a sign right now. Not when he was holding stuff back from Nicky.

"You could tell Meredith to leave," Garrett suggested.

"I considered it. Then dismissed it. There are several people in that house I don't like." She said Lady's name and covered it with a cough. "But the group therapy sessions are about to start. I'm hoping that after a few of those, some people will feel well enough to leave."

Garrett thought about that for a moment. "What if they *all* feel well enough to leave?"

"There's a waiting list. Six others want to come, but there's no room for them. Sorry," she added. "I know you want us out of there."

Not as much as he had a couple of weeks ago. At least, he didn't want Nicky gone. "You'll be going through the therapy, too?" he asked.

That got her staring at him again. "All right, spill it. What else did Roman tell you?"

Hell's Bells. He really just needed to keep his mouth shut.

Since he didn't want to be driving for this part of the conversation, Garrett pulled over near the end of Main Street. It was far enough away from the shops and foot traffic that Nicky and he would have some privacy. Not a kissing kind of privacy, but being out in the open like this might give him some willpower that he sorely needed whenever he was around Nicky.

"Kyle told Roman that your husband cheated on you," Garrett admitted.

He'd already had a few regrets in this conversation, and that was another one. The moment he said the words, Nicky got that look in her eyes. The sad, haunted one that was almost identical to the look she'd had at her folks' old place.

"He did cheat on me," she finally said, and she glanced away, her attention focused on the nothing that was going on outside the window. "That's something we have in common. And you know how you don't want to talk about what happened with Meredith? Well, I don't want to talk about this, either."

"I'm sorry." Garrett didn't know what else to say. Because, yes, it was something in common. Something he wished Nicky hadn't had to go through.

She huffed. Not the reaction he'd been expecting. He'd thought she might be on the verge of tears. However, there were no tears in her eyes when she turned back to him. Nor was there a sad, haunted look. She suddenly seemed very determined about something.

"I don't want you to feel sorry for me," she insisted. "In fact, there's only one thing I want you to feel when you look at me."

Garrett hesitated a second, trying to figure out what she meant by that. Maybe she wanted him to be put off by her past. But that wasn't what Garrett felt. Even if that would have been the safer option.

But apparently safe wasn't in the cards today.

He took hold of Nicky, and for the second time in two weeks, he kissed her.

CHAPTER ELEVEN

GARRETT DIDN'T THINK it was right for a man to lie to himself so he didn't try to justify this. It was wrong. Period. Even if he had been ready for a relationship, the timing sucked. Nicky was here to heal and get over her past.

He was reasonably sure that this kiss wouldn't help with that.

That didn't stop him.

He kissed her and just kept on kissing her. There it was again. That punch of attraction. Not that he actually had to kiss her to feel it. It came whenever he laid eyes on her, but the punch was significantly harder with his mouth on hers.

She tasted good. Like those memories that could always stir him in just the right place. Specifically, his groin. His dick rather liked the idea of this kiss and thought it was going to get lucky. It wasn't. The kiss would have to be the beginning, middle and end of this particular mistake.

Nicky came up with some mistakes of her own. She moved in as close as she could get considering she was still wearing her seat belt. That meant no real body-to-body contact, but she upped the stakes by running her tongue over his bottom lip. French. Just the way he liked his kisses.

She made a sound of pleasure, soft but potent because it revved up things even more for Garrett. He groped his way down to her waist to undo her seat belt, missed, and his hand slid right into her crotch. The next sound she made was one of pleasure. But a different kind.

"If you're trying to give me an orgasm, you nearly did it," she muttered against his mouth and went back for another round of kissing.

Garrett immediately got right back into the kiss, but he also couldn't get his mind off what she'd just said. Maybe that's why he didn't move his hand after he undid her seat belt. It would take a special kind of stupid to try to give a woman a hand job while parked on Main Street, but he toyed with the idea of what it would be like to feel and hear Nicky shatter.

Especially since he wasn't so sure she'd shattered the one time they'd been together.

His lovemaking skills had been nonexistent then. Plus, that'd been coupled with the fact that he hadn't even known Nicky had been a virgin.

"Why didn't you tell me that you hadn't been with a man before?" Garrett blurted out.

In hindsight, he wished he'd stapled his lips together instead of saying that.

She looked at him, blinked. "Is this something you really want to talk about right now?"

Easy answer. "No." And he hauled her back to him.

The kiss continued, but obviously he'd screwed up the mood because she pulled back, met him eye to eye. "I didn't tell you because I didn't think you would notice," she said.

All right. He had his answer, and he pulled her to

him again, without the seat belt keeping her at bay, so he finally got sweet contact. Her breasts landed against his chest. All in all, that was a very good place for them to be. It sent some signals straight to his dick.

Unfortunately, what she'd said sent some signals to his brain.

Now, it was Garrett who pulled back. "You didn't think I'd notice? Trust me, I noticed. For one thing, you yelped in pain, and you kept on wincing. I hurt you. That's not something a guy just forgets."

She stared at him, maybe questioning his guy-hood right now because she was clearly in position for him to shut the hell up and resume the kissing. With just a little nudge, he could have her breasts against his chest again. With a harder nudge, he could have her in his lap.

Something that couldn't happen, of course, but a man's dick could dream.

"You didn't hurt me," she muttered. Then, shook her head. "Okay, it hurt, but there were some good parts, too."

"Name one." He really wished he had that stapler because it was obvious neither of them wanted to discuss this. Yet, here they were.

"It started to feel good after a while." She didn't hesitate, which helped his ego some.

"There was no *a while* to it," he corrected, causing her to smile. He liked that smile and wished she would do it more often.

She glanced away. Moved slightly away, too. "It was still a wonderful experience for me. Not necessarily the act itself, but you held me afterward while you were cursing yourself. You do remember the cursing, don't you?"

He nodded. He remembered all right. Garrett had called himself a few choice names. Like *dickhead.* "If I'd known you were a virgin, I would have taken more care with you."

No, that wasn't the truth.

"I probably wouldn't have gone through with it," Garrett confessed. At least he would have liked to think that. Of course, after Nicky and he had started making out, his decision-making skills had taken a serious nosedive.

Nicky nodded as if she'd known that all along. And that made him frown. Then, curse.

"You didn't tell me because you knew I'd stop?" he asked.

"Don't judge," she scolded. "We weren't in the same places in our lives we are now. I was seventeen," Nicky emphasized. "And I was with Garrett Granger."

And trying to escape a hellhole of a life at home. Garrett certainly hadn't helped with that. She'd seen him as some kind of grand prize, and he'd been anything but. Still wasn't. Just minutes earlier he'd asked Roman about the halo effect of the Granger name. Roman had dismissed it, but Garrett certainly wasn't doing that.

That killed the rest of his "pulling her into his lap" mood.

"You're about to say you're sorry, aren't you?" Nicky asked but didn't wait for an answer. "You're beating yourself up for something you can't change. Stop doing that."

He was about to tell her that he deserved a good

ass kicking, but it became impossible to speak. That was because Nicky latched on to the back of his neck, snapped him to her and resumed kissing him.

Garrett had been certain that his make-out session with Nicky was a done deal. But he was wrong. With just the touch of her mouth to his, his body revved up again, and he was already considering the logistics of the lap idea. Nicky helped with that, too. She hooked her arm around him, angling their bodies and dragging him closer. So close that her left thigh landed against his. Not quite a lap but it stoked the fire into a full blaze.

Mercy. The memories came. Good ones this time. Of all the kissing and touching that had landed Nicky and him on that chaise in the library. Especially the touching. And Garrett reenacted some of those memories now by sliding his hand between them. Yeah, this was definitely a good memory.

He moved his hand over her breast, and even though she had on a shirt and a bra, he could still feel her nipple, all hard and puckered. He brushed it with his fingers, all the while deepening the kiss. It was good. But he knew how to make it a whole lot better. He put his hand beneath her top, pushed down the cup of her bra and touched her the way he wanted.

The way Nicky apparently wanted, too, because she moaned with pleasure.

It definitely wasn't those wincing sounds of pain that she'd made on the chaise. Nope. This was the moan of a woman who liked what he was doing.

So Garrett did more.

He wet his fingers with his tongue and touched her nipples some more. Both of them. He also kept watch because, while he was in the hot and heavy foreplay mindset, he also still had a partial brain. That brain kept reminding him that they were on Main Street. Thankfully, though, no one was around.

Garrett pulled her closer. Nicky cooperated. Still no lap maneuver, mainly because of the steering wheel, but she did end up straddling his thigh. That was a good position for him to lower his hand to the center of her jeans.

She cursed him. And that made him smile. Made him do it again, too. And again. He touched her through the layers of clothing but figured he was getting the right spot because she dropped her head on his shoulder.

And then she played dirty.

Nicky kissed his neck. Not just an ordinary kiss, either. She tongued it, and while she scooted closer and closer to his moving fingers, she did some moving of her own. Her hand went to the front of his jeans, and Garrett did his own version of moaning when she found the right spot. Of course, his *spot* was a lot easier to find because he now had a full-blown erection.

"We need to get a room," he grumbled. Or hell, maybe he could just pull into one of the alleys and finish this there. Something quick and dirty…

His brain kicked in again and gave him an image that brought that thought to a halt. The memory of Meredith's video. That had happened in a vehicle, too, and he'd been stunned that she would have done that in a public place.

Much as he was doing right now.

He had one hand up Nicky's shirt, another on her crotch, and they were only seconds away from creating a scene that would be YouTube-worthy. Definitely not good.

Nicky must have realized it, too, because she eased back. Eased away her hand, as well, and Garrett did the same.

"I think we got carried away," she said, her voice strained because she was breathing too fast.

That fast breathing was causing her breasts to rise and fall. Something that got his attention despite the fact he should be doing something to soften his hard-on. This was the opposite of softening.

Garrett couldn't force his attention off her and to a safer view. Nope. He was clearly still in stupid mode because he looked down at where her shirt had come open. Her breasts were right there for him to see, and her right nipple was peeking over the top of the bra cup that he'd pushed down.

But that wasn't all he saw.

There was a scar. And even though he didn't want to look, Garrett did. It wasn't an ordinary scar. No. This was a word, and he got just a glimpse of it before Nicky yanked the side of her shirt over it.

"Oh, God," she said. She made another sound. Definitely not a moan of pleasure. And while she was still fixing her shirt, she bolted from his truck and started running.

NICKY FIGURED THAT Garrett's state of arousal would slow him down, and it did. By the time he made it out of his truck, she was already halfway up the block. She had no idea where she was going, but she had to get out of there fast.

Fast, before the tears came.

Too late, though. They were already burning her eyes, making it hard for her to see, so Nicky ducked into the alley between the hardware store and the pharmacy. It'd been years since she'd gotten off the sidewalk of Main Street and ventured to the backs of the buildings, but as a teenager she'd done it a couple of times to avoid seeing her father.

Then a couple more times to avoid seeing Meredith and Garrett together.

Thankfully, there was no one in the alley. No one behind the businesses, either, so Nicky kept running. She didn't look back for fear that she would see Garrett, and she was in no shape to face him right now.

Her phone buzzed, and she took it out long enough to see that it was from Garrett. He was no doubt wanting to know all about the scar he'd seen on her breast. She let the call go to voice mail and hoped that would be enough of a clue for Garrett to give her some time.

Like maybe a couple of years.

Another secret out of the bag. And this was one she would have gladly kept for the rest of her life. She'd been a fool to think that making out with Garrett wouldn't have consequences. Especially making out in broad daylight.

She kept running until her side hurt and her breath came in short spurts. Nicky had no choice but to stop, and she leaned against a building. It took her a moment to realize which building it was.

The Longhorn Bar.

Great. She'd come full circle, and worse, she heard footsteps coming her way. Nicky gathered as much breath as she could manage and got ready to move again. Before she could do that though, Roman came around the corner.

Even though she didn't want to see him, it was better than if it had been Garrett.

Roman didn't seem surprised at all to see her. Nor did he hurry closer. He just strolled toward her in that laid-back way of his.

"Garrett just called me," Roman said. "He's looking for you, and he sounded worried."

Yes, he would be. Maybe disgusted, too, by what he'd seen.

"He didn't say what was wrong," Roman went on. "And I didn't ask." He paused. "Do you want me to ask?"

"No." She couldn't say that fast enough.

Roman made a fair-enough sound and stopped several feet away. He took out a handkerchief and handed it to her. What he didn't do was press her for anything. He just stood there while she dried away the old tears. Some fresh ones, too.

She had to get control of herself. Had to woman up. This was just part of the old memories and scars that had haunted her for way too long. She had to find a way to get past it.

"My son called me an old fart this morning," Roman tossed out there. "Of course, he didn't say it to my face. He mumbled it under his breath when I told him he couldn't have six friends over on a school night." He pressed his thumb against his chest. "Me, an old fart. Doesn't quite go with my badass image, huh?"

Nicky couldn't help it. She smiled. It didn't last, but that was okay. Even a brief smile gave her a moment to get her footing.

"I told you that for a reason," he went on. "Sometimes, what other people see aren't who or what we are." The corner of his mouth lifted. Heck, even his smile was badass. "Was that a good enough life lesson for you to stop crying? And don't think that was a story I just made up. He really did call me an old fart."

She nodded. "It was an adequate enough life lesson." It wasn't, not really, but at least talking to Roman was giving her time to reconstruct the wall that she was very good at building. She needed to keep up the repairs on that wall.

And not wear shirts that could easily come unbuttoned.

While she was at it, Nicky needed to rethink this whole lust thing with Garrett. When he was kissing her, she'd thought that sex could be a possibility. Even casual sex. But the only way that could happen would be in a dark room. No chance of that now. Garrett had gotten a look inside her shirt, and even if they did land in bed, that scar would always be between them.

"Better?" Roman asked when she handed him back his handkerchief.

"Yes," she lied.

The flat look he gave her proved he didn't believe her, but he didn't call her on it, either. "You want me to drive you back to Z.T.'s place?"

It was a generous offer, especially considering that Roman avoided the ranch so that he wouldn't run into his mother. She didn't like that he would be putting himself out like that, but there weren't a lot of options other than walking. She'd ridden into town with Sophie so her SUV was at the ranch.

"Yes, thank you," she said.

He didn't put his arm around her or anything. Maybe because he realized she was too fragile. A gesture like that would only start the tears again. Instead, he fell in step beside her as they made their way to the front of the Longhorn.

"Does this mean you've given up on the idea of having sex with my brother?" Roman came out and asked.

If any other man had been asking the question, she would have been surprised. But this was Roman. "He's probably given up on the idea of having sex with me."

"I doubt it." He glanced at her from the corner of his eye. "Garrett's always had a thing for you."

"Until he met Meredith," she quickly pointed out.

"I didn't say he was smart, only that he had a thing for you." Roman smiled, causing her to smile, too. "My advice? Don't give up on sex with him. Seems to me you could both use something to loosen you up a bit. You're both wound pretty tight right now."

Finally, something she couldn't argue with. Nicky felt like a coil, ready to snap. And she doubted sex was going to fix that.

She heard the voices when they were just a few steps away from Main Street, and Nicky stopped so she could make sure it wasn't Garrett. It wasn't. But she instantly recognized who they belonged to.

Gina and Kaylee.

They were walking down the sidewalk, and Kaylee had a book in her right hand. Kaylee immediately spotted her. She ran to Nicky, and she scooped up the little girl into her arms. The hug was the fastest way to improve Nicky's mood.

"We drove into town for ice cream and then stopped by the bookstore," Gina said, her gaze sliding from

Nicky to Roman. She extended her hand to Roman. "I'm Gina Simpson from the Widows' House. Car accident," she added as if that were part of a normal conversation. "I'm also Kaylee's nanny."

"Roman Granger." And though Gina didn't ask, he added, "I'm the black sheep of the family. Whatever you've heard about me is probably true."

"All I've heard is that you were nice enough to let us stay at the house when we were waiting for the cops to clear out the Widows' House." Judging from Gina's sly smile, though, she'd heard much, much more about Roman.

There was concern in Gina's eyes when she looked at Nicky. Appreciation when she looked at Roman. Roman had that effect on women, and even Kaylee didn't seem to be immune to that.

"Will read dis to me?" Kaylee asked, and she held out the book to him.

Roman was a father, but his son, Tate, was almost thirteen. It'd probably been a while since he'd read to a toddler. Still, he took the book from Kaylee, opened to the first page and started reading. Well, what reading there was to do anyway, considering it was a picture book about kittens, but Roman went through the handful of words and made a few sounds.

Most women would have been totally engrossed in a hot cowboy reading to a child, but Gina kept her attention on Nicky. Her eyes were no doubt still red from crying, but even if they hadn't been, Gina would have noticed there was something wrong.

Roman finished the book, handed it back to Kaylee, and she thanked him. "You still need that ride to the ranch?" he asked Nicky.

She shook her head when she spotted Gina's car parked just up the street. "I can go back with Gina."

He nodded but didn't move. Roman stared at her a moment longer as if considering one last time whether to get to the bottom of what had gone wrong, but he finally shrugged, mumbled a goodbye and walked away.

"I'm not sure how you can keep from drooling when you're talking to him," Gina commented. "But then, you've got something else on your mind. Garrett called me," she added a heartbeat later. "He's looking for you. Want to tell me why you're not letting him find you?"

Nicky checked to make sure Kaylee wasn't hanging on every word, but thankfully she was looking at her new book. "Garrett saw the scar" was all Nicky said.

Gina's gaze fired back to her, and her forehead bunched up. "God, I'm sorry. Should I ask how he reacted?"

"No. In fact, please don't ask anything else about it."

Gina wouldn't. That's why Nicky considered her to be such a good friend. She wouldn't ask, though Nicky was certain she wanted to know. One day, Nicky might show it to her.

But not today.

Today, she would hide the word a little bit longer. The word that had been carved into her skin.

Whore.

CHAPTER TWELVE

NICKY WAS ON the porch steps of her old house again, and even though she knew it was a dream, it felt real. Always did. This time there was progress, though. She marched right up the steps and made it all the way to the front door. Her feet cooperated.

The rest of her didn't, though.

She froze right in the doorway, and without the broken screen to partially block her view, she could see the living room. Not filled with dust and dead leaves, though. It was the way it'd been when she was a kid. Clean, everything in its place. In the adjacent dining room, she could see dinner on the table. Everything in place there, too, and if the plates hadn't been mismatched, it would have looked like a picture from a magazine.

The images came, and she tried to turn away. But tonight, there were no shields. No way to stop this. She was as helpless now as she'd been then.

He came at her, his hands already balled into fists. Her father. The man who had maybe once loved her. Maybe. But he didn't love her now. There was only hate in his eyes.

His face was red, partly from the booze, and he reeked of it. Not just his breath—Nicky could have sworn he was sweating it, too. That was the only thing that explained the stench.

She braced herself for the fist. And it came. It landed against her head. His favorite spot because it didn't leave a visible mark. Nothing for the town to see so they would know his secret. That he hated her and wanted to punish her.

Nicky felt the punch, and the pain ripped through her head. She didn't fight back. She'd learned the hard way that it only made it worse. Nor did she cry. Tears made it worse, too. She just lay there, silent and unmoving, where he'd beaten her down, and she prayed that tonight it would only be the one punch.

It wasn't.

He came at her again, but this time Nicky's own hoarse sob woke her from the dream.

"COCKSUCKER," D.M. SNARLED.

Nicky wasn't sure what D.M. was trying to convey, especially since that didn't seem to be an answer to the question: What do you miss most about your husband or partner?

The counselor, Cassie McCord, kept her attention on D.M. "Would you like to share more?" Cassie asked.

"My husband was a cocksucker," D.M. said after a few tics of her head. "I should have left him, but I kept thinking he'd change. He didn't. So, I guess what I miss is the hope that he'd change. There's no hope of that now with him six feet under."

"All right," Cassie said. She waited a few more seconds, but when D.M. didn't add anything else, she turned to the woman sitting next to D.M.

"I miss sleeping next to someone," Ruby, the suicide widow, said. "Especially during thunderstorms and cold weather." Her voice was soft and tentative, and she was staring at the floor instead of at Cassie or anyone else in the group.

There were eight other widows—and Meredith—in the group therapy circle in the parlor, and all eyes were on Ruby since it was her turn. All except Nicky made sounds of agreement, but that was because she was still thinking of the dream she'd had the night before. Sometimes the dream stayed with her, no matter how much she tried to shake it.

This was one of those times.

But she had to shake it. Had to focus and put herself back together. If not, everyone would think that she was too broken to figure out something as simple as what she missed most. It wasn't sleeping next to Patrick, that was for sure. Patrick was gone so much on business and then with his cheating, that they hadn't spent a lot of nights in the same bed. Even when they had, it hadn't felt as if he'd been there mentally.

"Brian was a cover hog, though," Ruby continued a moment later. "And sometimes he would sleepwalk and do number one on me. Urinate," she clarified. "But I suppose that's happened to everyone at one time or another."

No one made sounds of agreement, but Nicky was sure she made a face.

"Donkey dicks," D.M. mumbled.

That was probably the most accurate thing someone could have said because yes, Nicky was shocked, too.

"And I thought my man was a cocksucker," D.M. added. "At least he didn't use his cock-sucking ways to pee on me."

"Brian didn't know he was doing it, of course." Ruby, again. "And he rarely did number two, mostly just number one."

Everyone but Ruby and the counselor made a face.

Great day. Maybe Nicky's own marriage hadn't been so bad after all.

"Anyway, I don't miss the number one and number two," Ruby went on, "but I miss Brian. When I get to heaven and see him, the first thing I'm going to ask him is why he took that whole bottle of pills." Her jaw suddenly got tight. "And then I'm going to kick him in the balls for doing that."

Lady cheered, pumping her arm in the air as if she were at a sporting event. Since she was swigging on a beer, it added to the ambiance. "Anger is a natural response," Cassie assured Ruby. "And it's something you and I are going to try to work through in our private sessions."

Yes, those. Cassie had indeed agreed to do one-on-ones with whoever wanted them. Most did. Nicky included.

"And what about you?" Cassie prompted when she turned to Lizzie. "What do you miss most?"

Lizzie opened her mouth, closed it and opened it again. "I'm not sure. I don't want to say the wrong thing."

Nearly everyone in the room sighed. That's because not doing or saying the wrong thing was Lizzie's go-to response. The woman was afraid of her own shadow. Literally. Nicky had witnessed Lizzie shriek when the light slanted just right to make her look like a swamp monster on the kitchen wall. Of course, Nicky had nearly shrieked, too. That kitchen still had bad puking memories for her.

"There is no wrong thing that you can say," Cassie assured the woman. "This is just a session for me to get to know you better and for you to express some of your feelings."

Lizzie nodded but didn't look very confident about that. "I guess I just miss his smell. Bernie always smelled very nice." Lizzie began to tear up, and as she took another tissue from her purse, she motioned for the person next to her to continue.

It was Meredith.

Meredith took a long breath first. "I miss everything," she said. "Being part of a couple. Sharing a morning cup of coffee. Just having someone there who actually cared how my day was going."

Even though Meredith probably hadn't meant that as a dig to Nicky, it sort of felt like one. Though it shouldn't have. It'd been a week since Nicky's kissing incident with Garrett, and she hadn't spoken to him since. He'd called her twice, but she'd texted back to say that she was busy. Not a lie exactly but not the total truth, either.

She was avoiding him.

Because she didn't want to see the look of "poor pitiful Nicky" in his eyes. That's why she'd come here, to get away from pitying looks like that. And besides, if she saw Garrett, she could end up in his arms again. She'd discovered she became a little like Lizzie whenever she was around him. Weak and mindless.

"I'm hearing that the little things are what you miss most," Cassie prompted. "That's natural. Relationships are complex, filled with little and big moments." And with that counselor-ish comment, she turned to Nicky. "What do you miss about your late husband?"

It was her turn.

When she'd first come up with the idea of the Widows' House, Nicky had looked forward to this next step in the healing process, but this suddenly seemed like a really bad idea. Bringing all this back to the surface. Especially since she had so many other things to deal with. Too bad she hadn't insisted that Loretta take this particular session instead of babysitting Kaylee.

"I miss just having someone around," Nicky finally said.

That was code. What she missed was having the possibility of someone there who had lived up to her expectations. Especially since she hadn't set those expectations that high. That probably came from being the daughter of an alcoholic. As long as she wasn't getting beaten or berated, then life was good. But in Patrick's case, she'd added fidelity to her marital wish list. He hadn't beaten or berated her, but the man had definitely had trouble keeping his zipper up.

Cassie paused as if waiting for Nicky to continue, but when Nicky didn't volunteer more, the therapist looked at Gina.

"Kisses," Gina readily admitted. "I really miss being kissed. And snuggling. I miss talking about a good book or movie with Simon."

"I miss my husband's dick," Lady volunteered the second that Gina finished. "I miss sex." She dabbed her eyes, though Nicky wasn't sure there were actually any tears there. "When I was married, it was okay to have sex anytime I wanted. Now, when I'm with a man, people complain."

Lady quit dabbing and aimed a glare at the sisters who had indeed complained about the woman's rather vocal lovemaking. The frequency of it, too.

"Just because I'm having sex, it doesn't mean I'm not mourning my husband," Lady went on. "I am. I miss Derek in the worst possible way."

None of them doubted that, and none of them doubted that *the worst possible way* involved sex. Nicky certainly didn't judge her for that.

"I miss sex, too," Nicky admitted. Of course, she hadn't actually intended to admit that aloud. Or to have the image of Garrett's face pop into her head. Nor had she expected to get the attention of every woman in the room.

She glanced at their expressions and silently cursed. Clearly, they thought she was already getting her sex quota filled, and they obviously thought Garrett was the one doing the filling.

Ruby smiled, gave a dreamy sigh. "Rekindling an old flame is the best."

Yes, they thought it was Garrett doing the filling, and it probably wouldn't do any good to deny it. Still, Meredith looked at her as if waiting for Nicky to do just that. If Nicky had had any doubts that Meredith was here to get her man back, she didn't have them now.

Cassie turned to the last women in the group. The sisters. And she didn't say a word before the women burst out crying. Like Lady's Camel-Tow sex and Lizzie's shadow fears, this was normal, too. They cried a lot. But again, Nicky wasn't judging. She'd lost a husband, period, and she'd had Kaylee to help her get through it. These women had lost everything but each

other, and unlike hers, it appeared their marriages had
been good.

Nicky went to them as did some of the others, and
it started a group hug. Lizzie joined in on the crying.

"I don't miss that D-word," one of the sisters said,
her mouth tightening. This was Diana, who always sat
or stood between the other two. She was the middle
by age, as well, probably in her early forties. "I have
medorthophobia."

That stopped the hugs and generated plenty of puzzling looks.

"Fear of a penis?" Cassie asked.

"An erect P-word," Diana corrected. Mercy, the
woman couldn't even say it. "Aradia has it, too, and
Hera has phallophobia, fear of all Ps whether they're
erect or not."

Nicky, like the rest of the group, seemed stunned to
silence. Lady appeared ready to keel over from shock.
"As for me," Diana went on, "as long as the P-word is
just lying there like a sea urchin with jowls, I'm okay.
Mostly."

"So, what did you do?" Lady asked. "Screw your
honeys with the lights out, or did they sneak up on you
from behind so you wouldn't get a good look at their
sea urchin dicks?"

Aradia gasped. Hera glared. "No. We didn't do
A-sex," Diana explained.

Nicky was clueless as to what that meant. Anal sex,
maybe? Or had the woman meant that as a blanket
comment to indicate no sex whatsoever?

"We can explore those phobias in private sessions
if you like," Cassie suggested to the sisters. "There are

treatments for both, and all three of you could go on to have healthy sex lives."

"That probably wouldn't be a good idea," Diana explained. "This way, we can keep ourselves for our late husbands." Her sisters bobbed their heads in agreement.

"All right, then," Cassie said after taking a deep breath. "This is a great start, but our time is up for today. I need to get ready for the second group."

That was their cue to get moving, and after Nicky thanked her, she went in search of Loretta so she could relieve her of babysitting duties. But Nicky didn't make it far, only a few steps outside the parlor before Meredith stopped her.

"Is it true?" Meredith asked. "Are Garrett and you back together?"

Nicky wished she hadn't hesitated, but she did that only because Meredith's ballsy question threw her for a moment. "No."

Meredith just continued to stare at her. Not an ordinary stare, either. That was the look of a woman who didn't believe what she was hearing. "I'm worried about him," Meredith continued a moment later. "I know whenever he sees your daughter that it tears him up inside."

Nicky wished there was no possibility that was true. But she couldn't dismiss it. "And you believe I should stay away from him because of that?" She made certain that Meredith understood that it was a question.

Meredith stared at her. "I'm the bad guy here. I know that. I cheated on Garrett with your brother. It doesn't matter that Kyle was the only one and that I regret it all the way down to my soul. I'm still the bad guy. That means anything I say to you will carry no weight."

At that exact moment, Gina walked past them and mumbled "oatmeal." Since her friend had threatened to fatten up Meredith via the oatmeal, the comment was timely. Meredith, though, didn't seem to make the connection. She just gave Gina a wave as if passing on the offer to eat.

"But you want what you say to carry some weight," Nicky finished for her. "You want me to stay away from Garrett so that you can fix a marriage that I don't believe is fixable."

Meredith looked as if she'd slapped her. She pulled back her shoulders, kept staring at Nicky. "So, you two are together." She finally glanced away. "That explains some things." Nicky didn't get a chance to ask her what it explained because Meredith kept on talking. "How'd you get over the past? How did you stop loving your husband enough to start seeing another man?"

Those questions were like driving on the potholed trail that led to the Widows' House. "My situation wasn't the same as yours. My husband died, and that means there's no chance he'll be my husband again."

"So, if you've worked that out, why are you here?" Meredith asked. "Why did you start this place?"

Another pair of potholed questions. "I needed to work on me."

Meredith flexed her eyebrows as if not buying that, either. Probably because she thought Nicky was there to stake her claim to Garrett.

"Meredith, I'm not comfortable talking about Garrett with you. And if you're here because you want to make sure he doesn't end up with me, then I need to ask you to leave."

There. She'd found her backbone, and it felt pretty darn good.

"No, that's not why I'm here," Meredith assured her. Unlike before with the *slapped* reaction, her expression gave nothing away. She had a blank-canvas kind of face. "And even if I were, it's too late for it. I accept that you two are together."

Nicky wanted to throw up her hands. "Why do you keep saying that?"

Meredith made an isn't-it-obvious sound. "Because Garrett's waiting for you on the porch. I saw him from the window." She paused. "He brought you flowers."

GARRETT SAT IN one of the rocking chairs on the porch, staring at the box of flowers and wondering if this visit was a mistake. Since Nicky hadn't contacted him, that probably meant she wasn't ready to talk.

Yet, here he was.

This could backfire and send her running. And if so, he would just have to let her run and accept that Nicky might never be able to tell him why she had that scar.

Whore.

Not exactly a word someone would have purposely put on her breast. Well, unless alcohol had been involved. Still, even then it was a long shot. No, he had the sickening feeling that Nicky's dad was responsible. Even if he hadn't been the one to do the actual cutting, he was behind this. That made Garrett wonder just how bad the abuse had gotten before Nicky had finally managed to escape.

"They shouldn't be much longer," Loretta said from

the other side of the screen door, a new addition to the house. As were the six rocking chairs on the porch. "They'll be finishing up the group session soon."

Garrett thanked her for the update and went back to the box, staring again. He didn't mind waiting because the wait might help him figure out if he was doing the right thing by coming here.

"Any news on the d-e-a-d m-a-n?" Loretta asked.

He shook his head and wondered why she'd bothered to spell it out when no one else was around. "Clay's working on it, though. Nicky, too."

Loretta opened the screen door and came out slowly, and he didn't think it was his imagination that she was somewhat alarmed by what he'd just told her.

"Nicky?" Loretta questioned. "What is she doing?" She sounded very concerned, maybe because she thought Nicky had enough to handle. Which she did.

Hell. Why was that word cut into her skin?

"Nicky's doing internet searches," Garrett answered. "She's trying to find someone who might recognize the ring."

Loretta nodded, but she still didn't look okay with that. "She hasn't been sleeping well, you know. And it's not all because of the noise Lady makes when she's having s-e-x. Not that I'm judging her or anything."

Garrett was confused. "Who? Nicky or Lady?"

"Lady, of course. She won't change that picture on the side of her truck, and she yells Camel-Tow as if we don't remember that's the name of her company. I mean, really, she's preaching to the choir. If any of us need tow service, we'd go to her since we know her and all."

That didn't help any with his confusion. "Why isn't Nicky sleeping well?" he came out and asked.

"Oh, dear," she muttered as if she'd said too much. That didn't stop Loretta from saying more though. "I think it's because of you."

Great. Now he was adding more crap to her crap-riddled life. That got him rethinking this visit, and he stood, ready to make his way back to his truck. Before he could do that, though, the door opened and Kaylee came out.

No pink overalls for her today. She was dressed like a cowgirl in jeans and a vest, complete with a hat and white boots.

"Who am I?" Kaylee asked. She twirled around like a ballerina.

Obviously, this was some kind of game, but he didn't know the rules. "You're Kaylee?" he tried.

"No." She made a what-a-stupid-answer face and twirled again. Loretta tried to help by pointing. At him.

"I Gare-if," Kaylee announced just as he made the connection.

He wasn't sure if he was supposed to feel flattered by that, but he was. The only thing that didn't go was the red superhero cape, and she was carrying what appeared to be a chicken feather coated with glitter.

"That fortune-teller lady gave her the feather," Loretta explained. "And she loves it so much, she sleeps with it."

"Miz Vita," Kaylee added, showing him the feather. She also had a book under her arm, and she handed it to him. Garrett put the flower box on the floor so he could take it. "Read it to me like Roaming."

Garrett looked at Loretta for an interpretation of the last part.

"Your brother, Roman, read her that story," Loretta said. "Gina told me all about it."

Garrett nearly said "No, way." That wasn't something his brother would do, but he went with a better question instead. "When did Kaylee see Roman?"

"About two weeks ago."

Around the same time Nicky had run from him. Since Roman had been in town that day, maybe Nicky had run to him. Then, she'd had him read Kaylee a story.

And here his brother hadn't mentioned a word about it.

Kaylee tugged him back into the rocker and then immediately climbed into his lap. Along with poking him in the eye with the glitter feather. He hoped she hadn't been using that feather in any cow pies.

"I dress jus' like you." Kaylee used the feather to point to his jeans, boots and hat.

That eased some of the sting from the eye poke. Some of the sting from hearing about Roman reading a story. Though Garrett wasn't sure why he didn't approve of that. After all, it was good that Kaylee was getting that kind of attention. Even if it was from Roman.

And not from him.

"She goes on and on about you all the time," Loretta explained. "Gare-if this and Gare-if that."

"Gare-if," Kaylee said as if confirming that. She added a smile that put a warm spot in his chest.

Oh, man.

The memories came, but this time they were just a flash. Barely time for him to even see them. That was because Kaylee caught his chin and turned his face in the direction of the page she'd just opened.

"Read it to me, please," she said.

Like Roman, this wasn't exactly his strong suit, but Garrett went for it. It wasn't much of a story though because it was a book about counting kittens.

"'One kitty, two kitties, three and more,'" he read. "'Four kitties, four kitties, four, four, four. Mommy kitty, daddy kitty, more, more, more.'" He added a few mews to that, causing Kaylee to cackle with laughter.

She was such an easygoing kid. Sweet and loving. It bothered him that Nicky had said she was behind and that she needed a tutor. Then, he wondered why it bothered him. Kaylee wasn't his.

Garrett made it through the book and what had to have been six hundred kitten illustrations, and Kaylee applauded when he finished. She hugged him, too, and then looked up at him with those big blue eyes.

"Are you a daddy?" she asked.

Judging from Loretta's slight gasp, she'd obviously heard that he had lost a child, and she immediately hurried to take Kaylee away. But Garrett shook his head and motioned for Loretta to stop.

"I had a little girl," he answered. Then, he cursed that lump in his throat. "But she's in heaven with the angels." He hoped that wasn't too hard for her to understand.

It wasn't.

"Like my daddy," she said and hugged him again.

This time, that warmth settled into his heart, and even though part of him knew he should pull away, he didn't. Garrett put his arm around her and hugged her right back.

Kaylee looked up at him and smiled. Even though she didn't say it, he could almost hear her saying *I'll be your little girl*. That was impossible, of course.

Or was it?

The thought came like a whisper, but it soon took on a full head of steam. There was no reason why he couldn't get involved with Nicky. They were attracted to each other, and so what if they had shitty pasts? That didn't doom them to a shitty future together.

He frowned.

But it wasn't right to pursue Nicky just so he could have a daughter. *Her* daughter.

Except it wouldn't be just that. He went back to the attraction again. And Nicky and he had been lovers... once. People dated and hooked up with less than that going for them.

The whisper turned to a shout, and Garrett stood up, ready to go inside and kiss the living daylights out of Nicky. Not solely because of Kaylee, either. Kaylee was just a nice fringe benefit.

He stood Kaylee on the porch, kissed the top of her head and grabbed the flower box so he could give it to Nicky. He didn't have to go far, though, because at that moment, Nicky came out of the house.

"Meredith said you were here," Nicky greeted.

Hell, he hadn't wanted anything to kill his mood or the momentum, but the mention of his ex-wife nearly did it. To kick up that momentum again, he leaned in and kissed Nicky.

"Oh," Loretta muttered. She scooped up Kaylee. "This little one and I will give you some time alone."

Loretta made it sound as if he were about to strip

off all of Nicky's clothes and pull her to the floor, but
Garrett figured that could wait.

"I wanted to see you," he said. "Please don't run."

"Not today. I'm wearing flip-flops. Hard to run in
them."

He was glad she'd gone for something light. Maybe
that meant she'd listen to the rest of what he had to say.

"I'm sorry you got upset when you were in my
truck."

"I'm sorry you saw what you saw," she countered.
Definitely nothing light about that.

He waited to see if she was going to add an explanation to that, but when she didn't, Garrett went on with
what he wanted to say.

"Will you go out with me?" he asked.

It was a very simple question. Just six words with
very few syllables. But Nicky didn't jump to answer.
Instead, she looked over her shoulder where they could
see Loretta and Kaylee through the screen door. Loretta
was leading the little girl away from them.

"Why do you want to go out with me?" she countered.

He could also see the wheels turning in her head,
and he didn't like the direction they were turning. She
was connecting this to Kaylee. And while it might be
partially true, there was another truth here, as well.

Garrett tucked the flower box under his arm so he
could slip his hand around her waist, pull her to him
and kiss her. He didn't make it too hot in case Kaylee
happened to look back, but he made sure Nicky knew
she'd been kissed.

"That's why I want to go out with you," he said when
he broke the lip-lock and let go of her.

She certainly didn't jump to agree. Probably because she thought that eventually she was going to have to talk about that scar. She wouldn't, though. Garrett wouldn't ask her anything about that until she was ready to talk about it.

Nicky finally nodded.

He didn't have time to celebrate, though, because her gaze dropped to the box under his arm. He'd nearly forgotten about it, and he shifted it back to his hand.

"You brought me flowers?" she asked.

"No. Sorry." But he made a mental note to do that. "These aren't from me. A florist in Spring Hill delivered them to the house, and I brought them over."

She stopped in midreach, her fingers freezing just a few inches from the box. He'd never seen someone's expression change so fast. Nicky hadn't been exactly smiling after that kiss, but now the color drained from her face.

"Thank you," she said, but it didn't sound the least bit sincere.

Maybe because he was right there watching her, Nicky opened the box and glanced inside at the pair of yellow roses. She slammed the lid shut and mumbled another thank-you.

"There's a card," he said, taking it from his pocket. It was only about two inches wide and was in an envelope.

Nicky opened that, too, but again he thought she might be doing that for his benefit.

But why?

Why had flowers put that kind of pained expression on her face?

Hell. He hoped this wasn't from some old boyfriend.

Or maybe this was some kind of deal her late husband had set up, to have flowers delivered after he was gone.

Garrett hadn't read the card, but when Nicky pulled it from the envelope, he saw what was written there.

I'm sorry, but I can't stay away.

"I have to go," Nicky insisted, shoving the card into the flower box and going back inside.

And despite her assurances that she wouldn't run, that's exactly what Nicky did.

CHAPTER THIRTEEN

GINA WAITED IN the parlor, peering around the side of the door, waiting. If anyone saw her, they'd think she was snooping or had developed an extreme shy streak, but there was a purpose to this lurking.

She was looking for Meredith.

Since the woman wasn't in her room or in the yard, that meant she was somewhere in the house. Gina had already learned that this house was a maze where you could wander around for hours and not find what you were looking for, so she decided to plant herself and wait.

Lizzie walked by, and yes, she was crying. She'd been doing a lot of that lately, and Gina made a mental note to check on the woman. While she was at it, she'd check on Ruby, as well, and try not to make a funny face because of the things she'd learned about the woman during group sessions.

"There you are," Loretta said.

Gina nearly jumped out of her dress. She apparently sucked when it came to detection mode since Loretta had made it to within just an arm's length away and she hadn't heard the woman coming up behind her.

"That really nice cowboy asked me to give this to you," Loretta said, handing her a folded note. "I'm pretty sure he's one of Hester Walter's boys, but I don't know which one."

"Jake," Gina provided, and she glanced at the note. It was his phone number with a little cartoon drawing of a cowboy with seriously bowed legs and a phone pressed to his ear.

"Call me when you're ready for some coffee, a drink, dinner and/or mindless sex," he'd written beneath the drawing.

Gina tried not to smile. She failed.

"Those boys always did have the best manners," Loretta went on. "Hard workers, too. The Walters have been working for the Grangers since back in Z.T.'s days."

"You knew the boys well?" Gina asked.

"Well, enough..." Loretta stopped, and her eyes widened. "I need to get back to the mopping," she said, and scurried off.

Great. Either Loretta had some dirt on Jake and his family and hadn't wanted to tell or the woman had a skewed sense of urgency regarding floor cleanliness.

Gina made a third mental note to find out if Jake was some kind of con artist who charmed women to get their fortunes. If so, he was going to be sorely disappointed in her bank account. Probably her sex skills, as well, but she didn't intend to let things get that far between them.

She put the note in her pocket and finally spotted her prey. Meredith didn't see Gina. That was because she had her attention on her phone screen. Actually, she was glaring at it. She yelped out a sound of surprise when Gina caught her arm and pulled her into the parlor.

"Made any trips to the florist lately?" Gina came right out and asked her.

Either Meredith was genuinely surprised by the question or else she was faking it. Gina was leaning more toward the faking-it theory. She didn't trust Garrett's ex one bit.

"What are you talking about?" Meredith pulled her arm out of Gina's grip.

"Florist. Spring Hill." Gina made sure she added a little snark to that.

Though Meredith only shrugged. "Yes, I went there. The owner is an old friend of mine, and I stopped in to catch up with her. What—are you spying on me or something?"

"Or something," Gina grumbled.

She studied Meredith's eyes and saw no hint of deception or gaslighting. Still, something had to be going on because there had been two flower deliveries in just a little over a week. A record. One that Gina didn't want repeated.

"Does this have anything to do with the flowers Garrett brought Nicky?" Meredith asked.

"Does it?" Gina countered.

Meredith huffed. "Clearly, you think I've done something wrong, and I haven't."

"You're sure about that? Because it seems as if you did *something wrong* when you blew Kyle in the backseat of his car. And when you browbeat Nicky into letting you come here. Don't you think we all know what you're trying to do?"

Another huff and she folded her arms over her ample chest. "I'm just trying to get better, like the rest of you.

You don't see me accusing you of being here under false pretenses."

"Because I'm not," Gina assured her. "Nicky is my friend, and she's too nice to tell you to get lost, but I'm not."

They stood there, just staring at each other like two Old West gunslingers about to draw their weapons. Gina saw the exact moment that she won the showdown, and Meredith turned, ready to leave.

But she stopped.

"Why would Nicky get so upset over a flower delivery?" the woman pressed. Now, there was some snark to her tone. "Because if you think I had something to do with it—which I didn't—and if the flowers weren't from Garrett—which I don't think they were—then it means Nicky has a stalker or something."

Gina tried not to let her expression give anything away, but she wasn't good at this sort of thing. However, she was good at anticipating stuff, and when Meredith finally walked away, Gina suspected this was not the last she'd see of Garrett's troublemaking ex.

Nicky's secret could be about to bite her in the butt.

I'M SORRY, BUT I can't stay away.

For only a handful of words, they certainly packed a punch. One by one Nicky's secrets had come to light. All but this last one. And it was the worst of them all.

Nicky had put the flowers in the outside trash can as soon as she'd made her way through the house and out the back. She'd shoved them deep beneath the other garbage, but out of sight didn't mean they were out of mind. No. It'd been hours since she'd laid eyes on those flowers, and the image of them was just as fresh and unblemished as it had been when she'd first looked inside that box.

There was no one to call about this. Nothing she could do except pray that the *I can't stay away* didn't mean she would soon have a visitor.

She had worked so hard to keep her life together, and even though it felt cobbled, the pieces had seemed to fit. Even with Patrick's death. But then the flowers had started to arrive, and Nicky had to rethink everything.

Because she could lose everything.

She tried to force all the bad stuff aside and get to work on the plans for the party. Plans that were growing by leaps and bounds. When Nicky had first come up with the idea, she'd wanted to find a way to thank Belle for giving them the lease. Also a way to thank the ranch hands for having to work around them. Now that Loretta and Ruby were involved, the guest list had been expanded to include some local business owners and members of the historical society. Every day, it seemed as if they added someone else.

Like today.

Nicky glanced at the revised guest list and saw that the mayor and Clay had been included. She doubted either of them wanted to come, especially Clay since he'd been out here enough with the investigation. But maybe they'd felt it would be an insult to Belle if they declined. Since Belle would soon be Clay's mother-in-law, that was likely enough incentive. She didn't know the mayor's motive but hoped it wasn't to try to boot them out of town because of Lady's antics.

She put her head down on her desk, no longer fighting the tears that she felt coming on. But apparently the tears would have to wait after all because there was a knock at the door. She said another quick prayer that her visitor wasn't Garrett. And it wasn't. It was worse.

Meredith.

Nicky really did need to get more specific with the way she worded her prayers.

Meredith was alone, but she had a grip on the handle of a suitcase. One that she rolled into Nicky's office.

"I wanted you to know I'm leaving," Meredith said. "I just wanted to say I was sorry and that I hope Garrett and you won't be mad at me."

Until Meredith had mentioned Garrett, Nicky had thought this conversation was going well. But there was something in the way Meredith said his name that had bells clanging in Nicky's head.

"Why would Garrett be mad at you?" Nicky asked.

"Because he blames me for upsetting you. He called me right after you ran off with those flowers. Others here are upset with me, too."

Nicky hadn't realized Meredith had seen that little incident, but it was possible every single person in the house had. The eyes might be windows to the soul, but there were enough windows in the house to offer every Peeping Tom a great view.

"Garrett thought I had something to do with those flowers," Meredith went on. "He was venting, of course. Very pissed off that you were pissed off and he didn't know why."

"I'll set him straight," Nicky assured her. Of course, she wouldn't do that with the full truth, but she would let him know that Meredith wasn't responsible for this latest dark mood of hers.

"Thank you." But she shrugged, then huffed. "It won't do any good, though. He said the only reason I was here was to complicate your life. He really held up a mirror to my face with that. And that's why I'm leaving."

Nicky wanted to issue a good luck and give her a goodbye wave, but there was another component to this. One that Nicky didn't like.

"What about therapy? Will you continue that?" Nicky asked.

Meredith nodded, started to leave but then turned back around. "You'll make sure Garrett continues with his, too? His nightmares used to be pretty bad, and I doubt they've gotten any better."

"Garrett was in therapy?" Nicky asked. This was the first she was hearing about it, and it made her ache for him even more. He'd lost so much.

"Yes. We both were. There was all that pain and grief to work through. But he stopped seeing the counselor when she suggested that he and I do our sessions together. If you ask him to continue, though, he would probably do it."

Nicky doubted that. Besides, her own mental well-being wasn't in such stellar shape, so she should just stay out of it.

Even if it felt like the last thing she wanted to do.

Just like that, the memories of Garrett's kisses returned. He certainly hadn't needed therapy or adjustments in that department. Even after all these years, he'd found the right place to kiss. To touch. He had increased the heat in her even though it would have been better if all of that had stayed at room temperature.

"You seem distracted or something," Meredith commented.

She was, and she was getting a little tingly from

remembering those kisses, but Nicky denied it with a head shake. What she couldn't deny was that Meredith still wasn't leaving.

"Is something wrong?" Meredith pressed.

"No," Nicky assured her.

But Meredith continued before Nicky even got out that one-word response. "Because I saw how you reacted to the flowers. Gina and Garrett were upset about them, too." She paused. "If you have a stalker, you need to let the ranch hands know. You don't want someone getting hurt because you're trying to keep it a secret. If you tell them, they can be on the lookout if this stalker shows up here."

Nicky stood, trying to process what Meredith was saying and figure out what to address first. "Gina? A stalker?" She probably couldn't have verbalized that better, but Meredith's accusation had unbalanced her.

"Gina's upset with me for being here. And as for the stalker, it's something I figured out on my own. I mean, what else could it be?"

It could be worse than a stalker. And was worse. But Nicky kept that to herself.

"No one here is in danger. At least not because of me," Nicky added, mainly because Lady was stirring up some trouble with her sleeping around. The buzz was that some of the women in town were fed up with Lady encroaching on their cowboy territory.

"Oh," Meredith said. "All right, then. I must have read the signals wrong. I figured it had to be something like that for Gina and Garrett to be so angry."

She didn't volunteer anything, and she just stood there, looking at Meredith until the woman finally got the message—that it was time for her to leave. Meredith issued a crisp goodbye and headed out.

Nicky waited until she could no longer hear the woman's footsteps before she went in search of Gina. Apparently, Meredith and Gina had had a conversation, and Nicky wanted to know what'd been said to make Meredith believe she had a stalker. If Meredith thought that, then Garrett probably did, too.

Gina wasn't in her room with Kaylee where she'd last seen them, but there was a note saying that she'd taken Kaylee to her session with her tutor in San Antonio. They'd probably be gone most of the afternoon, but that would give Nicky time to pay Garrett a quick visit.

A visit that she immediately rethought.

She really didn't want to tell him about who was sending those roses. Didn't want to talk about the scar, either. Heck, most of the things going on in her life were off the conversational table with Garrett, but she felt as if she owed him something.

Nicky was on her way to the trail where her SUV was parked, but her phone buzzed with a text message. It was from a number she didn't recognize, and it caused her heart to start racing.

I'm sorry, but I can't stay away.

Since those words were right there in the front of her mind, Nicky half expected to see them repeated in the text. But no. This had nothing to do with flowers or staying away.

I think I might know who owns the wedding ring, the texter said. The one with "forever wrapped around you" engraved inside it. Call me so we can talk.

CHAPTER FOURTEEN

GARRETT SPOTTED TROUBLE coming his way. Two doses of it. His mother was walking up the hall toward his office, and out the window he saw Roman pull his motorcycle to a stop. Neither of them would want to see the other, and Garrett didn't want to see either of them.

Hell, what had happened now?

He wasn't in any mood to soothe some family squabbles or hear any more about the blasted party that Nicky was planning. Especially since it appeared his mother had taken over that planning and was now trying to involve him.

"I'm not here about the party," his mother said the moment she stepped in the doorway.

"Good." Well, maybe that was good. Garrett waited for the other shoe to drop because with his mother, there was always another shoe. "But you should know that Roman just got here."

"Yes, I called him."

"And he came?" Garrett sounded as surprised as he truly was. These were perhaps the end times because Garrett seriously doubted Roman and his mother had buried the hatchet.

"Yes, but if it's to say no, please try to talk him out of it."

Garrett just lifted his hands to let her know he didn't

have a clue what she was talking about. Roman obviously did, though.

"No," his brother said the moment he made it to the office. "I am not giving permission for a Widowers' House to be set up here. It doesn't matter that I don't live here, but I don't want the place to become a boarding house to strangers."

Garrett had considered several ways this chat might play out, but that wasn't one of them. "A Widowers' House?"

"It makes perfect sense," his mother insisted. "We've got widows in Z.T.'s house, and who better to understand what they're going through than men who've lost their spouses?"

"Counselors and other widows can better understand that," Roman snarled and then turned to Garrett.

Garrett couldn't agree more, and there was no chance he was going to try to convince Roman to change his mind. Besides, he suspected the real reason his mother wanted this was so she'd have a new pool of matchmaking candidates. The last thing Garrett wanted was to add a new set of strangers to the mix. He was just getting used to the old set of strangers.

"Look, I'm tired of being in the middle of this," Roman went on. "Tired of hearing about your being in a bad mood. Hell, I'm tired of Nicky's friend calling me about Meredith. I just want to be out of the FYI and 'could you please do this?' loops. For that to happen, I can either kill all of you or remind you one last time to quit bothering me. I've got a business to run and a son to raise, so quit pestering me with this kind of crap that I can't do anything about anyway."

"A son you've chosen to raise on your own," his mother said. She punctuated that with a know-it-all nod.

Damn. This was about to get ugly. His mom was about to launch into her usual nagging session about Roman not marrying Tate's mother. This despite the fact that neither Tate's mother nor Roman had wanted to get married.

But there was something else in what Roman said. Something that got Garrett's attention.

"Why would Nicky's friend call you about Meredith?" he asked his brother.

Roman gave him a flat look. "I just said a lot of things, and that's what you got out of it?"

"Yeah," Garrett admitted.

Roman continued to look at him, maybe because he thought Garrett would rethink that. He wouldn't. But he did do something to help with the Roman-Mom dispute.

"I don't want a Widowers' House," Garrett told her. "Sophie probably doesn't, either. After all, she'll be planning her wedding soon, and she'll likely want to get married here. No way would she want a bunch of people around when she's trying to do that."

It was as if a light went on over his mother's head. Of course, she knew Sophie was engaged and would soon marry. But maybe it was just occurring to her that wedding plans were a better way to spend her time than widow-widower matchmaking.

"Besides," Garrett added, and he went straight for the pay dirt, "think of all the gossip there'd be about you if you had a bunch of single men living under our roof. The Garden Guild would have a field day with it."

Some of the color blanched from his mother's face.

Since Belle was the queen of gossip, she knew just how vicious something like that could get.

"Fine," she said as if it were a great concession and she was giving up on her *dream*. "And you need a haircut," she added to Roman before she walked away. It wasn't a new insult. She seemed to bring it up every other visit.

Garrett didn't waste any time getting some clarification from his brother. "Now, tell me about Nicky's friend who called you."

"Gina," Roman quickly provided. However, he still had his attention on their mother who was making her way down the hall. "You don't think any of the widows put the crazy notion of a Widowers' House into her head?"

"Maybe Lady." But he doubted it. From what he was hearing, Lady had found an adequate pool of lovers right here in Wrangler's Creek. "Why did Gina call you?"

"Maybe because she saw me with Nicky. It was the day Nicky had been crying."

Probably when Garrett had seen the scar.

"Were you responsible for those tears Nicky was shedding?" Roman asked.

"No. Well, maybe." He scrubbed his hand over his face. "It's complicated."

"I gathered that. Hope it doesn't happen again. Nicky's got a lot going on in her life. Her kid is cute, but kids are work. So are ex-boyfriends who make her cry. I'm sure she loves her daughter, but the ex-boyfriend making her cry she can do without."

Garrett nearly mentioned the scar. Nearly. But it

wasn't his story to tell. Plus, he didn't know what the hell the story was even about.

"You read a book to Kaylee that same day," Garrett said a moment later. "Is that when Gina called you, too?"

"No, it was later. And how did you know I read her a book?"

This chat was moving like a sidewinder, and Garrett didn't want to sound petty, but he felt a little petty at the moment. "She told me. She calls you Roaming."

Roman smiled a little. Not his usual reaction. But then Kaylee could have that effect on even a badass. "Like I said, she's a cute kid."

True. A kid who kept finding her way into his lap. And his heart. Garrett wasn't sure he was ready for either, but Kaylee didn't seem to notice that.

"Now, back to Gina," Garrett prompted his brother. "Why did she call you?"

"She wanted to know if Meredith was capable of doing something sneaky and mean. I told her yes. Especially if she thought sneaky and mean would get you back."

Garrett felt his forehead bunch up. "What did Meredith do?"

"To heck if I know. Gina's call was a fishing expedition, but she was short on details. She just said something had happened at the Widows' House, and she wanted to make sure Meredith wasn't involved. I pressed her for more, and she finally said it was something involving flowers."

Yes, that. "Nicky got upset when some flowers were delivered for her. But she didn't say anything about them being from Meredith."

"They weren't from her," someone said.

Nicky.

Garrett hadn't seen or heard her come in, but she stepped into the doorway next to Roman. She volleyed glances between them as if she expected them to continue, but Garrett wanted her to do some talking. That said, he also didn't want her to run again.

"Meredith didn't send the flowers," she repeated. "They were from someone else. Why did Gina think Meredith had sent them?"

Apparently, Nicky had heard a great deal of the conversation. Roman only shrugged, though. "You'd have to ask her. Or Meredith."

"Meredith left."

Well, that was one problem solved. Garrett wouldn't have to risk running into his ex or having Meredith meddle in whatever was going on in Nicky's life.

"I'll talk to Gina," Nicky assured him. "I came to see your mother about the dinner."

She said the word *dinner* as if it were about as pleasant for her as it was for him. Once, it probably had been a fun idea, but it no longer was now that his mother and some of the other widows were involved.

"But I also wanted to talk to you," Nicky added, looking at Garrett.

Roman had some bad habits, but getting lost at the appropriate moment wasn't one of them. He mumbled a goodbye to Garrett, kissed Nicky on the cheek and headed out. Later, Garrett would ask him when he'd gotten so chummy with Nicky that he could give her a peck like that.

Later, he would figure out why he felt jealous of the peck.

Nicky didn't actually come into the office. She just stood there and bracketed her hands on the jamb. "I got a text and then a call from a woman who might know something about the wedding ring. The one that John Doe was wearing. She wants me to meet her at a café in Houston where she lives so we can show it to her. Then she can see if it belonged to her uncle, Felix."

"Clay knows about this?" he immediately asked.

Nicky nodded. "I called him right after I got off the phone with the woman. Candy Halverson is her name. She saw the post I put on Facebook."

This was perhaps the lead they'd been looking for. "She couldn't try to ID the ring from a picture?"

"No. She said she needed to see it because she remembered the ring fitting perfectly on her middle finger. She'd apparently tried it on a couple of times."

Finger size could easily change over the years, but maybe this woman would be able to tell them if it belonged to her uncle or not.

"Anyway," Nicky continued, "Clay can go on Friday, three days from now, and he asked if we wanted to go with him to the café where Ms. Halverson arranged for us to meet. I'd like to go. How about you?"

That would eat up an entire day. And it wouldn't really accomplish anything that Clay couldn't do on his own. But he would get to spend some time with Nicky. Especially if they drove up separately from Clay so they could have some time to talk.

Of course, talking hadn't worked great for them so far.

"I can join you if everything goes well on this cattle buying trip I have to make," he explained. "I'm leaving first thing in the morning and will be gone for two days."

"Oh," Nicky said.

"Disappointed that I won't be around?" He smiled, tried to make it sound like a joke.

"Yes."

Well, he certainly hadn't expected that response. Heck. Was something wrong? And why was that his go-to reaction whenever Nicky was around? Of course, his other go-to response was to want to kiss her again. That, despite the mess the last kiss had caused.

"I also wanted to say I was sorry," Nicky added a moment later. "For everything."

"That covers a lot of territory." He hoped that would sound a lot lighter than it had. "You want to talk about what happened in my truck? Or what happened on the porch with the flowers?"

"Not really." Then she gave a heavy sigh. "I know the scar has become the elephant in the room. But it won't make you feel better to hear about it."

"Will it make you feel better?"

"No." She sighed again. "It's not something many people know about. Gina and Patrick are the only ones. Patrick looked disgusted when he saw it. I figure disgust was your reaction, too, but you did a great job of hiding it."

"Not disgust," he assured her, and Garrett walked closer to her.

"Pity then. That was Gina's reaction. She cried."

He shook his head. "I wanted to punch the person who'd put it there," he corrected.

Nicky flinched just slightly. But it was more than enough for him to fill in the blanks.

Shit.

She'd done that to herself.

He knew nothing about cutters. Didn't know if it was a good idea to press her to talk about it or not. So, Garrett just stood there and waited.

"It happened a long time ago," she finally said. "And yes, I got help for it. Obviously, I wasn't thinking straight when I did that."

Obviously. Something else then occurred to him. "Does it have something to do with me, with what happened between us?"

He figured she'd rather eat glass than admit it, and that was why he was surprised when she nodded. Surprised, and he felt as if she'd slugged him.

"After you broke up with me, my father heard the gossip that we'd been together." Nicky spoke slowly, as if she'd rehearsed this but still wasn't certain she should be saying it. "That's the word he called me. I got upset. *Really* upset," she clarified. "And I took a razor blade and...well, you can figure out the rest."

He could indeed, and it made him sick to his stomach.

"Don't say you're sorry," she went on just as he'd been about to say it. "Because it wasn't your fault. Truth is, I don't think it had much to do with you."

"I was the straw that broke the camel's back," he mumbled.

She shrugged. "Anyway, believe it or not, it helped."

"How the hell could that have helped?" Garrett hadn't meant to blurt that out, but he just didn't get it. She'd cut herself. Deep enough to leave a scar. It must have bled. And it must have hurt.

"It got my mind off other things. Not just you," she

quickly added. "That was around the time of that police report about my father."

Definitely more straws.

"Again, don't say you're sorry," she repeated. "It happened a long time ago, and the only thing left of it is the scar."

That was plenty, and she no doubt got a reminder of that hellish time whenever she looked at it.

"Do the flowers have anything to do with the scar?" he asked.

The long, weary breath she took let him know that he'd just overstepped the limits of what she intended to tell him. "You know, I'm tired of all this gloom-and-doom talk."

Hell. He figured she was about to turn and run again. And he couldn't blame her. That's why it stunned him when she came closer, leaned in and brushed her mouth over his.

"Actually, I came to tell you that we should have sex." She kissed him again. "Think about it and get back to me."

GARRETT HAD NO idea if that was a real invitation or if it was just a ploy to get his mind off the dark and gloomy stuff she'd just mentioned.

If it was the latter, it'd worked.

His mind was off that and onto the two kisses Nicky had just stunned him with. Those kisses would have been her version of a farewell since she started to walk away, but Garrett put a stop to that. He moved in front of her to block her path.

And then he kissed her right back.

It wasn't one of those pecks, either, like Roman had

given her. Nor was it short and sweet like the ones she'd
given him. He kissed her, catching on to her waist
to pull her closer so that not only their mouths were
touching.

"I told you to think about it," Nicky reminded him
with her mouth still against his.

"I did. Trust me, that wasn't a subject I needed to
give a lot of thought."

Though it should have been. She was offering him
sex, which could make things more complicated than
they already were. It could make things worse for her.
Those were both valid arguments that he didn't stand
a chance of making after she pulled him back to her
to resume the kiss.

Garrett wanted to ask her why she'd had this change
of heart. Or ask her if she'd lost her mind. But he would
have had to stop kissing her to do that, and it suddenly
seemed like those questions could wait. Everything
could wait.

Including but not limited to his need for oxygen.

Man, she tasted good. Not something he could put
a label on, but whatever it was, it went straight to his
dick. Of course, just about everything Nicky said or
did had that effect on him these days. He'd had the hots
for her in high school, and the years hadn't cooled that
heat one little bit.

Without breaking the kiss, Garrett pulled her away
from the door and closed it. No way did he want Roman
or his mother returning to witness this. Not that he
cared if they knew, but he figured Nicky wouldn't want
anyone to see them. Especially since things seemed to
be escalating—fast.

The kissing quickly turned to groping, as good kissing usually did, and he backed her against the door to hold her in place so he could free up his hands. He'd learned his lesson about going after her top so he just caught her hips and aligned them with his.

Garrett liked that, but his erection was especially pleased with it. Nicky appeared to be, too, because she made one of those throaty sounds of pleasure that he'd heard her make in the truck. He wanted this to have a whole lot better outcome, though.

But what outcome exactly?

That question flashed through his head like a neon sign. Certain parts of him knew where they wanted to take this. Maybe pull her to the floor or up on the desk. Maybe just take her right against the door. However, the question came with a reminder.

He didn't have any condoms in his office.

As a general rule, he'd just never thought of mixing sex with business reports. That rule, however, was about to be broken. But perhaps not broken the way one specific part of him wanted it to be.

There were some condoms in his bedroom on the other side of the house. Old ones. And it would mean making a trek there to get them. There were potential pitfalls along the way: his mother, the housekeeper, Alice, Sophie and any number of women from town who'd shown up to cure his loneliness. Garrett would have risked it if he'd thought he could walk that far, but he wasn't going to get more than a few steps with this raging hard-on.

"Are you stopping?" Nicky asked.

And that's when Garrett realized he had slowed down. Not good when things seemed to be moving along nicely, at breakneck speed. Speed didn't allow much thinking time, and again, his dick thought that was stellar.

Too bad that part of him didn't often make wise choices.

His concerns faded considerably, though, when Nicky took her mouth to his neck. The woman was a witch and had a devil tongue. He was sure of it. Because with just a few flicks of that tongue, she rid him of doubts that he probably should have hung on to a little longer.

He didn't, though.

Garrett hoisted her up, putting his erection right in the V of her thighs, and he did some neck kissing of his own. He licked her neck, licked her breasts, too, but he stayed away from that general area and instead used some well-placed pressure to get his point across.

The point being that his hard-on was in search of a place to go.

Of course, it couldn't go anywhere right now, and that realization made it through the lust-haze in his brain. He reconsidered that trip to get a condom. Dismissed it when Nicky's gaze met his. He didn't see any doubts in her expression.

Not a one.

Which meant she was trusting him to do the right thing here. Knocking her up wouldn't be the right thing, Garrett repeated that to himself. But that didn't mean he couldn't do something to ease this pressure-cooker heat.

He slid her back down and placed his hand on the front of her jeans. This was definitely old school, reminiscent of times when he'd gotten to third and a half base, as Roman used to call it. Not quite a satisfactory ending, but it would take the edge off. For Nicky anyway. Next time he would plan better.

If there was a next time.

She might come to her senses and run again.

But she wasn't running now. She was moaning, making that sound of pleasure that was music to his erection. He used his erection, his hand, too, and his body to create some pressure right there in her spot that he was pretty sure wanted some pressure.

It did.

Because after Garrett added some kisses to her neck, he heard the hitch in Nicky's breath. Felt her tense. Then relax, all the while making those sounds. The ones that were driving him crazy.

He wanted to join in on this. Man, did he. But there was still pleasure in watching her come. Pleasure in her looking at him with that glazed, satisfied look in her eyes.

Which lasted only a surprisingly short time. Maybe a couple of seconds at most.

"We really just screwed up, didn't we?" she whispered.

Garrett could honestly say—no. Judging from his perspective and the ache in his groin, they hadn't screwed up nearly enough.

CHAPTER FIFTEEN

IT WAS TOO bad that Nicky couldn't bottle an orgasm so she could hang on to that slack feeling for a while. Of course, most adults with even a minimal sex drive probably felt that way. But after two days, the only thing that remained of the orgasm was the memory of it.

A really, really good memory.

Those moments with Garrett had given her a breather from life. A sort of stress reliever, though Garrett probably wouldn't be totally pleased since he'd gotten no such slack feeling.

She'd blown it with him. Not literally, though that would have been one possible way to finish off what'd happened in his office. But the problem was— it shouldn't have happened at all. She hadn't gone there to have hand sex with him. Nicky had gone there to tell him about the wedding ring and instead had ended up kissing him and offering herself to him.

Nicky blamed that on his jeans. Simply put, he looked hot in them. Always had. And she'd had no more success holding back two days ago than she had when they were in high school.

She heard the sound of laughter and looked out the window. It was Kaylee and Liam, Lizzie's son, playing on a Slip'N Slide underneath the sprinkler while Lizzie watched them. No Lady sunbathing today. The woman and her tow truck were actually away on a towing job. There were also no sounds of a bulldozer. The crew had finally finished the work on the pond and pasture, and the only sounds out there now, other than the laughter, was the occasional cow mooing.

The occasional sound of a vehicle, too.

Not Garrett, even though he was due back from his business trip today, and Nicky had thought he might visit. However, it was Gina. She'd been gone, as well, for two days to clear out a storage unit with her late husband's things and to do the last of the paperwork from his estate. That probably meant Gina wouldn't be in the best of moods since she and her husband had had a lot of debt, but Nicky needed to clear up some things with her.

Nicky put aside the Widows' House bills she'd been paying and went downstairs to meet her, but when Gina didn't come in, she went in search of her. Too bad she found the sisters along the way, and Diana stopped her.

"You have to do something about those cowboys," Diana exclaimed. Her sisters nodded. "You can see their Ps."

Only because of the group therapy session did Nicky realize they were talking about penises. Otherwise, she might have thought they meant peeing. Which, of course, would have still caused the sisters to see a penis or two.

"Uh, how and where are you seeing them? Because if it's when they're relieving themselves, then that's because they probably don't want to come in the house to use the bathrooms."

Hera made a "you, idiot" kind of huff. Diana patted her arms as if to calm her down. "We've never seen them relieving themselves, but we can see their Ps when their jeans are too tight. It's especially bad when they wear chaps."

Well, the chaps did frame their junk. No denying that. A woman would have to be blind not to notice it. And would need to be suffering from some penis-phobia not to appreciate it.

Diana took Nicky's hand and put a note in it. "That's a list of the cowboys with the biggest Ps. Please tell them to wear looser jeans. Or maybe wear aprons to cover their zippers."

Nicky had rather eat chaps and aprons before tell-ing anyone that, but she took the note and glanced at it. Garrett's name was there. So was Lawson's. And four others she didn't know.

"I'll see what I can do," Nicky assured them. It wasn't a lie. She would ensure that Lady didn't get her hands on this list because she would consider it some kind of carnal treasure map. But she might men-tion it to Garrett.

Might.

Since she was wearing shorts and a top without pockets, Nicky stuck the note in her bra.

"We'll put another copy of that on your desk in case you lose that one," Diana said.

Nicky thanked them, not very enthusiastically, though, and went in search of Gina again. She finally found her running through the sprinkler with the kids and laughing like a loon.

"Are you okay?" Nicky asked her. It was a valid question because, like her, Gina preferred to hide her emotions. Of course, Gina also liked playing with Kaylee, and her little girl had a way of improving people's moods.

"Everything went fine. No more paperwork."

Nicky heard it then. The sadness in Gina's voice. Signing those final papers had meant saying a final goodbye to her husband. It made Nicky wish that she'd called Gina while she'd been away, but she had figured Gina would be too busy to chat.

"I missed you," Nicky told her. "So did Kaylee. It's been a while since I've had to watch her pretty much on my own, and I'd forgotten what a handful she can be. You should press your boss for a raise." Nicky winked at her.

"I will. And I think I'll press her to have some fun, too." Gina hurried to Nicky, caught her hand and tried to pull her into the sprinkler, as well.

Nicky wanted to point out she wasn't dressed for such antics, but Gina wasn't, either. In fact, she was in a white cotton sundress.

"Come, Mommy." Kaylee caught her other hand, and Nicky quit resisting.

She ran into the sprinkler. No loon-giggling for her. The water was cold, and it immediately caused her clothes to stick to her. But since Kaylee, Gina and Liam were having a blast, she stayed put. Besides, this was her first chance to ask Gina what she'd been wanting to ask for two days.

Gina spoke first. "How'd your time go with Garrett?"

Of course, Gina could probably tell from the way Nicky had been acting that something sexual had gone on between them. Later, Nicky might fill her in on a few details, *very few*, but that could wait.

"Why didn't you tell me that you called Roman

about Meredith?" Nicky asked. She whispered it so that Lizzie wouldn't hear, though the woman wasn't listening. She had her face in a book.

Gina shrugged. "Didn't think it was important."

It was probably hard to give a "say what?" look with water dripping down her face, but Nicky thought she might have managed it.

"All right, it was important," Gina amended. She had a drippy face, too. "I didn't want you to know because I thought it would upset you. But I called him because I knew he'd tell me the truth."

"I would have told you the truth," Nicky assured her. She waited until Kaylee had moved a little farther away before she continued. "It wasn't Meredith who sent those flowers. Think it through. If she'd found out about me, do you think she would have kept something like that to herself?"

"No, probably not. She would have gone straight to Garrett with it. But I didn't know if she was one of those people who likes to play with her prey before she finishes it off."

Mercy, Nicky hoped not. "Meredith would have stayed if she was doing something like that. She can't play if she's not around."

When Kaylee ran past her, Nicky scooped her up, spun her around in the water spray and then placed her back on the ground. Her daughter laughed, and despite the serious conversation she was having with Gina, Nicky smiled. Being with Kaylee made everything more tolerable.

Well, almost everything.

"I did call the local florist to see if someone was ordering the roses from here in Wrangler's Creek," Nicky explained. "She said no." And Nicky believed her because the florist had then proceeded to give details of every order she'd had for the past month. No yellow roses. "I called around to find which delivery services had brought them, but I struck out on that, too."

"Why Mommy sad?" Kaylee asked.

Nicky hadn't even realized Kaylee was paying any attention to her, but clearly she was. She smiled, scooped her up and kissed her. "Mommy's sad because I can't stay out here and play. I have to go back in."

And finish this chat with Gina. Not just about the flowers, but she wanted to know why Gina was looking a lot happier than she probably was.

Lizzie glanced up from her book. "I'll watch her," she said to Nicky.

Nicky thanked her, and with Gina following, they scooped up a couple of the towels from the porch and went inside the house. But they didn't go far. They stood at the door.

"Don't worry," Gina said. "We'll all keep an eye on Kaylee. She's never out in the yard alone. Plus, the ranch hands are around. They'd spot anyone trying to get onto the ranch."

All of that was true, but it didn't assure Nicky that all was going to be well.

"I think you should tell Garrett about this," Gina went on.

But Nicky shook her head. "No. Not yet anyway. The roses didn't come for over a year, and maybe they'll stop coming again." Besides, she'd had her fill of spilling her dirty secrets to Garrett.

"Tell Clay then," Gina advised. "He should know what's going on. Just in case the worst happens."

Nicky knew she was right. But she couldn't even consider it right now. Or imagine what *the worst* could mean.

"How long has it been since you've had an orgasm?" Gina asked out of the blue. "With another person present," she added.

Obviously, Nicky hadn't been expecting that because she nearly choked on her own breath. Talk about a major change in subject.

"Why? What have you heard?" Nicky answered, caution in her voice.

Gina smiled. "Well, I hadn't heard *that*. But good for you. I always thought Garrett looked capable of inducing an orgasm or two."

He was capable. Even with her clothes on.

"He still looks as if he's been dropped in a dark pit of despair whenever he's around Kaylee," Nicky reminded her.

"You can get more orgasms from Garrett while he's still trying to work through his feeling for Kaylee. While he's still trying to work through his feelings for you, too."

Nicky looked at her. "Is there a reason you brought up this whole orgasm topic?"

"There is. Someone recently reminded me that they'd met their mindless sex quota. I haven't. Neither have you. It's something to consider." She gave Nicky's arm a pat.

And whether Nicky wanted to do it or not, she considered it.

"SHE'S LATE," CLAY SNARLED, glancing at his watch again.

Garrett checked the time, too. Yes, Candy Halverson was indeed late. Not by much, though. Only fifteen minutes. Maybe the woman would show up soon so they could get some answers about the John Doe.

Not that Garrett was thinking much about John Doe at the moment.

He was seated in the diner booth across the table from Nicky and was mentally playing the "what's wrong?" guessing game. Mentally was the only way he could play it because Clay was there, seated right beside him. As he had been on the entire drive from Wrangler's Creek to Houston.

Garrett should have come up with a way that he and Nicky could make the drive alone. But he just hadn't been able to figure out a good explanation to offer Clay about why he wanted to be alone with Nicky. Not without Clay realizing what was going on between them. Garrett wanted to figure that out first before having to explain it to someone else. Of course, since he hadn't had a chance to speak with her, he was trying to guess what could possibly be causing her to look as if she'd wallowed in a pity pit.

The near sex they'd had?

Her past?

His past?

Widowhood?

The attraction between them?

All of those could have put that sad look on her face so there really wasn't any reason for him to come up with more things to put on that list. But that's exactly what he was doing. This sadness seemed on a whole new level. Which meant it was probably the near sex.

She could be regretting it. He was, but probably not

in the same way. He was regretting that he hadn't been able to finish it.

Clay checked his watch again, huffed and stood. "I'll step outside and give Candy Halverson a call."

Since Clay didn't have to step outside to do that, it meant he was giving Nicky and him some time alone. But that seemed a little strange, too. Since Clay was a cop, he didn't wear a lot of emotions on his face, but Garrett got the feeling that Clay knew something about Nicky's mood.

"I told him about some things from my past," Nicky said, following Garrett's gaze, which was still on Clay. "I'd rather not get into it with you, though. I hope that's okay."

Since she wasn't exactly asking permission, Garrett just nodded. It had to be okay. Because he didn't have any right to make demands on Nicky, especially since she'd gotten upset when he'd seen that scar.

She looked down at her coffee cup, running her finger around the rim. "Would you consider what we did to be mindless sex?"

Well, the woman certainly knew how to keep him on his toes. "No. Mindless would have been more enjoyable for both of us. It would have involved clothing removal, a condom, more moaning. Oh, and actual sex."

The corner of her mouth lifted. "Yes. You're right." She paused. "Tell me about one of your ranch hands, Jake Walter. Is he a good guy?"

Garrett frowned. Cursed. "Are you thinking about having sex with Jake?"

"No, but Gina is. He asked her out."

He hadn't intended to make a sound of relief, but

he did. "Yeah, Jake's a good guy. I didn't realize Gina was looking for a lover."

"Not really looking for one, but sometimes the hormones want what the hormones want."

No disputing that. He'd been battling his since Nicky showed up in Wrangler's Creek.

"Jake's also on this list," Nicky said, taking a note from her purse. "Don't be flattered that your name's on there," she added.

"I can't be flattered if I don't know what it is." But he did look at the names. Lawson, Jake, Cash, Lucky McCord, him and the new guy that everyone called Tater.

"Consider me just the messenger, but I was afraid if I didn't mention it to you that one of the Ellery sisters would. They think everyone on that list has big Ds. And no, I don't mean dimples, deltoids or diaphragms. They want you to wear clothing that doesn't emphasize your assets."

She said it with a straight face, too.

Garrett laughed, though he knew this wasn't a joke. The sisters had been complaining to his mother about all sorts of things.

"They don't want the animals having sex, either," Garrett told her. "There isn't a lot of that going on at the ranch because we inseminate most of the herd, but every now and then we let a bull cover a cow or two to keep him happy." He stopped, grinned. "Big dicks, huh? The guys might want to frame the list if I tell them."

"And that's why you won't. That's why you won't smile, either." Though she appeared to be fighting her own smile. It was nice after the gloomy start to the day. "Trust me, it's not flattery when it comes from the sisters."

True. He wouldn't tell her that they'd objected to the hands riding stallions because the sisters could see horse dicks and had suggested they put diapers on them. They also wanted diapers on the cows, to cut down on the smell of shit. Apparently, they were not aware they were living on a working ranch.

"Lucky McCord doesn't work for me," Garrett told her. "He was at the ranch to pick up his wife, Cassie."

She nodded. "I remember. I also remember that Lucky had a thing for your sister at one time."

Garrett hadn't known that, but when it came to his kid sister's sex life, he preferred to believe it was non-existent. It was sort of like parent sex. Just not something he wanted in his head.

The door to the diner opened, and Clay came in with a woman. Candy Halverson, no doubt. She was in her early thirties, younger than Garrett thought she'd be. Since their John Doe had been dead for about twenty-one years at most, he hoped she could remember enough about the ring to give them an identity to go along with it.

Clay made the introductions, and Candy took the seat next to Nicky so that she was facing Clay and him.

"Garrett Granger?" Candy immediately questioned. "As in the owner of Granger Ranch?"

He nodded but felt uneasy with the question. They were a big operation, but Houston was three hours away. And Candy didn't look like a rancher or a cowboy groupie. Of course, Candy might know about him from Meredith's sex tape. That kept turning up like a bad penny.

"I didn't expect you to be here," Candy said, her question just as puzzling as that comment.

"The body was found on the ranch," he told her, though that really didn't explain why he had come. Wanting to spend time with Nicky wasn't something he intended to admit. Plus, he did need this cleared up. The story was attracting folks from the news media who wanted stories. Attracting more of those ghost hunters, too. Garrett didn't want either group out at Z.T.'s house to pester the widows.

And therefore give the Ellery sisters something else to complain about.

Clay took out the ring from a clear plastic evidence bag, and he put it on the table in front of Candy. "You can touch it," he said.

She did, after she leaned in and had a good, long look at it. When she finally did pick it up, Candy rotated it, reading the inscription.

"'Forever wrapped around you,'" she said in a whisper. She slipped the ring onto her right middle finger. The fit was perfect. "Yes, I'm pretty sure this belonged to my uncle."

"Pretty sure?" Clay questioned.

Like Garrett, he didn't want any qualifiers here. He wanted the woman to be certain.

"Sure enough." Candy took a deep breath. "His name is Felix Drummond. Was Felix Drummond," she corrected. "So, he's been at the ranch this whole time."

"Where did you think he was?" Garrett asked.

Candy lifted her shoulder, and he didn't think it was his imagination that she dodged his gaze. "We didn't know. When I was in middle school, he asked his wife for a divorce and then told us he was leaving.

I was heartbroken because he was my favorite uncle. I adored him. And so did his wife. We were all stunned when he did that."

"Did he actually file for a divorce?" Clay pressed.

"No. He just disappeared. So, of course, we thought he'd just gone on to his new life."

Well, he sure as heck hadn't. "When exactly did he go missing?" That from Nicky, and because Candy was visibly upset, she slid her hand over the woman's.

"I was in seventh grade so it must have been a little over twenty years ago."

Clay exchanged a glance with Garrett. The timeline fit as well as the ring had. So, they might finally be able to stop calling this guy John Doe.

"Twenty-one years?" Clay asked. "Because we found a receipt near his clothes that fits the timeframe."

She nodded. "His wife, Marie, is still alive but in a nursing home. I'm not sure how much she'd be able to tell you though since she has dementia. Both my folks are dead so asking them is out, too. But I used to keep diaries in those days. I'll look through them and try to pinpoint the exact date he left."

"Thanks, that'd be helpful." Clay paused. "Did your uncle have any health problems?"

"No." Something flickered in her eyes. "But I remember hearing my mother and Aunt Marie talk. They said Uncle Felix was leaving her to be with another woman."

And here he'd ended up at the ranch. Garrett didn't like the unsettling feeling he got in his stomach.

"The newspapers picked up the story of the body," Garrett explained. "You didn't see any of the articles?"

"No. I'm the mother of twin boys, and I'm a teacher.

I don't have a lot of free time. But I wish I had seen them, so I could tell my aunt. She's been waiting for him, you see. Waiting all this time for him to come back to her."

Candy looked at Garrett, and he saw something in her eyes. Not sadness. Not entirely anyway. More like anger.

"Your mother is still alive?" Candy asked him.

He nodded, felt that unsettled feeling go up a notch. "Why do you ask?"

"Because according to what I heard, Uncle Felix was having an affair with Belle Granger."

CHAPTER SIXTEEN

GINA READ NICKY'S text five times, and it still didn't make sense. Belle certainly didn't look like the affair-having type. But apparently that's what the dead guy's niece was accusing her of.

"Keep this quiet for now," Nicky had added in the text. "I'll be home in a few."

Nicky hadn't said if Garrett had called his mother about this, but she was betting he had. If he wasn't in shock, that is. Or maybe in denial. Hard for a man to accept something like this.

Especially since "this" was linked to a death.

Nicky also hadn't mentioned if Clay thought Belle had something to do with that death, but it was possible the police chief would investigate it as a homicide. And Belle wouldn't necessarily be the main suspect. The guy's wife would be. She'd watched enough cop shows to know that jealousy was a big motive.

Gina cringed. Poor guy. Poor Belle. And poor them. Because when the story broke, the place would probably be crawling with reporters. Considering Nicky's situation, that wasn't a good idea. Best not to draw any more attention to herself or to this place.

She looked up from her phone to make sure Kaylee was still napping. The little girl was sacked out on a quilt on the floor. It had become her favorite napping place, mainly because it was also her favorite place to play. She was asleep amid the strewn books, tea party makings and dolls.

Gina made her way back down the stairs, intending to go to Nicky's office so she could see if there was any paperwork she could do for her, but she came to a stop when she saw Jake in the doorway. Not alone, either. The Ellery sisters were there with him.

"Is everything okay?" Gina immediately asked.

Jake held up a blue apron. "They want me to wear this. Apparently, my man parts offend them."

One of the sisters gasped. "Talk to him," the gasping sister told Gina, and the trio hurried away.

"I'm sorry," Gina told Jake right off. "Did they show you the list?"

He patted his shirt pocket. "They gave me a copy so I could help them *address* it. I'll put that in a special place when I get back to the bunkhouse."

She could only sigh and silently curse the sisters. Dick size was not something she wanted to be discussing with a flirting, hot cowboy who made her body remember something very important.

That he was a man. One with a dick.

And she was a woman. One who on occasion liked a dick.

"The sisters want me to stop the cow sex, too," Jake went on. "And they said if I didn't, they would go out in the pasture and shoo the bull away. Not a good idea, by the way. Bulls tend to get testy when interrupted."

Gina hoped the sisters wouldn't indeed try to stop something like that, but with them, you never knew. They had become the prude police of the Widows' House.

"If you think they'll listen to you, tell them to especially avoid any bull with a nose ring." He touched her own nose ring. "We only put those in the more rambunctious ones."

"Why are you here?" Gina asked Jake just to be saying something. While she was at it, she stepped back so that he wouldn't touch her nose ring again. It seemed intimate.

Felt it, too.

Maybe speaking would prevent her from drooling. But he was certainly drool-worthy in those chaps, jeans and denim shirt. He smelled like warm saddle leather and other things, manly things.

"Garrett called and asked me to come," Jake answered. "I'm supposed to see if his mother is here."

Because Gina was spinning a sex dream of him in her head, it took a moment for her to get that. "No. At least I don't think she is. I've been upstairs, though, with Kaylee so it's possible she came in."

But if she had—why? Was Belle returning to the scene of the crime?

"Follow me," Gina instructed, and she immediately started leading Jake through the house and toward the kitchen. Not that she was certain Belle would go there. If she had indeed had something to do with John Doe's death, that should be the last place she'd go. Still, it was a starting point.

Cassie was in the middle of a group session so Gina shut the door but not before hearing Lady talk about missing blow jobs. Jake didn't comment. But she got another flash of that dimple.

"Have you reconsidered going out with me?" he

asked. "I mean, since I made the well-endowed list, that should give you some incentive."

She already had enough incentive. The attraction. But she held up her hand to show him that she was still wearing her wedding ring. Gina wouldn't mention that she'd nearly taken it off after she had finished signing the final papers regarding her husband's estate. Nor would she bring up the sex conversation she'd had with Nicky. No, it was best to mull on this a little longer.

She stopped in the formal dining room just short of the kitchen, and she turned to tell Jake that she needed more time.

Or not.

That was because he leaned in and kissed her. It was a test kiss, like someone dipping their toe in the water to check the temperature. He must have decided the temp was just fine because he dove in for more.

And Gina let him.

It'd been a year since she'd been kissed and never by a cowboy. She was suddenly regretful that she hadn't added that to her personal résumé sooner.

He was smiling when he pulled back, and Gina realized she was still leaning in. As if waiting for more. More was out. Because if he came back for thirds, she might insist on getting a look at his overly endowed man parts.

"All right, I'll go out with you," she heard herself say. It was the lust talking, but it was making some sense. Well, as much sense as lust could make. Still, a date wasn't a lifelong commitment. It was just a date.

She hadn't thought that smile could get any better, but it did. And while she would have liked to have stayed put and continued this kissing/smiling/flirting session, the timing was all wrong.

"We should be looking for Belle," Gina reminded him. Reminded herself, too. And she forced herself to get moving again.

Belle wasn't in the kitchen, but the back door leading to the yard was wide-open so Gina went there. Only to smack right into Nicky. She really had meant she'd be home in a few when she'd sent that text.

"I don't think Belle is here," Gina told her right off. "And Garrett must be worried about her because he sent Jake here to look for her."

Nicky thrust her purse into Gina's hands. "I just saw her out on the trail. She's on horseback—wearing a dress and heels. And she was crying. I would have followed her, but I can't get the SUV down there."

Jake cursed. "I'll go after her."

"No. I will," Nicky insisted. "If you don't mind, I'll take your horse."

He made a you're-welcome-to-it gesture, and Nicky took off running.

NICKY HADN'T RIDDEN a horse in years, but that didn't stop her. She climbed into the saddle and got the stallion moving. She moved, too, bouncing like a jumping bean and trying to keep control of the animal.

She hadn't heard what Garrett said to his mother when he called her shortly after Candy had dropped that bombshell. Garrett had stepped outside to make that call while Clay finished talking to Candy. But Nicky had watched Garrett's body language, and she could tell he'd asked Belle one very important question.

Is it true?

Judging from the fact that Belle was on the run, Nicky thought that it might be.

She heard the creek waters just ahead. Heard the crying, as well. And Nicky finally spotted the woman by the water's edge. Belle definitely looked out of place with her blue flowered dress and white shoes. Nicky got off the horse, leaving it next to Belle's, and went to her.

"Please tell me you don't believe I could do something this horrible," Belle said, looking up at Nicky.

Nicky sat down beside her and decided it was best just to put her arms around the woman and try to calm her down.

"Garrett said the man's niece believed I was having an affair with him," Belle went on. "I wasn't. I'm not that kind of woman."

"I'm sure Garrett knows that," Nicky assured her.

"Then why would he call me and tell me what that Candy person said?"

"Because he wanted to let you know what we'd learned." She paused. "We're not even sure the man we found is Felix Drummond. Clay said there'll have to be tests done. And if it is indeed Felix, the cops will have to piece together what happened."

"Well, I don't know what happened," Belle insisted while more tears came. She stopped, turned to Nicky. "Wait, yes, I do."

Everything inside Nicky went still, and she braced herself in case this was about to be some kind of confession. She considered asking Belle to go to the police station with her, but that would probably only send the woman into flight mode again.

"I think Matilda must be behind all of this," Belle

went on. "She probably used my name when she was meeting with that man, and now his family thinks I'm responsible for what happened to him."

That would have made sense if Felix had died twenty years earlier when Matilda had lived in Z.T.'s house. And maybe he had. If she went with her theory that the receipt could have been a misprint. Or maybe someone dropped it there later. Nicky didn't know who exactly would have done that, but it was possible.

"Why don't we go back to your house?" Nicky suggested. "And you can tell Clay and Garrett everything you just told me. They'll believe you, and we can get all of this straightened out."

Belle looked at her, blinked. "You think so?"

"Yes. Of course." She wasn't certain of that at all, but Garrett and Sophie were probably worried sick by now. She fired off a text to Garrett to let him know they were on their way back.

Nicky helped Belle to her feet, and they started walking. They didn't get back on the horses, but instead led them along the trail toward the house. It would make the trip longer, but it would save Belle from having to get back in the saddle in that dress.

"If I'd wanted to cheat," Belle went on, "I wouldn't have had to look outside Wrangler's Creek for a man, you know? There were plenty of hands, especially Hester Walter. That man was such a looker. His boys are, too."

Nicky made a sound of agreement. "His son, Jake, lent me his horse to come after you." And judging from his and Gina's body language, there was something going on between them. Nicky hoped that something was sex.

Belle made a sound that was part whimper, part sob. "I suppose everyone knows I went on the run."

Probably. But Nicky kept that to herself, too.

"Of course, they might just think I was out for a late-afternoon ride," Belle went on. She wiped away her tears, hiked up her chin. "I do that sometimes."

Yes, but she likely didn't do it in heels. Nicky caught her when Belle stumbled on one of the rocks that littered the trail and then maneuvered her around some animal poop.

"Did you ever think about cheating on your husband?" Belle asked.

"No," Nicky answered honestly. Maybe because he'd been doing enough cheating for both of them. "My marriage wasn't a good one, but I would have just divorced him if I'd wanted to be with another man."

"My point exactly. I mean, we're not in the Dark Ages. There's absolutely no reason for me to have done something like sneak around and have sex with another man. I'm not prudish like the Ellery sisters," Belle continued. "But I mean a woman only needs one man to take care of things down there." She made a vague motion toward her panty region.

Nicky really didn't like talking about this with Garrett's mom, but there was no polite way to stop her. Plus, Belle was going through hell and back right now and just needed to keep on venting.

Which she did.

"And you know how I feel about a girl's first," she added. "The first is the one who joins together with your soul."

Interesting outlook. And Nicky hoped that Belle wasn't fishing for details about Garrett. It didn't help, though, when Belle said his name. Not just any ordinary way of saying it, either. It came on one of those whimpering sobs.

"This must be just tearing Garrett apart," Belle said. "It's probably bringing back all sorts of memories about what went on with Meredith."

Mercy, she hadn't even thought of that. But Belle was right. Heck, it was bringing back memories for her, too, and she hadn't gone through anything nearly as public as Garrett had.

They kept walking, kept dodging rocks and poop.

And some footprints.

They weren't Nicky's, either. That sent a tingle of alarm through her until she reminded herself that it could be prints from one of the hands. It could mean nothing, and she had enough trouble in her life without borrowing more. Still, she sent a text to Gina to tell her that she'd not only found Belle but that she should keep close watch on Kaylee.

"I need to go see this niece," Belle said a few seconds later. "And the man's wife. I need to tell her I had nothing to do with this."

According to Candy, the wife was in a nursing home and had dementia so a visit probably wasn't a wise idea, but she doubted Belle would want to hear that right now. So, they just kept walking while Belle continued to declare her innocence. When they made it to Nicky's SUV, she helped her inside and started back down the trail toward the ranch house.

"Oh, my," Belle said. "The party you're giving. It's in just three days."

"We can cancel it. Don't worry. I can take care of that." Gladly take care of it since the dinner had snowballed way past the thank-you stage and was now just something she wished she'd never thought up in the first place.

"Lord, no. Canceling is the worst thing you can do. Then, everyone will be certain I'm guilty, that I have something to hide."

Nicky wanted to point out that Belle wasn't in any shape for a party, but she held her tongue. Maybe Sophie could better deal with this. And speaking of Sophie, Nicky spotted her on the front porch the moment she pulled into the driveway. Sophie hurried out to them.

And Garrett was right behind her.

"I didn't do this," Belle said when she got out.

"Of course you didn't," Sophie assured her. She put her arm around her mother and got her moving to the house. "Everyone knows that."

Belle's shoulders slumped with relief, and the relief got a little better when Garrett made it to them and hugged her, too.

"I'm sorry," he said. "I shouldn't have called you. I should have waited until I was here to tell you."

Nicky could see that he was beating himself up about that. But he'd had a good reason for what he'd done. Candy hadn't exactly seemed like a woman who was going to keep any of this a secret, and she might have called Belle herself. This wasn't news that Belle would have wanted to hear, period, but it would have been harder coming from a stranger. Especially a stranger who was accusing her of something like this.

Nicky texted Gina again to let her know where she was and that Belle was safe and sound, and then she went to Garrett, to tell him that she'd be at the Wid-

ows' House if he wanted to talk. However, he looped
his arm around her and started inside, following along
behind Sophie and his mom. After she made sure everyone was okay, Nicky would say goodbye in an effort
to give them some privacy to deal with this.

"Thank you for finding her," he said.

"I just happened to see her when I got back to Z.T.'s.
She was on the ranch trail that runs by the house. Is
Clay inside?"

Garrett shook his head. "He went back to the station. He thought maybe it'd be best to delay questioning my mother until morning."

It would be. Especially since Clay had mentioned
needing to fingerprint Belle to see if she was a match
to a partial print that had been on the gas receipt.

"Are *you* okay?" she whispered.

He looked at her, closing the front door behind them
once they were all in the foyer. "I don't like my mother
going through this."

"I meant because of Meredith."

Garrett's eyebrow lifted. "Actually, I didn't even
think of her. I was more worried about how this would
affect my mother. And you."

Nicky might not have believed that if he hadn't
kissed her. Well, it wasn't really a kiss. More like a
peck, but it was enough to convince her that this hadn't
brought back the bad memories as Belle and she had
feared.

"Why don't you wait for me in my office? I can get
my mom settled," he said. "And then we can talk."
But he didn't move. Garrett just stood there, looking
at her. "I've thought about your offer, and yes, I want
to have sex with you.

CHAPTER SEVENTEEN

GARRETT WAS SOMEWHAT out of practice when it came to romance, but he was pretty sure what he'd said to Nicky had been a major bust. Yes, she'd offered him sex, and they'd carried through on that.

More or less.

But he'd wanted more. Lots more. In hindsight though, he could have tweaked the way he accepted her offer. Tweaked the timing, too, because it had clearly stunned Nicky. When he'd walked away from her, her mouth had been open, her forehead bunched up, and she'd looked as if someone had just shot her with a Taser.

Definitely not the reaction he'd wanted.

Garrett had wanted a dreamy look in her eyes. Maybe even for her to return the kiss with a little body-to-body contact, but he'd obviously sprung this on her the wrong way. To Nicky this probably seemed like some kind of knee-jerk reaction. After all, he'd just learned the dead guy's niece thought his mother had been having an affair with him.

It wasn't true.

Garrett had no doubts about that.

And no, he didn't feel that way just because he thought his mother incapable of something like that or because she was totally devoted to his father. His father had been a jerk, and his mother was human. But if she'd decided to have an affair, it wouldn't have been in Z.T.'s place. The spiders and dust alone would have put her off that notion. No, there was something else going on with the dead guy, but Garrett knew he wouldn't get any answers about that from his mom.

"Drink," he told his mother, and he handed her the glass of whiskey.

He'd flavored it with enough honey to make it go down easier, but she still made a face when she drank it. Garrett immediately fixed her another one. He didn't want her drunk, but he did want her relaxed enough so she could go to sleep. And, no, he didn't want that solely so he could go and see Nicky. His mother needed to get some rest, and maybe in the morning she'd have a better perspective on this.

"Those busybodies from the Garden Club are probably stitching a scarlet letter for me right now," Belle said. She had vacillated between what people were thinking and doing to what she wanted to be doing.

And what she wanted was to confront Candy and her aunt.

Then confront anyone who'd known Matilda.

Then hire Vita to talk to the spirits and sort this all out.

Garrett was positive that Vita was not the way to go. Neither was a visit to Felix's wife. Their best course of action was to let Clay do his job.

If his mother's fingerprint matched the one on the receipt, then things were going to get even more complicated. That still wouldn't mean she'd had an affair with the man, but she could be covering for someone. Or hell, maybe she'd just touched the receipt and the touching had nothing to do with anything else. But it might not look that way to Clay. Belle was his soon-to-be mother-in-law, but as chief of police, he still had to do his job.

Sophie helped their mother into bed, fluffing up the pillows behind her neck and back. His sister looked ready for Belle to nod off, too, but then they'd been at this for what felt like six years. It'd only been a couple of hours, but his mother had a way of stopping time.

"I don't want this to spoil the widows' dinner," Belle went on. She turned to Garrett. "Make sure Nicky doesn't try to cancel."

He was hoping that canceling was exactly what she had in mind. No way did Nicky, Sophie or he want to sit through a dinner where his mother was a juicy morsel of gossip.

"Drink," Garrett reminded her, and with some wincing and face making, his mother finished off the second whiskey.

"I also don't want this to affect either of you," Belle went on. "Sophie, you should go through with your wedding plans as if nothing happened. Because nothing has. And Garrett, you should keep on seeing Nicky. She was all torn up about this. I could tell."

Hell. His timing had sucked even more than he'd realized. Of course, this would affect her.

"Oh, the poor thing," his mother went on. "I could just see it on Nicky's face. I'm sure this made her think about her own husband cheating on her."

Garrett was about to get another wave of feeling like shit, but then something hit him. "How'd you know Nicky's husband had cheated on her?"

"Meredith," his mother said on a sigh. "She called

a while back. I'm sure she's still trying to get in your pants, by the way. My advice is to keep your zipper shut tight around her. Woo." She touched her fingers to her head. "Boy howdy, I'm sure feeling those drinks now."

"Uh, how would Meredith have known about Nicky's husband?" Sophie asked.

Belle shrugged. But Garrett knew the answer. She almost certainly got it from pillow talk with Kyle.

"Meredith thought because Garrett and Nicky have similar histories, that it would draw Garrett to Nicky," Belle went on. "Meredith didn't want Nicky to be hurt again."

Wrong. She didn't give a rat's ass about Nicky being hurt. She only wanted to drive a wedge between Nicky and him. Well, it wouldn't work.

Except tonight there was a different wedge.

Garrett didn't doubt that his mother had truly seen an upset look in Nicky's eyes, and he certainly hadn't improved things with her. He needed to fix that. And ask her about that date.

"Go ahead," Sophie said to him. "I'll stay with Mom until she falls asleep."

Garrett hadn't said a word about seeing Nicky, but his sister wasn't stupid. She must have known what was going on. He thanked her, kissed his mother on the cheek and went to his office. He threw open the door, expecting Nicky to be there.

She wasn't.

But there was a note on the center of his desk. "I went back to Z.T.'s to put Kaylee to bed. Come over if you're feeling up to it. If not, I'll see you tomorrow."

Well, at least she didn't sound upset. In fact, the note

sounded almost casual. Definitely no teardrop stains or any signs that she was troubled by what had gone on.

And then he looked in the trash can.

There were at least a dozen pieces of notepaper, all crumpled up into tight little balls. He unwadded one of them and saw a different version of the note that Nicky had left for him.

"I had to go. Needed some time to—"

That was it. Garrett took out the others, opening each of them, and it showed him the pattern of a woman who was tied up in just as many knots as he was.

Are you sure about what you said?

You probably need some alone time…

Did I really offer you sex? LOL. In hindsight, that was way too forward…

Hugs for the mess with your mother. I'm here if you need me.

And the final one: "Garrett,"

Nothing followed his name but that comma which meant she'd intended to say something but had changed her mind. Obviously, Nicky wasn't feeling as casual as she sounded in the message she actually left on his desk.

Garrett considered just texting her to let her know he'd see her tomorrow. But he dismissed it just as quickly. He started for the door and purposely didn't grab a condom from his desk drawer. Condoms he'd bought on his business trip. Having one of those in his pocket would be just too much temptation, considering Nicky definitely wasn't convinced that sex was the way to go. Yes, she'd been the one to offer sex, but those discarded notes he'd found told him that she might be having second thoughts about that.

Since it was dark and starting to rain, Garrett took his truck rather than walk, but he turned off his headlights as he approached the house. No need to announce to all the widows he was there even though he was dead certain that someone would see him and gossip about it. That was another reason to make this visit short and sweet. Of course, then the gossip would be speculation that he had "premature" issues.

He parked behind the line of vehicles and made his way to the front door. Locked. A surprise since it was barely 9:00 p.m., but then the women probably did that automatically since most were used to living in the city. He went to the back door, found that it was locked, too, and was about to text Nicky when the door flew open.

And there she was.

"I saw you drive up," she said in a whisper, and she stepped back so he could come inside.

"Is everyone already in bed?" he asked.

"Either that or in their rooms. All but Lady, who's on a date. You got my note," she added.

He didn't mention that he'd read all of them. Instead, he nodded. He also put his hands in his pockets so he wouldn't be tempted to touch her. She certainly looked good enough to touch in her pale yellow pj's. He'd never considered pj's to be especially hot, but they were on her.

"I can't stay," he said right off. What he meant, though, was that he wouldn't stay. "Mom told me you got upset, that the cheating brought up bad memories for you. If I'd known that, I wouldn't have said to you what I did. And I'd like for us to go to a movie or something."

Garrett winced. He should have put some pauses in there and not run all of that together. He sounded like a fumbling teenager.

"I was upset because I thought the reminder of cheating would upset *you*," she said.

He looked at her to make sure this wasn't another attempt like the discarded notes, something she was saying to try to make him feel better. But while he was looking, Nicky clarified things for him.

She hooked her fingers over his belt buckle, pulled him closer and kissed him.

All right. That was pretty clear.

And Garrett took things from there. He snapped her to him and kissed her right back.

Garrett knew he wasn't thinking straight right now. One kiss from Nicky could do that to him. But he really hoped this wasn't some kind of extreme reaction to the crappy day they'd had.

He pulled back, just to give her a chance to stop, but she still had her hand on his rodeo buckle and used that to yank him right back to her. All in all, it wasn't a bad place to be.

Until he remembered he hadn't brought that condom with him.

Clearly, he wouldn't qualify for the Boy Scouts since he was never prepared when it came to Nicky.

Garrett tried to tell her about the condom problem, but it was hard to talk with the tongue play that was going on. The moving, too. At first Garrett thought

Nicky was responsible for that, but then he realized he was the one doing it. He inched her away from the door and out of the kitchen.

He suddenly got a jolt of déjà vu. On the night he'd taken Nicky's virginity, the kissing had started in the kitchen, and they'd kissed their way to the library. Exactly what they were doing now. The difference was back then they were young and stupid, and he'd had a condom.

Nicky broke the kiss when they made it to the foyer and the stairs, and she glanced around again, as if making sure they didn't have an audience. There wasn't anyone that he could see, but Garrett's vision was a little blurred thanks to the way Nicky kept brushing her body against his.

Since the kissing and body touching were driving him crazy and slowing them down, Garrett scooped her up. Just to cool things down, he considered taking her upstairs to her bedroom, but he wasn't sure if Kaylee was asleep in that same room. So, he let his homing-pigeon senses lead him to the library. The moment he stood Nicky on the floor, she shut the door, locked it and hauled him right back to her.

She wasn't giving him any time to think. No time for her to think, either. And he wanted to do something to make sure she had thought about this and that it was the right thing for her to do. Then, his hand landed on her butt, and he forgot all about the need to think. Hell, he forgot how to breathe.

Garrett just went with it. He kissed her the way he'd been dreaming of kissing her. Long, slow and deep. Actually, that was the way he'd been dreaming of having sex with her, too, and with that reminder every part of his body started getting ready to fulfill that dream.

Except it couldn't happen.

"No condom," he said.

"I have one." She patted the pocket on her pajama top. "I got it from Lady's room."

He'd never wanted to kiss the nympho tow truck owner, but Garrett would have had she been there. Then, he would have promptly told her to get lost because it was time for him to do something that he hoped Nicky didn't regret when she came to her senses.

The lights were off, and he kept it that way. Even though he would have loved to see her naked, he didn't want to risk the scar playing into this. Didn't want to risk any old memories of the pain she'd had on that chaise, either. That didn't leave many options. A desk, a spindly-looking chair, the floor or the wall.

He chose the floor.

Still kissing her, Garrett dragged her down, and the foreplay went into serious overdrive. Her hands were all over the place while she tried to unbutton his shirt and unzip him. She bumped into his hands, nearly kneed him in the groin, all the while continuing the kisses.

As she'd done in his truck, her mouth went to his neck, and he would have enjoyed it a whole lot more if she hadn't been fumbling with his zipper. Plain and simple, she was awful at that, and rather than risk things ending by accidental hand job, Garrett turned her on her back, pinning both her hands so that he could shove up her top.

She wasn't wearing a bra, but since he felt her tense a little, he kept her breasts covered. For the most part anyway. He did do a tongue flick on one of her nipples before he kissed her stomach and shimmied down her pajama bottoms and panties. He had to let go of her hands to finish that, but she was apparently done with the fumbling because she was reacting to the stomach kisses.

Good.

Garrett got an even better reaction from her by kissing her right between her legs.

He got a reaction all right. She bucked beneath him, made a sweet *take-me* sound that was music to his ears. So he continued kissing her there. Pleasuring her, pleasuring himself and giving him some time to strip her naked.

There was just enough moonlight sneaking through the windows for him to see her. Not the scar. But everything else. With all his clumsy teenage moves, he hadn't taken the time to appreciate this seventeen years ago, but he damn sure appreciated it now.

That didn't last, though.

She cursed him, latched on to his hair and pulled him back to her. Not gently, either. Nicky kissed him, hard, cursing his clothes, as well, so Garrett helped with those. He managed to get off his shirt, mostly anyway. He freed one arm, gave up when it started to eat up too much time.

Because right now, time wasn't on their side.

There was a raging need. An ache so deep that Garrett knew there was only one cure. And the cure required a condom.

While Nicky unzipped him and shoved his jeans off his hips, Garrett fished around on the floor for her pajama top. It wasn't easy to find in the dark, and Nicky had started to torture him again by freeing him from his boxers. Things had been moving pretty fast before that, but this sped things up further and created a new urgency for him to find that blasted condom.

He finally fished it from the pocket and had to wrestle Nicky back into place because she was trying to give his dick some "special" kisses. He was already too primed so he got the condom on with every intention of finishing this the right way.

Something he hadn't done seventeen years ago since he hadn't lasted long enough to make her climax.

He pushed inside her, his brain nearly exploding. The rest of his body wanted to explode, too, but he made sure he held off. Nicky did no such thing. She hooked her legs around him and moved right into the thrusts. There certainly didn't seem to be any pain tonight, just the pleasure.

Good.

Because Garrett was feeling plenty of pleasure, too.

He moved and moved and moved, making sure that this time he hit just the right spot. A spot he hadn't even known existed the last time they'd been together like this. But he knew it now, and after a few of those well-placed thrusts, he gave her the first and only orgasm that she'd gotten from having actual sex with him.

Judging from the bad name she called him and the sounds she made, it was a good one, too.

It certainly was for Garrett when a few seconds later, he let Nicky give him an orgasm right back.

CHAPTER EIGHTEEN

NICKY WOKE UP with a jolt. Literally. Her shoulder and hip smacked against the floor, hard, and that was when she realized she'd fallen off the chaise. When she also realized she'd been sleeping on that same piece of uncomfortable furniture.

And she'd been sleeping there with Garrett.

The sound of her fall must have alerted him because he grunted. He obviously wasn't awake yet. The sound of her groaning and groping to get up must have alerted him further because he finally opened one eye.

Then he cursed a blue streak when he saw her.

"Are you all right?" he asked, pulling her back onto the chaise.

She'd been about to say no, that she might have dislocated her hip, but apparently Garrett was the cure for that. Especially since he was naked. She was, as well, from the waist down, and she got a nice reminder of how good his naked body could feel when he pulled her against him.

He yawned, scrubbed his hand over his face. All mundane things if he'd been any other man, but she could see that Garrett didn't fall anywhere in the ordinary category. That sent her in search of a kiss. Until it hit her.

She could see him.

Clearly.

That was because the sunlight was pouring through the window. Jeez Louise. It was morning. And now that her ears weren't ringing from the fall, she could hear some movement on the floor above them. Out in the hall, too. It sounded as if everyone in the house was up.

Garrett must have realized it, too, because he scrambled off the chaise. Just as the doorknob rattled. That sent Nicky scrambling, as well.

"Yoo hoo!" someone called out. Loretta. She was testing the knob again and then knocked on the door.

Nicky debated if she should just stay quiet, and then Loretta might just go away. Or not.

"Nicky, if you're in there, I need to see you," Loretta added.

That caused Garrett to move even faster, which was a good thing since he had more clothes to put on than she did. She only had to locate her pajama bottoms and panties. She managed the first but couldn't find the second.

"It's really important, Nicky," Loretta went on and tested the knob again.

Lord, Nicky hoped she hadn't found another skeleton. Since the woman's knocking was getting more insistent, Nicky pulled on the pajama bottoms, sans panties, and motioned for Garrett to move to the side of the room. There was another locked door there, one that led to a sitting room, and he could dress in there and try to sneak his way through the house so that no one would know where he'd spent the night. Not that Nicky was ashamed of what'd happened, but she really didn't want to be the focus of this kind of gossip. Gossip that her daughter might overhear.

"I'm coming," Nicky called out to Loretta.

When Nicky opened the door, she stretched and yawned as if she'd just awakened and hoped she didn't have any visible hickeys or anything. That would be rather hard to explain now that Garrett was no longer in sight.

"I was reading and fell asleep," Nicky lied. She yawned again.

Loretta nodded as if she had no trouble believing that. "I heard that the chief found out about the d-e-a-d m-a-n, that his name is Felix something or other."

"Yes. Felix Drummond. His niece ID'd the wedding ring."

Loretta let out a long breath and glanced in the hall. "Well, that's good. I mean, now that we know who he is, we can start putting all this behind us."

Nicky wasn't sure of that at all. There was still the investigation to figure out the cause of death and to prove that Garrett's mom wasn't involved. Nor was she sure why Loretta had spelled out those two words when there was no one else around to hear.

"Clay still has some questions about how the man got here, but it's a start," Nicky said.

"Is that why Garrett is here?" Loretta asked. "Because of Clay's questions?"

Nicky was certain she looked like one of those proverbial deer caught in headlights. "Garrett's here?"

"Uh, yes," he answered. He strode toward them from the direction of the sitting room. Apparently, he hadn't gotten around to making his way out of the house. "I drove over, hoping everyone would be up. I wanted to give Nicky the latest update."

Even though Garrett was clothed, he still looked as

if he'd just climbed out of bed with someone after a night of sex. That meant Nicky probably looked as if she'd had two nights of sex since she was still wearing her pj's.

Loretta didn't leave. She stayed there, apparently waiting to hear the update he'd just mentioned. An update that probably didn't exist since he hadn't been home all night.

"I'll be taking my mom to see Clay this morning," Garrett said as if carefully choosing his words. "He wants her fingerprints to compare with the partial on the receipt. He doesn't expect it to be a match, but this is standard procedure."

Well, that was definitely an update. One that Nicky was surprised he would tell her in front of Loretta. But maybe he knew it would get around when folks saw Belle going into the police station.

"Oh, dear," Loretta murmured. "Belle has to be so upset about this."

"She is." Garrett checked his watch. "That's why I should get back." He slipped on his hat, ready to leave, but then someone called out to him.

"Gare-if!" Kaylee squealed.

Her daughter came barreling down the stairs. As much as she could barrel considering she was wearing another bulky outfit that she'd obviously taken from the trunk.

"Who am I?" Kaylee asked, doing her standard twirl when she was playing this particular game. She didn't seem to notice the way Nicky was dressed.

But Gina noticed all right.

Her friend gave her a sly smile. The smile was tempered a bit with a narrow-eyed warning directed at Garrett. A warning for him not to break her heart again. However, that ship had sailed way out into the ocean. Because Nicky was certain another heartbreak was in her near future.

Well, maybe.

It was probably a postorgasmic thought, but maybe Garrett and she could have an affair. Nothing permanent or with strings. Just sex. It would be a start anyway, and far better than a broken heart.

"Who am I?" Kaylee repeated with another twirl.

Nicky pulled her attention back to her daughter and studied the clothes. Kaylee was wearing a small floral print old lady dress, complete with a pearl necklace that Nicky hoped was fake. Someone, probably Gina, had gathered Kaylee's hair into a granny bun.

Since Loretta was standing right next to her in an old lady dress, granny bun and pearl necklace, this was easy. But Nicky tried to make it seem hard in case Loretta was insulted by Kaylee's interpretation of her.

"It's Miss Cunningham," Kaylee announced, and she did a decent job of pronouncing the woman's name.

Loretta stared at her as if trying to make the connection and then smiled. "Of course you are. She's sweet as Texas tea," she added to Nicky. Loretta checked her watch, as well. "But I need to be going. I'll stop by to see Belle before I head into San Antonio. I need to check on my house, which I'm renting out, and see some friends. I'll be back in plenty of time to help you with the party."

Nicky groaned before she could stop herself. She certainly hadn't forgotten about the party, but thankfully it wasn't until tomorrow night. Maybe by then, this situation with Belle would be cleared up.

Kaylee waved goodbye to both Garrett and Loretta before she went back up the stairs. That was where Nicky needed to go so she could shower and get dressed.

"You're here early," Gina commented to Garrett.

Garrett nodded. "Like I told Loretta, I was giving Nicky an update from Clay." He tipped his hat and headed for the door.

His lie would have been a whole lot more effective if Nicky's panties hadn't been caught on the heel of his right cowboy boot.

Nicky considered running after him, but at that moment the sisters walked by. No sense in drawing attention to something like that. If the panties fell off in the yard or on the trail, everyone would assume they belonged to Lady.

"So?" Gina said the moment the sisters were out of earshot.

"You want details or the big picture?" Nicky asked her.

"Both."

Nicky didn't intend to get too specific. "Garrett came over, and we ended up in here again. It was better this time. Much, much better."

Gina smiled. "You look well pleasured."

She was. Well, her body was anyway. But the doubts started to come. And the realization that if she wanted to continue this with Garrett, then she needed to tell him the whole truth.

"I think I'm falling in love with him," Nicky admitted. "I know. Bad idea," she added when Gina's smile faded.

"It could be." Coming from Gina that was practically an endorsement for Nicky to take the plunge. She patted Nicky's arm. "Just talk to him. Tell him about the flowers, about who's sending them and why. After everything else that's gone on, it probably won't even cause him to raise an eyebrow."

Yes, it would. Because she didn't have a stellar track record with him when it came to her secrets. And this was a secret with life-altering consequences.

One that could possibly send her to jail.

Thankfully, Nicky didn't have time to wallow in that depressing thought because Kaylee came back downstairs. No more granny buns and pearls, but she'd gotten into the markers again because she was sporting a red nose and a hat made completely of fake yellow flowers. The flowers had frayed and mushed together, making it look a little like a blond wig.

"Who am I?" Kaylee asked, complete with twirl.

But this time, Nicky wasn't trying to guess. Her attention was on the shirt that Kaylee was using as a dress.

A man's plaid shirt.

It matched the suit and the hat brim on the dead man they'd found in the closet.

"I a clown," Kaylee proudly announced.

"Where did you get that shirt?" Nicky asked her, and then she tried to soften her expression so she wouldn't alarm Kaylee.

"In de trunk." She blended it together like one word, but Nicky had no trouble understanding what her daughter was saying.

Apparently, Gina made the connection, too. "You think that belongs to Felix Drummond?"

Nicky doubted it was a coincidence that the pattern matched. "Where in the trunk did you find it?" she asked Kaylee.

"Way, way, way at the bottom." She took a wallet from one of the pockets and a small box from the other. "With dis." The box contained the pearls that she was certain her daughter had been wearing earlier.

"This wallet and necklace were with that shirt?" Nicky pressed.

Kaylee nodded. She took off the shirt and proceeded to wrap the box and wallet inside it. "Way, way, way at the bottom," she repeated.

"You think he was trying to hide it?" Gina asked. "Maybe because the pearls were a present?"

That was as good a guess as any, and maybe the CSIs hadn't found it because it'd been buried deep in the box. Of course, they also might not have found it because they'd had to go through heaven knew how many boxes and trunks filled with clothes.

Nicky took the shirt, wallet and necklace from Kaylee. "I'll take them to Clay."

First, though, she had to get dressed, and she was about to head upstairs to do that when the wallet fell open, and she saw the driver's license that was still in place behind a clear plastic screen. She also saw the name.

And that name wasn't Felix Drummond.

GARRETT HAD TO hand it to his mother. She was dealing with this a lot better than he'd ever thought she would. Maybe the honeyed shots of booze had helped. Or maybe Sophie had managed to sneak something into Belle's morning tea before she left for Austin.

Either way, Belle hadn't ducked down in the seat on

the drive to the police station. In fact, she'd smiled and waved at everyone they drove past on Main Street. For the most part, people had smiled and waved back, but that didn't mean they weren't whispering about this situation. He only hoped the gossip stayed at a whisper and that none of the guests brought a side dish of meanness with them when they came to the party at the Widows' House.

Garrett had had no luck talking his mother out of cohosting that event, but he hadn't given up yet. In fact, when he was done with this visit, he was going to ask Nicky about canceling the dinner party.

Of course, that wasn't the only reason he wanted to see her.

He wanted to talk. And kiss her. He didn't like the way he'd had to rush out of there a few hours ago. Also hadn't liked that he'd come home with her panties caught on his boot. He especially hadn't liked that his mother had been the one to notice those undergarments.

Thankfully, his mother hadn't asked for any details, but that was probably because Garrett had rushed off to the shower. He was betting, though, that the subject would come up soon enough.

"What are your thoughts about crabs?" his mother asked when he parked in front of the police station.

Garrett doubted she meant anything sexual so he went with the obvious. "For the party?"

"What else?" Belle kept right on talking as they got out of his truck. "It's not too late for Alice and me to make crab cakes. That would be a nice addition to the menu. After we're finished here, let's stop by the store and see if Leland can get them for us in time."

Well, at least the party gave her something to think about, something other than what was about to go on inside.

"Remember, Clay will need to fingerprint you," he reminded her.

He doubted she needed that reminder, though. Nor had she forgotten about it. That's why she'd brought a pair of white gloves with her. She probably meant to wear them afterward in case her fingers still had ink on them.

They walked in, getting everyone's attention in the squad room. The two deputies—Rowdy Culpepper and his sister, Reena. And Ellie Stoddermeyer, the receptionist. Judging from their somber looks, they knew what was going on.

"The chief's waiting for you in his office," Reena said. "Nicky Marlow's with him."

That caused Garrett to stop. "Why is Nicky here?"

Reena shook her head. Rowdy lifted a shoulder. "She wouldn't tell us," Ellie said. "Nicky always was the secretive sort." She glanced at Belle. "That seems to be going around."

Normally, Garrett could just let that kind of snide remark roll off his back, but he was suddenly in a dick kind of mood. "By the way, Ellie, you left your panties in my truck."

And with that, Belle and he continued toward Clay's office. Sometimes, it didn't take many words to make a dick-ish statement. Reena gasped, probably already reaching for her phone to tell everyone she knew about this. Rowdy chuckled. And despite Ellie rattling off a protest that they weren't her panties, few people would want to believe her.

"Liar, liar, pants on fire," his mom mumbled. "But thank you."

Of course, now he would have to live with the rumors that he was having sex with a woman twenty years older than he was, but it'd been worth it to see that gob-smacked look on Ellie's face.

When they stepped into Clay's office, Nicky stood, immediately going to his mother and hugging her.

"Thank you for coming," Belle told her. Now, the tears came to her eyes. "Sophie had a business meeting that she couldn't get out of, but I'm so glad you're here. I hope you don't believe the awful thing that man's niece said about me."

"I don't." And Nicky said it without a shred of doubt.

Garrett didn't have doubts, either, but Belle was his mother. He wondered what had caused this faith in Nicky.

Then, he saw the shirt.

There was no mistaking that plaid. Either this was the dead guy's missing shirt or else it was an eerie coincidence.

"Kaylee found it," Nicky explained. "It was in the trunk of clothes in her room. Along with his wallet and some pearls. I can't be sure, though, that the pearls went with the shirt or wallet. It could have just been in the trunk along with the other things."

Clay nodded in agreement. "According to his driver's license," the chief went on, "his name was Donny Ray Pittman. His family last saw him twenty-one years ago, which meshes with the date on the receipt. He was a widower and a minister, originally from New Orleans, but he'd been living in San Antonio shortly before he disappeared. In fact, his family didn't report him missing because they thought he moved to Mexico or someplace else to do missionary work."

Obviously, his mom was having some trouble processing all of that because she groped behind her, feeling for a chair, and when she located one, she sank down onto it. "Donny Ray Pittman," she repeated. "I've never heard that name before. What was he doing on the ranch?"

"We don't know yet, but I'm hoping his family will be able to remember something about that."

Garrett hoped that, too, but he had a question of his own. Several of them. "Why didn't the CSIs find that shirt? And who the hell is Felix Drummond? Was that some kind of alias that Donny Ray was using?"

But that last question didn't make sense. Because his niece knew him as Felix, not Donny Ray.

It hit Garrett then.

"That woman wasn't his niece," Garrett concluded.

"She wasn't," Clay verified. "She had an uncle named Felix all right. He passed away of a heart attack and is buried in Houston. He was never a missing person, and there's absolutely nothing to connect him to Wrangler's Creek or your ranch."

Even with the extra info, it took Garrett a few seconds to piece this together. "Candy was trying to scam my mother?"

"Looks that way," Clay verified. "Or maybe she's just one of those people out for attention. Either way, I suspect you'll be getting a call or visit from her soon. She might want money to stay quiet."

Hell. He wanted to wring this Candy's neck for doing this. That witch had put his mother through a nightmare and all for money or attention? "Can you arrest her for this?"

"I'd love to, but right now the only charges I'd have against her are lying to a cop. She'd get a slap on the wrist. Plus, she could always claim that her uncle did have a ring like that but she was mistaken about the name of his lover." Clay paused long enough to gather his breath. "And as for the CSIs, there were plenty of places they had to search, and I guess they just didn't look deep enough in that trunk."

Probably because they would have expected it to be closer to the top since no one had been living in the house when Donny Ray had been there. That didn't explain why this man had put the shirt in the trunk. Or if it was even he who did. No way to know that unless they found out why he'd come to the ranch.

His mother moved to the edge of her seat. "But why would this woman say that I was the one cavorting with her uncle? How did she even know my name?"

"The Grangers are rich," Clay reminded her. "She could have read about the body being found, and with just a little research, she could have figured out that you would be about the right age to have had an affair. An affair that you still wouldn't have wanted anyone to know about after all these years."

True. And someone out there might feel the same way. They might want to keep an affair hidden. But who? Because it certainly wasn't his mother.

"I'm so sorry," Nicky said, and that's when he noticed there were tears in her eyes, too. "I didn't think of something like this happening."

Probably because he was still reeling from the other things he'd just learned, Garrett didn't make the connection right away. But Nicky was blaming herself for posting anything about the dead man's ring on social media.

He went to her, pulling her into his arms, and he brushed a kiss on her forehead. It was a seamless gesture, so easy and natural that Clay and his mom seemed to pick up on the intimate vibe right away. Of course, his mother already had an inkling of that vibe because of the panties.

"You didn't know this would happen," Garrett assured her.

"You were only trying to help," his mother added, and she got in on the hug, as well.

"But I should have known it could attract someone crazy," Nicky insisted.

Clay shook his head. "Hey, I didn't pick up on anything crazy, and I'm a cop. My suggestion is for you to keep an eye out for her, and if she shows up or calls, get in touch with me right away."

They would. But that left Garrett with yet one more question. "Are we sure our John Doe is really Donny Ray Pittman?"

"Not yet, but now we can get his dental records to see if there's a match. I'll also start showing his picture around town. Someone might remember seeing him."

In a way it felt as if they were back at the beginning, but now that Clay had a photo, it would help. Of course, that still might not explain what the man was doing at the ranch so Garrett would look back in old employment records and see if the guy had ever worked for them.

"There's no need to fingerprint your mother," Clay

went on. "In fact, why don't you go ahead and take her back home?"

"Yes," his mother softly agreed. "I think I'd like to go get those crabs now."

Garrett figured it wasn't a good idea to advise her against that. Maybe she needed to do some party planning to get her mind off all the other things.

She hugged Nicky, and Garrett opened the door for both Nicky and his mom, but Nicky shook her head. "I need to talk to Clay a little while longer," she said. "Paperwork."

Since Clay hadn't asked him or Belle to do any paperwork, he was instantly suspicious. But then, maybe Clay wanted her to sign something since Kaylee had been the one to find the items.

He stepped out and shut the door, but his mother didn't head for the exit. "I need to go to the little girl's room," she said. But since that required her to walk right past Ellie, Garrett wondered if Belle also wanted to dole out a little nanny-nanny-boo-boo expression.

Garrett had already had his Ellie dig for the day, so he checked his phone instead, reading through the latest email on a cattle purchase. What he hadn't intended to do was hear what Nicky was saying.

But he did.

"I think it's time for me to get a restraining order," she said.

No way to unhear that, and even though Garrett knew it was wrong, he just stood there and listened.

"Another flower delivery came," Nicky added.

The flowers. Yeah, he remembered those. He also remembered the stark expression they'd put on Nicky's face. He'd suspected then that maybe she had some kind of stalker, and the restraining order went a long way toward proving that theory.

Hell.

Was someone trying to hurt her? It had to be more than just a persistent old lover or someone she'd rejected or she wouldn't have come to Clay with it. It sickened him to think that she could be in danger.

And, no, that didn't have anything to do with them having sex.

It went beyond that. Nicky had already been through too much to be put through another round by this flower-sending stalker.

"I think it's a smart move," Clay answered. "These kinds of things can escalate. I think it would also be wise for you to alert the ranch hands and the other women in the house. And Garrett, of course."

Garrett didn't catch what she said, but he hoped it was a yes, that she would indeed do that. But what if she didn't? He could alert the hands himself, but he didn't even have a description of this guy.

Not yet anyway.

But one way or the other, he would get it. This asshole, whoever he was, wasn't getting near Nicky.

CHAPTER NINETEEN

PART OF NICKY wished this were one of her dreams. It wasn't. But like the dreams, she found herself at her family's old house. Why she'd stopped here, she didn't know, but the house was like some kind of magnet that kept pulling her back.

She wasn't sure there were any answers or fixes here. Nothing to help with the nightmares, nothing she could use to repair herself. Still, she got out of her SUV and walked to the porch. Like the last time, she stopped on the second step.

Maybe her need to be here had something to do with the restraining order she had just filed. Perhaps being in the police station had brought some of it back. Not that she'd spent much time there. She hadn't been the one to file the original charges against her father. A schoolteacher had done that because, the night before, her father's fist had missed the side of her head and had landed on her cheek.

Nicky had tried to cover up the bruise, but there hadn't been enough concealer to do that. She also hadn't had the courage to go through with filing charges. Her mother had convinced her that the safest thing for her to do was to let it go. And Nicky had.

Well, she'd let go of the charges anyway. Letting

go of the shit he'd doled out wasn't something she'd managed just yet.

She forced herself up another step. Only one more to go, and then it was just a couple of feet to the front door. But she froze again. Too bad the freezing didn't stop the images. In the blink of an eye, she was a teenager again. Beaten and broken. With little hope.

Until Garrett.

He'd given her an incredible amount of hope. And it didn't matter that he had taken it away just a few weeks later. Garrett had been the one who'd taught her that she wasn't all those names that her father had called her, that she was Nicky Henderson, someone capable of doing more than not crying out when punched.

Nicky heard the sound of a car engine, and she immediately blinked back the tears. Unlike the nights when she'd been punched, she hadn't managed the fine art of not crying all these years later. She hoped it wasn't Garrett. No way did she want him to see her like this.

Thankfully, it was Gina, and she had Kaylee with her. They were out of Gina's car and were making their way to her.

That dried up her tears faster than anything could have. Garrett might have been the one to give her hope, but her daughter had given her the real love she'd never had.

"Are you okay?" Gina asked her.

"Fine." This time it was only a partial lie. And Nicky walked off the steps so she could hug her little girl.

Or rather the little girl who was now hers.

One day, she'd have to tell Kaylee the truth.

One day.

CRABS.

There were at least two dozen of them in an aluminum tub filled with ice, and they were still alive and moving. Nicky wasn't sure how Belle had managed to get them, and she didn't especially want to thank the woman for it, either. Even though Belle had included a note with the delivery that Alice and she would be by that afternoon to prepare them for the party tonight, that meant Nicky had to store them for a couple of hours. Not an easy feat, what with the fridge already crammed full of other foods that needed to be prepped.

The next time she got an idea to throw a party, Nicky intended to go to the pasture, find a large rock and hit herself on the head with it. But maybe her lousy mood had more to do with her visit to the police station and the old house than it did with live crustaceans.

Still, the crabs were contributing to this mess in their own way. So was the fact that Nicky seemed to be the sole person on kitchen duty today.

Where was Loretta when Nicky needed her? Or any of the women for that matter? It seemed as if all of them were giving the kitchen a wide berth. Maybe because they, too, had lost their enthusiasm for this joyous event that was now only eight hours away.

"Who am I?" Kaylee said, running into the kitchen. She twirled, of course, still obviously thrilled with this game that now made Nicky's stomach knot. She couldn't help remembering the last outfit, the one that'd belonged to the dead guy.

There was a bright spot in Kaylee having found that, though. Now they knew that Candy—if that was even her real name—was a liar and a possible scammer. Nicky wouldn't forgive herself for allowing that woman into the Grangers' lives, but maybe this would be the end of it. At least the end of Felix Drummond. Now they had to find out if and how Donny Ray fit into all this.

"Who am I?" Kaylee repeated, outstretching her arms.

She was wearing jeans, a plain white top, flip flops that were many sizes too big for her. Her hair was in a ponytail, though more of it was out of the scrunchie than in it. Kaylee pointed to her face, specifically to the deep frown that was on her mouth.

Nicky was certain that only deepened her own frown.

"You're Mommy," Nicky said.

Judging from the way Kaylee squealed, she was right. She was definitely in the frowning, moping zone. Again.

Her rotten mood was one of the reasons Nicky had wanted to come here, and apparently she still had some searching to do to find her happy place. The only time she felt it was when she was with Kaylee. And Garrett. But she couldn't stay in an orgasmic state with him forever.

Nicky scooped up Kaylee, gave her a big sloppy kiss, and it improved both their expressions. When she put the little girl back down, Kaylee went running off, probably to find another set of clothes with which to play dress up. Nicky intended to join her, but first she had to make room in the fridge for the crabs.

"There you are," someone said, coming into the kitchen. Cassie. She'd likely just finished the group session. The one that Nicky had missed for the third time in a row. "You look busy."

Good. That was better than looking unhappy. "Just

getting ready for tonight's party. Apparently, we're having crabs. If they don't escape first." Several had broken the rubber band restraints on their claws.

Cassie smiled in that soft way that only therapists and good grade school teachers could manage. Nicky felt a lecture coming on, except it wouldn't actually feel like a lecture, more like a life lesson.

"I have three kids, a dream job and an equally dreamy husband," Cassie said. "He made the Ellery sisters' best endowed list," she added.

Now Nicky smiled. "Lucky McCord. Yes, I've seen him." Though she hadn't paid any attention to the endowed part. Well, not much attention anyway.

"Then you know I'm truly lucky." Cassie's smile faded. "I suspect you didn't get that luck factor in your family or relationships, and that's why I'd like for you to continue with the sessions—either group or private ones."

Yep, a life lesson, and judging from the way Cassie offered her services, she had an inkling as to what had gone on. "You heard about my father?"

Cassie shrugged. "I've heard some things." She walked closer. "My father is an asshole who owns a strip club called the Slippery Pole. My mother's on her sixth marriage. So, obviously I didn't get the luck in the parent department. No physical abuse, just some bullying and neglect. Would you like some advice on how to get past it?"

Nicky was suddenly hanging on every word. Cassie was a respected therapist. In fact, she'd once had a hugely successful practice that catered to celebrities.

"I'm listening," Nicky assured her.

"Well, this is a treatment you probably won't find in

a textbook, but it's worked for me. You should go to the place that gives you the most grief. The one that comes to you in nightmares. And you stand there, and while staring it down, you invite all the demons to step up."

Nicky was totally on board until that last part. "Excuse me?"

Cassie gave a confirming nod. "You invite those demons to show you their wrinkly demon balls. Since you're about to show them yours. Trust me, your balls are bigger than theirs—metaphorically speaking, of course. Because they're just old watery demons, and you're a woman with what is now a luck-filled life."

She had indeed had some luck. With Kaylee. With her career. With this house.

"And after you've brought forth those demons," Cassie continued, "then, you yell these words in a very loud, firm voice. 'Screw you, asshole,'" and then she whispered in Nicky's ear, "'Screw you in the ass! And screw all those other demon assholes with you!'"

Cassie pulled back, shrugged. "I'm not sure why, but there's something cathartic about shouting the curse words."

Nicky was certain she looked skeptical. "And that works?" she asked.

"It did for me. Of course, I was yelling at a strip club that had a neon sign with blinking boobs so I didn't draw that much attention. Still, I got my point across—that I didn't intend to let the past take another dump on me. My current life is too good for that shit."

With that, Cassie gave her arm a gentle squeeze. "If you need someone to go with you to the asshole place, just let me know. You'd never know it to look at me, but I'm pretty good at kicking demon balls."

Cassie walked out just as Garrett walked in. Nicky wasn't sure if he'd heard any of the conversation, but judging from his bunched up forehead, he had. Or maybe he was just looking at the tub of crabs she'd set on the floor.

"Sorry about those," he said, tipping his head to the tub. "My mother doesn't always think things through. You want me to take them back to the house and find some fridge space there?"

It was a generous offer, but Nicky wanted to re-arrange some things and try to fit them here first. She started to do just that when her phone dinged. A text from Gina to let her know she was taking Kay-lee to her tutor appointment. Nicky considered going with them, but it was obvious Garrett had something on his mind.

"Cassie was just giving me advice on how to handle some of the memories and nightmares," she admitted.

He shook his head. "I didn't know you had night-mares."

Oh, mercy. She hadn't wanted to drag him down with her. "Hey, I have good dreams, too." She shoved aside some plastic bags of veggies and picked up the tub. It wasn't heavy, but the crabs were making a loud rattling sound against the metal. "Recently, those dreams have included you."

That had the intended effect. He smiled a little, brushed a kiss on her mouth. It would have been a much nicer kiss if there hadn't been snapping crabs between them. She hoped that wasn't some kind of metaphor for her life.

"By the way, Candy did call my mother," Garrett went on. "And yes, she asked her for money to keep things quiet. My mother tried to record the conversation, but she had the sound muted on her phone. Not to worry, though. Clay said the call is enough for him to alert Houston PD, and they'll set up a sting operation for extortion. That way, they can arrest Candy."

Good. That was something at least. If the woman got jail time, maybe she wouldn't try to do this to anyone else.

"Did you get all the paperwork done for Clay?" Garrett asked.

Her heart skipped a beat or two, but then she remembered telling Garrett that she had paperwork to fill out for the police. And she had. That wasn't a lie. What she'd omitted was that the paperwork included a restraining order.

One that she needed to tell Garrett about.

But maybe not right now. She had several demons to exorcise, and she had to work her way up to that one.

Nicky pushed the tub in the fridge, but she didn't quite get all the crabs inside. One plopped out, landing on the floor. This was the one that'd managed to get out of the rubber bands, and it scurried beneath the wooden prep table that was anchored against the wall. Garrett went after it while Nicky managed to prevent other escapees. She shut the door with a hard shove.

"It's way the hell underneath there," Garrett said, getting back to an upright position. "If you get me a broom, I'll try to get it out."

"No need." She went to him, leaned in and kissed Garrett, hoping that he wouldn't insist on talking. He didn't. Garrett cooperated and kissed her right back.

Nicky caught his hand, leading him toward the stairs. "Come on. I want to show you something."

CHAPTER TWENTY

IN THEORY THIS had been a good idea, but Nicky had lost some of her confidence by the time Garrett and she made it to her bedroom. No way to hide in the daylight. It helped when Garrett kissed her.

A lot.

It gave her a reminder of why she'd wanted to get naked. And with Kaylee out for her tutoring session, Garrett and she might be able to fit in sex along with some soul-baring. Of course, he might not want the sex once he'd seen her without her clothes. He'd gotten a glimpse of the scar. But only a glimpse. It wasn't exactly a turn-on to see it up close.

He kept kissing her. Touching her, too. A reminder that their notion of foreplay was short but potent. She wanted the potency, wanted every part of this, but Nicky eased back from him. She caught his hand, led him to the bed and had him sit. She stepped back before he could pull her onto the bed with him.

"Just watch," she instructed.

She was wearing her usual jeans, top and flip-flops so she pulled off the top, sending it sailing to the floor. He got that look in his eyes. The lust look. But what she wanted him to see was the scar, so Nicky took off her bra, dropped it and kicked it aside.

His lust-look only intensified, and when he reached

for her again, Nicky let him inch her closer to him. Now, he'd see the scar and he would know that her body was damaged goods. He would look at her the way Patrick had.

And Garrett did stare at it, all the while bringing her closer and closer until he touched his mouth to that awful word. But he didn't just touch. He kissed her there.

Nicky had never thought of that part of her body as a hot spot, but she certainly had to consider it now.

Garrett didn't say anything. He just kept kissing her. He used his tongue. And his hands. He unzipped her jeans, slid both them and her panties off and eased her onto the bed next to him.

Now she couldn't hide behind her clothes, and Garrett took full advantage of that. He slid his gaze over her. Head to toe, lingering a bit in her midsection. But if he was lingering on the scar, it didn't show in his expression.

He took her hand, put it on the front of his jeans. "If you want me naked, you need to get busy."

It was the perfect thing to do and say. And she did want him naked. She suddenly wanted that in the worst way.

He didn't help with his clothes. He just continued to kiss her, thereby making it tricky because it was hard to undress a guy when he was kissing his way down her body. Still, she managed it and would have tossed his jeans if Garrett hadn't stopped her and taken a condom from the pocket.

Great day.

Here, she'd nearly forgotten about safe sex. Thankfully, he had remembered. And also thankfully, he knew how to get the condom on fast so they could get to the best part. For a quickie, though, he certainly didn't move very fast. Garrett took his time, kissing his way back up her body before gathering her into his arms.

Long, slow strokes. Holding her as if she were fine, precious crystal that might shatter in his hands. There was no urgency, no demands. Just this need that she felt all the way to the soles of her feet.

Maybe in her soul, as well.

There were no demons now. No scars. Just Garrett as he moved inside her and made her feel only the good.

Sex.

Gina could sense it in the air. No doubt sex between Garrett and Nicky, and that's why she tiptoed upstairs when she went to put an already sleeping Kaylee down for her nap. If Garrett was in there with Nicky, Gina didn't want to disturb them.

Nicky would probably think Gina had used her ESP to come up with that sex theory. But this was a no-ESP-required observation. Nicky was falling hard for Garrett. Whether that was good or bad was yet to be determined, but falling hard for a guy meant sex.

For most people anyway.

There were the sisters and their various penis phobias. And there was her. No phobias, but as long as she still felt married, sex was out. That thought was right at the forefront of her mind when she came out of Kaylee's room and saw Jake standing there in the hall.

"Nicky told me that she saw you headed up this way," Jake greeted.

Gina looked back at Nicky's closed bedroom door. Maybe she'd been wrong about the sex after all.

"Nicky said she saw you from the window and that you were carrying Kaylee to put her down for her nap," he went on. "She didn't come out to help because she has a crab cornered in the kitchen. But she said I was to tell you that she'd check on Kaylee in a half hour or so. In the meantime, no one should wear open-toed shoes in the kitchen because the crab is really pissed off."

Gina just nodded. She got what he was saying, but it was a little hard to think because her mind was sharing his explanation with her thoughts of sex. Thoughts of her body's reaction to seeing him, too.

Her girl part, which she'd recently named Sissy, came to life.

She quickly tried to rein it in, but Sissy seemed to know what she wanted. Gina, however, wasn't convinced, and that's why she tried to do some damage control. She said the first thing that came to mind.

"I'm a widow." Not her best effort, but sadly it was not her worst, either. "And we haven't even gone on that date yet."

"There'll be plenty of time for dates. Heck, we could even consider this one. And as for the widow part, yes you are one. A widow with a great ass. Great smile, too." How could he make that sound so sizzling hot? "I dream about your smile."

Best to keep this on the light side. "Really? Because I dream about your ass." It just happened to be the truth.

He chuckled. "Better than dreaming that I am an ass. Which I'm not, by the way." He paused. "I told

Nicky I was coming up here to have some mindless sex with you, and she wished us luck."

Gina wasn't sure if that was a joke or not. Probably not. Nicky would have indeed said that. Now that Nicky was getting laid, it was likely her wish that her friends get laid, too.

"Before you say no or think about saying no, just let me kiss you," Jake offered.

She couldn't object to that, especially since Gina really wanted him to kiss her. And he gave her one all right. He slipped his arm around the back of her neck, drew her to him, and French-kissed her. She would no longer need an eyelash curler because Jake had managed to curl them for her.

It wasn't an ordinary kiss. The man probably wasn't capable of anything that fell into the ordinary category. It lasted a long time. Maybe days. And even though Gina could no longer breathe, she didn't care. Nor did she put up a fuss when he stepped into her bedroom, taking her with him.

No objection, either, when he shut the door.

Best for them not to be making out in the hall in case someone came upstairs. And there was no doubt about it—they were making out. Gina certainly wasn't stopping him. After several more kisses, she knew something else.

They were going to have sex.

It didn't matter that she could be making a mistake. She'd rather make a mistake with him than make what could be a bigger blunder by turning him down and regretting it for the rest of her life. Of course, that was the need and lust talking.

Gina slipped off her ring, putting it in her dress

pocket just seconds before Jake started ridding her of her clothes. It'd been a while since she'd undressed a man, but since this was a quickie, that didn't matter. They got off all the clothes. And that's when Jake put on the condom.

He took her right there against the door. A first for her. And he didn't treat her like a widow. Nope. He treated her like a lover.

A needy one who was desperate for an orgasm.

Which she was.

Apparently worse than desperate because it only took a couple of thrusts before Gina felt herself soar and then shatter into all those lovely orgasmic pieces. Just the way she preferred to shatter.

Jake smiled, kissed her, and then got to work on his own shattering. It didn't take long for him, either, maybe because her own muscles helped him out. He buried his face against her neck, kissing her there, too, and let himself finish what he'd started.

Gina waited, letting herself ease back down to the real world. She figured it wouldn't take Jake long before his legs gave out. After all, he had hoisted her up for the door sex and was carrying all of her weight. He moved all right but not to put her down on the floor. He carried her to the bed.

"How was that for some mindless sex?" he asked.

"Not bad." Again, she kept it light. Easy to do now that her body was slack and boneless. "You earned your place on the sisters' overly endowed list."

He chuckled. "We could go for a round of *mindful* sex if you like."

She nearly laughed. Then, hesitated. "What's the difference?"

"This."

Jake eased her onto the bed, kissing her again. This time, it was slow and easy. This time, he was letting her savor the feel and taste of him.

"Too much?" Jake asked, pulling back and meeting her gaze.

She should probably say yes, should probably give herself a week or two to catch her breath. But she didn't. Gina eased him back to her and added some *mindful* of her own to their next quickie.

GARRETT WAS PROBABLY going to get kicked out of the man club for this, but that round of sex with Nicky had left him feeling, well, confused. Normally, he wouldn't mind much of anything after sex, but he'd gotten the feeling that Nicky had wanted to do a whole lot more than show him her scar.

She hadn't, though. She hadn't exactly kicked him out of her room after sex, but it'd been close to that. Maybe because she had party food preparations on her mind. Or it was possible she didn't want Gina and Kaylee returning to find them naked and in bed. Either way, he wished there'd been more time.

He needed to tell her that the scar didn't bother him. Well, it did. But not in the way she probably thought it did. He wasn't grossed out by it or anything. However, it riled him that she'd gone through such hell that this had seemed like a solution. He didn't want her ever having to rely on that kind of fix again.

His phone rang as he drove back up the ranch trail to his house. It wasn't Nicky but rather Sophie. Garrett answered and put the call on speaker.

"Candy called Mom again," Sophie said right off.

"That horrible woman is at the diner in Wrangler's Creek."

"She's here in town? Why?"

"My guess is she thought it would get her the money faster. She told Mom to bring her twenty grand."

It wasn't much by Granger standards, but he was betting Candy planned on milking his mom for a whole lot more. Heck, this might have gone on for years if his mother had indeed done something wrong. But she hadn't.

"Mom and I are headed to the diner now," Sophie went on. "So is Clay."

He cursed, then realized this was a good thing. It would finally put an end to this part of the investigation. "I can be there in less than ten minutes." Seven if he didn't hit too many potholes on the trail.

"No need. In fact, it's probably best if you don't come. Clay will go through the back of the diner so he can watch what's going on. He'll have one of the deputies with him. Mom and I are supposed to go in as if we plan to pay her and then record Candy demanding money. After that happens, Clay will come out and arrest her. If Candy sees you, she might chicken out. You can be scary sometimes."

"I'm not fucking scary," he snarled, which only proved his sister's point. Candy might run if she saw the scowl that was on his face right now, and he wasn't sure he could rein that in. Candy would definitely feel less threatened by two women.

But there was a problem.

"Does Clay think this is safe?" Garrett asked. "What if Candy has a gun or something?"

"He wouldn't let us do this if it weren't safe."

True. Clay was both a cop and in love with Sophie. He would do anything to protect her.

"And he'll be right there, watching us," she added. "Gotta go. We just arrived at the diner. I'll call you back as soon as it's over."

She hung up, not giving him a chance to continue arguing about this. Not that he had an argument he hadn't already voiced, but it didn't matter. Despite everything his sister had just said, he would drive to the diner, keeping out of sight so he could be there if something went wrong.

That plan came to a halt, though, when Garrett started to drive past his house and spotted the woman on the porch.

Hell.

His first thought was this was Candy, that she'd come here rather than the diner. Some kind of bait and switch. His second thought was to get his phone ready to record her in case she demanded the money from him instead of his mother.

But it wasn't Candy.

Garrett saw that as he pulled into the driveway and the woman stood. She had graying brown hair, was probably in her late forties or early fifties and had a sturdy build. She was also tall. Even though she was wearing flats, she was probably close to his six-two.

She was dressed well in a blue skirt and matching top. Definitely not a derelict who'd wandered onto the property. She also didn't look like a politician or like she was trying to sell something. However, despite the nice appearance, there was a hard look in her eyes. Maybe she was a widow looking for Nicky. Nicky hadn't mentioned any new arrivals, but with Meredith's departure, that meant there was a room open.

"Are you one of the Grangers?" she asked the moment he stepped from his truck.

He nodded. "Garrett. And you are?" He didn't bother to sound friendly, mainly because he didn't like the vibe he was getting from her. She was scowling as much as he was.

And then he got a bad thought. This woman could be working with Candy. Maybe Candy had sent her here to get money while she was doing the same to his mother at the diner. Just in case that was the plan, Garrett hit the record button on his phone and slipped it into his shirt pocket.

"I'm Doris Stokes," she said.

The name meant nothing to him but neither had Candy's until a couple of days ago.

"Can I come in?" the woman asked. But it wasn't really a request. More like a demand. "Because we need to talk."

"We can talk out here." No way did he want her in his home. "What's this about anyway?"

Her mouth tightened a little, probably because he wasn't being very hospitable—if she turned out to be one of his mom's long lost friends, then he'd apologize.

Doris paused for several moments, but she didn't take her gaze from his. "It's about Nicky Marlow."

So, maybe she was a widow after all. "What about her?"

"She's a liar," Doris said, and this time she didn't pause.

All right. That was a start. Not a good one, though. A knot tightened in his gut. Here he'd assumed that the reason Nicky wanted the restraining order was because of a stalker. A male stalker. Maybe an old boyfriend. But it could be this woman.

"Are you the one who's been sending Nicky flowers?" he came out and asked.

Doris pulled back her shoulders, clearly surprised by what he'd just said, but what she didn't do was deny it. She searched his eyes, maybe trying to figure out how much he knew about all of this.

He didn't know much.

No way, though, would he tell Doris that.

"Why the flowers?" he asked.

She had to get her jaw unclenched so she could speak. "Because I don't want her to forget what she's done."

Garrett didn't respond. He just waited, hoping Doris would continue. He didn't have to wait long.

"Nicky's not Kaylee's mother. She stole her from me, and I intend to get her back."

CHAPTER TWENTY-ONE

THE THUNDER CAUSED Nicky to curse. From the sound of it, the storm was moving in sooner than expected, and that meant there might be a full downpour when the party guests were arriving. It also meant the trail would become a bog. At least Lady's tow truck was there if anyone needed to be pulled out.

Nicky hurried into the kitchen to grab the last of the plates, but she was careful about where she was stepping. She hadn't managed to catch the escaped crab, and she didn't want the critter pinching her toes.

It seemed a silly thing to worry about, since the crab had been bound for the boiling pot, but she hoped he wasn't hungry wherever he was. In case he was, she'd put a few baby spinach leaves under the prep table, along with a shallow bowl of water. And she hoped that no one thought she was an idiot for doing that.

Alice, Belle and Ruby were also in the kitchen, finishing up the various dishes. Including the other crabs, which were now crab cakes. Despite the A/C, the room was sticky hot, and Nicky felt the sweat trickle down her back.

She hadn't asked Garrett's mom about how things had gone with Candy. She hadn't wanted to bring up anything unpleasant, especially since Belle was in a good mood. Maybe that meant Candy was under arrest and had been locked up.

She took the plates to the formal dining room table, and thankfully Ginger was there to arrange things. Some of the other women were doing the same to another table they'd set up in the parlor. Since none of the rooms were large enough to accommodate a lot of guests, there'd be plenty of mingling.

Nicky's phone dinged, and when she pulled her phone from her pocket, she saw that the text was from an unknown number. Her stomach automatically started to churn because that was how Doris usually contacted her.

And this had to be Doris all right.

There was no greeting, no name, just the text: I'll be in touch soon.

Even though there was no profanity or threats, Nicky knew that it was exactly that—a threat.

"Where's Loretta?" Ginger asked, drawing Nicky's attention back to her and the party prep. "She knows how to fold the napkins into cute shapes."

"She had a meeting with her lawyer in San Antonio. Something to do with her husband's estate."

Nicky checked the time. It was less than an hour before the guests would start arriving, and Loretta had said she would be back by now. Unless she got there soon, there wouldn't be any cute-shaped napkins.

She pushed aside the effects of that text message and made a quick check of the bar area that D.M. and Lady were setting up. It wasn't perfect, mainly because the two had been testing out new cocktail recipes all day, but it would have to do. At least Lady wasn't off somewhere satisfying her sexual urges.

As Nicky had done earlier with Garrett.

As Nicky suspected Gina had done, too.

Her friend was doing an inordinate amount of smiling while she dusted and did a final cleaning check. Nicky was smiling, as well, but she didn't think Garrett was doing the same thing. The sex had been great as usual, but she knew that when he arrived at the house he'd wanted to talk. That would happen soon.

Tomorrow, probably.

But first she had to get through this night.

While she texted Loretta to make sure she was okay, Nicky headed upstairs to change her clothes. She looked in on Kaylee first, and her little girl and the sitter, Piper, were playing Kaylee's favorite game of dress up. Since this was Piper's first time watching Kaylee, Nicky would be looking in on them often, but Piper was the mayor's daughter, a college freshman, and everyone had raved about her babysitting skills. She certainly had figured out the way to Kaylee's heart because her daughter seemed to be having fun.

Nicky wasn't going to interrupt that fun, but she thought of something she needed to tell Piper. The problem was how to word it so that it didn't frighten her or Kaylee. Nicky took out her phone, scrolled to the picture that she'd given Clay for the restraining order, and showed it to Piper.

"If this woman happens to show up, you need to let me know right away," Nicky whispered to her.

Piper's eyes widened a little. "Is she a widow you've kicked out of here? Because I heard a couple of them had left."

One had left. Meredith. And Nicky hadn't actually kicked her out. "She just shouldn't be here," Nicky settled for saying. "And she probably won't come. I wanted you to know just in case."

Piper nodded and suddenly didn't look as at ease as she had a few moments earlier. Nicky started to assure her that the woman wasn't dangerous, but she was. Anyone who wanted to take Kaylee fell into the dangerous category.

There was an advantage to being in such a sprawling house. Kaylee's room wasn't exactly easy to find, and even with the guests who'd be coming and going, Doris would stand out because no one from town would recognize her. With her height and size, she wouldn't be able to just blend in, either. Still, Nicky wished she hadn't planned this stupid party.

I'll be in touch soon, Doris had texted.

But Nicky prayed that was an empty threat.

She took a quick shower, dressed and even managed to put on some makeup before she heard the doorbell. Obviously, someone had arrived early. She checked her phone as she headed downstairs. Still no response from Loretta, and while Nicky wasn't ready to sound the alarm just yet, she was concerned. Maybe Loretta was driving and hadn't checked her messages yet.

"It's the mayor and some men I don't know," Lady said as she passed Nicky at the bottom of the stairs.

Nicky had been expecting the mayor—Belle had invited him—but she was a little surprised that there were men on the guest list that Lady didn't know. Nicky figured Lady had become acquainted with everyone in or near Wrangler's Creek who had a penis.

There was another rumble of thunder. Some lightning. And Nicky saw that Belle was taking a wet umbrella from the mayor. Nicky greeted him and left it to

Belle to show him around when she spotted the other
three men that Nicky didn't recognize.

And that immediately set off alarms.

No. Not this. Not tonight.

Had Doris sent them?

Nicky went to them, trying to keep hold of her composure. "Who are you?" she asked, and no, she didn't
exactly sound like a welcoming hostess.

The men didn't answer. Unlike the mayor, they obviously hadn't had umbrellas because they were wet.
Not just their hair but their clothes, as well. They also
had plenty of mud on their shoes and the bottom of
their pants.

"I'm Barry," the one in the middle said. "These are
my brothers, Bobby and Bennie."

That still didn't explain who they were, and Nicky
didn't get a chance to demand more information. That's
because there was a shrieking sound, followed by a
thud, and she whirled around to see the Ellery sisters.
Two of them anyway. It took Nicky a second to spot
the third one, Diana, who was now on the floor. She
appeared to have fainted, but despite this, her sisters
weren't doing anything to help her. That's because they
were gaping at the men.

"Hera," one of the men said.

"Aradia," another said.

"Diana," the third one, Barry, said. He didn't go to
the woman, either.

"Bobby," Hera said.

"Bennie," Aradia said. Even though her voice had
hardly any sound, Nicky heard her. So did the others
in the house because suddenly all the widows, Belle,

Alice and the mayor were there. Like Nicky, they'd obviously figured out there was a huge problem here.

Three of them.

"I'm going to take a wild guess that these men are your husbands." But it wasn't much of a guess. The men wore wedding bands that were identical to the ones the sisters were wearing. There was also the emotion. In the time that the sisters had been at the house, none had ever seemed to get their pulses elevated above a resting rate.

Their pulses were clearly elevated now.

Even Diana who was regaining consciousness but appeared to be moving to the hyperventilation stage.

"How? Why?" the sisters asked, and there were some *oh God*s and *oh dear*s thrown in there.

Judging from the way the men dodged their gazes, there wasn't going to be a happy answer. Such as they'd gotten lost or had amnesia and had just now found their way back or recovered.

After nearly two years.

"Our boat didn't capsize," Bennie finally said. "We made it look that way so we could, well, disappear."

"Why?" That came as a collective question from the sisters, followed by some sobs.

"We just weren't thinking straight," one of the men said. "We were drunk and made a bad decision."

"Bullshit." That came from D.M. For a woman of so few words, she nailed it every time since her BS meant she knew they were lying.

The sisters' shock was quickly wearing off, and since Nicky wasn't sure what they would do, she walked between the sisters and their husbands. Probably not a stellar idea, but Gina joined her.

"Why don't all of you go into the library so you can talk?" Nicky suggested.

If anyone heard her, they didn't acknowledge it.

"Why?" Diana repeated in a gusty breath. Hera's breath was gusting now, too, but she sounded more like a snorting bull.

"Because we wanted out," Barry finally admitted. "And because we knew you wouldn't give us a divorce. We didn't want to hurt you and thought this was the best way to go about it."

"You shit heads," Lady snarled. It was the first and only time Nicky had ever heard Lady defend the sisters. "They've been here grieving. Where the hell have you been?"

"Florida," Bennie answered, his attention on the floor and not his sobbing wife. "But we ran out of money, and we didn't have any other place to go. We couldn't get jobs because we didn't have fake IDs. We were living off the cash we took with us." He paused. "You have no idea how hard it is to be married to them."

No one in the room argued with that, but that didn't stop Lady from flinging another *shit heads* at them. Nicky went to Diana, took her arm and got her moving toward the library. Thankfully, Gina managed to get the other two sisters to follow, and Belle and D.M. did the same to the men. Maybe once they talked, they could work all of this out.

Or not.

Making a feral sound, Diana launched herself at Barry. Gina caught the woman in midlaunch, whirling her around and practically slinging her into the library.

"No violence," Gina warned them.

"These F-word heads made us think they were dead," Hera said, no longer sobbing. Her eyes were narrowed to tiny slits. "What would you do if your husband had done that to you?"

"I would have killed the ass wipe," Lady quickly volunteered. That only fueled the narrowed eyes, the snorting breaths and the G-rated profanity. Diana called the men chicken caca.

"I would have hit him with a shovel and buried him in the swamp," D.M. contributed.

Nicky hoped that was the last of the answers to Hera's question.

It wasn't.

"I would have given him a chance to explain." That from Ruby. Nicky wanted to kiss her. It didn't last though. "And if he told me that he'd faked his death to get away from me, then I would have asked D.M. to help me hit him with a shovel and bury him in the swamp."

Nicky groaned. It was too bad Cassie wasn't here yet, or she could have asked her to do an emergency therapy session. Since it might be a while before the therapist arrived, Nicky just went with the "least collateral damage" approach.

"You three get on that side of the room," Nicky ordered the men. "And you get over there." She pointed to the other side for the sisters. "There'll be no violence, no shovels, no grave digging and only minimal name calling. Hey, you deserve some name calling," she added when one of the men groaned.

The doorbell rang, causing Nicky to do her own groaning. Obviously, she would have to let the guests know what was going on and let them decide if they wanted to stay for a free sideshow. She also needed to call Clay and get him out here, though he was likely already on his way with Sophie.

Nicky glanced around and pointed to the mayor, Gina, Belle and Alice. "Could the four of you stay here and mediate? You get the door," she added to Lady and D.M.

The pair weren't exactly the best greeters, but Nicky needed to make that call to Clay. When she stepped out in the hall to do that, she saw Jake. Thank God. He was big enough to hold back at least a couple of the sisters if a fight broke out. She was about to fill him in on what was happening, but he spoke first.

"What happened to Loretta?" he asked.

Nicky had to shake her head. "I'm not sure. Is she here yet?"

"No. She's in town. I just drove by the police station and saw Loretta through the window. Reena was with her, and she had Loretta in handcuffs."

GARRETT HAD THOUGHT if he arrived early to the party that he could get a moment alone with Nicky. But it didn't look like that was likely. Someone was shouting.

Lady and another widow were in the foyer, greeting Herman from the hardware store and Fred, the pharmacist. No sign of Nicky, though, or the people who were shouting.

A woman called someone a doodle head.

"The sisters' husbands faked their deaths," Lady informed him. And she called them dickheads instead of the shouted version.

Oh, man. That couldn't have been the start that Nicky had wanted to the party. But, of course, with what he had to tell her, this party was going to be over fast.

"Nicky was outside the library last time I saw her," Lady added, and she winked at Garrett. Maybe innocent flirting, but it was probably a reminder that if things didn't work out between Nicky and him, then she was available. He wasn't interested in Lady.

But he wasn't so sure things were going to work out with Nicky, either.

After they talked, she'd probably be anxious to get Kaylee out of there. Get herself out, too.

"By the way," he told Lady. "The trail from the road to this house is pure mud right now. Cars are stuck, and no one can get in or out."

Lady smiled. "I'll bet those judgmental bats from the Garden Guild won't mind my Camel-Tow sign now."

Yes, they would still mind, but they wouldn't turn down a tow.

He went in search of Nicky and found her just outside the library, and she had her phone in hand. She looked up at him, their gazes connecting, and she must not have picked up on his tense body language because she hugged him.

"Thank God you're here," she said. "Clay's not answering his phone. Do you have another number for him? A private one. I don't want to talk to any of the deputies."

"Why? You want him to arrest the sisters' husbands?"

"No. Maybe," she amended when the yelling went up a notch. "But I need to check on Loretta. Jake said he saw her in the police station in handcuffs. Have you heard anything about that?"

"No." Hell. Was there some kind of bad juju in the air?

He hoped Vita hadn't put some kind of creepy spell on the place. He got confirmation that might be true when he heard something crash against the wall. At first, he thought someone had thrown something, but one of the sisters had one of the men—her husband probably—against the wall. For a small-statured woman, she'd done a pretty decent body slam.

His mother and the mayor were trying to get the sister off the man. Jake was holding back the other two sisters who were clawing and biting at him to get loose. The other two men were trying to open the window. Maybe to escape. Gina was shouting for everyone to stop.

"Stop it!" Garrett yelled.

His yell worked a lot better than Gina's. The sisters with Jake stopped fighting. The one trying to choke her husband let up on that, too. Everyone seemed to pause to gather their breath, and they looked at him as if waiting for some further instructions.

Garrett really hadn't planned that far ahead, but it was obvious that there needed to be some cooling off. That probably wouldn't happen if the husbands and wives were in the same room.

He pointed to the men. "All of you, out of here. You can go wait in whatever vehicle you used to get here."

"It's stuck in the mud," one of them said.

"Tough. Wait in it anyway. If you get lucky and manage a tow from Lady, then you can go into town and wait there."

The men didn't argue with that. In fact, they seemed relieved to get the heck out of there. The sisters were a different story, though. One of them hadn't given up on gouging out her husband's eyes because she went after him again. Since Jake still had his hands full with the other two, Garrett took this one.

She kicked him in the shin, then socked him on his funny bone.

And Garrett could have sworn he saw flippin' stars.

"Go, now!" he shouted to the men, and he held the combative woman back long enough for them to hightail it out of there.

"You piece of cow dung!" the woman yelled.

She added a few more choice labels, but she must have spent every drop of her energy doing that because then she sagged against him. If Garrett hadn't taken hold of her, she would have dropped to the floor.

Nicky took over for him by pulling the woman into her arms. "Diana, you just need to take a moment. And when you think this through, you'll see the silver lining in this. Your husband is alive."

Diana looked at her, blinked, and then the tears started. Her sisters began to cry, too, and even though Garrett wasn't a crying expert, these didn't seem to be tears of relief.

"I'm not a widow," Diana muttered. Again, Garrett wasn't picking up on any sense of relief. Just the opposite, in fact.

"And neither are we," one of the other sisters said. That brought on even harder crying.

Maybe they'd enjoyed not having their loser husbands around. Hell, maybe they just liked having people feel sorry for them. Garrett still felt sorry for them, but it had nothing to do with their marital status.

Diana lifted her chin, and it appeared she was trying to steel herself. "We'll go upstairs, pack our things, and then we'll leave tonight." She pulled away from Nicky and started out of the room.

"Wait." Nicky stepped in front of her. "You don't have to leave right away. Stay at least until morning."

"Of course we have to go. This is the Widows' House, and it wouldn't be right if we stayed. We have husbands, and it would be a slap in the face to everyone else here if we stayed."

It wasn't an especially good argument considering that Meredith had stayed here and Lady was nowhere near grieving mode. But clearly the sisters had made up their minds because they joined hands and walked out, each mumbling something about finding a more appropriate support group to suit their emotional needs.

He didn't want to tell them that they probably wouldn't get far because they appeared to be satisfied with their stoic exit. But with the trail in such bad shape, they wouldn't be able to drive anywhere, and Lady might be too busy to give them a tow. Hell, the woman might be outside right now screwing the sisters' husbands.

Nicky stood there, watching them as if she might go to them, but she stayed put when his mother and Gina went upstairs with them. Nicky tried to call Clay again. Because Garrett was standing so close to her, he heard it go to voice mail.

"I'll try Sophie," he said, taking out his own phone. After that, though, he was talking to Nicky.

"By the way, what happened with Candy?" Nicky

asked in a whisper. "I didn't want to ask Belle because I didn't want to upset her."

"Everything went as planned. Candy demanded money, and Clay arrested her."

"And he didn't say anything about Loretta?"

"Not a word." Garrett doubted that Loretta had anything to do with Candy, but maybe she did. If there hadn't been other pressing things to deal with, he would have asked Nicky about that possibility. "Look, I know this is a bad time, but we have to talk."

"About Loretta?"

"No." And he didn't want to get into it with a possible audience around.

He took her out of the library and went in search of a private place to talk. In a house built like a giant ant farm, that shouldn't have been a problem, but it was.

Ginger was in the kitchen. Ruby, in the foyer. There were guests in the parlor and dining room, so Garrett headed for the back porch. There was a tin roof covering it so they wouldn't get wet, but he had to nix that when lightning zagged through the night sky.

"Can you at least tell me what's wrong?" Nicky asked as Garrett took her into the back hall. At least no one was there.

He stopped, turned to face her. "After I got back home, I got a visit from someone named Doris."

There'd already been plenty of concern on Nicky's face, but his words only made her expression worse. There was a hitch in her breath, and she dropped back a step. "She told you?"

He nodded, not even sure what he'd heard from Doris was the actual truth. "She told me her side of the story. Now, I'd like to hear yours."

"Oh, God," Nicky whispered, and she turned away from him. "I was going to tell you. I was. But the timing was never right." She paused. "Kaylee doesn't know."

Yeah, he'd figured that out, but before he could ask anything else, he heard more shouting. Not from the sisters this time. It was Lady.

"Uh, Nicky? You really need to get out here."

Nicky didn't budge, but she did when she heard the next voice.

Loretta.

"Nicky, I need to see you," the woman said. "I've got to leave the Widows' House right now."

CHAPTER TWENTY-TWO

NICKY DEFINITELY DIDN'T want to do this right now Loretta was obviously in some kind of trouble, and while the conversation with Garrett was important, it could wait.

Not long, though.

But it could wait long enough for her to find out why Loretta had been taken into police custody. Nicky also needed to know how and why Loretta had been released and why she was back here at the house. Besides, Loretta might need a lawyer for whatever it was she had done.

There was no mystery about Nicky's final secret. It was out. And it was obvious that Garrett was upset. She'd lied to him by omission, and it probably had felt like a punch to the stomach because she'd started up an affair with him without telling him about Kaylee.

"I won't be long," Nicky said to him, but that might be another lie. If Loretta had been arrested for something serious, she might have to go back to the police station with her. At least until Loretta could get another attorney there.

Garrett didn't insist on her staying put, probably because he, too, was concerned about Loretta. He followed Nicky back to the front of the house, and she immediately saw Clay, Sophie and Loretta. At least Loretta wasn't in handcuffs, but her eyes were red from crying, and she looked pale and shaky.

In addition to the tears, both Loretta and Clay were soaking wet and muddy.

"I didn't kill him," Loretta volunteered right away.

Nicky hadn't been certain what the woman might say, but she certainly hadn't expected that. Oh, mercy. Had Loretta been implicated in a murder?

"I was just meeting him here," Loretta went on, but it was hard to understand her through the sobs. Also hard to hear because even more people were coming into the room. Belle was one of them, and she was clearly waiting for some answers like the rest of them.

"You need to start from the beginning," Clay reminded Loretta, and he led her into the nearby parlor and had her sit down. Of course, everyone went in there, too, but Loretta didn't seem to notice that this wasn't going to be a private conversation.

Loretta nodded, took a sip of whatever it was that D.M. handed her. She spit it right back out in the glass and made a face. Apparently, the cocktail experiment was a bust. In the grand scheme of things, that was small potatoes, but all the bits and pieces of this crappy night were starting to feel like dead weight on Nicky's shoulders.

"I knew Donny Ray, and we came here to…visit with each other," Loretta finally said. That part came through loud and clear, and it helped Nicky start to fill in some blanks.

Loretta and Donny Ray had been lovers. Here, at Z.T.'s place. Since it had also been Nicky and Garrett's tryst location, it was hard to fault the woman for that, but she could fault her some for the rest of it.

"Belle didn't know we came here," Loretta went on. "No one did. I knew this place would be unlocked and that we'd have some…privacy. So we'd use the trail to get here."

Nicky shook her head. "But no one found a vehicle belonging to Donny Ray or anyone else for that matter."

"That's because he rode a motorcycle. He would always hide it in the woods. It's probably still out there somewhere."

"Or it could have been stolen," Clay quickly pointed out. "Reena said the Penningtons had teenage boys around that time, and their land was close to the Grangers' Ranch."

He was right, but the Penningtons had moved to Florida well over a year ago, and their sons had left long before that. Clay would have to track them down to question them.

But there was also another possibility.

"My brother could have taken it," Nicky suggested. "He was always coming home with spare parts and junk that he'd find. And one day he pulled out a motorcycle from our old shed, and he rode off. I can ask him if he found it in the woods." She turned to Loretta. "Why didn't you say something when you found the body?"

"Because I didn't know it was Donny Ray. I swear I didn't," she added, glancing at some of the others in the room. "Donny Ray and I had had an argument because I wouldn't move to Mexico with him, so when I showed up and he wasn't here, I thought it was over between us for good. I left and didn't come back until the day we made this place the Widows' House."

Garrett shook his head. "But when you saw the skeleton, you must have had an inkling that it was Donny Ray."

"I didn't. I don't ever remember him wearing shorts like that. A suit like that, either. But he was always playing the goofball. You know, dressing up funny the way Kaylee does sometimes. Once he showed up looking like a cowboy. Another time, like a mobster from one of those old James Cagney movies."

It was possible he was trying to disguise himself. After all, Donny Ray was a minister, and he was meeting his lover. Then again, maybe he just hadn't outgrown a love of playing dress up.

"Any idea why Donny Ray would have put some of his clothes in the library and others in the trunk upstairs in the room Kaylee's using?" Nicky asked.

Loretta sighed. "That was another game of his." She paused, blushed. "He would hide my clothes, too, and after we had our intimate time, he'd have me look for them. I think he liked the idea of us running around the house in just our birthday suits. Sometimes, though, that would lead to even more intimate times."

Of course it would, but Nicky couldn't imagine the prudish Loretta prancing around the house naked. In fact, she was glad she was having a hard time imagining it.

"What about his wedding ring?" Judging from Garrett's tone, he had as many questions as Nicky did. And he wasn't especially pleased with any of this.

"Of course, Donny Ray had a wedding ring because he was a widower," Loretta answered, "but I didn't know what was engraved inside it. It looked just like an ordinary wedding ring to me."

It did on the outside. And Nicky supposed that it

was reasonable that a widower wouldn't have taken off his ring to show his lover. But that brought her to a gray area.

"Why come here to Z.T.'s?" Nicky pressed. "Why not just go to his place or yours…"

Loretta glanced away. And Nicky knew why.

"Did Donny Ray know you were married at the time?" Nicky added.

Loretta nodded. "He didn't approve. He wanted me to leave my husband. And I considered it. I'm not a loose woman like…some people around here." She glanced at Lady. "It's just I'd fallen out of love with my husband but couldn't divorce him. That wouldn't have sat well with my family." Her gaze landed on Garrett for that.

Maybe the looks were Loretta's way of judging, but at least Lady wasn't sleeping around on a husband, and Garrett hadn't done that to Meredith, either.

Loretta stopped long enough to wipe away more tears. Belle gave her a tissue. Lady offered her another drink, a green one this time. Loretta took the tissue but declined the drink.

"When I saw that skeleton in the closet, I didn't want to believe it was Donny Ray," Loretta went on. "It hurt too much to think that he might have died here, in pain, waiting for me."

"There wasn't any trauma to the body," Clay interjected, "so he probably died of a heart attack. I don't even think he fell or anything because none of the pots or pans on the shelves around him had been disturbed. If he'd fallen, he probably would have tried to catch on to something and would have toppled things."

Well, that meant there'd likely be no charges against

Loretta, but still, this would eat away at her for the rest of her life. Nicky tried not to be frustrated with the woman because she doubted Loretta was lying about any of this, but if Loretta had just let them know that it could be Donny Ray, then Garrett and his family wouldn't have had to deal with the likes of Candy.

"Jake said he saw Reena cuff her. Why did she do that?" Nicky asked Clay. She tried not to sound like a lawyer whose client hadn't been handled properly.

Clay looked as if he wanted to curse. "She jumped the gun. Loretta came in and said she killed a man so Reena reacted without getting to the bottom of it first."

"I meant I felt responsible for his death," Loretta corrected. "I still do."

Nicky let out a long breath and gave the woman a hug. It seemed to help, and Loretta got to her feet. "I had Clay drive me over. We had to walk quite a ways, though, because of all the stuck cars. Anyway, he said he'll take me to a friend's house in San Antonio."

"I can do it," Jake volunteered. He looked at Clay. "You should probably stick around here for a while in case the Ellery sisters run into the Ellery brothers again. The one that stands in the middle said something about finding some rusty pliers. She can't be up to anything good if she's looking for something like that."

Clay gave another "I want to curse so badly" huff even though he likely didn't know what was going on with the Ellerys. That was something Nicky was going to have to fill him in on. At least he knew about Doris since he'd been the one to help her fill out the paperwork for a restraining order against the woman.

"I'll get my things packed," Loretta said, heading for the stairs.

Nicky had already made this offer to the sisters, but she made it again to Loretta. "Why don't you at least stay until morning or until the storm has passed."

Loretta frantically shook her head. "I can't stay. Now that I know Donny Ray died here. You'll just have one less widow in the house."

Four less, Nicky mentally corrected. There'd be a lot of empty beds tonight. And considering the way Garrett had looked at her earlier, he wouldn't be sharing hers.

"Let's talk," she whispered to him. She stood, faced the others. "Help yourselves to the party food, and if you don't want to have to go back out in the storm, find a place to crash here." She turned but then stopped. "Oh, and watch out for the loose crab in the kitchen."

Now that she'd given that invitation and warning to everyone, she motioned for Garrett to follow her. Nicky didn't want to go upstairs where Kaylee and the sitter were because she didn't want them to overhear her. She also didn't want to run into Loretta or the sisters again. Her empathy reservoir was drained right now.

But at least some things were settled.

Candy was out of the picture. They knew more or less what'd happened to Donny Ray. And despite the ruckus the Ellery brothers had caused with their arrival, there hadn't been any injuries. Heck, once the sisters got over the shock of no longer being widows, they might even be able to reconcile with their spouses. If the men could get over those penis phobias, that is.

There was no one in the library so Nicky went there. Ironic that Garrett and she kept ending up there, but at least it had doors, and she made sure both were shut.

"What exactly did Doris want?" she asked.

"Kaylee," he answered without hesitation. "She believes she has the right to raise her."

Nicky felt the chill go through her, head to toe. Another irony because she rarely felt anything but heat around Garrett.

She sank down onto the foot of the chaise, and since she would need it, Nicky took a deep breath. "No, she doesn't have that right." She looked up at Garrett. "What exactly did she tell you?"

He also drew in a long breath. "That she was Kaylee's grandmother. Is she?"

"Yes. But Kaylee is also my late husband's child." There, she'd said it aloud. Now, for the rest. "You already know that Patrick had affairs. Several of them. Well, about three years ago, I saw some papers from my insurance company. Patrick usually handled that, but that time I opened it before he did. Anyway, someone claiming to be me had used my insurance card for a hospital stay."

"Kaylee's birth mother?" he asked.

Nicky nodded. "At first, I thought it was just a case of identity theft, but when I showed it to Patrick, he admitted that the woman was Shanda Stokes, and the baby was his. Needless to say, I was stunned, and while I was still reeling, he brought the baby home. Shanda had abandoned her in the hospital."

Garrett cursed and sat on the chair across from her. "Shanda allowed you to adopt her?"

She nodded again. "Shanda wanted money for her, and we paid." Or rather Nicky had paid her. "Patrick wasn't exactly thrilled with the idea of being a father, but he'd brought Kaylee home because he didn't want the hospital questioning anything about the birth since he knew about the insurance fraud. He's the one who'd given Shanda my medical card and had helped her get a fake ID so she could use it."

Garrett said some profanity under his breath. Nicky had often cursed Patrick for what he'd done, but if he hadn't, she might not have Kaylee today.

"Kaylee doesn't know any of this by the way," Nicky went on. "I'll tell her eventually, of course, when she gets a little older."

Nicky wasn't certain when that would be, but the therapist she'd visited about it had said that Nicky would know when the time was right.

"I've saved some photos of Shanda and Patrick so I can show them to her," Nicky went on. "It's all official, by the way. Shanda put my name on the birth certificate as Kaylee's mother, but I wanted to legally adopt her. Shanda agreed, eventually."

"After another payoff?"

Nicky made a sound of agreement. "At the time, I just wanted her out of our lives and thought it was money well spent. In hindsight, I wish I'd had her prosecuted. It probably would have saved her life because two days after I gave her the money, she died of a drug overdose."

He groaned softly, shook his head. "How does Doris fit into all of this?"

"Doris didn't even know her daughter had had a baby until she showed up for the funeral, but when she heard about Kaylee, she pieced things together. Heck, it's possible that Shanda even mentioned Patrick to her. Either way, Doris knew."

"And she wanted her," Garrett finished for her.

"She did." Nicky had to pause. "Doris felt as if she'd failed with Shanda and she wanted a second chance at motherhood. I didn't want to give her a chance to screw up another child's life."

Nicky tried to tamp down the memories. Both those from her childhood and the ones that Shanda had bought into her life. "Shanda's father was an alcoholic. He beat her. He berated her. Remind you of anyone?" She didn't wait for Garrett to answer. "And Doris let that happen just as my mother did."

A muscle flickered in Garrett's jaw. "Please tell me Shanda's shit head father isn't in the picture."

"He's not. He died the year before Kaylee was born." That was something at least. But in some ways, he'd be easier to fight. "Shanda's father had a police record. Doris doesn't. There's nothing on paper for me to convince a judge that she would be a bad grandmother. But I don't believe she wants to be only a grandmother. I believe Doris wants to be Kaylee's *mother*."

"So do I," Garrett said without hesitation.

Nicky lifted her head, looked at him. "Did she say or do something?" She got to her feet when the panic started to roll through her. "She's not coming after Kaylee, is she?"

He stood, too, met her gaze. "I heard you mention the restraining order to Clay." He held up his hands in defense. "I wasn't actually eavesdropping, but I was standing outside the door at the police station when you told him."

Of course. Garrett and Belle had been there because of Candy's accusations. She hated that he'd overheard it, mainly because he'd gotten no explanation to go along with it. Unless he'd heard everything she'd said to Clay, but Nicky doubted it.

"There's a problem," Nicky went on. "And it's the

reason I didn't tell you all of this right from the start. Doris is claiming that I allowed Shanda to use my insurance card, that I willingly gave it to her. If I had done that, I could be arrested since it's illegal. But I swear I had no idea Shanda even existed before Kaylee was born. I certainly didn't let her use my insurance. I'm not rich, but I had plenty enough money to have paid for her medical expenses without resorting to breaking the law."

He stayed quiet a moment, obviously processing all of that. "I believe you, but since both Patrick and Shanda are dead, they can't tell Doris the truth."

"She doesn't want the truth. She wants her granddaughter."

And she wanted her enough to keep sending those stupid flowers and texts.

"Doris sends me those yellow roses because they were Shanda's favorite," Nicky continued. "Apparently, Shanda even had a rose tattoo. Doris would probably say she sends them as a way of keeping her daughter alive."

Garrett nodded. "She mentioned that. Along with saying she didn't want you to forget."

A burst of air left her mouth. It wasn't from humor though. "As if I could. And I don't want to forget her. Shanda was a young and troubled woman. Barely twenty-one. And she was Patrick's client. He was trying to get her out of some drug charges when they met."

"Drugs?" Garrett repeated. And he didn't have to say anything else for her to know what she was asking.

"Yes, she used them when she was pregnant with Kaylee. That's probably why she has some delays, but the delays aren't permanent. She's catching up."

"Thanks to you," he said.

Nicky didn't want any thanks. She loved her daughter more than life itself, and it was a privilege to do whatever it took to help her. If she ever had a biological child of her own, she'd never love that child or anyone else more than Kaylee.

"If Doris ever did pursue guardianship," Nicky added a moment later, "she'd have to fight me in court for that because as I said, Patrick and I did legally adopt Kaylee before he passed away. The only thing that's holding Doris back from a lawsuit is money. She's not broke, but she doesn't have the cash for something like this."

Nicky could have sworn that the air changed in the room. Something had certainly changed.

"Shit." Garrett squeezed his eyes shut and groaned. "Nicky, I'm so sorry."

She shook her head. There were some bad ideas going through her mind, and she hoped Garrett hadn't done what she thought he had.

"Please tell me you didn't pay her off." Nicky's voice barely had any sound. That's because her breath was stalled in her lungs.

"I did," he said, reaching for her. But Nicky stepped back. "I gave her fifty thousand. I told her to leave town and never come back."

"Oh, God," Nicky said and she repeated it several times because she didn't know what else to say. "She'll be back. She always comes back."

The words from Doris's text came back to her.

I'll be in touch soon.

With Garrett's money, the woman certainly would be.

CHAPTER TWENTY-THREE

NICKY HURRIED OUT of the room, running again, and Garrett didn't stop her. That was because he didn't know what to say to her. He was still trying to wrap his head around what he'd done.

And what he'd done was screw up big-time.

Of course, he hadn't known that was what he was doing when he forked over the money to Doris. He'd thought he was ridding Nicky and Kaylee of a problem. One in the guise of a money-grubbing granny.

Even though he didn't know Doris, he had smelled trouble all over her, and apparently his nose had been right. But now that she had cash, she would go after Kaylee. Maybe not because she even wanted to raise her but simply because she didn't want Nicky to have her.

Garrett hadn't missed the venom in Doris's voice and eyes. Venom all aimed at Nicky. Probably because Nicky was the only one alive that Doris could blame for her daughter's death. He cursed Doris.

He cursed Shanda, as well, for using drugs while she was pregnant.

"Oh, dear," he heard his mother say.

Crap. He didn't want to deal with her or anyone else right now. But there she was. Already making her way into the library.

"I came in here to ask if you'd catch the crab, clean up the horse poop and talk to Lady," his mother continued, "but I can see I caught you at a bad time."

The biggest understatement in the history of understatements.

Despite his mother's having recognized his bad mood, she didn't leave. Did nothing to improve it, either. "The crab has started charging at anyone who goes into the kitchen, and I need to get more snickerdoodles from the counter. It just gets madder when you throw things at it to get it to move."

Garrett groaned, buried his face in his hands. "Mom—"

"And as for the poop, well, Jake left his horse beneath the porch awning, and it pooped," she continued as if he hadn't even spoken. "Then, there's Lady. She's trying to get into the mayor's pants."

Garrett seriously doubted the mayor minded that since he was divorced and not seeing anyone, but even if he minded, it wasn't Garrett's problem.

"Of course, you know about Nicky," his mother tossed out there.

That got him to lower his hands. "What about her?"

"Well, she was crying, and she told Gina to stay with Kaylee and the sitter, in case some woman shows up. I really hope we don't have any more surprise guests because we've had enough of that malarkey."

Yeah, they had. "I need to check on Nicky," he said, heading for the door.

"She's not here. After she told Gina to watch Kaylee, she left. She said she was going to find some woman named Doris."

Hell's Texas Bells.

"The trail is blocked, and there's a bad storm raging," Garrett grumbled. "There's no way she could have left."

"Not by car, but she took Jake's horse. That's when she noticed the poop. Anyway, she said she was going to ride the horse to the ranch and get a vehicle there."

Garrett fished his keys from his pocket. He only hoped he'd parked far enough away from the mud that he could still get out of there. If not, he'd have to walk through the pasture. At night. In a storm. No, nothing stupid about that, but he had to find Nicky and try to make things right.

Somehow.

He stopped again when something else occurred to him. "How does Nicky even know where to find Doris?" Garrett asked his mother, not expecting her to have a clue.

But she did.

"Nicky called her on the way out the door, and she's meeting the woman in town."

NICKY WAS SOAKED by the time she rode Jake's mare to the ranch. Soaked and pissed off. She'd known it could come to this, but she hadn't thought it would play out with Doris actually having the money to go after Kaylee.

Her conversation with Doris had been short and not friendly. "I want to see you now," Nicky had demanded.

"Good, I want to see you, too. I'm at the lawyer's office on Main Street in town. He stayed open late just for me." That was it, all that Doris had said, before she'd ended the call.

Nicky didn't know the lawyer, Seth Rodriguez,

since he'd only been in Wrangler's Creek a couple of months. That meant he didn't have any ties to the Grangers and might be hungry for business. Since she now had cash, Doris could have easily enticed him to stay late and take her case.

She took the horse to the barn, thankful that a hand was still there to tend to the mare, and despite the hand's offer to get her a towel, Nicky declined and had instead asked to use a vehicle. Any vehicle. The hand had given her the keys to a spare truck they used to haul hay.

She got started on the drive to town, but the weather didn't cooperate. The rain came down even harder, and despite the windshield wipers going at full speed, it was still hard to see. She forced herself to drive slowly even though she didn't want to lose another minute before confronting the woman.

But what was she going to say to her?

It'd been nearly thirty minutes since she'd called Doris, and that was enough time for the lawyer to have started the initial paperwork for Doris's custody suit. The woman would almost certainly accuse Nicky of abetting her husband to commit insurance fraud. And that meant Nicky would need her own lawyer not just to defend herself but to make sure Doris never got her hands on Kaylee.

The panic continued to build, and she realized part of the reason she couldn't see so well was because she was crying. She wouldn't lose her daughter. She just couldn't.

By the time she made it to Main Street, Nicky knew she had to rein in her emotions, especially the tears. They wouldn't help, and in fact could hurt. She didn't want Doris's lawyer to think she was on the verge of losing it. Even though it felt as if she was.

She tried not to blame Garrett for this. Because he hadn't known what Doris would do with the money. He'd no doubt believed he was fixing things, and after Nicky had calmed down some, she might be able to thank him. But not now.

Nicky pulled to a stop in front of the lawyer's office, and her stomach dropped a little when she didn't see any lights on. She hurried out of the truck, tested the doorknob.

Locked.

And there was a closed sign in the window.

She knocked, waited. No answer. So she knocked again. It wasn't a large office, just a reception area with two other rooms behind that. The doors to both of those rooms were open, and there didn't appear to be anyone in them. No way could Doris and the lawyer have finished up so quickly. So where the heck was she?

Since there wasn't any kind of awning over the lawyer's office, Nicky got back in Jake's truck to call Doris. No answer. It went straight to voice mail. She tried the number for the lawyer that was on the sign outside the office, but just like the call to Doris, he didn't answer.

What was going on?

It was too much to hope that Doris had been lying about seeing a lawyer. But maybe Seth had turned her down and sent her on her way. If so, Nicky had no idea where she would go. Judging from what Patrick had told her, Doris moved around a lot, and Nicky didn't even know where she was living these days.

Doris could be anywhere.

That didn't settle her stomach or calm the panic. In fact, it made it worse. Nicky had geared herself up for a fight. A verbal one anyway. And now she might have to wait days or longer to find out Doris's plan. It was possible the woman was on her way to San Antonio PD to try to convince the cops there to arrest Nicky.

She sent off a text to Gina to remind her to keep watch in case Doris showed up there. At least if she did, she wouldn't be able to get through on the trail, and by now Gina had almost certainly alerted everyone in the house to be on the lookout for the woman. Of course, Doris wouldn't need to resort to such measures as an attempted kidnapping because she might have the law on her side. Nicky doubted the courts would give the woman custody, but Doris might end up with visitation rights. Or even more. Split custody since Nicky had no biological connection to her little girl.

The tears came again. So did the anger. No matter what it took, Nicky would fight this.

She started the drive back to Z.T.'s and tried not to think of all the things that could go wrong. But it was too late. She was already thinking of them, but instead of it leaving her feeling defeated, Nicky tried to steel herself up. It was working.

Until she saw her old house.

Even though it was just a gray blob in the curtain of rain, she could still see it well enough for the flash-backs to come. She cursed, started to speed up so she wouldn't have to look at it for long. But something inside her snapped. Not like a dry twig, either. But the kind of snapping a person did when they were mad as hell and weren't going to take it anymore.

She turned into the driveway so fast that she nearly

went into a skid, and then Nicky hit the brakes. In that short period of time, her anger had grown by leaps and bounds. She felt like a pressure cooker ready to blow. That was probably why she didn't have any trouble marching right up the porch steps.

Nicky didn't even pause at the door. She threw it open, ready to scream. And she did that all right.

When a mouse scurried across her shoe.

She screamed like a little girl, in fact, and ran to the other side of the room.

At least she was fully inside now, and she might not have been able to do that so easily if it hadn't been for the mouse. Thankfully, it stayed put and didn't come toward her, but she kept her attention on it just in case.

The place was dark and wet. Literally. The ceiling was dripping, and the water had puddled on the floor in spots. Even over the sound of the rain on the old roof, she still heard the crunching sound and looked down. Thanks to a flash of lightning, she saw the clump of dead bugs.

Nicky's courage dipped a little, dipped even more when she realized some of the bugs in the pile were still alive. Some squashed ones were beneath her feet, too. That didn't discourage her, though, from what she had to do.

"Screw you, assholes!" she shouted just as Cassie had told her to do. Of course, Cassie had meant for this to help her deal with her childhood. Still, Nicky included Doris in that message.

She yelled it again, adding the part about the demons, including all the profanity that Cassie had told her to use. In fact, Nicky repeated it, and she just kept shouting it, her voice echoing through the empty house.

Even the bugs and the mouse ran for cover. The mouse darted into a hole in the wall near the fireplace. Bugs scurried. Heck, it felt as if the walls themselves were rattling.

And Nicky kept on yelling.

THE FIRST THING Garrett heard when he stopped his truck was Nicky screaming. He hurried out, running toward the house, only to realize she was actually cursing.

"Screw you in the demon ass!"

He'd never heard her use that kind of language, and he assumed the worst. That she was in a shouting match with Doris, and judging from the rage in Nicky's voice, it was about to get really ugly.

"Nicky?" he called out to her, and he scrambled across the wet porch and into the house. He really wanted to settle some things right here, right now. But there was no Doris.

Just Nicky.

She had her fist raised at the ceiling, the very place where she was aiming all that profanity.

"Garrett," she said on a rise of breath. Actually, her breath was gusting, and she was shaking. He peeled off his jacket and slipped it around her. "What are you doing here?"

Since that'd been what he was about to ask her, he just repeated her question. He also glanced around to see if Doris was hiding somewhere. She wasn't. In fact, the only other signs of life he saw were two mice in the corner. He wasn't sure mice could actually cower, but that was what they appeared to be doing.

Nicky didn't cower, but she glanced away from him

and relaxed her fists. "Cassie McCord said I should do this."

All right. Cassie was a therapist so maybe this was some kind of tried-and-true approach to dealing with the past. "I didn't know demons had assholes," he mumbled because he wasn't sure what else to say.

Her gaze slashed to his, and while she didn't look ready to laugh just yet, she no longer seemed to be on the verge of internal combustion.

"Did it help?" he asked.

She lifted her shoulder. "It didn't hurt."

Well, that was a start. The fact that she was actually inside this place was a start, too. At least he hoped it was. Maybe he could try fixing a few demons of his own.

"Screw you!" he yelled at the ceiling. "And F-you and everything that's ever taken a dump on us."

"F-you?" Her mouth quivered a little.

"A tribute to the Ellery sisters and their G-rated profanity."

"Yeah, I figured that out." She paused while he shouted it again. "Did it help?"

He thought about it for a moment. "Actually, it did." Though Garrett had no clue why it would.

The relief didn't last, though, because there was a flash of lightning, and he saw Nicky's wet face. He seriously doubted that was solely from the rain. No, she'd been crying.

"I'm sorry." And Garrett would say it a thousand times more if it would help.

"F-you!" she shouted. Not at him but rather at the ceiling again. "That one was for Doris," she added.

Yeah, he figured some of the cursing had been because of the woman. Some of the tears, too. But he'd also likely been responsible for some of those tears.

"Did you see her?" he asked.

Nicky shook her head, pushed her wet hair from her face and yelled out again. Garrett added his own round, aiming it at Meredith. Then, at himself.

This time, though, the ceiling responded.

There was a sharp groaning sound. Not human, thank God. But it wasn't a good sound, either. Because the ceiling was collapsing and falling in chunks to the floor. One of those chunks nearly landed right on Nicky's head, but Garrett pulled her out of the way in time.

He didn't stop. Garrett hooked his arm around her waist and got them running. Not only to the porch since its roof was falling, too. He hurried Nicky out into the yard and to his truck. The moment they shut the truck doors, there was another loud groan, much louder than the first.

And the house disappeared.

It was like something right out of a horror movie, as if the fates had gobbled it up. One second it was there, and the next it wasn't. All that was left was a pile of wood, shingles and glass.

"Shit," Nicky said, staring out the window at the heap.

His sentiments exactly. "Maybe the demons took their assholes and left." At least Garrett had managed to get them out of there in time. They could have been seriously hurt, or worse.

"Are you okay?" he asked. Nicky's gaze was frozen on the remains of the house. Perhaps she was in shock, and while he considered taking her to the ER just to be checked out, he dismissed it when he saw her smile.

It wasn't one of her dazzling smiles. This was more like one of relief. The kind of smile a person offered after completing a marathon and then puking.

She nodded. "I'm okay with this."

This, being her past. Hell, if he'd known having the house gone would help, he would have bought it and burned it down years ago. Maybe, though, the timing had to be right for this sort of thing. Ironic that this would happen when the rest of her life was falling apart.

"I want you to know that I'll do anything I can to help you with this," he said. That applied not only to Doris but to everything else that crossed Nicky's path.

She stared at him, and Garrett tried to prepare himself in case she started yelling those profanities at him. But she didn't yell. Nicky moved across the seat, put her arm around him and kissed him.

For the past couple of hours, he'd been feeling like crap, and it had gotten progressively worse as the night unfolded. But that eased the feeling. Hell, it eased everything.

Garrett felt the punch of relief. Nicky didn't hate him after all. She wasn't so pissed off at him that she couldn't kiss him. Well, unless she'd put on poison lipstick like in the spy movies. However, this didn't feel like a get-revenge kiss. This felt more like a kiss of comfort.

And of attraction, too.

That was the next thing Garrett felt—the heat. Which was a good thing because he was wet and cold, and Nicky had his jacket. He wanted her to keep it on because she had to be cold, as well, but he welcomed the warmth from her body when she landed against him.

"I'm sorry," he repeated. "I didn't know money would cause this much trouble."

She put her hand on his cheek, met his gaze. "Why did you pay her?"

Obvious question but he wasn't sure there was an easy answer. "I didn't want her anywhere near Kaylee." There was more emotion in his voice than he wanted. More emotion inside him, too. "This doesn't have anything to do with my daughter. It's all about Kaylee. I just feel...protective of her."

Nicky didn't say anything for several long moments and then she nodded. He thought that might be the beginning of a much needed conversation, but Nicky did something else that was much needed instead.

She kissed him again.

And again.

And she just kept on kissing him. Touching him, too—her hand landed on his chest, and her fingers began to play with the muscles there.

Now, his dick got involved, especially when Nicky pulled him closer and practically climbed into his lap. All in all, it was a good place to be.

Unlike the kissing session in town, there was no one else around. And with the rain sheeting down the windows, no one could see in, either. Still, he needed to make sure this wasn't some kind of kneejerk reaction on her part. After all, she'd just had that F-ing yelling session, and the house had nearly fallen down on top of them.

"Are you sure you're okay?" he asked.

She huffed softly. "I'm not happy about the money you gave her, but that's not something I can change. I can just go forward, now that's finished." Nicky tipped her head to the wrecked house. "There are a lot of things in my life that are up in the air right now, but how I feel about you isn't one of those things."

"It's not?" Because he wasn't totally certain as to how he felt about her.

"It's not," she confirmed. "Your first reaction when you saw me in the house was to give me your jacket. You tried to protect my daughter. That's the man you are. A good one. And I'd be stupid and living in the past not to feel what I feel for you."

He would have pressed her on that, but she continued to kiss him. "We don't have much time," she added. "I need to get back to check on Kaylee."

So, this was a quickie. His dick liked that idea a lot, but he kept going back to the things that she'd just said. That probably would have stayed on his mind if she hadn't lowered her hand to his zipper. It was a cliché, but a man couldn't think with both his dick and brain at the same time, and his dick won out.

Garrett pulled her all the way onto his lap and did some touching of his own.

Sex in a truck posed some logistical problems. There were plenty of things to catch his knees and elbows. Plus, the seat size sucked. But since the first place they'd had sex was on that rickety chaise, he knew they could manage this.

Nicky managed it by dropping down onto the seat and pulling him on top of her. For once she was wearing a dress. Probably something she'd put on for the party, but it was much easier than jeans when it came to panty removal. Of course, he wouldn't be able to get her totally naked, but he could maybe do that later after he got her back to Z.T.'s and kicked out the rest of the party guests.

Despite his urgency, Garrett took the time to kiss her neck and the tops of her breasts. He would have lingered a little longer if she hadn't unzipped him.

"Please tell me you have a condom," she said.

"I do. I put one in my wallet."

Actually, he'd put two in there, which made his wallet so bulky that it'd barely fit in his jeans pocket. But he had wanted to be prepared when it came to Nicky. Garrett tugged and pulled at the wallet to get it out. He also felt something else in his front pocket. Easy to feel because it was now sandwiched between Nicky's and his thighs.

It was his phone.

"By the way," she whispered, her voice all breath and silk. "I'm in love with you."

Part of him, not his dick part, realized this was not going to be the best response for him to say to Nicky. Not after she'd just told him she loved him. But it was a response that would make her life a whole lot better.

Garrett took out his phone and held it up for her to see. "I know how to fix this mess with Doris."

CHAPTER TWENTY-FOUR

NICKY PACED BECAUSE she couldn't stop herself from moving. If she stopped, she might start crying again. It wasn't every night a woman learned she might lose her daughter, got to confront her demons, told a man she was in love with him and then also found out that man might be the very one to prevent her from losing her child.

At least she wasn't soaking wet as she paced in the Wrangler's Creek Police Station while she waited for Clay to bring in Doris. That was the good news. The bad news was that the only spare clothes in the building had belonged to the deputy, Rowdy. They were baggy gray gym shorts and a T-shirt with the high school logo. Since Rowdy was in his thirties, these were no doubt relics from his days at Wrangler's Creek High.

Judging from the smell of them, they hadn't been washed in all that time.

But at least she was dry, and if what Clay told them was accurate, he'd be arriving soon with Doris. He'd tracked down the woman at the San Antonio PD where she'd gone to file a complaint against Nicky. Instead of that complaint, though, Doris would be facing her own charges.

Well, maybe.

Garrett had recorded her saying that she would

accept money to leave Kaylee alone, but something like that might not hold up in court. Maybe, though, it would be enough to get the woman to back off.

Garrett came back into Clay's office with yet another cup of coffee for her. Nicky took it, not because she needed the caffeine. She had already had enough that she could probably run on foot to San Antonio and get Doris. However, it was hot and gave her hands something to do other than tremble. She wasn't cold, but the bone-deep emotion was catching up with her.

He kissed her forehead, eased her into his arms, mindful not to spill her coffee. Again, he was being nice. Garrett was indeed a good man, as she'd pointed out to him in the truck. She'd also mention the "I'm in love with you," as well, but he hadn't reacted to it. She doubted it was because he hadn't heard her.

Maybe at that exact moment Garrett had remembered the recording on his phone. Or maybe it was a good time for him to remember it since he didn't want to have to respond to what she'd said. Too bad. Because she wanted to know how he felt.

But she wasn't sure her heart was strong enough right now if he gave it another stomping.

"You're sure you're up to facing Doris tonight?" Garrett asked. "It's late, and Clay could hold her until morning. You could talk to her after you've gotten some sleep."

"I won't get any sleep."

Since he made a quick sound of agreement, that was possibly true for him, too. Nicky wanted to be there not only when Clay questioned Doris but when he brought her in, as well.

Garrett brushed another kiss on her forehead. "How long has it been since you've seen her?"

"Over a year. Before that she would call several times a week, and a couple of times she actually came to my house and tried to see Kaylee. That's when I moved."

"A year," Garrett repeated. "Considering how much she claims to want and love her granddaughter, that's a long time to go without any contact."

"Well, she wasn't in jail or anything like that. I did internet searches," she added.

"Is she the sort to have gotten involved with a man who could have, well, distracted her from all that grandmotherly love?"

Nicky had to shrug. "Shanda did tell Patrick she didn't want her mother to get her hands on Kaylee, so you might be onto something."

Her phone rang, the sound shooting through the room. Nicky realized just how on edge she was when she gasped. She wanted to gasp again when she saw Gina's name on the screen. Since it was close to midnight, Nicky prayed that nothing was wrong.

"Everything's fine here," Gina said right off the bat. That took Nicky's heart out of her throat. "Kaylee is sacked out, and the guests who couldn't make it out are all settled in. Ruby even caught the crab. She named him Herman and made a box for her new pet."

Nicky had to smile. "Did you mention to Ruby that she'd eaten some of Herman's friends?"

"No. She seemed eager to have something to take care of. So, how are you?"

Garrett stepped out, maybe to give her some privacy, and that's when Nicky spilled it. "I told Garrett that I loved him."

Silence on the other end of the line. "And?" Gina said a moment later.

"And nothing. We ended up here so we could tell Clay about Doris." Nicky paused. "Maybe that's for the best. I mean, how do I know that it wasn't just the emotion talking?"

"It was the emotion. That's what love is. And you're not the sort of woman to say that just for the sake of saying it."

No, she wasn't. And it was true. Damn it. While she was F-wording all those demons at the old house, she should have added some F-yous for love. Because love didn't make things better. It complicated everything and made your heart hurt.

Though the heart pain could be indigestion from the party food she'd sampled.

Still, there was a metaphorical hurt, too.

"So, what are you going to do about Garrett?" Gina asked.

She hadn't really thought about it, but this seemed the safe thing to do. "I'll give him some space, some time to figure out if he wants to date me or something."

"Date you? Date you!" Judging from the way Gina howled that twice, she thought dating was a bad idea. "He's had sex with you. You're well past the dating stage."

It certainly didn't feel like it. Not on Garrett's part anyway.

Nicky heard the voices in the squad room, and one of those voices belonged to Clay. "I have to go. I'll be back in touch as soon as I can," she added and ended the call.

She put her coffee on Clay's desk and hurried out into the squad room. With the way her day had gone, Nicky half expected for Doris not to be with him. But she was.

Doris hadn't fared much better with the storm than Nicky had. The woman's hair was wet and stuck to her head. Her mascara had run down her face all the way to her mouth. And her clothes were clinging to her body. Nicky smirked at her.

Doris smirked back, and that's when Nicky remembered she was wearing Rowdy's gym uniform. But at least it wasn't wet and clinging to her.

"You sent your lackey cowboy cop friend to bring me in?" Doris snarled.

"Last I heard that's what we lackeys do," Clay grumbled. His sour expression said it all. This had not been a pleasant drive from San Antonio. "Come on back to my office," he instructed.

"I don't want to go to your office. I want you to take these cuffs off me now so I can call my lawyer."

Nicky hadn't noticed the cuffs, but she looked at Clay for an explanation. "She didn't cooperate when I asked her to come with me. It's illegal not to cooperate with someone in law enforcement."

"Because you're a lackey!" Doris yelled.

"You've already established that. Now, cooperate and walk to my office. Then, I'll consider removing the cuffs. But I have to tell you that we lackeys sometimes lose cuff keys."

Doris gave him a you-wouldn't-dare glare, but she

did go with Clay to his office. Nicky and Garrett followed them in.

Clay took the key from his pocket and held it up for Doris to see. "Here's the one and only warning you'll get. If you try to assault anyone or if you even look as if that's what you're going to do, then the cuffs go back on."

He waited until Doris gave a crisp nod before he took off the cuffs. In the same motion, he turned his phone in her direction. "You can call your lawyer now."

Doris's jaw tightened. "I don't have one yet, but I will first thing in the morning. That local yokel lackey lawyer you've got here refused to take my case."

Nicky wanted to cheer. Seth hadn't taken the case, which meant there hadn't been any paperwork filed.

"Sit," Clay told the woman. "I'll get you a phone book so you can look up numbers for a whole bunch of lawyers."

He went back into the squad room but not before giving Doris another warning glare. He was good at them, too.

"The cop said you recorded our conversation," Doris said to Garrett. "He even played it for me. That proves nothing."

"Yeah, it does. It proves you asked me for money to leave Kaylee alone. I think they call that extortion."

"I didn't demand it. I only mentioned that it would be nice if I had some extra cash."

"So you can try to take my daughter," Nicky supplied at the same moment Garrett said, "So, you can get custody of Kaylee and then maybe have enough left over for a fling with some guy who'll dump you after a couple of months. Then, you could come back to Nicky and extort more money from her if she wants Kaylee back."

Doris's eyes narrowed. "I won't dignify that with a response. Did Nicky tell you about the insurance fraud?"

"You mean your daughter's insurance fraud? The one you probably knew about because after all, Shanda was *your* daughter. Nicky never met Shanda before Kaylee was born."

Doris moved to the edge of her seat. "Prove it."

"I will. That's what good PIs are for."

Garrett wrote something down on a piece of paper and handed it to her. "That's what I'm worth, give or take a million or two. And no, I'm not offering you another penny of it. That's just to let you know what you're up against. I have lawyers on retainer. Good ones. That fifty grand I gave you will run out very fast when you butt heads with them. I will have them tie you up in court for so long that the stick up your ass will petrify."

Clay came back in the room, lifted an eyebrow because he'd likely heard that, and he dropped an old thick phone book on the desk next to her.

"You're threatening me," Doris said to Garrett. "He's threatening me," she repeated to Clay.

Clay only shrugged. "No crime against a man mentioning petrified ass sticks."

Nicky wrote down her own figures on a note and slid it toward Doris. "That's what I'm worth." It was a drop in the bucket compared to Garrett's, and even that drop was exaggerated.

Nicky went closer. Doris stood, towering over her,

but Nicky didn't let her size intimidate her. She was fighting for her daughter here.

"I'll use that money and every lawyer friend I have to stop you," Nicky assured her. "I didn't survive a dickhead of a father just for my little girl to end up with the likes of you."

"The likes of me!" Doris shouted.

Clay dangled the cuffs. "Remember that part about not looking like you're about to commit an assault."

Doris didn't calm down, but she didn't come closer, either. She volleyed her gaze among the three of them. No doubt trying to figure out her next move.

"I want that recording destroyed," Doris finally said.

She might as well have asked for the moon. "Lackey cowboy cops don't destroy evidence in a criminal investigation. Now, Nicky and Garrett are going to leave so they can get some rest. You're going to stay and give me a statement. I've already got theirs, and the recording, of course. Seems to me I've got a very easy case to prove."

Doris just stood there.

"Let me spell this out for you," Nicky told her. "You will never—*never*—get your hands on my daughter."

Doris glanced at the cuffs that Clay was still dangling. She then looked at the two notes with the money figures that Nicky and Garrett had written down.

"We lackeys stick together," Nicky added, staring down the woman.

Nicky managed a smile, and she took hold of Garrett's arm and walked out. Her father might not have been proud, but even he would have had to admit something.

That tonight, she'd finally grown a pair.

SEX WITH NICKY—one of Garrett's favorite things. And he was really into the best part of the favorite thing. Just a few more thrusts inside all that heat and he'd be whistling Dixie.

Whatever the heck that meant.

He frowned, not liking that the whistling metaphor was interrupting this. So were the sounds. It was like a dozen footsteps coming at him at once. And that's when Garrett realized this was a dream.

His eyes flew open, and he jackknifed to a sitting position. Not a good idea. Not with a raging hard-on. Also not with real people making those real footstep sounds. There was a group of women coming at him, and none of them was Nicky.

He looked around for her but realized he'd been sleeping on the chaise in the library at Z.T.'s house. His back hurt. Butt, too. His erection wasn't feeling especially happy, either, at being interrupted by, well, whatever the devil this was.

There was Lady, Ruby, Ginger, D.M. and his mother. All of them pattering their way toward him.

"I told you he'd be up by now," his mother said. "He never sleeps this late. Garrett is always up with the chickens."

Well, he was up all right, but there were no chickens involved. He fumbled around, located a blanket and pulled it over his lap. It probably didn't hide what he wanted hidden, but it was the best he could do since he couldn't stand up and walk out of there.

"Where's Nicky?" he asked.

His mother smiled at the others. "Told you he'd ask about her right off. Ah, young love."

Garrett didn't smile, though. That was because he

remembered Nicky telling him she loved him. No, not that she loved him but rather was *in love* with him.

Big difference.

"Last I saw Nicky she was in the kitchen," Ruby said. "Say hello to Herman." She thrust the box toward him, and he saw the crab inside. Both the crab and Ruby's maternal expression looked creepy.

Lady scowled at the crab before turning to Garrett. "I just wanted to pop in to say goodbye before I left. Yes, I'm leaving," she added as if everyone would be upset about that. The Garden Guild certainly wouldn't be.

"Why'd you decide to go?" he asked. And he wondered if he could talk her into leaving sooner. Talk all of them into leaving so he could locate a cold shower and then see Nicky.

"Well, all that towing last night made me remember how much I love doing that. It works out the sexual frustrations, you know. I think that's why I've been so horny since I've been here."

His mother and Ginger groaned. D.M. was cleaning her fingernails with a pocketknife.

"Bullshit," D.M. said, followed with a tic motion of her head. "Breathing makes you horny."

Lady gave them the same look she'd given the crab before she continued with Garrett. "Anyway, I'm also expanding the towing business to include roadside repairs. I've already got ideas for signs and logos." She fanned her right hand in the air. "'Let's Hook Up' with a picture of a tow hook. Then, on the other side, I could put 'Panties in Your Crack over a Flat Tire?—I Won't Jack You Off.'" Lady grinned. "What do you think?"

Garrett didn't want to endorse crappy advertisements like that, but if he tried to dissuade her, it would only lengthen this conversation. "Those work for me."

Lady aimed smirks at the other women who clearly had done the right thing by attempting to dissuade her, and she moved in on Garrett as if to kiss him goodbye. But he waved her off.

"Morning breath," he said.

That seemed to satisfy Lady, perhaps a first since her arrival at the ranch, and she gave him a smile before leaving. One down, too many to go.

"That crab looks hungry or something," Garrett told Ruby, and after she glanced down at it, she nodded and hurried off.

"Bullshit," D.M. grumbled. "But it was a good use of bullshit," she added before she left.

He was thinning the herd and looked at Ginger next. "Could you please give me a moment alone with my mom?"

"Oh, of course. You want to talk about being in love with Nicky."

"Uh, no. But we have other things to discuss." Hopefully something that would soften him up enough so he could stand. But it did make him wonder where they'd gotten this notion of him being in love with Nicky. He doubted Nicky had said anything, so maybe it was just wishful thinking on their parts.

"The sisters are gone," his mother said after Ginger had left. "I think they're going to try to work things out with their husbands."

"Really?" Garrett hadn't thought much more could surprise him. "You believe the sisters can get past the fact that the men faked their deaths so they wouldn't have to be around their wives?"

Belle shrugged. "It's either that or divorce, and those women don't look like the divorce type to me."

Yeah, she was right about that. "Are you okay about how things turned out with Loretta?" he asked.

She gave another sigh, sank down on the chaise next to him. "No. I don't like that she sneaked around and saw that man in this house, but I forgive her, and I'm hoping she'll come back."

"You think she could be here after everything that happened?"

She shrugged. "People stay lots of places where unpleasant things happened. Well, everyone but your brother. Roman ran away from home and didn't come back."

Roman hadn't exactly run, but anything that Garrett said would only cause his mother to go on the defensive. Deep in her heart she had to know that it'd been a mistake to judge Roman for not marrying the mother of his son. But maybe she'd lived with the mistake for so long that it was hard to admit it.

"Anyway, Jake let us know that he got Loretta back to her house safe and sound. He did seem a little worried about her, though. It's a big house, and she's all alone there. Poor dear never was able to have kids, you know."

"You should call her and talk to her," Garrett suggested.

His mother eyed him with suspicion in a way that only a mother could do. "Is this about Nicky?"

Garrett couldn't see much of a correlation between his comment about calling Loretta and Nicky, but he nodded anyway, kissed his mother's cheek. "I should check on her."

"Yes, you should." His mother stood. "She needs cheering up. She was all down in the dumps this morning, I could tell. It's as if something didn't go her way. Any idea what?"

"No," he lied. But it put a knot in his stomach to hear she was down. Of course, after everything that'd happened, that was probably normal.

"Well, if she truly wants to leave," his mother went on, "please tell her that I'll run the place for her. I don't want to give up on the widows who need help."

That hit him like a bag of bricks. "Leave? Did Nicky say she was leaving?"

"I'm certain I heard her mention something about that," Belle said while she was walking away.

Well, hell.

When had she come to that decision? When they'd gotten back to the house the night before, she'd been wiped out and headed straight for bed, but she hadn't said a thing about either *L* word.

Love or leaving.

That got Garrett off the chaise, and he went in search of an unoccupied bathroom. There were five in the house, and maybe because so many of the widows had left, the first one he tried was empty. He hurried in, showered in record time and nearly ran into Kaylee when he opened the door.

"Gare-if. I got a boo-boo." She held out her arm for him to see the scratch. It was small, barely visible, but clearly it was causing her distress. She was looking at it as if her arm might need to be amputated.

"I'm sorry. Does it hurt?"

She nodded, then shook her head. "It hurts a little bitty."

Well, that was some hurt that he didn't want her to feel. He went through the medicine cabinet, not sure what he would find, but it had obviously been stocked. He took out some antiseptic cream and a Band-Aid and doctored it. He kissed the top of the bandage when he was done.

"All better," she said, hugging him.

There it was again. That raw emotion, except it no longer felt as raw as it once had. It felt somewhat sweet, warm and gooey. Which made it sound a little like a cookie straight from the oven. But he also felt something else.

Fiercely protective of this little girl.

Yeah, he'd use every penny of his Granger money to make sure she stayed with Nicky.

Kaylee didn't let go after a few hugging moments so Garrett scooped her up in his arms. She might need some mommy TLC, as well, so he went in search of Nicky.

She wasn't in the kitchen so he tried her room. Not there, either. And she wasn't in the parlor.

"There you are," Gina said when he came out of one of the rooms. But her comment was clearly meant for Kaylee because she reached out her hands for the girl. Kaylee, though, shook her head and tightened her grip around Garrett.

"She's got a boo-boo," Garrett explained.

Gina peeked beneath the bandage and saw that it was okay. "Cowboys say *boo-boo*?" she asked, her mouth quivering a little.

"This cowboy does. My manhood can withstand that kind of hit."

Gina didn't smile, and he could feel the tension

between them return. It was nothing like that sweet, warm and gooey vibe he'd gotten from Kaylee.

"One of the sisters found rusty pliers before she left," Gina whispered. "If you make Nicky cry again, I might consider using them on you."

"Nicky cried?" Garrett obviously said that louder than he'd intended because he noticed alarm on Kaylee's face. He was certain there was alarm on his face, too, because first his mother had said Nicky might be leaving and now he heard she'd been crying.

Gina nodded. "She's on the front porch."

Since he didn't want Kaylee there for a crying/leaving conversation, he kissed her cheek and handed her to Gina.

"I love you," Kaylee said.

"I love you, too," Garrett answered without thinking.

"See?" Gina asked. "That wasn't so hard, was it?"

No, it wasn't. And he'd meant it. But what he felt for Kaylee had nothing to do with Nicky. Well, almost nothing.

Garrett headed for the porch, trying to prepare himself for Nicky's tears. And he found her all right. But she wasn't crying.

His mouth went dry.

And where the hell had all the air gone?

She was sitting on the top step, leaning against the porch railing. Barefooted and wearing shorts and a sleeveless top that exposed a lot of the skin on her arms and legs. The morning sun was hitting her just right, haloing all that blond hair that fell loose on the tops of her shoulders. She looked like some kind of nature goddess who'd stopped for a bite to eat.

And what she was eating was a snickerdoodle.

She not only looked amazing, but she smelled that way, too.

Nicky was also smiling, and that smile stayed on her mouth even after she saw him. "You're up," she said, and she patted the spot next to her.

Well, if this was her way of saying goodbye, then she seemed darn happy about it. Which pissed him off a little. Garrett tried not to show that, but crap on a cracker, he didn't want her to be happy about going.

"Clay just called," she continued. "It's official. He's arrested Doris, and she wants to work out a plea deal. He says the only way he'll agree to that is for the charges to stay on her record. That should make it next to impossible for her to win a custody suit."

Maybe that was why Nicky was smiling. It was good news. And maybe that good news had temporarily dried up her tears.

"Doris didn't have the money on her," Nicky went on. "And she claims she's already spent it so you might be out fifty grand. I'll pay you back, of course, but it might take a while."

"I don't want you to pay me back. I spent that much on bull sperm last month."

She made a face.

"Hey, cows need sperm," he added.

Nicky smiled again. "You should suggest that slogan to Lady."

"I would, but she'd probably like it enough to use it." He paused, took the piece of the cookie she offered him. "By the way, I don't want any damn space."

Garrett certainly didn't smile. Good grief. It was as

if he needed Language 101 when he was around Nicky. Best to give her more of a reference for that.

"I heard what you said to Gina when you were on the phone in Clay's office," he explained. "Someone should tell him he needs thicker walls."

Well, she sure as hell wasn't smiling now. "What else did you hear?"

"Every word," he admitted. "Not Gina's words, though, because you didn't have it on speaker, but I'm sure she was bad-mouthing me because of the way I acted when you told me you loved me. I acted that way because I really did remember the recording on my phone, and because...well, because I didn't know what else to say."

Her next smile didn't quite make it to her eyes. She brushed a kiss on his lips, but it was too chaste for a Nicky kiss. "By not knowing what to say, you said it all."

"Say what?" He apparently needed Language 101 interpretation skills, too.

"If the answer wasn't obvious..."

Oh.

That.

He heard the movement behind him and saw that they now had an audience. Most of the women, including his mother, were now watching from the windows. No doubt listening, too, because D.M. had raised the window a few inches. Plenty of space for the group to find out just how he was going to fix this. The only ones missing were Gina and Kaylee.

"My granddaddy used to say if you find yourself in a hole, then quit digging," Garrett told Nicky, and he leaned in and kissed her. Not one of those pecks, either. This was a hole-getting-out-of kiss. At least he hoped it was.

It did leave Nicky a little breathless, and it gave him the beginnings of another hard-on. So it was a good kiss after all. It was a start, but he knew he needed more.

"You know that answer you just mentioned?" he asked. "Well, I didn't know the answer last night, but I do now. First, though, I want to ask you out on a date. Several of them. In fact, I want to ask you out for Friday and Saturday nights for the next six months."

Nicky stared at him. "That's your answer?"

"Part of it. More like an introductory offer. I'm in love with you."

There. He'd said it. And better yet, he meant it. Garrett expected that to get Nicky jumping into his arms for some more of those kisses. Maybe some celebratory sex, too, if he could get her away from their audience.

An audience who was celebrating with whispers and soft happy squeals. Apparently, this was the outcome they'd wanted. It was an outcome Garrett was pretty damn pleased about, as well. Except for one thing. Nicky hadn't said those words right back to him.

His heart stopped.

And he felt the panic start to race through him. He didn't think that was a sugar hit from the cookie, either.

"Say something," he insisted to Nicky. "Say the right thing," he amended.

She leaned in, put her mouth to his ear. "I'm in love with you."

Just like that, the panic vanished. His heart started to beat again, and he kissed Nicky, hauling her onto his lap. He kept the kiss as tame as he could manage, considering that he was suddenly starving. And not for any more of that cookie.

But for Nicky.

He stood while he still could and pulled her into his arms. "We can take things slow," he said to her, knowing that wasn't going to happen.

Apparently, someone else felt the same way because a voice came from the window. D.M.'s voice. And she muttered one very appropriate word.

"Bullshit."

* * * * *

Now, turn the page for a special bonus story,
ONE GOOD COWBOY, also set in
Wrangler's Creek,
by USA TODAY *bestselling author*
Delores Fossen...

ONE GOOD COWBOY

CHAPTER ONE

THERE WAS A cowboy lying on the bar of the Longhorn Saloon. From the doorway, Evie Martin stared at his tall, lean body.

This wasn't good.

She needed to get to work, but first she would apparently have to deal with a passed-out drunk. A drunk who wore faded jeans, an unbuttoned denim shirt and scuff-toed cowboy boots, and had a pair of red lace panties partially covering his face. His last moments of consciousness had probably been exciting, to say the least.

The rain spat against her back, and Evie stepped inside to save the few dry places left on her jeans and top. A trio of overhead whirling fans spilled cool, brisk air onto her.

She tiptoed around the toppled chairs, peanut shells and other assorted food remains. The floor was gluey, so sticky in spots that she had to work her shoes loose a couple of times.

Bud Wiser—his real name—was in the corner eyeballing the mess much as she was except there was even more dread on his craggy face because he worked for Evie's father, Dale, who owned the Longhorn. That meant Bud was going to have to clean this up.

Evie took a deep breath before she spoke. "What happened here?"

"It was a bachelor party, of sorts." Bud had a broom in one hand and a mop and pail in the other. "Don't think it was planned. It just sorta sprung up real late last night, and everybody in town including the Busby boys got in on it."

Well, she hoped whoever had done the "springing up" had paid for this. If not, her father was going to have a cow or two. "Is that why you called me, so I could smooth things over with my dad?" Because it was highly likely her dad didn't know. He didn't work Wednesday nights so none of this had happened on his shift.

"Nope. I called you because of the note pinned to the cowboy's chest. The cowboy with the red panties on his face," Bud added.

There was no need for that clarification since there was only one such cowboy in the room. But what she did need was clarification as to why he would be wearing a note that had anything to do with her.

Evie stopped just short of the bar, reached over and raked the panties off his face. They landed on his neck. Still, he didn't move, but it gave her a better look at him. And in this case, a better look was all she needed to know who he was.

Carson Rowley.

A cattle broker from San Antonio and the absolute last person she expected to find passed out like this. If Evie had been guessing who was likely to end up here, she would have put every other adult in Wrangler's Creek on her list, including the town's three ministers. At the top of that list would have been Bennie Martindale, Carson's business partner.

Bennie was also her on-again, off-again boyfriend.

This kind of "sprung-up" party was exactly something he would have done. Ditto for being on the bar with the red panties.

Evie checked out the note next. And yes, it was pinned to Carson's shirt. Someone had scrawled, "Call Evie and tell her I'm sorry." There was no signature.

She gave Carson's arm a shake, and as if hinged at the waist, he snapped to a sitting position. His bloodshot eyes flared open to reveal stormy blue irises. Like some angry force to be reckoned with, he growled and wrenched his mouth into a jagged line.

"Had too much to drink?" she asked.

He groaned again. This one had a *you think?* smart-aleck quality to it. He grabbed the panties off his neck and looked at them as if they were a UFO. For a second she thought he was about to ask her how they'd gotten there.

Or if they were hers.

But instead he groaned again, tossed the panties on the floor and got off the bar. He winced every inch of the way before his feet landed on the floor.

"There's a stampede going on in my head," he grumbled.

Not surprising. Also not surprising that Carson still managed to look hot despite the wincing and groaning. Of course, he always had that effect on her. Forbidden fruit and all that. Not that he would have given in to anything forbidden. Nope. Not Carson. He was a good guy and as loyal as a brother to Bennie.

Even when Bennie didn't deserve such loyalty.

"Want to explain this?" she asked, touching the note.

Not a good idea because he shifted just as she touched. Since his shirt was still wide-open, she ended up fingering his chest. He noticed, too. Carson spun toward her. Then, he groaned because the spinning had probably caused that stampede in his head to get even worse.

He looked down at the note much as he'd done with the panties. When he groaned again, she could tell that whatever had gone on here was coming back to him and that it wasn't especially something he wanted to share with her.

"Did Bennie get you drunk and leave you here?" Evie went behind the bar and started a pot of coffee, which she figured Carson was going to need.

Carson didn't jump to verify that, which meant the answer was yes. "Is my truck in the parking lot?"

"No. Sorry. When I drove up, the only vehicle out there was Bud's old car." And speaking of Bud, he'd started in on the cleaning.

"Then I'll need to call for a ride." He looked up at her, maybe some of the fog clearing in his head. "Aren't you supposed to be at work?"

"Soon."

Which meant she'd need to text her boss, Garrett Granger, and let him know she was going to be a little late. He wouldn't bust her chops about it, but since she was his bookkeeper and Garrett ran the biggest ranch in the county, there would be work that needed to be done. Also, it was tax season, and Evie knew the paperwork would just pile up if she wasn't there to help Garrett put out some fires.

First though, she had this particular fire to put out.

"I need you to tell me what happened so I can explain this to my father," Evie pressed.

Carson certainly didn't jump to do that, but he nearly wrenched the coffee from her hand when she poured him a cup. Despite it being scalding hot, he had two long sips, paused and then looked at her.

"Bennie ran off with a stripper," he finally said.

That wasn't nearly as surprising as finding Carson on the bar, but Evie figured there was a lot more that went with that comment. She poured herself some coffee and went back around the bar so she could face him.

"Ran off as in eloped?" she asked.

His mouth tightened and twisted as if he were at war with the words he was about to say. "Yes. God, Evie, I'm so sorry."

Evie was thankful for his apology, but it wasn't necessary. "Are those her panties?"

"Yeah. She had a purse full of the damn things and was handing them out like party favors."

Evie figured that wasn't all the stripper had been handing out. Especially not to Bennie. She'd always said Bennie could charm the underpants off a nun, but in this case, he probably hadn't even had to turn on that dazzling smile to accomplish that.

Carson stared at her. Well, as much of a stare as he could manage, considering he was still having trouble focusing. "You're not crying or carrying on."

She dismissed that with a shrug. "I quit crying and carrying on about Bennie years ago."

But apparently no one had noticed that. According to everyone who knew her, she was still Bennie's girl. She could thank her mother and Bennie's foster mom for perpetuating that myth.

"You're really not upset?" Carson asked in the same tone he might have used trying to determine if she were an alien.

She huffed and nearly blurted out that there were only two things upsetting her right now. This mess, which he had yet to explain, and the fact Carson had never noticed that she practically threw herself at him.

Because she had the hots for him. So very bad.

Evie hadn't been as obvious about her attraction as the stripper probably had been, but she'd tried to send out all the signals that she was interested in him. Flirting, smiles, visits to his office when she knew Bennie wouldn't be there. Carson had maybe picked up on those signals, too, but he'd ignored them because of his loyalty to Bennie.

That "Bennie's girl" label was like a flashing neon sign looped around her neck and drowning her. Probably drowning Bennie, too. But this stripper thing might help with that.

"I don't think it's too late to fix this," Carson went on after gulping down more coffee. "I mean, Bennie likely sobered up before he got to Vegas so he could get married."

Vegas. Yep, that sounded like Bennie, too. "How did his so-called bachelor party end up here?"

Even though Bennie and Carson had both been raised in Wrangler's Creek, they now lived nearly an hour away in San Antonio where they ran their cattle broker business. The only time Bennie came back to town was to see her. The only time Carson came to town was to do business with Garrett since Carson and Bennie supplied some of the Granger Ranch's livestock. When Carson was in Wrangler's Creek, he usually stopped by the Longhorn, and she would see him then if that's when she happened to be working her second job as bookkeeper for her father.

Carson dodged her gaze. Not a good sign. She had to put her fingers underneath his chin and lift it to see what was going on in his eyes. Whatever it was, it was something he didn't want to tell her.

"Bennie came to Wrangler's Creek to break off things with you for good," Carson confessed. "He said he just couldn't stay with you to please my mom."

Thank God. It was about time that Bennie grew a pair about that. Of course, it was possible Carson's mom, Ida, wasn't going to believe him. Yes, Ida thought of Bennie as her own son and knew his faults, but the woman must have believed that Evie could somehow make him less irresponsible.

Evie figured that would take a miracle.

Evie's own mom was part of the problem, too. In her mom's mind, if you lost your virginity to a guy, you were noosed to him forever.

Even if that de-virging had happened a decade ago.

And even if it'd been more than a year since Bennie had been in her bed.

In hindsight, it had been a mistake to let her mom see her sneaking inside the house after getting out of Bennie's car. Evie had been just seventeen then and had walked into an ambush. Her mother had been waiting for her and had spotted the love bites on her neck. The one on the top of her left boob, too, since her shirt had slipped off her shoulder. Her mom had taken that as a future marriage proposal from Bennie.

"You're not upset," Carson repeated. "Well, you

should be. Bennie acted like an ass. And he did it at a time like this."

Uh-oh. He got that look in his eyes, and Evie knew what was coming. The "poor, pitiful you" attitude that she didn't want. It was second only to the "Bennie's girl" label.

"How are you doing, by the way?" Carson asked a heartbeat later.

Bingo. There it was. The sympathy. Over the past year, *sympathy* had become a very ugly word to her.

Ever since she'd been diagnosed with kidney cancer.

She'd gone through the surgery to remove the tumor, the treatments to make sure it didn't come back, and still none of that had been as bad as those looks of sympathy. People treated her like glass.

As if she were damaged.

Broken.

And that hurt more than the cancer had.

"I'm so tired of this," she mumbled.

Carson nodded. "Yeah, Bennie can be irresponsible. Don't worry. I'll go after him and fix it."

He would. Carson would fix this the way he had the other times Bennie had cheated and done something reckless. Bennie wasn't blood kin to Carson, but Carson's folks had practically raised Bennie when he'd been a troubled teen. No way would Carson drop his "good guy" label to let this stay unfixed and hook up with her.

Sometimes, labels sucked.

"I didn't mean I was tired of Bennie's shenanigans," Evie corrected. "Bennie's just Bennie. He screws up. You bail him out. And for reasons I'll never understand, your mom and my mom think Bennie and I are the perfect match. Well, we're not."

"That's the shock talking." Carson touched her arm, rubbed gently as if to soothe her. "Once it wears off—"

"It's not Bennie I want, it's you," she blurted out.

This was another example of hindsight being twenty-twenty. It just hadn't been a good idea to spring this on Carson like that. Even if he knew she was attracted to him—and she highly suspected he did—Carson was dealing with a hangover and the guilt over having his best friend's "girl" throw herself at him.

Evie decided what the heck. Since she was throwing, she might as well go for broke. She caught on to the front of Carson's shirt, balling the fabric into her fist, pulled him to her and did the unthinkable.

She kissed him.

CHAPTER TWO

THE KISS HIT Carson hard and fast. And it was so good that it stunned him into not reacting faster. Too bad. Because he got the sweet taste of Evie before he remembered this couldn't be happening.

Carson stepped back, hoping he looked merely surprised and not aroused. If Evie looked in the direction of his zipper, though, she'd know just how her kiss had affected him.

"Bennie…" he reminded her.

"Is married to a stripper," she reminded him right back.

Maybe. But even if Bennie had done something stupid like marrying that woman, Carson was sure he would come to his senses and try to work out things with Evie. He always did. Everybody in Wrangler's Creek knew Bennie and Evie were destined to be together. Carson couldn't screw that up.

Even if that kiss had sucker punched him with a doubt or two.

Doubts aside, he had to do the right thing here. After everything she'd been through, Evie deserved that. Of course, there were times, like now, when he thought she deserved better than Bennie but that was his semi-erection talking.

Man, when he screwed up, he went for the gold medal in screwing up. First, he'd followed Bennie here to Wrangler's Creek to get him from a bachelor's party at the strip club just up the road. That party had been for Bennie's friend Jake Monroe but Bennie had called Carson to come and get him because he'd had too much to drink.

Bennie hadn't been alone, either.

A stripper had been with him, and that was when Carson made his second mistake. Bennie had tried to talk Carson into taking them home. To meet Carson's mom. Since that would have gone over like a lead balloon, Carson had taken them to the Longhorn instead.

After that, things were fuzzy.

Carson remembered ordering a virgin margarita. Which clearly wasn't virgin. Also clearly, he'd had more than one of them. Somewhere along the way, his common sense had gone out to take a leak and hadn't come back because he'd ended up joining in on Bennie's celebration.

Even while drunk, it hadn't seemed a good idea, though.

Now he knew it'd been a damn stupid one.

Carson gulped some more coffee, hoping it would ease the stampede in his head to a mere gallop. It didn't. But he couldn't take the time for the caffeine to work. He needed to get started on this before his mom found out.

Too late.

There was some movement in the open doorway of the Longhorn, and he watched as three people hurried in out of the rain. Evie's dad, Roy. Her mother, LuAnn, and Carson's own mother, Ida.

The trio was already scowling.

Of course, none of them was aiming a scowl at Evie, only him. He doubted the facial expressions were about his aroused state, either, but just in case, he lowered his coffee mug to the front of his jeans.

LuAnn and Ida had been friends since birth, as they liked to tell people. They'd been born on the same day, only a few minutes apart, and as preemies, they'd shared an incubator since the hospital only had one at the time. They'd had double weddings. Ida, however, had gotten pregnant with Carson almost immediately. LuAnn hadn't had Evie—or rather Evette Elise—until eight years later. Both women had stopped after just one child.

If there'd been a picture in the dictionary of helicopter moms, LuAnn's and Ida's faces would have been there.

It'd been the age gap that had made LuAnn and Ida decide that Carson and Evie weren't right for each other but that Bennie was, since Evie and he were the same age. Carson could see their logic and maybe would have agreed with it.

If Evie hadn't deserved better, that was.

"Baby Girl," LuAnn said, rushing to Evie. "We're gonna make this right."

"I promise, we will," Ida added. "Bennie shouldn't have treated you this way, what with your c-a-n-c-e-r and all."

To the best of Carson's knowledge his mom had never actually said the word aloud in front of Evie. Maybe Ida couldn't bring herself to say it. Either that, or she thought Evie couldn't spell and therefore didn't know what she was talking about.

Evie's father didn't get in on the conversation. He just kept scowling, but that was because he was looking at the mess left by the partiers. Carson took out his wallet, emptied the entire contents onto the bar.

"If that's not enough, send me a bill," Carson offered.

That still didn't get the scowl off Roy's face, and the gaze he'd been volleying around the mess finally settled on Carson. "You couldn't stop Bennie from doing this?"

"The situation got away from me," Carson settled for saying. He thought maybe that'd happened in between his seventh and eight shots of tequila.

Roy's gaze went from the coffee mug to the red panties on the floor. Back to Carson's mouth.

Hell, Carson hoped he didn't look as if he'd just been kissed.

"I've been trying to call Bennie," Ida went on, "but he's not answering."

No surprise. Bennie was probably either still drunk or having wild sex with his stripper-wife. Either way, Carson needed to track him down. And get to work. That was going to be hard to do when he didn't have a clue where his truck was. It was possible that Bennie had used it to go somewhere. Hopefully, though, he'd gotten someone sober to drive it.

"You can drop me off at the Granger Ranch," Evie said to him, clearly figuring out what was on his mind. "Then, you can use my car."

Normally, Carson wouldn't have wanted to put her out like that, but he did need a vehicle, and he certainly didn't want his mom chauffeuring him around. Especially since he didn't want her to hear the things he was going to say to Bennie when he finally got a chance to talk to him.

"Don't cry about this," LuAnn said, giving Evie another hug.

Carson had never seen a woman further from tears.

In fact, Evie was smiling. A small Mona Lisa smile, but it let him know that Bennie hadn't done as much damage as Carson had thought. Then again, maybe it was the worst kind of damage. After all, Evie had kissed him, and that had opened a really bad Pandora's box. That kiss had seemed to be some kind of declaration that she not only wasn't going back to the way things were but that she also was coming after him.

While Evie and he got out of there, Carson tried to call Bennie. No luck. It went straight to voice mail.

"Call me, you dumbass idiot," Carson snarled into the phone. "Things have gone to hell in a handbasket here in Wrangler's Creek." He added some profanity that he hoped would spur Bennie to call him as soon as he heard the message.

Evie chuckled and ran to her car. Even though it was only a few feet from the Longhorn, Carson still got wet because the rain was coming down pretty hard. Good. Maybe it'd wash away some of the tequila smell and help clear his head.

"Hell in a handbasket, huh?" Evie repeated. She started the engine as soon as he had on his seat belt. "Did you mean Bennie's marriage or that kiss?"

"Both," he answered honestly.

Evie smiled again and drove away from the Longhorn with her parents and his mom watching them from the doorway. "I've been wanting to kiss you for a while. Seemed like a good time."

She was yanking his chain. On the last part of that, anyway. "Bennie's like a kid brother to me, and you're—"

Her narrowed gaze slashed to his. "If you say *Bennie's girl*, I'm going to pull over and kiss you again.

This time, I'll make it French with some possible groping involved."

He frowned and wished that sounded unappealing.
It didn't. In fact, it appealed to every part of his body.
One part in particular.

"You're in a weird mood," Carson grumbled.

She lifted her shoulder. "Post-cancer awareness. I
realized life's too short not to do what you want to
do. I don't want to be Bennie's girl. I don't want to be
anybody's girl."

All right. That spelled it out for him. At least Carson thought it did until she continued.

"I want to be someone's *woman*," Evie added a moment later. "Someone's lover. Preferably someone I'm
incredibly attracted to even if that someone won't look
at me because he's too good of a man to do something
he'd consider low-down and dirty."

Yeah, that was it in a nutshell.

Carson didn't confirm it, but Evie huffed. "Bennie's
not in love with me," she went on, "and I'm not in love
with him. He still calls himself my boyfriend because
he feels sorry for me. Personally, I think he'd be relieved if I got you drunk and hauled you off to bed."

The images came, shoving aside the fog, and for a
couple of seconds, he could see Evie naked and riding
him hard. Hell, he could feel it, too. And that's why he
looked away from her.

"Your parents wouldn't be relieved about that," he
reminded her. "Neither would my mom."

She stayed quiet a moment, then groaned. Because
she knew it was true. He might have a "good guy"
label, but Evie wasn't exactly a bad girl. She'd toed
just as many lines as he had.

Still quiet and now with no trace of that smile, Evie took the turn toward the Granger Ranch, and the place came into view. Most people just called it sprawling, and it fit. Miles of pastures and white fences. Barns, corrals, stables and the house that also qualified as sprawling.

"If you don't mind, I'd rather not see Garrett," Carson said. After all, he had to do business with the man. "What are the chances he'll be at the ranch this morning?"

"A hundred percent. He's waiting on me so we can finish the quarterly taxes."

Great. Since Garrett also ran a business, Granger Western, miles away in Austin, Carson was hoping that was where he would be. No such luck, though. Because Garrett was sipping a cup of coffee on the front porch. It would be too rude for Carson just to let Evie out and then drive away, so he bit the bullet. Once she'd come to a stop in the circular drive that fronted the house, Carson joined her as she made her way to the porch.

"Sorry I'm late," she said.

But Garrett waved it off. "Is it true?" Garrett asked her. "Did Bennie elope with a stripper?" Before she could even confirm it, Garrett pulled her into his arms. "God, Evie, I'm so sorry."

That *I'm so sorry* seemed to apply to more than just Bennie, and Carson got a glimpse of what Evie had been going through. People were indeed treating her with kid gloves. That was probably okay while she was going through treatments and such, but it was likely wearing thin.

"You want me to call Sophie and have her come out?" Garrett asked her.

Sophie was his sister and Evie's friend, and while it would have been nice to talk this out with her, Sophie was busy with work at the family business in Austin. "Thank you but no. I'll call her later."

Garrett nodded, but he didn't look so caring and sympathetic when he turned to Carson. "You're going to fix this?" Garrett snapped, and the snap was for Carson. Garrett's expression quickly softened again, though. No doubt because he remembered he had a younger brother, Roman, who made Bennie look like a choirboy.

"I'll certainly try." And his first attempt to do that came before he had even finished giving Garrett that assurance.

Carson's phone buzzed, and when he saw Bennie's name on the screen, he stepped to the side of the porch to take it. Of course, Evie and Garrett would still be able to hear him, but thankfully they went inside.

"Where the hell are you?" Carson demanded the second he answered.

"Uh, I'm not sure. A hotel room, I think."

Carson wanted to curse a blue streak along with knocking Bennie upside the head. "Is the stripper with you?"

"Who? Car, I'm not feeling so great. I think I'm gonna puke."

"You can puke after you've answered my questions. Where are you, and did you marry that stripper?"

Bennie didn't answer. At least not with words. Carson heard a retching sound. Followed by something else. A woman's voice.

"You poor thing," she purred. "Let Gigi make it all better."

Hell. Carson hadn't actually remembered the stripper's name until now. But that was the woman with the stash of red panties all right. "Gigi?" he yelled into the phone.

"Car?" she said, and he hated hearing his nickname purr from this woman's pouty lips.

"Yeah, it's me. Where the hell are you?"

"Vegas, I think, but I can't talk right now. Bennie just puked on the petunia."

Carson had no idea if that was code for her lady part or if it was maybe a pseudo bridal bouquet. It didn't matter. He needed answers.

"Did Bennie and you get married?" he pressed.

But he was talking to the air because Gigi, her petunia and the puking Bennie were no longer on the line. Cursing, he tried to call Bennie back, but like before it went to voice mail.

"Well? What's the verdict?" Evie asked.

With all the cursing and the rain hitting the tin roof, Carson hadn't even known that she'd stepped back onto the porch with him. He shook his head. "Bennie couldn't talk, but he's with the stripper. Don't know, though, if they're married or not."

If not knowing bothered her in the least, she didn't show it. "I'm sure they'll be okay."

She went to him, took his hand and dropped her keys into his palm. "Forgot to give these to you. Garrett's going to drive me to the Longhorn when I'm done here because I have a couple of hours of work to do for my dad."

"Not cleaning, I hope, because I can hire some extra help."

She waved that off. "I'll call some of the Busbys and get them to help Bud. It'll be cleaned up before afternoon opening."

Yeah, but he still owed her dad another apology.

Probably a whole bunch of other people, too. The only saving grace about the night was that he hadn't ended up with a stripper.

"When you bring back my car, you want to go for some coffee or something?" she asked.

Carson didn't have to think long or hard on that. "It's probably not a good idea."

Well, unless he could talk her into giving Bennie a second chance. Or in Bennie's case, it was more like a sixteenth chance. Of course, for it to do any good, he'd have to verify that Bennie wasn't married.

And Carson would have to put his own feelings aside, too.

Because he didn't want Evie with Bennie.

That kiss was responsible for the way he was feeling. It had put doubts in his head, and right now there was enough going on up there without adding doubts to the mix.

She smiled again. That evil Mona Lisa smile. "Consider this," she said. "We can please our folks, maybe Bennie, too, if we keep our hands off each other. You could hang on to your 'good guy' label and I can continue being Bennie's girl. Or you can meet me after work and we can figure out how we can make a go of this."

"This?" Carson questioned.

"Sex," Evie answered without hesitation.

And with that smile still on her hot little mouth, she turned and went inside, leaving him to wonder where the hell the rug was that she'd just pulled from beneath his feet.

CHAPTER THREE

"You did what?" Sophie Granger asked Evie.

Even from the other end of a phone line, Evie had no trouble hearing her friend's surprise. Sophie's concern, too. Concern that Evie hoped to nip in the bud. While she was at it, she wanted to do some sympathy nipping, too, because Evie figured that would soon surface in this conversation.

"I threw myself at Carson," Evie repeated.

Yep, she had. Evie had thrown down the sexual gauntlet to Carson, and now she had to see if he would do anything about it. She had to accept that he wouldn't, that he would put Bennie and his reputation ahead of her.

And if that happened, it meant she had made a fool of herself for nothing.

It also meant she'd misread the signals, that maybe Carson wasn't actually feeling what she'd been feeling for him for years. If so, that was going to hurt. Because she suspected those feelings went past the mere attraction stage.

"The timing seemed right for me to do that," Evie explained. "And I'm expecting him to show up at the Longhorn any minute now." At least she was *hoping* he would show.

"Uh, are you sure about that?" Sophie asked. "Don't get me wrong. I've wanted you to dump Bennie for a long time. Yes, he's charming, and he's got that whole bad boy, hot cowboy thing going on, but I don't think he's the settling down type." She paused. "Is that why you asked out Carson, because you want to settle down?"

Sophie probably thought that since she knew all about Evie's quest to grab some gusto in life. "For starters, I just want to make out with Carson. From what I could tell, he's a really good kisser."

"He looks like he would be, and he's got a great butt, too. I just want you to think before you leap. You know, make sure this is what you want and that it's not some kind of knee-jerk reaction."

"It's not knee-jerk. And yes, settling down is at the back of my mind. Funny, though, that I'd never thought of settling down with Bennie, but my mind can weave some very sweet fantasies when it comes to Carson."

Sophie chuckled. "Then go for it."

It was the exact reaction Evie wanted her friend to have. Sophie was probably the only person who knew her who would approve of this.

"Gotta go," Sophie said. "Let me know if any of those fantasies come true," she added, ending the call.

Evie put her phone on the table and checked the time again. Carson was late. He'd texted her earlier to say that he'd meet her at the Longhorn to return her car. He hadn't said a peep about sex, but then phone messages probably weren't the best way to converse about that sort of thing.

"Want to talk about it?" her father asked. Since he'd come by the booth where she was waiting three times, it was obvious he was worried about her.

She hated that, the worry. The fear in his eyes. He loved her, and nearly losing her had cut him to the core.

Her mother, too, of course, but at least her dad hadn't tried to smother her.

Well, not as much as her mother, anyway.

"I'm fine, really." Evie forced a smile.

Her dad would know it was forced, and that was probably why he lingered a moment. He didn't sit down, though, because he was manning the bar, and while there were only two customers at this early hour—four o'clock—he wouldn't want to be seen lollygagging. Like Carson, he had that whole reputation thing to uphold.

"You do know your mom and I want the best for you," he added. "We want the best for Bennie, too, because we've always thought of him as part of the family."

And there was the problem. It was hard to oust a family member even after he'd run off with a stripper, and in their minds Bennie had also broken her heart.

"What if I don't think of Bennie as family?" she threw out there. "What if I'm actually glad this happened?"

He sighed, patted her arm. "Once you get past the shock, you'll be thinking a little clearer."

Now she sighed. Part of her just wanted to scream that Bennie wasn't right for her, but if her folks couldn't see that now, they would never see it. Screaming wouldn't help. And that meant she had to come up with another way. One that didn't crush them but still kept what was left of her dignity intact.

She'd already run into at least a half-dozen people today who had upped those "poor, pitiful Evie" looks. Not only had she had cancer—which was always spoken in a whisper or spelled out as Ida did—but now she'd lost her man.

The door opened, and Carson finally came in. The relief she felt was instant. At least until she saw his face. Something was wrong, and he was possibly trying to figure out how to turn down her offer of sex.

Her father walked away as Carson slid into the seat across from her after asking her father to bring him a beer. "Still want to have sex?" Carson asked.

She nearly choked on her own breath. "Uh, yes." Evie hadn't meant to sound hesitant, but something was wrong. "That's not exactly a 'let's have sex' look in your eyes."

He mumbled some profanity and stared at his hands that he had balled up on the table, but he didn't say anything else until her father had served him the beer and left them alone.

Even though her father was now out of earshot, Carson still whispered, "I don't want you crying, upset or having a setback."

That again. "And you thought sex would help." Evie huffed, then shrugged. "Sex with you probably would."

He didn't smile as she'd hoped he would. In fact, Carson was wound very tight right now. Heck, he probably needed sex more than she did.

"Let me guess," she went on. "Bennie really did marry the stripper, and all day you've been dealing with the fallout from that."

Carson didn't answer right away. "Yeah. The marriage is legal, but I told Bennie to get to a lawyer for an annulment. Whether he will or not is anyone's guess." He drank some beer, looked at her over the rim. "I'm so sorry."

"You're not Bennie's keeper, even if I'm sure at times it feels that way." She paused. "Is there any chance Bennie's actually in love with this woman?"

"None. He met her last night at Jake Monroe's bachelor party. That's why we were there at the strip joint.

Trust me, I wouldn't have had even a drink if I'd known the lap dance she gave him was going to turn into this."

Bennie probably hadn't known it, either. A lap dance coupled with tequila shots could maybe feel like love. Temporarily, anyway.

"This Gigi's not a bad person," he continued. "By that I mean she doesn't have a police record. I checked. She's one of those rare people who really is working her way through college. Does it bother you to hear about her?" Carson tacked onto that.

"Not in the least. I really am not going to fall into a pit of despair."

Carson stared at her as if trying to figure out if it was true. He finally glanced away, cursed. "I have to tell my mom."

Which meant her own mom would soon know. Evie's eyes widened when she realized the end result of that. Maybe there'd be some despair after all.

Well, crud.

"Yeah," Carson agreed. "Either your mom will work extra hard to keep you with Bennie, or she'll wash her hands of him."

"She'll only do that after much whining," she finished for him. "Then, she'll start playing matchmaker with a vengeance."

That wouldn't have been so bad if she would start the matching with Carson. But she wouldn't. Not with her mother thinking Carson was too old for her. There was no telling what Carson's mom and her mom could cook up.

"Mom's gotten worse about micromanaging me," Evie said. "This certainly won't help."

"She's gotten worse because you were sick?" he asked.

She nodded, considered moving the conversation back to the sex offer he'd made when he first sat down. But with a despair-pit looming, Carson needed to know the big picture.

"After I was diagnosed, I'd never seen my mom like that. Always crying and searching the internet for new treatments. She even asked Vita Banchini to do a healing spell for me."

Carson didn't gasp, but it was close. Vita was a strange old woman who lived in a trailer at the edge of town. She claimed to be able to see the future, do magic potions and stop bad stuff from happening—if she wanted to stop it, that is. Most people were either terrified of her or thought she needed to be in the loony bin. Some just wanted to buy her laundry detergent since she always reeked of herbs and other unidentifiable things. It was a testament to her mother's gloomy state of mind that she'd go to the woman for help.

"Vita made these smelly poultice bags that my mom kept stashing around my house. And, of course, she wanted me to move back home. If the treatments hadn't worked, I might have had to do that, too." She shuddered a little.

"But they did work." He stared at her. Paused again. "Were you scared?"

"Terrified." She winced because she hadn't wanted to admit that to anyone. Not even herself. Now that Carson had that big picture, it was time to move on to something else. "Are you seeing anyone?" That resulted in another wincing. Not very subtle, but it got that worried look out of his eyes.

"I was. She's a doctor in San Antonio, but we broke things off a while back. She wanted to move to the next level, and I wasn't ready."

Evie had heard bits and pieces about that when she'd walked in on conversations between "the moms." Ida was definitely pushing both Bennie and Carson into getting married.

"Maybe we need to stage a revolt." Evie wasn't exactly joking.

"You mean by us seeing each other?" He certainly didn't sound as appalled or shocked by the idea as he had earlier in the day. "And that way if it doesn't work out, then we can blame it on the shock of Bennie's marriage. Maybe the aftermath of your illness, too."

Evie smiled, then frowned. "You've given this some thought. Any chance you think we could succeed?"

"No."

She wished that he had at least hesitated a little.

"Because I'll feel guilty," he went on. "Our moms will make our lives a living hell. And because eventually Bennie will sober up, come to his senses and do what it takes to win you back."

Evie thought about that for a few seconds. "All of that is possibly true. *Probably* true," she amended. "Except for the part about Bennie winning me back. Not going to happen. But our moms will certainly make us miserable while trying to set us on the paths that they're convinced are right for us. That's why I think we should kiss just so we can consider if it's worth the effort."

Carson's eyebrow came up. "We've already kissed, this morning."

"That wasn't a kiss. That was a test-drive."

He kept staring at her, probably trying to think of some way to wiggle out of this. And he wiggled all right. Sort of, anyway. Carson came off the seat and leaned across the table. He slid his hand around the back of her head.

And he kissed her.

Man, oh, man, this wasn't a test-drive. It was a full-on lip-lock with his mouth firmly on hers. All in all, it was a really good place for his mouth to be because it sent a nice swirl of heat through her.

He didn't stop with just a swirl, though. Carson pressed harder, deepening the kiss, and he did what she'd threatened earlier.

Carson made it French.

Just the way she liked her kisses. Well, she would have if they hadn't been sitting in her family's bar.

That nice swirl of heat—which was at a much higher temperature than just moments ago—was best suited for a more private place. Preferably one with a bed. But even without the privacy and the bed, when Carson finally pulled back, she felt as if she'd had an orgasm or two.

"You're really good at that," she said, smiling.

However, he wasn't smiling. Nor was Carson still looking at her as if he wanted to have her for dinner. His attention was to his right.

And the two people who were standing there.

The two scowling mothers.

Evie could say with complete certainty that neither of their moms was gleeful about that orgasm-inducing kiss.

CARSON FELT AS if he'd developed a sudden, severe case of ADD. He couldn't focus, couldn't think, and this wasn't a good time for that to happen. He had a pile of work to do and some fires to put out, and he wasn't getting any of it done.

The first fire was Bennie, but for the flame-dousing to start, Bennie had to answer his phone. When he did, Carson hoped like the devil that Bennie had gotten an annulment and was on his way back to Texas.

Fires number two and three were connected. And he'd been the one to start those. It'd begun when he had kissed Evie the day before in the Longhorn. It'd been a really stupid thing to do, but when she'd sat there, looking both beautiful and bothered, he hadn't been able to resist.

If he had resisted, fire number three wouldn't exist.

The moms' disapproval.

Of course, Ida and LuAnn hadn't wanted Carson to French-kiss Evie. Especially not in public. They probably had rationalized that at least if it'd happened behind closed doors, then word wouldn't get back to Bennie and it wouldn't spoil the chances of a Bennie and Evie reconciliation.

Even if it was getting obvious that neither Bennie nor Evie wanted that.

That put Carson between a rock and a hard place. He kept thinking about kissing Evie. About doing more to her than just kissing, as well. But life was not going to be fun if he did that.

Nope.

So it was best if he backed off from the kissing or the thinking about kissing and gave Evie some time to sort out her feelings. Carson still wasn't sure that kiss was an actual desire to be with him instead of her merely going for that whole life-zest thing.

Now that she knew she was actually going to have a life, that was.

He needed to make sure that she couldn't get that *zest* from Bennie. Of course, that would leave him out of the running for any future kisses with Evie. Until yesterday, Carson wouldn't have thought that was a bad thing, but he was sure thinking it at the moment.

There was a knock at his office door, followed by his assistant, Merrilee, saying, "You got visitors, boss man."

The door opened, and Carson steeled himself because he expected to see the moms walk in. But it was Garrett Granger. Good thing Carson had done the steeling because Garrett looked a little pissed off. He came in, shutting the door behind him.

"Evie," Garrett said right off the bat.

"I know you're here to lecture me. I haven't been around Wrangler's Creek much and didn't see her when she was so sick. She's been through too much, and I should just back off and let her work things out with Bennie."

Garrett's scowl turned to a frown. "No, actually I was here about some cows I need to sell, and I wondered if Evie had called you about them for me."

"Uh, no. She didn't mention any cows." But it might have been hard for her to talk what with him kissing her.

The corner of Garrett's mouth lifted in a half smile. "You got a guilty conscience or something?"

Or something. What Carson had was an attraction for Evie that was occupying way too much of his thoughts.

"I just happened to be in San Antonio on business," Garrett went on, "and thought I'd drop by the request in person. I need to get rid of this particular herd because I've got some calves coming in." He dropped a purchase order on Carson's desk.

Carson glanced through it, nodded. "Let me make some calls, but I'm almost positive that I can have a buyer for you by the end of the week. Is that soon enough?"

Garrett nodded and kept staring. "Are you going to hook up with Evie or not?" he asked. "Gossip," he added. "When you kiss a woman in the Longhorn, it doesn't tend to stay secret for long."

Carson knew that, too. Also knew the right thing to do was to nip this in the bud right now by telling Garrett that no, he wasn't going to hook up with Evie. But the words just sort of stuck there in his throat, causing Garrett to half smile again.

"I always thought she deserved something better," Garrett said. And with that, he walked out, causing Carson to wonder if he fell into that better category.

Probably not.

Because he could cause her more trouble than she needed.

And speaking of trouble, his phone buzzed, and he saw Bennie's name on the screen. Carson answered it so fast that he damn near spilled his coffee.

"You'd better have good news," Carson snarled.

"Some. I remembered where I left your truck. It's at the San Antonio airport. Don't worry—I didn't drive it there. Gigi did because she wasn't drinking."

No, she'd been too busy showering red panties around the bar. "Where are you now?"

"Still in Vegas."

And then Carson heard a sound he sure as hell didn't want to hear. Giggling. Familiar giggling at that. Because he'd heard it enough at the Longhorn during Bennie's so-called bachelor party.

"Is Gigi there with you?" Carson demanded.

Bennie didn't answer right away, but Carson could hear some heavy breathing and some moans. The kind of sounds a man might make if he was on the verge of having sex.

"Can I call you back?" Bennie asked, still breathing and moaning.

"No. You can tell me how the appointment went with the lawyer, the one you'll be using for your annulment."

"Oh, that went fine. Gigi and I signed the papers, and the lawyer said the judge should grant the annulment in about six weeks. I just got a few more things to finish up here, and I'll be home."

Carson was stunned to silence for a moment. All of that sounded, well, responsible. If he graded on a curve, that was, and curve grading was par for the course with Bennie.

"Evie," Carson said when she walked through the door. At first, he thought she was a figment of his imagination, but she was the real deal.

And mercy, she looked amazing.

She was wearing what a lot of Wrangler's Creek women wore. Jeans, boots and a red top, but on her they looked amazing. No need to grade Evie on a curve.

"Evie," Bennie repeated because he obviously thought Carson was talking to him. "Uh, can you break up with her for me? No, wait. That's not right. I'll man up and do it when I get back. Gotta go." And with some additional moans coupled with giggling, Bennie ended the call.

"Was that Bennie?" she asked. "I didn't hear any of the conversation, but you always get that look on your face when you're talking to him. I like the look you had, though, a couple of seconds prior to that."

The gaping stare where he'd been admiring the fit of her jeans. And her breasts. Her face, too. Hell, no use naming parts. He'd been admiring all of her.

No way did he want to tell her what Bennie had just said. Carson needed a chance to figure out how to go about it. Or decide if he just wanted to put this back in Bennie's lap. Besides, if he told Evie that Bennie was getting an annulment but still breaking things off with her, it would put some dents in that sexual attraction barrier between them.

Carson needed some time to think about those barriers, as well. And decide if he even wanted them in place.

"Did your mom give you a hard time about me?" he asked.

Just as she knew his "I've got the hots for you" face, he knew her "yes, Mom did" face, but as Evie usually did, she just shrugged. "A year ago all this drama would have sent me in search of ways to keep the peace. I've sort of given up on that. I mean, for my mom to get what she wants, I have to settle for Bennie."

Yeah, and she would be settling, all right.

"How about your mom?" Evie said, turning the tables on him. "Was she upset, too?"

"Oh, yes," he readily admitted. "Bennie will always be her baby boy." He paused, trying not to remember just how this had twisted at her. "She reminded me that I'm the responsible one and that I didn't have the challenges growing up that Bennie did."

"Ouch. She played the troubled teen guilt card on you."

Now, he shrugged. "I deserved it. After all, I'm the one who kissed you."

"Only after I kissed you. You know, for two people

with so many doubts about seeing each other, we certainly have done our share of kissing."

Carson laughed before he could stop himself. Evie smiled. One of those smiles that reminded him of just how good she tasted.

She held his gaze for a couple of seconds before Evie cleared her throat. "I came to drop this off," she said, taking a small box from her purse. "It's a necklace that Bennie gave me. I don't feel right about keeping it, and I wasn't sure if I'd see him anytime soon."

"You'll see him," he insisted, but they both knew that might be a lie. If Bennie was still fooling around with his soon-to-be ex-wife, then it might be days before he came back to Texas. Months before he made it back to Wrangler's Creek.

"Actually, I'd rather not. Returning the necklace is my way of breaking up with him."

"You could try calling him," Carson pointed out.

"What, and interrupt his honeymoon?" She put that last word in quotes. If she was the least bit bothered by Bennie's marital predicament, Evie wasn't showing it.

"Come to dinner at my house tomorrow night," she threw out there.

He was instantly suspicious. And interested. "Dinner?" he repeated.

"Dinner," she verified, the smile returning. "Kissing and sex are optional," Evie added over her shoulder as she headed for the door.

Carson watched her walk away and knew one thing was for certain.

If he had dinner with Evie, sex wouldn't be optional. For better or worse, sex was going to happen.

CHAPTER FOUR

"THIS IS GOING to lead to sex," Sophie said.

"Maybe," Evie admitted. "But there are no guarantees with Carson. I have a couple of strikes against me." She had her phone sandwiched between her shoulder and ear, and despite the rattling around she was doing in the kitchen, she had no trouble hearing Sophie's sigh from the other end of the line.

"I just don't want you hurt. Remember to guard your heart."

"Too late." Evie winced. Because it was also too late to take back that comment. She certainly hadn't meant to blurt it out like that, but her nerves and the margarita she'd been sipping had lowered her defenses.

"Carson could get hurt, too," Sophie went on. "Have you considered that?"

"No." Actually, she hadn't. But Evie considered it now. She honestly didn't know what Carson thought of her. Well, other than it was obvious he was attracted to her. However, what if they had sex and it ended badly?

As in ending their friendship?

Great. Now, she was tipsy from the drink, tingling from the attraction and worried that she'd just screwed up big-time.

"Just talk this out with him," Sophie went on. "Make

sure you're on the same page before you even kiss him. Because once you kiss him, you'll be a goner."

Yes, a goner with an orgasm.

Evie's phone beeped, indicating she had another call, and she groaned when she saw her mother's name pop up. "Gotta go, Sophie. If I don't take this call from my mom, she'll keep bugging me all night. Thanks for the advice, though."

Talk before kissing. Definitely something she would do.

She ended the call with Sophie and switched to her mom. As usual, her mother started speaking before Evie even managed a hello.

"Just got off the phone with Ida, and Bennie's still in Vegas," her mom said. "Have you told him you want him to come home?"

"No. Actually, I haven't spoken to Bennie since his elopement."

"Well, you should. Bennie and you—"

"Are finished," Evie interrupted. Since her mom seemed to be gearing up for a lecture, Evie decided to keep interrupting her. "Do you really think I want him back after he ran off with a stripper? Plus, Bennie and I haven't actually been together in a long time."

"But that's only because you were going through the treatments. Of course, you weren't thinking about love and sex and stuff."

Her mother hurried over that last handful of words. It couldn't be comfortable for her to talk about sex with her daughter, but it was doubly uncomfortable for Evie to talk about it with her mother. That was why she changed the subject.

"Carson is coming over for dinner," Evie said. "He should be here any minute now."

The silence on the other end of the line told her loads. Of course, she hadn't needed the silence to know that her mother disapproved.

"Carson's too old for you," her mom finally said.

"Maybe ten years ago he was, but I'm twenty-eight now, and he's thirty-six." There wasn't much more to add, which was a good thing, because she spotted Carson's truck pulling up in front of her house. "Bye, Mom. I'll call you tomorrow."

And since her mother had terrible boundaries about such things, Evie turned off the ringer on her phone before she went to the door.

She had no neighbors, which meant there was no one around to see Carson and feed that tidbit to the gossip mill. In fact, that was one of the reasons she'd bought the old farmhouse that sat in the middle of ten acres.

Evie threw open the door and took a moment to admire the view. And what a view it was. Carson, standing on her porch, flowers in hand and looking good enough to classify as dessert.

It was raining again so his hair was damp and rumpled from having to run from his truck. There were a few drops on his face, too. He smelled like some kind of expensive bottle of sin.

Just the way she preferred her men to smell.

"I was afraid you wouldn't come," she admitted.

"I was afraid I would," he admitted right back.

Obviously, he'd been doing some soul-searching, and she hoped that didn't mean he was about to turn around and leave. But he didn't. He stepped in, handing her the flowers. His gaze skirted around the house before settling on her. He definitely wasn't smiling.

"Garrett and I had a talk on my drive over," he said. "He's worried about you getting a broken heart out of this, and he advised me to talk to you before we do anything stupid."

"Apparently, Garrett and his sister are of a like mind because I just had a similar chat with Sophie."

He nodded. "It makes sense."

She nodded, too, because it did. Then she waited for him to get this talk started. But he didn't.

Carson cursed. "Screw the talk," he snarled. And she wasn't sure who was more surprised when he dragged her to him and kissed her.

CARSON KNEW IF he thought about what he was doing, he'd stop. And that's exactly why he didn't think about it. He wasn't the sort to bury his head in the sand, but he sure as hell was going to be that sort right now.

Evie went a little stiff at first. No doubt because she hadn't realized he was about to kiss her. But soon the stiffness vanished, and she melted against him. There would have been some nice body-to-body contact if she hadn't been holding the flowers. They squished between them.

Carson pulled out the flowers, dropping them in the general direction of the table by the door. He had no idea if that was where they actually landed because he didn't take his attention off Evie. Specifically, this kiss. He'd spent a very frustrating last two days with the Bennie fiasco and his body burning for her, and Carson took out all the frustration and fire in the lip-lock.

All in all, it was a darn good way to relieve some

stress. A darn good way to get a hard-on, too. But that seemed to come with the territory whenever he was around Evie.

She made a sound of pleasure. Then, not of pleasure. "Something's burning," she said.

Maybe his jeans were on fire. Hell, maybe *he* was on fire. But judging from the way she pulled away from him and ran to the kitchen, he wasn't the one who'd ignited into flames, yet. But there was something on the stove that looked and smelled way past the well-done stage.

"I burned the beef stir-fry," she grumbled, moving the skillet off the burner and onto the back of the stove.

"That's okay. I wasn't hungry." Not hungry for food, anyway.

The kitchen had plenty of smoke in it, so when Evie turned to start back to him, she looked a little like a goddess walking through otherworldly mist. But she didn't feel like a mythical goddess. It was a flesh-and-blood woman who slipped right back into his arms and picked up where they'd left off. The moment would have been perfect if the smoke alarm hadn't gone off, and if they both hadn't started coughing like fools.

She cursed, and coughing she turned on the fans, threw open the windows. Evie didn't stop there—she caught on to his hand and led him out the back to a porch that overlooked what had once been a pasture. Behind that he could see the creek. No smoke out here to make them cough, and Evie kept it that way by shutting the door. No rain on them, either, since the porch roof would keep them dry.

"Sorry," she said.

"I'm not. I can kiss you just as much out here as I could in there."

She smiled. It was that smile he really liked, too, because it had a sexy edge to it. Most people probably never thought of Evie as someone who could have down and dirty sex, but Carson was betting that beneath the bookkeeper exterior, there was the heart of a lap dancer.

Not that he wanted a lap dance.

Well, maybe after he did something about this first erection and took care of a few of Evie's needs. And he was certain she had them because she'd already said she'd gone a year without sex.

Carson set out to fix that by pulling her to him again. She had already started in that direction, and they crashed into each other. Mouths crashed, too, and he probably would have registered some pain if she hadn't tasted so damn good. That quelled any doubts that started to creep into his mind. But what really helped was when she caught on to his rodeo buckle, her fingers dipping down into his jeans.

Into his boxers, too.

Of course, her fingers couldn't venture far since he was still zipped up, but they could remedy that soon enough. First, though, he wanted more of the foreplay.

Carson kissed her, all the while nudging and adjusting her position so that their parts were aligned. Yeah. That's what his erection wanted. Well, actually it wanted full-blown sex, but it was occupied for now so he could shove up her top and play a little.

He lowered his head, kissed the tops of her breasts. She clearly liked that because she called him a bad name, latched on to fistfuls of his hair and anchored him in the general area of her torso. Thankfully, Carson still had her other breast to play with.

The urgency kept notching up a little, and then it notched up a lot when he went even lower and kissed her stomach. Where he found something, well, interesting.

A little gold navel ring.

He looked up at her, managing to raise his eyebrow. It looked as if it'd been there for a while.

"A friend talked me into getting it when I turned twenty-one," she said. "There were tequila shots involved."

Well, at least it'd been a less wild option than getting a tattoo, which would have been much harder to remove. And the gold felt good against his tongue when he flicked it. It jiggled a little. Evie jiggled some, too, wiggling closer to get to his mouth. So, he flicked it again. And then did some French-kissing below the navel ring.

Below her panty line, too.

There was some pain involved in that since she didn't let go of his hair, but it was worth it.

"It's still too smoky to go inside," she managed to say.

Yeah, and he didn't want to get caught up in a coughing fit. Didn't want to wait, either, so he did a logistics check. There wasn't anyone in the pasture, no one by the creek, either, and there was a white-painted porch swing. It even had an old blanket draped across the back of it.

That's where Carson headed.

He didn't let go of Evie, though, when he got moving. He just kept kissing her. She kept pulling his hair, and they did a hard landing on the porch swing.

With her in his lap.

His erection really liked that.

It liked it even better, though, when she went after his belt and zipper. She only got him partially undone when she stopped, and he followed her gaze to the tattoo on his hip.

An embarrassing tattoo of a red cherry with a stem that pointed right to his erection.

"There were tequila shots involved," he explained. "And some really bad advice from the tat artist."

She smiled, managed to get her mouth down there, and she did some tongue action on the tat. Of course, any kind of tonguing in that general area was going to make him even harder, but because this was Evie, he reached a whole new level of hardness.

Since that was a definite escalation from foreplay, Carson shifted his attention from kisses to getting her naked. Well, partially naked, anyway. It was probably best if they didn't strip down completely out here.

He did keep her top shoved up and her bra pushed down because he liked being able to drop a few kisses on her breasts and that navel ring. But he also unzipped her. Since she was trying to do the same to him, it turned into a hand bumping contest, which had the potential to end all of this a little sooner than Carson wanted.

That's why he caught her right wrist, finished unzipping her, and then helped her shimmy out of those jeans and her panties.

He saw the scar where she'd had the surgery to remove one of her kidneys. A reminder that he should be taking things a lot easier than he had been. But Evie shot that notion to hell and back when she unzipped him and latched on to him with a vengeance.

This wasn't a woman who had gentleness in mind.

So Carson gave her what she wanted. After he fished out a condom from his pocket, that was. She tried to help with that, too, and he wanted to tell her that she really sucked at that. It became more of a hand job.

Considering what he really wanted was a "job" from that part of her that was only a few inches away, it made him start throbbing. He was within seconds of begging for mercy when she finally finished.

"Let's play," she whispered, her voice all hot and silky.

He only got a few seconds to savor that look and her incredible face because she did something else incredible. She guided him inside her.

Hell, yeah. This was what both Carson and his erection wanted.

She laughed, an evil little laugh that made her evil little smile seem like foreplay. And she started to move. Evie caught on to the back of the swing, and the motion of her hips caused the swing to move, too. The gentle rocking motion combined with Evie's thrusts nearly took off the top of his head.

Carson did manage to get in that kiss. First to her breast. Then he hooked his hand around the back of her neck to pull her to him for a kiss. The timing was perfect.

The swing moved.

Evie moved.

And all the foreplay, kisses and touches created a flash of scalding pleasure. First for Evie. Then for Carson.

He gathered her close and took every last bit of that pleasure, knowing that it wouldn't be long before he had some music to face.

pocket, of course, and if it didn't ring, she might get a phone spam. She wasted another ... but it was ... would be much better if it ... could ...

... attempted to talk to you. She said a ... mine. About their sexual ... wait and you might get something out ... at ...

She ... having to talk, but was calm and ... than the ... She wanted her message to ... together ...

CHAPTER FIVE

EVIE WAS POSSIBLY PARALYZED. Either that or every part of her body had gone numb. Too bad because she was on the porch swing with Carson, and she would have liked to at least feel all those incredible muscles in his chest and stomach. As it was, the best she could manage was a sound that was part grunt, part groan.

Carson seemed to be having trouble moving, too. That was probably because after he'd come back from the bathroom an hour ago, they'd tried to curl up on the swing rather than go back inside the still smoky, smelly house. The swing was a great reading spot for one person, but it wasn't meant for post-sex cuddling.

She forced herself to move, located his mouth and kissed him. "Thank you for not treating me like a sick person."

His eyes had been half-closed before she said that, but that got them fully open. "Should I have been gentler with you?"

"Nope. I'm all healed. When you saw the scar, I thought you were going to hesitate."

"I did hesitate," Carson admitted. "But hesitation doesn't stand a chance against you."

She smiled, pulled him closer and just savored the moment. At least she savored it as much as she could, considering his phone buzzed again. It was in his pocket, on vibrate, and if it didn't stop, she might get another orgasm. She wanted another one, but Carson would be much better at it.

"I'm supposed to talk to you," he said a moment later. "About that possible broken heart you might get out of this."

Since everything inside her was calm and slack from the orgasm, she actually felt relaxed enough to consider it. She wanted to dismiss the possibility, but the truth was, she couldn't.

"Do Sophie and Garrett think a broken heart will cause my cancer to come back?" she asked, only half-serious. "Because I doubt there's a correlation."

"They don't want you down and depressed," he clarified.

"Ah. That. Well, I did have some serious blues when I was going through treatment and contemplating my possible mortality. It was while I was doing all that contemplating that I decided I wanted to have sex with you."

He stayed quiet a moment. "Sex," Carson repeated. Except he didn't just repeat it. His tone made it sound as if he was saying, "Only sex?"

As in—*that's all you want this to be?*

Even though he hadn't come out and asked, they were good questions. She didn't have anything that remotely qualified as good answers. Because, yes, she did want more from him, but that was a lot to spring on a man who'd just had sex with her for the first time. Even though she'd known Carson her entire life, they hadn't ever gone on a real date.

His phone buzzed again, and since it had only been a few minutes since the last call, Carson must have decided he needed to at least look at his screen. Groaning, he maneuvered himself to a sitting position so he could pull his phone from his pocket.

"Bennie," he said after cursing. "Four missed calls from him. I've got a missed call from my mom, too."

She knew what that meant. Carson needed to find out what Bennie wanted, and she doubted that he preferred to have their conversation with her half-naked and coiled around him. That was her cue to get up.

Easier said than done.

She finally managed to stand. Then staggered. She wasn't very graceful because she was also naked from the waist down. Even though Carson was about to make that call, he still took a moment to hook his arm around her and kiss her. It was a sweet way to end the lovemaking.

Which she hoped was only round one.

Evie gathered up her clothes and took them inside so she could dress. Carson stayed on the porch to make his call. What she needed was a good air freshener for the burned smell and a shower. But as she was heading past the kitchen counter, she noticed her own phone.

Six missed calls from her mom.

Sheez, that was extreme even for her mother. Since it appeared that Carson had managed to get in touch with Bennie—he was talking to *someone*, anyway— Evie decided to have a quick chat with her mother just to make sure the sky hadn't fallen. However, before she could press the number, a new call came in, and an unfamiliar number popped up on the screen. She instantly got a weird feeling about this. Not a good kind of weird, either.

ONE GOOD COWBOY

"Evie?" a woman said once she'd answered the call. "Look, you don't know me, but—"

"You're Gigi, Bennie's wife," Evie supplied. She placed the call on speaker so she could set aside her phone to put on her clothes.

"Uh, yes. Just how mad are you right now?"

Since that seemed like a trick question, Evie decided it was best to go with a question of her own. "Is there a reason you're calling?"

"Yes," Gigi answered without hesitating. "It's Bennie. God, Evie, I'm so scared. I don't know what to do. I'm on my way to Wrangler's Creek, but I'm not sure where to start looking."

That got her attention. "What's wrong? What happened?" And because they were talking about Bennie, Evie's mind started to come up with all sorts of bad scenarios. The man certainly had a knack for getting into trouble.

"So you haven't seen Bennie? I'd hoped he would go to you. Or Carson. Where's Carson? I've been trying to call him."

Evie glanced out the kitchen window at the porch to see him putting his belt back on. "He's here at my house," she settled for saying. "And I think he's talking to Bennie on the phone right now."

"Good." And Gigi repeated that along with a "Thank God. Because I've been so worried."

"I'm picking up on that. Tell me what happened."

"That's just it. I don't know. Bennie and I flew back to San Antonio earlier today. We went to his house, and a few minutes later, Ida, his foster mom, showed up. She was really, really mad."

"I can imagine. Did Ida have words with Bennie?"

"Yes. A lot of words. She said he'd better work out things with you or else. But she didn't say what *else* would be. Did I mention she was mad? Sorry, yes, I did. It's hard to concentrate because I'm worried. Because right after she left, Bennie got so upset, he left, too. He said he had to go to Wrangler's Creek. That was hours ago. I tried to call him, but he didn't answer."

"Do you believe something bad happened to Bennie?" Evie asked.

"Maybe. He was so down when he left. You know, he had that really sad look in his eyes." It sounded as if she was choking back a sob. "Are you back together with him, and you just don't want to tell me?"

Oh, so that's what had the woman in tears. "We're not back together. And it'll stay that way."

But it did bother her that Bennie and Ida had gotten into it. Now, Evie just needed to find out what the argument was about. Since that was probably either Ida or Bennie on the phone with Carson, she'd soon find out.

"Let me talk to Carson, and I'll get back to you," she promised Gigi.

She ended the call just as Carson came back inside the house. He still had his phone pressed to his ear and was mumbling profanity under his breath. He didn't stop in the kitchen, where she was, but instead headed straight for the front door and he threw it open. For a moment, Evie thought he was just going to storm to his truck and leave her standing there to wonder what the heck was going on.

However, Evie soon figured out why he'd opened the door.

Bennie was standing on her front porch.

ALL CARSON HAD wanted was to spend the evening with
Evie. An evening that included maybe something to
eat that wasn't burned and another round of sex. But
seeing Bennie had Carson facing a hard truth.

That the sex shouldn't have happened.

At least it shouldn't have happened tonight. Evie
had enough on her plate without adding a new relationship to the mix.

"How'd you know I was here?" Bennie asked him.

Carson held up his phone. "I'd missed your calls,
but when I tried to phone you back, you didn't answer.
That's when I called Mom. She said you were on your
way over."

Actually, what Ida had said was that Bennie was
going to see Evie to patch things up with her. But Bennie looked as if he needed some mental patching up
of his own. He was soaked to the bone, hunched over
and shivering, and his bloodshot eyes told Carson that
he probably hadn't slept much since this whole fiasco
started.

Bennie shifted his attention from Carson to Evie.
"Can I come in?"

She didn't jump to say yes. Maybe because she was
as surprised by this visit as Carson was. But after a
very loud sigh, she stepped to the side to let him in.

"I'll get you a towel," she said and immediately
walked away.

Bennie waited until she was out of earshot before
he spoke. "Did Ida tell you she was mad?"

"Oh, yeah. She made that perfectly clear." Now it
was Carson who sighed. "But here's the deal. You can't
live your life to please Ida."

Bennie shook his head. "She did so much for me, and it twists at my gut to know I've disappointed her."

His mother had moved well past the disappointment stage, but Carson kept that to himself. "I can talk to her, try to smooth things over." It wouldn't be easy to do that, and it would probably take a decade or more, but Carson figured eventually she would forgive Bennie.

Evie came back, carrying a stack of towels, and she put them on the entry table. Right next to the flowers Carson had brought her. Bennie noticed those flowers, too, when he reached for one of the towels. That sent Bennie's gaze volleying between the two of them. Bennie wasn't stupid—about things like this, anyway—so he had probably figured out what had gone on. Especially since both Evie and he looked, well, like unmade beds with their wrinkled clothes and rumpled hair.

"Gigi just called me," Evie explained. "She's very worried about you. You should let her know that you're okay."

"I'm not okay," Bennie corrected. He dried his face, and his attention settled on Evie. "Will you hate me if I tell you that I really care for Gigi?" he asked her.

No sigh this time but rather a huff. "Bennie, I hated you before all of this." But she quickly waved that off. "Correction, I didn't love you before this. Actually, I'm not even sure I liked you very much. So if you're asking me for permission to stay married to your wife, you've got it."

That caused Bennie to do more of those volleying looks. "I thought you'd be more upset."

Welcome to the club. Her reaction had been an eye-opener to Carson, too. A couple of days ago, he'd thought of Evie as a fragile woman recovering from cancer. Now she was a strong, hot babe with a navel ring.

And Carson wanted her.

Bad.

Of course, this probably wasn't the time to give her a long, heated look, but it was hard to tamp that down. He'd thought if he had sex with her, that it would cool things between them. But no. It had actually made the attraction worse.

"Say, are you two…together?" Bennie asked.

It was the million-dollar question, and Carson didn't have an answer. Apparently, neither did Evie because she shrugged. Maybe she would have come up with something. Carson might have as well, but the sound of the approaching car caused them all to look at the front of the house.

Bennie cursed. "That's Gigi." He tossed down the towel and hurried outside to her.

"Are we together?" Evie asked at the same time Carson said, "Are we together?"

They stared at each other a moment.

"I asked first," she said at the same time that he said, "I asked first."

She laughed, and man, he hated to admit it, but that was the right answer. So was the smile that followed. And the kiss she dropped on his mouth.

The kiss was the best answer of all.

Carson might have slid right into that kiss, too, if Gigi and Bennie hadn't interrupted them, soaking wet. Bennie must have met his bride at her car. Evie handed them both a towel.

No smile or laugh for Gigi. The woman had obviously been crying, and she was eyeing Evie as if she were the enemy.

"Did you mean it when you said Bennie and you weren't back together?" Gigi asked her.

"I did. As far as I'm concerned, you two have a green light to do whatever it is you've been doing."

"And Carson and you want that same green light," Bennie concluded before Gigi could say anything.

That was pretty much it as far as Carson was concerned, but they weren't the only players in this.

"Ida and LuAnn," Evie said, taking the words right out of his mouth.

For a moment Carson thought they were just on the same wavelength. But no. There was a tad more to it than that. Evie hadn't said the names because they were on her mind.

It was because she'd seen the approaching car.

The moms had arrived.

CHAPTER SIX

"BE STRONG," EVIE WHISPERED. She wasn't just giving advice to herself but to all of them. They were going to have to steel themselves, grow a pair, weather the storm or do whatever cliché would work.

Too bad she just couldn't turn mean girl and tell Ida and her mom to get a life. One that didn't involve pestering their children, foster children and the poor stripper who'd married into this chaos. But Evie couldn't do that.

Because she loved them.

And even if the moms had a funny way of showing it, they loved them, too. Well, with the exception of Gigi. Pole dancing in stilettos and glitter thongs would seem easy peasy compared to this.

Bennie stepped protectively in front of Gigi. Carson did the same to her, but Evie just huffed and stepped out in front of them all.

"I'm the one least likely to catch flak," she reminded them. "Hey, there's nothing wrong with a woman using cancer to her benefit," she added when they gave her a blank stare.

Evie ignored them, grabbed two more towels and went to the porch to greet the moms. She also made a mental note to give umbrellas for Christmas since none of her visitors seemed to have one.

"Mom," Evie greeted, hugging her. "Miss Ida." She hugged her, too. That caused both women to give her a blank stare, as well. They all possibly thought she'd gone insane. But the truth was, Evie had never seen things clearer.

"It stinks in here," her mother said. "Did something burn?" But her observation and question went unanswered because Ida spoke right over her.

"Is that the stripper?" Ida asked, her mouth pinched so tight that it sort of resembled a cat's butt. Best not to mention that comparison, though, to Ida.

"Yes, this is Gigi, Bennie's wife," Evie said. "Gigi, this is my mom, LuAnn, and Bennie's foster mom, Ida."

The moms clearly didn't like her polite introductions, and when they stepped into the living room, they gave Gigi a wide berth. Since Gigi looked terrified, she probably didn't mind that so much.

Ida didn't waste any time, first doling out a scowl to Carson and then turning to Bennie. "How could you do this to Evie? She has c-a-n-c-e-r."

"*Had* c-a-n-c-e-r," Evie corrected, but Ida ignored that as she always did.

"Look at her." Ida pointed to Evie. "You broke her heart pulling a stunt like this. And you did it all because of the likes of her." That pointing finger went in a cowering Gigi's direction.

"I know," Bennie admitted. "And I'm sorry. I really didn't mean for this to happen. Believe me, I'm as surprised by all of this as you two are."

"Surprised?" Ida howled. "You should be ashamed. I didn't raise you to do junk like this, though heaven knows I've given you plenty of freedom. Too much freedom, and look where that's landed us."

Ida finally stopped when LuAnn nudged her and then tipped her head at Carson and Evie. For the first time since this little visit had started, the moms looked Carson over from head to toe.

Though their mothers' minds likely didn't go straight to sex, they probably got the idea when they noticed Carson wasn't fully zipped. Heck, neither was she, Evie realized when she glanced down at her jeans. Plus, she was only wearing one shoe. And there were a couple of buttons missing on Carson's shirt.

All of that could have perhaps been explained if there hadn't been a hickey on his chest.

"What went on here?" Ida asked. She spoke the words slowly as if spelling them out.

Carson huffed and stepped to Evie's side. "Sex went on," he admitted. "Sex between Evie and me."

Evie braced herself for howls of protests. Maybe even a fainting or two. But the moms just stared at them. Bennie and Gigi were doing their share of staring, too.

"Good sex," Evie added because it seemed as if they were waiting to hear more.

Ida shook her head. "But you have c-a-n-c-e-r."

"Had," Evie tried one more time, and she got right in Ida's face and repeated it. "But I'm fine now. I've finished all my treatments, and the doctors don't expect it to return. Even if it does, I'll deal with it. While I hopefully have more sex with your son."

That stunned everyone to silence again, and Evie wished she'd worded that better. Or at least she wished that until she looked at Carson. He smiled at her, causing her to go all warm and gooey inside. The warmth and gooeyness didn't last, though, when her mother took hold of her arm and turned her to face her.

"You slept with Carson?" she asked. It was the same tone a person might use when asking about an impending zombie apocalypse. "You hardly know each other."

Evie frowned. That was her mother's argument? "I've known Carson for as long as I can remember."

"I mean, you don't *know* each other," LuAnn corrected.

"I know Evie has a navel ring," Carson spoke up. "If you flick it with your tongue, it jiggles."

"And Carson has a cherry tat on his hip," Evie supplied.

Apparently, this was startling news to everyone in the room, but Evie thought that was excellent proof of carnal knowledge.

"You had sex with Carson?" Bennie asked at the same time Gigi, her mom and Ida asked the identical question.

"Yes," Carson and Evie answered in unison. He slipped his arm around her and waited for the responses.

They didn't have to wait long.

Gigi released a breath of relief. Bennie's mouth dropped open. Her mother reached down, yanked up Evie's zipper and huffed. Ida burst into tears. Evie and Carson groaned.

"Does this mean you're okay with me being married to Gigi?" Bennie asked Evie.

"Yes," she said without hesitation.

Gigi ran to Evie, kissed her and then threw herself

into Bennie's arms to kiss him. Bennie did some kissing right back.

That only caused Ida to cry even more. Caused her mother to scowl harder. And Carson groaned even louder before he went to his mom and pulled her into his arms.

"I love you," Carson told her.

She looked up at him, blinked back the tears. "But?"

"But I'm tired of you meddling."

"So am I," Bennie spoke up. Apparently, he'd grown that pair he needed for this.

"Me, too," Gigi agreed. "Because I love Bennie, and I want to be with him."

Ida turned those teary eyes on Evie, probably hoping that she would disagree with the others.

"Sick and tired of it," Evie verified. But because she truly did love this woman, she went to Ida and hugged her. Since Carson still had his arm around Ida, it meant Evie hugged him, too.

"Try to see it this way." Carson looked at his mom, then at LuAnn. "You always wanted your kids to fall in love. Well, I'm Ida's kid, and Evie is yours."

"You're in love?" Gigi, Bennie, Ida and LuAnn all said in unison.

Evie would have said it, too, but she was stunned to silence.

Carson smiled. "I *could* be in love with her, easily." He leaned in and kissed Evie. "We just need a few dates first. And if it works out, then you both get what you want."

Yes, and Evie would, too. She was certain of it. Because what she wanted was Carson. She let him know that with a kiss.

Probably not the best time for it, though, considering they were inches away from their mothers. Still, it gave her some nice tingles in her body and made her wish they'd all leave so she could spend some time alone with Carson.

"You really think you two could fall in love?" That from Ida.

Evie and Carson nodded.

"And the age difference doesn't bother you?" Ida, again.

This time some head shakes from Carson and her.

"And everyone is okay with Gigi and me?" That from Bennie.

Carson and Evie repeated their nods. LuAnn eventually added a nod. Ida either nodded or got a sudden muscle twitch in her neck, but they all decided to take it as a nod because there were breaths of relief. Smiles. And kisses.

Evie liked the kisses from Carson best of all.

"So it's settled," Bennie concluded. He apparently liked kisses from Gigi best of all, but he didn't budge. He was perhaps waiting for someone to tell him it was okay to haul his bride off to the nearest bed.

As long as it wasn't Evie's bed, she was perfectly fine with that. Because she had plans for her bed. Plans that involved Carson.

They all looked at each other, and Evie saw the exact moment that Ida gave in to the notion that her decades-long plan was shot to pieces. But there was a new glimmer in her eyes.

Ida was no doubt planning Carson and Evie's wedding. Possibly planning grandchildren, too. Well, let her plan. Evie was looking forward to those dates that Carson had mentioned. Obviously so was he because he landed one of those chrome-melting kisses on Evie's mouth.

The kiss stopped, though, when LuAnn cleared her throat.

It occurred to Evie then that her mother didn't have wedding planning in her eyes. No, there was something else going on, and it was obvious her mother had not put all of this to rest.

"So, is it true?" LuAnn asked.

Evie braced herself for a rehashing of everything that had already been hashed. "Yes, I care for Carson. I have for years. And yes, we want to try to make a go of this."

LuAnn shook her head. "No. I got that. But is the other thing true?"

Evie figured this was about sex. Maybe safe sex. It was possible Carson and she were about to get a thoroughly embarrassing lecture about condom use. Evie was certain of it, but then her mother leaned in and asked her a question:

"Do you really have a navel ring?"

It was hard, very hard, but Evie managed to choke back a laugh. Carson was less successful, so rather than let her mother think they were laughing at her— which they were—Evie just pulled Carson to her and kissed him.

* * * * *

Caitlyn eased the newborn into her arms. Of course, it wasn't the first time she'd held her, but without the coat around her, she could feel just how tiny and fragile she was.

Drury went through the coat pockets, coming up empty each time, and he turned his attention to the bow on the baby's headband.

"Hell," he mumbled.

Caitlyn watched as he gently slipped off the headband, and she saw it then.

"It's a tracking device," he said. "That's how the man was able to follow you."

Caitlyn shook her head. "I should have noticed it. Drury. I'm so sorry."

"Save it." He tossed the headband onto the coffee table. "In case I missed something, don't use the blanket to wrap her." He pulled a throw off the back of the sofa and handed it to her. "Use this."

"Where are we going?" she asked, draping it over the baby.

"Away from here. And fast." He took out his phone and sent a text. Probably to Grayson. "I don't want any other hired guns coming to the ranch. Every one of my cousins has wives and kids, and they're all right here on the grounds."

That didn't help steady her heartbeat.

Drury led her to the back door, grabbing a remote control from the kitchen counter. He used it to open the detached garage, and he stepped out onto the porch to look around.

The rain was still coming down hard, but the porch was covered so the baby was staying dry. However, she was starting to squirm, maybe because Caitlyn's dress was damp, and it was perhaps cool against her. She needed dry clothes. Baby supplies.

And a safe place to take her.

But where?

The sheriff's office certainly didn't seem like an ideal location since the man's partners could go looking for her there.

"Wait here in the doorway, and I'll pull the car up to the steps," Drury said. He'd already started to walk away but then stopped and turned back around to face her. "So help me, you'd better not try to run."

Since she was indeed thinking just that, Caitlyn wondered if he'd read her mind. Or maybe he could just see the desperation on her face.

Because she didn't know what else to do, Caitlyn did wait. And she prayed. She trusted Drury, but her trust wouldn't do a darn thing to protect him or the baby.

He hurried to the garage, and it took only a few seconds before she heard the engine turn on. Only a few seconds more before he pulled the car to the steps with the passenger's side facing her.

The moment Drury threw open the door and frantically motioned for her to get in, she knew something was wrong.

"Someone's coming," Drury said.

Caitlyn saw the headlights then. There was a car on the road. And it was speeding right toward them.

Find out just how far they'll go
to keep the baby safe in DRURY
by Delores Fossen,
available in April 2017
wherever Harlequin Intrigue books are sold.

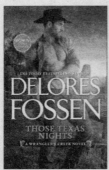 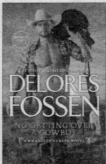 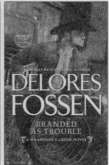

  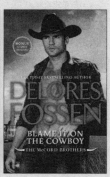

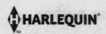

INTRIGUE

EDGE-OF-YOUR-SEAT INTRIGUE, FEARLESS ROMANCE.

Save **$1.00**

on the purchase of ANY Harlequin® Intrigue book.

Available wherever books are sold, including most bookstores, supermarkets, drugstores and discount stores.

Save **$1.00**

on the purchase of any Harlequin® Intrigue book.

Coupon valid until June 30, 2017.
Redeemable at participating outlets in the U.S. and Canada only.
Not redeemable at Barnes & Noble stores. Limit one coupon per customer.

Get 2 Free Books,
<u>Plus</u> 2 Free Gifts -
just for trying the *Reader Service!*